FIRST EDITION 2015

ISBN – 13:978-0692587621
ISBN – 10:0692587624

Contact information:
Judy Barker Austin
P. O. Box 94
Centerville, IA 52544 52544
judybarkeraustin.highroad@gmail.com

Also written by Ros Barker and available on createspace.com and amazon.com: *Mind's Eye*

Also written by Judy Barker Austin and available on createspace.com and amazon.com: *Always Take The High Road In Your Professional, Personal, And Financial Life* and *Things My Mama Said*

ACKNOWLEDGEMENT
AND THANKS

This book is dedicated to all the people who are willing to get out of their comfort zone and follow their dreams.

This book is written by a truck driver and a retired teacher. We don't have a degree in English. We decided one day to write a novel and so we did. We didn't start off with a news article, or a short story, or a magazine article. We started out with a novel.

We worked on the book during the years of 2002 – 2005 and then it sat dormant for ten years until we decided to publish it in 2015. We hope you enjoy it.

We want to thank all our friends and family members for their encouragement, as well as Stone Ronson for his poetic contributions.

THE
GOD COMPLEX

FAMILY SECRETS

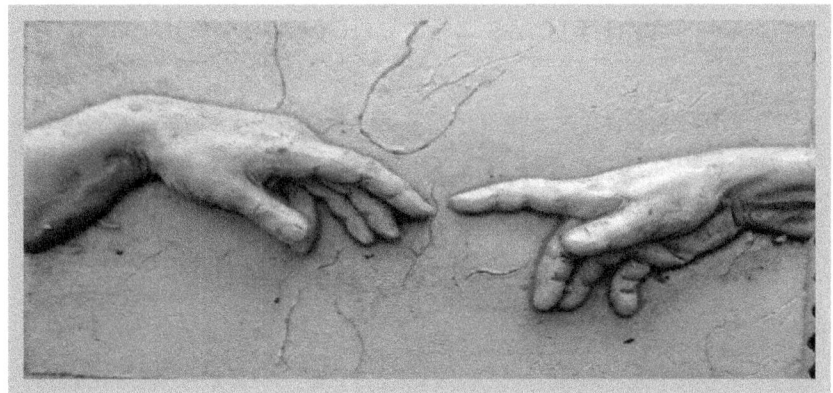

A NOVEL

BY
ROS BARKER
AND
JUDY BARKER AUSTIN

THE THREE

Three men, once friends, while in their youth
Chose different paths to follow.
All orphaned at an early age
With tears and pride to swallow.

The first one's path went straight and true
For God's favor he had won.
His touch was like the Midas King
He was their "Golden Son."

The second one's path went up and down
He stumbled, but no one mocked.
He did not fall and so they bragged
"He's solid as a rock."

The third one's path went straight downhill
He stumbled, and then he fell.
He could not pick himself back up
And he was bound for Hell.

PART ONE –
RUSSELLVILLE, ALABAMA
JUNE 2000

Chapter One

Peter sat at his grandfather's bedside mesmerized by the fragile, brittle shell that poorly represented the strong, physically fit man who had raised him. Even physically spent, Papa still exuded a royal elegance coupled with a commanding spirit that permeated the antique-filled bedroom.

"We hid so much from you about us . . . about you . . . about our true wealth," whispered Papa as a lock of white hair fell down and nestled between his intelligent, piercing eyes. At ninety-five, Papa still sported a full head of white, not gray, hair. He wore it longer than other male senior citizens in the area despite his barber's constant prodding to wear a shorter and more mature style. Peter, had hair as dark as Papa's was white worn in what could be called a military cut.

Peter held back tears as he wondered if his grandfather would live to see another sunrise. Dawn was his Papa's favorite time of day. As far back as Peter could remember, Papa faithfully rose early enough to witness each new day's sunrise.

Because Papa was now bedridden, Peter had hung a gorgeous sunrise portrait of Loch Ness Scotland on the wall across from where Papa lay propped up by a bevy of assorted pillows on a massive, ornately carved canopy bed. Each morning Peter stopped by to check on his grandfather, and they enjoyed discussing the majesty and beauty of the sunrise in the portrait. Peter selected this particular Scottish portrait because Papa was an immigrant from Scotland and believed it might remind Papa of happy times in his homeland.

Papa was a popular and respected man in Franklin County. Local and state officials had pleaded with him since the `50s to run for public office, but he had never so much as run for city council or even deacon in his church.

"Maybe Anna and I should have told you, but we kept it all from you."

Peter couldn't help but smile as his grandfather referred to Gramma Joanna by the shortened version of her name. He hadn't had much to smile about since a frantic Jim Davis, Russellville's Chief of Police, had called back in March.

"I need your help," begged Chief Davis. "I know you're not going to believe this, but Papa's been in another accident. He ran two cars and a chicken truck off the road before he finally ended up in a ditch on Highway 24 across from the Parade Gas Station. He's hurt and refuses to let Clyde, the ambulance driver, take him to the hospital. When Clyde gets too close, Papa pelts him with rocks from the ditch. Papa must have a good throwing arm because Clyde already has a split lip and a swollen eye. Can you get out here and talk some sense into him?"

"Sure, Jim," mumbled Peter. "I'll be right there."

It was the third time in two weeks Papa and his 1979 Cadillac Fleetwood had caused an accident. Chief Davis warned Papa one more would result in his driver's license being revoked and explained this to him at the last accident scene. Papa had stomped the accelerator instead of the brakes at a downtown red light broadsiding a van transporting elderly contestants to the senior citizen center for their annual and highly anticipated *Most Unusual Hat* day. No one was injured, but it was quite a sight to see so many disheveled, pissed-off old folks lined up along Jackson Avenue with their prized, unusual hats all ruined. Papa's Cadillac wasn't even dented by the accident while the van required extensive bodywork.

Peter had left his office and driven as fast as he could to the scene of the accident. Before he opened the door of his Dodge Ramcharger, he heard Papa rant and rave as he threatened to have the Chief fired. When a rock zoomed by his head, Peter called out for Papa to behave. No matter how much Peter reasoned with Papa, he could not talk him into going to the hospital. Papa wanted to go home.

"A hospital is for sick people. I'm not sick," Papa had argued. "If you go into a hospital and you're not sick, you will be by the time you come out, if you come out at all. Doctors bury their mistakes."

Papa hated hospitals to the point where Peter believed Papa actually had a phobia. As far as Peter knew, Papa had never been in a hospital. Peter finally gave in to Papa, paid Clyde extra to transport Papa home, and hired a private medical team to care for Papa until he got his strength back.

Despite superb medical treatment for three months, Papa had not recovered his strength. He had given up, almost willing himself to die. He had lost sixty pounds and could barely speak above a whisper.

"You listen to me, young prince," commanded Papa as he struggled to regain his grandson's attention.

Papa and Gramma Joanna had always called Peter *Prince,* or *young prince.* Peter didn't like it, but, at least, they only used those endearments in private. Even though Peter was twenty-eight, he still cringed at the thought of anyone finding out about his nickname. *Prince*, thought Peter, *was a dog's name.*

"When Harold presents my new will, you will be displeased," whispered Papa losing the physical strength he had accumulated a few minutes earlier. "I did not leave you everything, but I have provided very well for you."

Papa prayed for sufficient strength to continue as he remembered when Peter was thirteen and Anna passed away. As she died, he promised to reveal their family secrets to young Peter. It was the only promise to her he'd never kept. Numerous times, he'd attempted to tell Peter about their secrets, but each time he'd been afraid of the effect it would have on the young prince.

"Papa, please. You don't have to explain anything," pleaded Peter. "You know I don't and never have cared about money."

"You must listen, Peter. I have not always been so good."

Peter knew how ethical Papa was in both personal and private life. Peter often felt the tremendous weight on his shoulders as he strived to live up to the principles his Papa had taught him. "Papa . . . That's not true. You . . ."

"You don't understand," Papa interrupted. "But I have tried to make amends. That is why I left so much to our employees. There is more . . . so . . . much . . . more . . ." Papa again labored with what he knew he must tell Peter. His grandson was a good man, not perfect by any means, but a kind man. There were times he and Anna reluctantly reined the boy in, but those rebellious incidents had been few and far between. Besides--Alan usually caused them. Peter, Eric, and Alan had been inseparable growing up. Eric and Alan had spent about as much time at the Stacia house as Peter had. Even with bad influences, Papa felt Peter had grown into a man of noble character.

"Papa, don't try so hard. You need to . . ."

"You will have great power." Papa interrupted. "Use this power for good, not evil. God will guide you . . . I have set you free . . . Young Prince in the back of my Bible in an envelope are three keys . . . I meant to tell you, to protect you, and now . . . I fear . . . I fear it's too late." Papa's voice had continued to grow weaker and softer with his last whispered words. Papa shut his eyes, relaxed his face, and started to breathe in short, shallow breaths. Several times Peter thought Papa stopped breathing, but each time was relieved to see his grandfather's chest raise and lower again. Peter didn't know how long he sat there, afraid to move before Papa spoke again. This time, though, Papa did not open his eyes.

"Young prince?"

"Yes, Papa?"

"Will you read me the prayer in my Bible? You know the one. Anna's Prayer?"

"Yes, Papa. I'll read it.

Peter gently opened the tattered Holy Bible on the nightstand and immediately saw the prayer. Every morning his grandmother took the prayer from her Bible, sat in her chair in the living room, and prayed as tears streamed down her face. Peter never understood why this particular prayer affected his Gramma Joanna in the way it did. As he looked at the prayer, he saw many words smeared beyond recognition where his grandmother's tears had fallen on the parchment. It was inconsequential that many of the words were unreadable because she had known the poem by heart, as did Papa, and as did Peter.

Papa smiled as Peter recited . . .

Give patience, Lord to us Thy children
In these dark, stormy days to bear
The persecution of our people
The tortures falling to our share.

Give strength, just God, to us who need it
The persecutors to forgive
Our heavy, painful cross to carry
And Thy great meekness to achieve.

When we are plundered and insulted
In days of mutinous unrest
We turn for help to Thee, Christ-Savior,
That we may stand the bitter test.

Lord of the world, God of Creation,
Give us Thy blessing through our prayer
Give peace of heart to us, O Master,
This hour of utmost dread to bear.

And on the threshold of the grave
Breathe power divine into our clay
That we, Thy children, may find strength
In meekness for our foes to pray.

As Peter picked up Papa's Bible to return the prayer, an envelope fell to the floor He retrieved it, tore it open, and found three unusual keys inside. As he turned the keys over and over in his hands, questions filled his head. *What are these keys for? Why hadn't Papa given them to me before now? What did Papa mean when he said there were family secrets?*

For the first time in his life, he felt weak and helpless. He realized he was not ready to relinquish Papa's guidance, wisdom, and love.

He mulled all these things over in his mind oblivious that during the reading of the poem his beloved Papa, and greatest man he'd ever known, had reached that clearing at the end of his path.

In a room nearby, Papa's private duty nurse and housekeeper heard a bloodcurdling wail and ran into the bedroom to find Peter sobbing and tightly holding Papa's frail body.

Chapter Two

" . . . Papa emigrated from Scotland to the United States in the early twenties. He moved to Alabama in 1946 where he later built Stacia Homes. When I was very young, my parents were killed in a boating accident, so my grandparents raised me as their own son. My grandmother passed away when I was 13, and Papa became both mother and father to me. I will truly miss this man of God. Goodbye, Papa. I love you," whispered Peter as he ended the eulogy and proudly walked to the back of the auditorium with tears streaming down his face.

Peter wiped his eyes with a tissue provided by an attractive brunette with violet eyes, glanced around the auditorium, and observed the lack of a dry eye in the gathering at Papa's memorial service. It was obvious Peter was not the only one who loved and admired Papa. One by one common people mixed with county and state dignitaries, employees, local business leaders, close friends, and many individuals Peter had never before meet filed past professing how much they would miss his grandfather. Peter stood proudly supported by his wife Lila on his right side and his best friend Eric on his left.

"Pete, you know how much I loved Papa," said Eric once the procession thinned out. "He was like a father to me."

Eric's parents were transients who had worked for Papa only a couple of months. They left Eric in Papa's care when they departed suddenly for a funeral in Ohio and couldn't afford to take Eric with them. Papa and Gramma Joanna agreed to watch after the boy until they came back. After six weeks passed and Eric's parents hadn't returned, Papa and Gramma Joanna felt they were too old to care for both Peter and Eric. Since their housekeeper, Ms. Velma Sandusky, had become quite attached to little Eric, she offered to keep him. Every Christmas and every birthday, Eric sat close to the door of their little home with his small leather suitcase neatly packed knowing this would be the day his parents would come back for him. They would have kind faces and apologize for not writing him or calling. After all, they had worked hard and saved money all these years to have enough to care for their precious son.

Ms. Velma officially adopted him when he was eleven, and Eric realized no one was coming for him. He spent the rest of his youth with Peter and their childhood friend, Alan, at Peter's house with Velma close by cooking and cleaning for the Stacias. When Velma died, he moved into a room of his own at the Stacia home. When Papa gave Peter and Lila that home as their wedding gift, Papa made Peter and Lila promise Eric's room would always be there for Eric to use if he ever needed it. "He's Family, Young Prince," said Papa. "No matter what happens you always take care of The Family. Someday they may be all you have." They kept that promise. Even though Eric moved out when Peter and Lila married, he still occasionally stayed in his room.

"I know, Eric. He loved you as much as he loved me," Peter whispered as a tall, thin, and distinguished older man approached them.

"Pete, I'm sorry," consoled Harold Jardi, Papa's attorney. "Papa was a good man."

"Thanks, Harold."

"He was so proud of you," bragged Harold in his soft, aristocratic southern drawl. "He often confided how he admired your level-headed commitment to your goals, your assertiveness and pride in the company, and your many athletic accomplishments."

Peter tensed as out of the corner of his eye he noticed Alan Chipenski coming toward him. Harold noted Peter's change in body language and gently, but firmly, guided Peter away from Chipenski's direction to a more private corner of the auditorium. Peter and Alan no longer got along, and the last thing Harold wanted was a fight at Papa's memorial service. "Forget Chipenski for now," replied Harold. "Pete, we've more important things to take care of. We need to get together tomorrow and go over the employees' part of Papa's will."

"Do we have to do it tomorrow?" Peter asked as he turned to gratefully watch Alan Chipenski leave the auditorium through a side door. "Tomorrow is the deadline for an important OSHA report. We'll be fined substantially if it's not submitted on time. Payroll checks have to be signed, and work schedules and supply orders have to be completed by the end of the day."

"Pete, this can't wait," insisted Harold. "My instructions are to do this on the first business day following his memorial service, which would be tomorrow."

Peter remembered how before Papa died he had mentioned something about making amends, as if Papa could have ever done anything he needed to atone for. Peter reluctantly agreed with Harold and asked, "What time should we get all the employees together?"

"Nine in the morning sounds good to me."

"I'll call Dillon and have him get in touch with everyone," said Peter, who knew Dillon Marshall, his good friend and plant supervisor, would take care of whatever was needed. He then turned and waved for Eric, Lila, and Lila's parents to join him as he climbed into the limousine poised to speed off for Papa's private burial at Spark's Chapel.

Chapter Three

Peter arose early the next morning and left before Lila awoke. He thought about how special Papa's memorial service had been and was overwhelmed by the large number in attendance. Instead of flowers, thousands of dollars had already poured into the Hemophilia Foundation and Leukemia Research Foundation in Papa's name.

After breakfast at the local "greasy spoon" restaurant, where he ate his daily heart attack special of two fried eggs, country ham, fried potatoes, cheese grits, sawmill gravy, buttermilk biscuits, and black coffee, Peter headed toward Stacia Homes. He planned to double-check weekly payroll figures before his office manager, Geneva, cut employee checks for him to sign. Although Geneva wanted to order one of those stamps she could use to stamp his signature, he had refused. She thought it was a waste of his time, but he enjoyed looking at and signing each individual check. After he signed the checks, he would complete the OSHA report he'd almost finished before Papa had passed away.

Once sitting in his small, paneled office, he glanced at the mountain of phone messages and decided they were lower on his priority list than the report that had to be e-mailed before noon. He would sort through the messages after the employee meeting and respond to the most important ones after lunch. Most of them, he was sure, were to show him encouragement and support in his recent loss.

Since the supply order usually took him a couple of hours to complete, he would tackle it after lunch along with next week's work schedules. With a little luck, he would easily be out of his office by five o'clock, that is, if this employee meeting didn't take up too much time.

At five minutes before nine, Harold knocked on Peter's office door. "Come on in, Harold, and have a seat," said Peter not taking his eyes off the computer screen. "I'm finishing up a report." Harold sat down and watched as Peter keyed the last few computations into the computer. Peter then attached his report to a brief transmittal memo and pushed enter to send it all to Washington, D.C.

"I guess it's time to start the meeting," sighed Peter as he glanced at his watch.

Peter and Harold left Peter's office and continued over to where Dillon had set up a microphone, small table, and several folding chairs. As Peter and Harold walked to the microphone, Dillon went to stand by Geneva. Peter briefly waved at Jennifer Brown, Harold's paralegal, sitting at the small wooden table with a stack of papers and several voucher books.

All eyes were on Peter as he made a few short announcements that included a new safety procedure starting after the Fourth of July holiday, plans to hire twenty-five additional employees, and a remodeling update of the onsite daycare center.

After answering a few questions, Peter thanked the employees for their kind words, cards, and prayers he and Lila had received during Papa's recent accident and passing. He then introduced Harold, even though he needed no introduction, and left to stand next to Dillon, who smiled and nodded encouragement to Peter. Dillon was one of the few people, besides Peter, who Papa explicitly trusted. Peter nodded back as they both turned their attention to Harold.

Harold took his reading glasses out of his coat pocket, shook the glasses to open them up, and gingerly placed them on his thin nose. He tapped on the microphone to ensure it was turned on and said, "As you all know, Mr. Stacia recently passed away. I have been instructed to read part of his will at an employee gathering. So if you would please be silent, I'll get started." He tore open the folder and began to read in his most eloquent and formal voice. "This is the final Will and Testament of Peter Stacia the first, concerning the employees of Stacia Homes. To Geneva Marie Childers, office manager since 1965, I leave a retirement trust for $1.5 million, the lake house located at 198 Lakeview Shores Drive, in Muscle Shoals, Alabama, the Mercedes Benz 450 SL currently titled to Stacia Homes, and the cabin cruiser moored in Steenson Hollow Marina."

There was a collective gasp from the people assembled on the plant floor. Immediately they chattered among themselves, as no one supposed Papa could possibly leave that much money to anyone.

"Geneva," Harold continued, "You have given me the best part of your life. Retire and enjoy the boat and home with your husband, children, and grandchildren. Thank you for always being there for me."

Questions started to fly. "Can you believe Miss Geneva gets all that?" wailed Margie Carmichael. "What do I get? I've given Papa a good portion of my life, also." A few nervous chuckles came from those who heard her comments and knew about Margie's complete lack of character.

"To the employees of Stacia Homes," Harold bellowed, as he had to raise the volume of his voice a few notches to drown out the rumblings of the employees, "I leave each of you a check for $100,000 and 49 percent of the company to be equally divided among all current employees. This does not include Dillon, Geneva, or Peter."

The face of each employee showed doubt and skepticism. Many turned to look at an incredulous Les Simpson. He had worked for Stacia Homes only two weeks. Today he would receive his first paycheck. Les quit a plant in Red Bay that made motor homes after working there fifteen years. His wife, Belinda, had pitched a fit when she heard about what he had done. She thought he'd ruined any chance for retirement pay. *Well*, thought Les, *she will sing a different and sweeter tune when I get home and wave that $100,000 check up under her nose.* He grinned from ear to ear and ignored whispers of how it wasn't fair for him to get the same amount as those who had worked there half their lives.

"What's this about company shares?" asked several employees at the same time. Charlie Zills, who was known to sell everything he got his hands on, yelled out, "Yeah, how much them shares worth?"

"When do we get checks?" added Joe Kramer, a supervisor on the verge of declaring bankruptcy.

Each employee continued to battle with what he or she had heard and what each had expected to hear at the reading of Papa's will. Comments and gasps continued to roar through the plant in waves. Soon it was hard for anyone to hear what Harold was reading.

"HOLD ON!" threatened Harold. "Wait until I finish, and I will answer each question individually. If I hear another word from anyone else, it'll be months before y'all get anything. I'll see to that. I guarantee you." The employees quieted down and remained silent until the complete reading of Papa's will.

"To Dillon Marshall and his daughter, Madeline Rose, I leave the sum of $1 million and 51 percent of the company. Dillon, you now have complete control of the company with all financial and fiduciary responsibilities."

Peter was visibly shaken. Papa told him he would be displeased, but he had not expected this. Harold glanced over to make sure Peter was okay before he cleared his throat and continued, "Run the company well, Dillon."

Harold paused as he watched Dillon and Geneva help each other sit in chairs provided by Peter and Jennifer. Dillon and Geneva clung to each other with wet unbelieving eyes as tears of affection and gratitude toward Papa ran down their cheeks. "To Harold Jardi, my attorney and close friend for the past twenty years, I leave $900,000."

There was an awkward moment as Harold looked up in disbelief. His face and neck had quickly turned as red as the crimson *Roll Tide Roll* banner on the wall behind him. *Nine hundred thousand dollars? What couldn't he do with that kind of money? His law practice had always provided him a good living, but it had been hard raising three kids. He and his wife, Brenda, had sacrificed so much. Well--the time for sacrifice was over. They could take that trip to France they had always dreamed about. They could . . . They could . . .*

Harold was brought back to reality as Jennifer handed him a cup of water. "Here, Harold, drink this," prompted Jennifer. "You look like you're about to have a heart attack." Harold gulped down the water. He took a deep breath, exhaled, and continued to read. "To Harold Jardi, my attorney and close friend for the past twenty years, I leave . . . I leave $900,000. You have been a good friend, Harold. Thank you for all your good advice."

Harold removed his glasses, wiped his moist eyes with his sleeve, returned his reading glasses to their perch on his now reddened nose, and cleared his throat several times before he was able to continue. The employees patiently waited until Harold pulled himself together.

"All my other assets, I leave to Peter, my grandson. Peter, you have five hours to clear out your office. Don't take this as a slight to your ability to run the company. You did a great job, but I am setting you free to accomplish even greater things. You will understand soon. For almost 50 years, the employees of Stacia homes have supported me and mine. I think of you as My Family, and I always take care of Family. I hope my appreciation was expressed here today.

Thanks to all of you, and I pray God will bless you and your families as he has blessed me and mine here in this new world."

As Harold stuffed the will back into its folder, no one said a word. Everyone in the room turned to look at Peter, who stared straight ahead and refused to make eye contact with anyone. Papa had fired him posthumously. Now it was Dillon and Geneva helping *him* sit down. As soon as Peter was seated and had somewhat regained his composure, the chattering started again. Within a few seconds, the chattering became a roar so loud it took Harold several minutes to regain control of the meeting.

"QUIET, everyone. SILENCE!" Harold yelled. "Jennifer will fill out a voucher for each of you to redeem at Citizen's Bank for your $100,000 cashier's check. As she calls your name, please come forward."

While Jennifer sat behind the little table ready to handle the employees, Harold strolled over and bent down to quietly say to Peter, "Pete, you need to come by my office. Papa left me another sealed folder to go over with you privately."

"Harold," Peter said as he still refused to make eye contact. "What's the use? Papa gave away more than $40 million with almost $30 million in cash. There won't, there can't be anything left. Where did he get $30 million in cash, anyway?"

"I don't know," replied Harold as he sat down next to Peter. "Papa gave me those two sealed folders back in January and told me I was not allowed to open either until I received instructions. One had the word "employees" written across the top and the other one had your name. He told me to destroy the old will I had made for him right after your grandmother died. Yesterday morning, only hours before the memorial service, I received a call that money had been wired from Chase Manhattan Bank in New York City to Citizen's Bank in Russellville. I was told to schedule an employee meeting the day after the memorial service to read what's in the employees' sealed folder. I was also instructed to bring at least one voucher for each of the 237 employees. I had no idea what the vouchers were for or any idea I would receive anything, especially $900,000." Harold's voice trailed off as he once again thought about what that money could buy.

"Chase Manhattan? New York City?" Peter asked looking puzzled. "Papa hasn't been to New York since he emigrated from Scotland."

"Harold?" questioned Peter as he finally turned to face the lawyer. "Did Papa ever mention anything to you about some keys he planned to give me?"

"I can't say I remember anything about any keys," answered Harold as he stood up. "But I have to go now. Can you come by the office before lunch on Monday to go over the information in that folder?"

"All right, Harold. I'll drop by first thing Monday morning. It's not like I have to be at work anymore," said Peter standing up to tower over Harold. "I'm a free man. I've been fired from the only job I've ever had. My own Papa kicked me out of the company I've loved so much and worked for my entire life. How could a man who said he loved me, and that he always took care of Family, do that and give me only five hours to clear out my office? I've not only lost Papa but also my reason for getting up every morning."

"Pete, don't take it so hard," reassured Harold as he reached up to pat Peter's slumped shoulders. "I'm sure everything will work out for you. Somehow, it always does."

Peter nodded his head, mumbled a few words of thanks, and headed straight to his office to gather his belongings. As he entered the small paneled room, his thoughts once again wandered back to what Papa had revealed before he died. Papa said he would be free to do what he wanted. Peter didn't know if he was going to like this new freedom. What could Papa have possibly meant about having power? He didn't have any power. In fact, he felt powerless.

And what was the deal with those keys? What surprises would they divulge?

He sat at the cluttered desk and looked at a picture of Papa and Gramma taken only days before Gramma's death. They both wore the easy, loving smile Peter had always seen directed toward him. For the first time, he noticed how much Papa and Gramma looked like one another. They could easily pass for brother and sister. It seemed he had heard an old saying about how the longer people live together; the more they looked like each other. What would Gramma think if she knew Papa had fired her precious young prince and thrown him out into the street? For the first time in his life, he felt anger and resentment toward his Papa. For the second time in less than a week, Peter sobbed. This time, it was out of "frustration," not "grief."

* * *

THIS MAZE

Why'd this happen? How'd I fall?
I thought that all was well.
I hit a low and didn't know the night was closing in.
A little nap, a lapse in time, has burned up all the light.

I'm in a maze without a map
Or way to navigate.
But in the dark, way deep inside, I feel a bit of hope.
A tiny ember in my soul still glows to help me cope.

I have the logs, I've found some wood.
The big stuff's all in place.
A breath of air and tiny spark
Could burn me from this maze.

~~~Stone Ronson

* * *

Chapter Four

Peter was not one to feel sorry for himself for long so he hurriedly packed everything away and called the moving company. Taking one last look around, he slowly closed the door to his office leaving through the back entryway. Several reporters from local newspapers had called and others stood outside the front door interviewing employees and waiting to get comments from Peter. It had not taken very long for the whole town of Russellville to find out about the unusually large sum of money Papa had given away and how he had fired his only relative in the family business. Peter had asked Geneva and Dillon to refrain from commenting to the press and to tell them he would have no comments. He wasn't in the mood to talk to any of his former employees and certainly not the press.

Peter was hurt and confused as he drove away. He was hurt because he was no longer a part of Stacia Homes and confused as to where all that money came from. *Where did Papa get $30 million in cash? What other assets could there possibly be? Of course, there was the home on Wilson Boulevard and the farm in Vina, but since when did Papa have a lake home in Muscle Shoals? Papa had lied and hidden things from him. What else in his life was a lie?*

It was time for lunch, or dinner, as people in Alabama usually called it. Peter pulled his cell phone out and called Lila. "*You have reached the Stacia residence. Leave a name and number and we will return your call as soon as possible,*" he heard Lila's sultry voice say. Why wasn't she there? She always went home for lunch. Maybe she was waiting for a patient to leave. She was a nurse at her parents' clinic that catered to the growing Hispanic population where her ability to speak fluent Spanish was a definite plus. Peter assumed she'd be home in a few more minutes, so he left a message, "*Lila? Hey, Babe. If you can meet me for lunch, give me a call. Love you.*"

Lila, the things you could say about her, and sexy didn't even come close. Twenty-five years old, 5'11", with legs all the way to there. The epitome of a woman, she exuded sexuality in a way most women could only dream about. Lila's skin was the color of copper and her features were Asian. Long dark hair framed her face, and her body was perfect, as Mother Nature intended. She carried herself with a unique confidence reserved only for those who were truly beautiful.

Peter first met his wife when he was 11 and she was 8 and went by the name, "Lillie." Sometime in her teens, she had decided she didn't like "Lillie" or her given name, "Lillian," and had settled on the name, "Lila." She had spent the summer in Russellville with her grandmother while her parents were relocating from Germany to Tuscaloosa. Peter and Lila never saw each other again until he spotted her on campus at the University of Alabama one fall afternoon when he was a senior, and she was a freshman. He immediately recognized her as "Lillie" who had crashed the "fearsome threesome" of him, Eric, and Alan, and had turned it into a "fearsome foursome." When he called out her name, he could tell she recognized him, too. They had laughed until their sides hurt as they discussed some of the things the fearsome foursome had gotten into that summer of '83.

When he asked her to go out with him, she tilted her head to one side, laughed aloud, and miserably shot him down by teasing, "I don't date dumb jocks."

Dumb Jocks? Does she not know who I am? Peter had thought. *Although I play football, I'm not a dumb jock. I have a 4.0 GPA and am in school on an academic scholarship. Besides, she's only some freshman. What do freshmen know anyway? How dare she? She's just as stubborn as she was when she was 8 years old.* Even after this humiliating rejection, Peter refused to take no for an answer and over the next several months had made it a point to ask her out at every opportunity.

Then came the day Lila finally relented. "Pick me up at my house at 8 P.M."

"Where is your house?"

"If I'm important enough, you'll find me."

How was he going to find out where she lived in a few short hours? He already knew she wasn't listed in the telephone book because he had already looked there. There were no listings for Volores. He was about to give up when he knew what to do. He would call his best friend, Eric, who had recently been hired as an officer for the Russellville Police Department. Peter called Eric and pleaded, "Eric, I've got to have a girl's address, and I need it now."

"A girl?" Eric laughed. "Please tell me it's not Lillie. "She keeps telling you to get lost, doesn't she?"

"It's Lila, Eric. Now she goes by the name, Lila," said a determined Peter. "Look. She finally said she'd go out with me, but as a test, I have to find out where she lives in time to pick her up at eight."

"Tonight?"

"Yes. Tonight."

"I can't make any promises," said Eric, his delight at the request evident. "I'll try, but you'll have to give me a name. So she goes by Lila, right?"

"Yes. Lila Volores," Peter said, spelling Volores for Eric.

"Volores is an unusual name. She shouldn't be too hard to find. That is, if she has an Alabama driver's license."

Peter could hear Eric type the request into his state-issued computer. "I have a Lillian Marie Volores. The computer says her last known address is 1106 Coventry, Tuscaloosa, Alabama."

"Thanks, man. I owe you one. I'll see you later."

"Glad to be of help. Don't forget my Iron Bowl tickets."

"If my date with Lila turns out as well as I think it will," said Peter before he hung up, "I'll get you tickets to the SEC Championship game."

Peter showed up at 1106 Coventry at precisely 8 P.M., rang the bell, and stood there nervously. "I'll get it," he heard a deep voice call out. Seconds later the biggest man he had ever met in his life opened the door. He was immense. The man had to stand at least seven feet tall and weigh more than 350 pounds. Peter was three inches shorter and 80 pounds lighter; this giant made Peter feel like a small child.

"May I help you?" he asked.

"We–Well . . ."

"Speak up, son. I don't have all night to stand out here and look at your pretty face."

"I–uh–I'm here to pick up Lila."

"Come on in. She'll be ready soon."

A petite Asian woman came over and took Peter's hand. She said, "I am Mrs. Volores, and you must be Peter."

"Yes, Ma'am."

"Lila has talked about you for years."

"She has?"

"Oh, yes. She never forgot about that boy, Pete, she had met in Russellville so many years ago. She always said you were going to grow up to be as big as the Colonel."

"The Colonel?" Peter asked, gesturing to Mr. Volores.

"That's right," growled Colonel Volores. "We've sat in the stands at every football game for the past four years while she pined for you. We had almost given up on ever meeting you."

"That's odd," Peter said. "She barely speaks to me."

"Well, that's Lila for you. She kept up with you all these years and never let you know it. I think she's got every newspaper clipping of every newspaper you've ever been in," confessed the Colonel. "Now don't let her know I told about her little secret. Anyway, I'm Colonel Adam Volores, and this is my wife."

"Pleased to meet you. I'm Peter, but I guess you already knew that. Most people call me Pete." He could hardly believe the same Lila the Colonel had described was the one who had rejected his advances for months. The Colonel motioned toward a chair in which a stunned Peter spent thirty minutes waiting before Lila finally breezed into the room wearing a pair of form-fitting black jeans and a red sweater. "I guess I was wrong about you. You may not be a dumb jock, after all," she said smiling radiantly.

"What's that about dumb jocks?" asked Colonel Volores.

"Oh, Daddy. It's just a joke."

"I'll have you know I played football and maintained a GPA good enough to get me into medical school."

"I know, Daddy. I also can remember everything you ever said about all you sacrificed to get through college and medical school. You grew up poor and walked to school and back in knee deep snow, uphill both ways," she said as she barely stifled her laughter.

"There wasn't knee-deep snow in Russellville Alabama," said the Colonel with a grin as he bent down and lightly kissed the top of her head.

"You went to medical school? I thought you were a Colonel," Peter asked.

"I am--well--I was. I graduated from medical school at The University of Alabama at Birmingham." The Colonel sat down in his favorite recliner with a groan. "After that I joined the Marines and went to Vietnam where I met Ming Toi."

"Ming Toi?" Peter asked.

Mrs. Volores proudly waved and said, "That would be me."

"Then we moved to Germany where I was a doctor until I moved here to start my present practice. Everyone calls me Colonel instead of Doctor," said the Colonel with a grin.

"I think we need to go before they start telling gory Marine Corps tales," said Lila, as she grabbed Peter by the arm to rush him toward the door. They walked out the door and down the sidewalk to Peter's baby, a 1988 Dodge Ramcharger he'd had since his sixteenth birthday.

"Wow. Now that's what I call a ride," exclaimed Lila.

"You like it?"

"I love a good 4 by 4."

"We have a change of plans, then."

"Why do we need a change of plans?"

"I had planned dinner and a movie, but there is a truck and tractor pull in town. Would you rather go there?"

"Sure, Peter. That sounds much better than a movie."

The tractor pull was already underway when they arrived. Of course, Bigfoot was there with a group of curious people crowded around. When Peter and Lila walked over to join the crowd, all eyes were on them. They were a striking couple. The person who first came up with the expression "tall, dark, and handsome" must have had Peter in mind. The closest thing to a flaw in Peter's appearance was a birthmark on his right cheek. The day after his seventh birthday, he had run home from school in tears because the kids teased him about it, along with his height, and called him Frankenstein. Gramma Joanna immediately explained it was a unique mark just like the one on Peter the Great, the Great Russian Czar. She had also told him Peter the Great was very tall. His Gramma always knew what to say to make him feel better. From that day on, Peter believed his birthmark and height made him special.

Peter and Lila stopped at the concession stand where they both ordered what they would later fondly refer to as the "biggest and greasiest hot dog" either had ever eaten. They both devoured the big dog before they could even get to their seats. "Now that's what I like," Peter had exclaimed with relief as Lila smiled, "A lady with an appetite." He had dated far too many girls who considered food something to toy with instead of enjoy. He had a big appetite and was pleased to see Lila also did. As they sat down, the second round of the competition started. After about fifteen minutes, Lila looked over at Peter and said, "This is exactly what I expected, a true redneck experience."

"We could still catch a movie," Peter said with a grin.

"No. I want to stay here!"

They found conversation easy, while at the same time, exciting. Being with Lila was everything Peter had imagined it would be.

Suddenly, Peter was no longer reminiscing. His cell phone was pressed to his ear and ringing. He heard Eric's voice and realized he had called Eric's private work line. Eric was now the Sheriff of Franklin County. Even subconsciously, Peter knew he could always count on Eric. In fact, Peter often called Eric "the rock" because of how strong and solid he was during those times when Peter had needed him, and now Peter needed his friend more than ever before.

* * *

A lie that is half-truth is the darkest of all lies.

~~~Alfred Lord Tennyson

* * *

Chapter Five

Sheriff Eric Sandusky was having a bad day.

It had started out much like the others with the uncompromising pile of paperwork. He hated paperwork. He had no idea being Sheriff would require so much paperwork. He glanced up from yet another undelivered summons to see Doris, one of his deputies, enter his office.

"What now, Doris? More paperwork?" Doris noticed how the Sheriff's full lips turned slightly up at the corners of his mouth, as he got ready to ask the next question. "Or has Miss Sarah called with yet another claim her next door neighbor is a Peeping Tom?"

Sheriff Eric Sandusky was a *fine looking specimen* according to the female citizens of Franklin County, and Doris agreed with them. Doris also acknowledged his lips were not the only thing that was *full.* Eric had the *full package.* He had great looks, great personality, great sense of humor, and a great flair for cooking when prodded. On more than one occasion, Doris had been asked by her single friends what she had done to get to work with that hunk, Sheriff Eric Sandusky. On those occasions, Doris smiled and replied she was happily married to a wonderful man and to her Eric Sandusky was just her boss.

Doris and Eric laughed as they thought about how Sarah Boyd had already called the Sheriff's department three times this week to complain how Tom Berry, yes his first name really was Tom, was hiding in the bushes of her back yard peeping in her windows. Three times a deputy was dispatched to Sarah's house, and three times there was no sign of Tom anywhere near her house or even his own. Each time there wasn't even a sign of Tom Berry's car, and no one but Tom Berry drove his restored, green `68 Ford Mustang with its shiny black vinyl top.

Doris shook her head and said with a smile, "No, Miss Sarah is behaving herself this morning. We do have a few more summons to deliver, but the secretary will bring those in later. This is different. I believe it could be substantially more important than Miss Sarah and her Peeping Tom. Georgia Hubbard just left you a package."

Georgia was an undercover snitch in Eric's attempt to crack down on drugs in Franklin County. Enforcement of drug laws had been the central plank in Eric's campaign platform. Eric hated drugs. He had never, not even once, used any illegal drug in any form. Sometimes he even felt guilty when he took an aspirin. He hated what drugs did to innocent victims. Georgia was a young prostitute who agreed to work with the Sheriff's Department to gather evidence against a drug dealer she called Da' Man. This drug dealer had recently beat her up, and she was bent on revenge.

"What do you think is in the package?" asked the Sheriff.

"It's a videotape, sir. Georgia said she had stolen it from Da' Man. He called it his insurance policy--in case someone threatened to turn him in.

"Did she say what was on it?" asked Eric, who had now perked up. Finally, there was something to take him away from his tedious, never-ending paperwork.

"No, she didn't. Do you want me to put it in the VCR?" asked Doris.

"Yeah, go ahead." Eric's outlook brightened as he anticipated they might finally find out who Da' Man was and have evidence to put him away for good.

Doris put the tape in, and Eric picked up and pushed play on the remote control for the combination TV/VCR. A grainy image of a small room came into focus. On a couch in the room sat a familiar pot-bellied man with slightly graying hair. He held a package wrapped in butcher paper. He sat stiffly on the couch until the second man came into focus. This second man, with long dark hair, was Eric's childhood friend, Alan.

"Good evening," said the second man. "Did you bring the stuff?"

"I sure did," said the man on the couch. "Did you bring the money?"

As Eric pressed the pause button, his bright outlook disappeared. "I don't believe it, Alan Chipenski." Eric sighed as he reluctantly pushed the play button on the remote.

Alan exchanged packages with the man on the couch. Eric knew the man on the couch was Russellville's Chief of Police, Jim Davis.

"Sheriff," said Doris. "It's Chief Davis."

Eric felt like he'd been run over by a truck. Georgia had really done her job well--perhaps too well. He looked up at the ceiling and silently prayed it wouldn't get any worse. As Eric brought his eyes back to stare at the TV, Doris stepped in closer. Alan's package contained two bricks of a white powder. Alan took out a knife and impaled one of the bricks bringing out a little of the white powder on the point of the blade. He put the point of the knife up to a light, looked at it, and then touched the edge to his tongue.

"Alan is Da' Man?" asked Doris. She knew Eric and Alan had grown up together.

"That seems to be true," said Eric. Eric knew Alan had not been a model citizen--after all, he had never been a model child. Alan always pulled childhood pranks, skipped school, and as a teenager lived life on the edge, but Eric had not expected anything like this. He, Alan, and Peter had spent many a good time together as boys. Unfortunately, they shared the common bond of losing their fathers at a young age. In their second grade play, they won starring roles as The Three Musketeers. At the end of the performance as they stood in line with the rest of the cast members to shake hands, several visiting relatives of other cast members, asked if the three boys were brothers. All three of them had laughed, punched each other, and said something under their breath about cooties.

Eric remembered how Mrs. Scott, who ran the downtown drug store, had told Ms. Velma the three musketeers looked enough alike to pass as triplets. It had been so funny to him--especially when Velma told her to go back to her *own* drug store and buy her *own* self some new *spectacles*. When Eric asked what *spectacles* were, Alan quickly whispered *spectacles* were what an octopus used to grab you and squeeze you to death. Eric hadn't understood why Ms. Velma wanted Mrs. Scott to get new *spectacles*. Had she squeezed so many little boys that her *spectacles* were worn out, and could a drug store really sell *spectacles*? Where did Mrs. Scott get them, and what did she do with the rest of the octopus after she cut off its *spectacles*? From then on, Eric never felt the same toward Mrs. Scott and even today avoided the drug store as much as possible.

On the Russellville Middle School football team, they were called the *Triple Threat*. Eric was quarterback, Peter a lineman, and Alan, the smaller and more muscular of the three, played fullback. Eric and Peter continued to play in high school, but Alan decided the required conditioning summer workouts cramped his style. Around the same time, Alan started hating Peter because Peter had more stuff and a better life than he. More and more of Alan's pranks were turned toward Peter. Then add the complication of Alan's mother, Louise, a known prostitute and drug addict who had been that way as far back as the three of them could remember.

It all culminated during their 11th-grade year, Peter and Alan had gotten into a disagreement that led to a fight. To this day Eric still didn't know what happened exactly. Peter exploded over a joke about Dillon Marshall's girlfriend, Nicole Sheridan. Before anyone could get between them, the fight was on. Eric still couldn't exactly figure out, why Peter exploded over Nicole Sheridan. Later on, Dillon got Nicole pregnant, married her, and dropped out of high school. Nicole died in labor, and Dillon raised his daughter, Madeline Rose, by himself. He'd had it tough for quite a while until Papa had hired him. After high school Peter and Eric remained best friends, but Peter had never forgiven Alan for the joke, and anytime there was contact between the two it was bad. Alan resented Eric almost as much as he hated Peter. Although Peter would just as soon see Alan in a coffin, Eric had never quite given up on his childhood friend. He believed deep down one day Alan would wise up.

"This is good stuff," complimented Alan. Alan's voice brought Eric and Doris' attention once again to the TV screen.

Police Chief Jim Davis opened his package revealing a stack of one hundred dollar bills. As he counted them, he turned to Alan and teased, "It's always a pleasure doing business with Da' Man."

Alan smirked when he heard the nickname he had recently acquired.

"You know I can get you more," Chief Davis continued. "I have a very good connection; but if we continue to do business, the next order needs to be twice as large. Can you handle that?"

"Handle it? Of course, I can," bragged Alan. "After all, I am Da' Man."

"Yeah, yeah. That's enough of that," said the Chief. "Where's that sweet little thang you've been talking about?"

"She's upstairs."

"How old is she?"

"Twelve, maybe thirteen."

At this point, Eric paused the tape for the second time. He thought he was going to be sick. There wasn't any way the two men he thought he knew could be the same two men on this tape. Hadn't they attended church off and on together? Of course, with Alan, it was more off than on, but Jim was there every Sunday. Only last week the three of them had attended the annual charity fishing expedition at Bear Creek Dam. He thought about the times they had met together to plan community service activities for Russellville and all of Franklin County. This was impossible. He didn't want to see any more. He glanced at Doris, who by this time had absolutely no color in her face. "Doris, are you okay?" asked Eric.

Doris, the only female Deputy in Franklin County, knew this was a true test of her ability to be a Deputy. She had to be calm and professional. As a wave of nausea passed over her, she forced herself to stand up straight. She then stated in a strong voice, much stronger than she actually felt, "Sure thing, Sheriff." With a slight pause, she quickly added, "Now Sheriff, we really do need to finish. We have to watch the whole tape." Her firm declaration brought Sheriff Eric Sandusky back to the present, and before he fully comprehended what he was doing, he had already pushed the play button.

"I'd like to try her," said the Chief.

"You know you don't get it free."

"How much will it cost?"

"Since we're business partners, you get a deal. For a hundred, I assure you, she'll do anything you ask."

"Is she good?"

"She's worth it."

"Here's the hundred," said the Chief as he slipped a bill out of the stack and handed it back to Alan.

"Hey you," Alan yelled, "get your ass over here!"

A thin young girl whose breasts were barely budding came gingerly into the picture. "Take off your clothes." The girl didn't hesitate but quickly removed the little amount of apparel she wore.

The Chief of Police pulled the young girl into his lap.

"Jim, think she'll work?"

"Yeah, I believe she will."

"Take her upstairs," said Alan. "She knows what to do."

Alan watched as the Chief followed the young girl up a set of stairs that groaned under the weight of his heavy frame.

Eric threw the remote against the wall shattering it into several pieces as Eric and Doris watched the batteries roll under a chair. "Has anyone else seen this?" Eric asked.

"No. Only you and me," said Doris, whose cheeks by this time had returned to their original rosy color. She sat down and contemplated why she ever wanted to become a Deputy.

Eric and Doris sat in a catatonic state before Eric finally came to his senses and commanded, "Doris, let's keep this between you and me until I tell you otherwise. You are not to tell anyone about this tape. I mean no one. I have to figure out where to go with it."

"What about the rest of the department? Do we tell them?"

"No, if this gets out, things could very well spiral out of control. I want Alan and the Chief to get what they deserve. Let's keep quiet about what we saw on that tape. Understand?"

"Yes, sir."

"Didn't that security company last month leave us some audio transmitters? The ones shaped like a fancy hairpin?"

"Yes, sir."

"Get one, and call in Georgia."

Eric and Doris continued to plan what Georgia would need, and need to do, to gather enough evidence to put Alan and the Chief away for good. "Give the hairpin to her and make sure she understands she must wear it all the time. Explain how serious the situation is," said Eric.

"Consider it done, sir," said Doris. "Sheriff?"

"Yes, Doris?"

"Don't those transmitters need the battery changed every two days?"

"Yeah. We'll have to deal with that somehow. Once again, don't tell anyone about this tape or our plans, not even Andy." Andy was Eric's Chief Deputy Sheriff, and it would be highly unusual for Eric to keep something from Andy.

"Yes, sir."

"Doris?"

"Yes, sir."

"You're a damn good Deputy. Don't let anyone ever tell you otherwise. You've handled this situation a lot better than I have."

"Don't sell yourself short," Doris stated, noticeably touched by the Sheriff's compliment. "There's not a finer man in Franklin County than you. Besides, you're by far the best Sheriff this county's ever had."

When Doris left the room, Eric walked around his desk and ejected the tape. He grabbed the tape, used a secret combination to open the safe that sat on the floor next to his desk, placed the tape into the safe, and shut the door with vengeance he didn't even know he possessed. He then glanced at the hole in the wall and then at the pieces of the remote and thought how stupid it had been to throw it. Now he'd have to walk to the TV/VCR and turn it on and off manually, but that and a hole in the wall were the least of his worries. After he took a few seconds to calm down, he gently pulled on the door of the safe to make sure it was locked. He sat back down in his office chair and plopped his feet on his desk. With eyes closed tightly Eric thought, *no one said this job was going to be easy.*

His thoughts were cut short as the phone on his desk rang. The fact it rang without first going through his secretary meant it was from either Pete or Lila.

"Hello," he said as his feet came back down to the floor. The line was silent. "Peter, is that you? Is anything wrong?"

Peter was indeed on the other end of the line. "Everything's wrong," said Peter weakly. "Do you have time to meet at *Our Place?*"

Our Place was a run-down barbecue shack a couple of miles outside the city limits sitting astride the county line. The parking lot and porch to *Our Place* was in *dry* Franklin County, the dining room and kitchen were in *wet* Colbert County. As you looked at the building, you just knew it could fall in any minute, but they served the best ribs south of the Mason-Dixon Line. It was a dump with a health department rating of 78. Several times Lucille, the health department representative, had tried to shut it down. Each time local executives who ate there regularly rallied together to keep it open. Wasn't it funny how the best food always came from restaurants with the lowest scores?

"Same here," said Eric. "I can be there in about thirty minutes. I definitely need a break from this place."

"Why?" Peter teased. "Have you given too many traffic tickets today?" Peter was starting to feel better. Picking on his best friend always lifted his spirits.

"Now, Pete. You know that's not in my job description. I reserve my time for more important issues," Eric quickly retorted.

"Like tracking down peeping toms and catching stray dogs? I hear you're the best dog catcher Franklin County's ever elected." Peter laughed for the first time in several days.

"Sure thing. Just captured a poodle," Eric also laughed.

"Okay then, poodle man. I'll see you in a few."

Peter and Eric hung up.

Peter put the truck in gear and let out on the clutch. The oversized tires barked a bit as he accelerated onto US 43. Only a few miles before Peter got to Our Place, Lila called.

"Hey, Hon. What's going on?" she asked.

"I'm on my way to eat lunch with Eric at Our Place. Do you have time to join us?" said Peter trying to keep the worry and hurt from the morning's meeting out of his voice.

"Always," she laughed. "I always have time for you."

"Want me to order you a drink?"

"We have surgery scheduled for 3 P.M. I don't think Daddy would appreciate being assisted by an inebriated nurse."

"Okay, then. We'll be inside. Love you, sweetie."

"Love you, too. Bye."

As Peter turned off Highway 43 into the restaurant's gravel parking lot, he saw Eric get out of a patrol car.

"Hey, Pete. When are ya gonna get a new ride?" yelled Eric. "You've had that old Dodge since high school."

"You're one to talk," said Peter as he slowly strode toward Eric. "What about you? When are you gonna drive something besides that old Chevy Blazer Papa got you?"

They laughed as they walked up the uneven steps to the restaurant's rickety porch. As Eric reached to open the door, Alan Chipenski thrust his way out.

"You had no business at Papa's service," shouted Peter to Alan as Alan walked down the stairs.

"Don't think I'm going to let some nigger lover tell me where I can and can't go," insulted Alan as he continued to swagger toward his Pontiac Trans Am. "By the way whenever you get finished with that nigger whore you're shacked up with let me know so I can put her to work servicing truck . . ."

Alan never finished his sentence. Peter, as quick as a big cat, shoved Eric aside and hurdled down the stairs, grabbing Alan by his long ponytail and spinning him around. Peter slapped Alan hard and grabbed Alan by the neck, with one mighty heave lifted and dangled Alan's 6'3" frame several inches off the ground.

Alan responded the only way he could, he spit a mouthful of blood and saliva directly into Peter's face.

Peter drew back to hit him again with his free hand, but this time it would be with a closed fist.

"Don't, Peter," pleaded Eric. "He's not worth it."

Peter looked at Eric, shrugged, and then tossed Alan out onto the gravel lot. Alan landed face first taking about a dollar's worth of hide off his chin and other cheek.

Alan lay there only for a split second before he jumped to his feet and sputtered, "Sheriff, arrest that man."

"For what?" Eric asked innocently.

"He assaulted me!"

"When were you assaulted?" questioned Eric, as he hoped he didn't say anything that would give away what he now knew about Alan.

"You always did take his side," challenged Alan. "It happened, and you saw it."

"Alan, I didn't see anything but you attacking Peter. If you say another word, I'll arrest you and make sure you spend at least forty-eight hours in lockup, paid for by the fine citizens of Franklin County."

"I'm going to swear out a warrant for both of you. I'm on my way to see Chief Davis at the police station right now," stammered Alan.

"No. You're not," Eric stated as calmly as he could. "Here's what you're going to do. You'll get your ass away from here, and you'll get it away from here right now! If you show up at any station in Franklin County for any reason, I'll make sure you don't get out of jail until your court date."

"Court date?" Alan seemed to think about this for a minute.

"Yeah, your court date. If I hear another word about this, I will arrest you personally for assault."

"You're crazy! I haven't assaulted anyone."

"You haven't? I'll swear up and down you did. When I tell Judge Pilgrim how you attacked Mr. Stacia, who had no choice but to defend his self, who do you think he will believe? Will he believe the honorable Sheriff Eric Sandusky or Alan Chipenski, the town troublemaker? Now get out of here before I handcuff you and haul you down to the county jail."

"Mark my words. One of these days, I will be one important man," threatened Alan said as he held a hand over his bloody face, "and I promise you'll get yours."

"I won't hold my breath, Chipenski, get your ass out of here!" Eric said as he turned to shove Peter inside the restaurant.

"I don't know who ended up with the worse end of that little ordeal--me or Alan," winced Peter as he examined his throbbing hand. "But, thanks."

"Thanks for what?" Eric asked. "You did all the work, and I did all the talking. I'm the perfect politician. Right?"

"Yeah. We make quite the team, don't we?"

"Man, you hit Alan hard. I don't think I have ever seen anyone slapped like that. You have to remember your own strength, big-un. This ain't the championship game in New Orleans. If you had closed your fist, you'd have killed him."

"I wish I had killed him."

"Pete, you know what I'd have to do if you did."

"You wouldn't, would you?" Peter looked slightly uncertain.

"What? Would I arrest you for killing that? Oh, yeah. I would arrest you, but we'd screw up the evidence worse than the LAPD did during the OJ Simpson trial. No jury in Franklin County would ever convict you."

"I wish he were at least in prison."

"I can't really elaborate on it, but I received information today with the potential to put him there."

"What kind of information?"

"A good source tells me he's been pimping and running drugs."

"I don't want to say I told you so, but, I told you so."

"How's your hand?"

"I didn't break it this time; so I guess I'll survive."

Peter picked up a napkin and wiped the blood and spit off his face as they sat at a table and looked through a window which had not been washed since it was installed. They watched Alan fire up his Trans Am and leave in a spray of gravel that knocked out the passenger side window of Eric's cruiser.

"Are you going to let him get away with that?" exclaimed Peter.

"Right now I am," said Eric. "I don't want him to file any harassment charges to mess up the case I'm building against him. I want to see him behind bars for good."

An elderly black man walked up to the table. "Good evenin', gentlemen," said Mr. Freeman.

"Good evenin', Mr. Freeman," Peter and Eric said.

"Sorry about your grandfather, Pete."

"Thanks."

"What can I get ya'll to drink?"

"I'll take sweet tea," said Eric.

"And you, Peter?"

"I'll have the same, and bring one for Lila, too."

"And how is that fine lady of yours?"

"You can ask her yourself when she gets here. Just promise me you won't flirt with her."

"I can't promise you that. If I was a few years younger, and I didn't have all this here gray around my head, you might have a time holdin' on to her."

"I hear you were quite the lady's man a few years back."

"I was. I was." In one fluid motion, Mr. Freeman put his thumbs under his red suspenders, lifted his chin, reared his shoulders back, and puffed out his chest. As he held his breath, he was for an instant transported back in time to an era where he had more hair, less arthritis, and three different women who competed for the honor of his presence. "Anyway, that was before I met Delmar." At the name of his wife, he exhaled and his shoulders went back to their regular slumped position. "Her Christian butt straightened out this so called lady's man, just like Lila straightened out you." Mr. Freeman patted Peter on his back and headed for the kitchen. "I'll be right back. I'm thinking you'll be wantin' some of my famous ribs with that tea."

"You know it," Peter and Eric said simultaneously.

"So, what's been so bad about your day?" asked Peter as he watched Mr. Freeman enter the double swinging doors into the kitchen. "It couldn't have been as bad as mine."

"Nothing really. I was feeling kind of down and out. Everything's fine now." Eric had decided not to tell Peter about the tape of Alan and the Police Chief. Peter already knew more than he needed to know. "I was just having another one of my 'why did I run for Sheriff, anyway' days."

"I hear you," said Peter. "First Papa dies, and now I'm unemployed."

"Unemployed?"

"Yeah, unemployed. Papa fired me this morning through his will. He left the plant to the employees with Dillon in charge."

"Really? He left the plant to the employees?"

Peter summarized what happened that morning.

"Peter, I'm so sorry. I can't believe Papa did that to you," consoled Eric. "And you got nothing?"

"I get what's left. I'll find out how much when I meet with Harold Monday, but there's something else."

"What, Pete?"

"I found some keys in Papa's Bible I've never seen before."

"They're probably keys to some old cars he used to have."

"No. These keys are . . ."

Peter was interrupted as Mr. Freeman brought them their tea.

"Pete, why did he give all that money to the employees?" asked Eric quietly. "That's over $25 million. I knew the plant did good business, but I didn't know it was that good."

"It wasn't. We never had more than $800,000 in all our accounts."

"So where did it come from?"

"Your guess is as good as mine. Harold said it was transferred from Chase Manhattan Bank."

"Chase Manhattan in New York?"

"Yeah."

As they looked out the same unwashed window, they saw an older model blue BMW pull into the parking lot. "There's Lila," said Eric.

"Have you told Lila about all this?" questioned Eric.

"Not yet."

Lila looked awesome as she wiggled out of the sports car. Even wearing scrubs and very little makeup she commanded and got attention. Her long hair was pulled back into a ponytail which accented the uniqueness of her flawless skin and almond shaped eyes. She walked across the parking lot with the grace of a gazelle. When she opened the door, Peter got up, led her to the table, and pulled out her chair.

Lila sat down and asked. "How's my favorite twin towers?"

Peter and Eric looked at each other and laughed. "Since Pete has joined the ranks of the unemployed, I am about to offer him a job as assistant dog catcher," said Eric.

"What? You own a company," said Lila as she turned toward Peter with concern in her eyes. "You can't be unemployed."

"Oh yes I can be," said Peter, as he repeated what he had told Eric only minutes earlier. "I feel totally betrayed. I'm beginning to believe my whole life is a lie."

"Let's try to look at the bright side of this. Okay?" Lila said, with tears in her eyes, as Peter nodded. "It can't get any worse, and you won't have to run Stacia Homes anymore. Right?"

"That's right," agreed Peter.

"Then you'll have more time to get me in the family way, sweetie," Lila concluded as she leaned over to kiss Peter.

"You do have a point. How soon can we get started?" said Peter returning her kiss and feeling more than ready to get started.

"That's enough of that," interrupted Eric. "Is that all you two can talk about?"

Lila was prepared to make one of her famous comeback remarks when she noticed blood on Peter's shirt. "Is that blood?"

"Yes. But it's not mine."

Before Peter could say anything else, Eric said, "He had a little–ah . . . let us say . . . an altercation with a Mr. Alan Chipenski."

"Jackass!" said Lila disgust evident on her face. "What was it about?" she asked as she gave Peter a look that could almost kill.

"It was nothing," Peter lied. "It didn't mean a damn thing."

Lila would have to wait until later to give Peter a piece of her mind as Mr. Freeman returned with their order and they turned their full attention to the plate of steaming ribs.

* * *

You can't have a good day with a bad attitude,
and you can't have a bad day with a good attitude.

~~~Anonymous

* * *

Chapter Six

In contrast to Peter and Eric's "bad" day, Lori Cochran was in the middle of a fabulous day.

Lori lived in Moulton, Alabama, twenty miles east of Russellville. She was a real estate agent and after having a fine year was having one fine vacation.

Lori had done nothing all morning except lie in the sun and work on her already perfect tan. As she rubbed on suntan oil, she drew envious stares from some of the other girls and appreciative looks from all the men. *This is the life*, she thought; *and this cruise is an excellent gesture on the part of Mitchell Realty*. Her all-expense-paid cruise had been a bonus for being top salesperson for the year. The sale of the little lake cottage had put her over the top.

Only ten days from the fiscal year end, Lori trailed Taylor Reese by $55,000. The cottage, listed for almost a year, had no real prospects. It had been priced too high for the current depressed market when Mr. Max Partain walked into the real estate office.

His appearance was a bit unorthodox. He had long hair and a beard, but his beard was neatly trimmed and his hair was clean and pulled back into a long ponytail. His clothes were nondescript, but he wore expensive shoes. You could always tell a lot about people by the shoes they wore--especially men. Helen Mitchell had taught Lori that men who wore expensive shoes could afford to buy property. Her last client had wasted her time. After she had driven him all around Lawrence County for a full week, she discovered the poor loser couldn't afford a happy meal at McDonald's. She should have noticed his $29.95 Reeboks.

She bubbled in her best patented real estate agent voice, "I'm Lori. How may I help you today?"

Max asked to look at some secluded properties, and the cottage was the first one to enter Lori's mind. As she showed him the listing, she described the property. Located in Franklin County with a Belgreen address, it was the only house on a secluded gravel road close to Cedar Creek, one of the local BCDA lakes. The small two bedroom/one bath cabin needed quite a bit of work, although it did seem structurally sound.

The original owner of the cottage was Helen Mitchell's friend who died and left it to his only living relative, a nephew, who was a New Jersey attorney. The attorney had no interest in the house or anything else in Alabama and mistakenly assumed property values in Alabama were comparable to that of New Jersey. Subsequently, he priced the cabin at $92,000. He refused to back down on the price, and it remained empty last year with no serious prospects. Only a week before Max waltzed in, with cautious prodding from Helen, the attorney finally agreed to reduce the price to $60,000.

After Lori had shown the house to Max, he affirmed it was exactly what he wanted and immediately offered $51,000.

Lori contacted the attorney in New Jersey and relayed the offer. Three days and several counter offers later, Max and the attorney agreed on a purchase price of $56,500. Max plunked down five stacks of hundred dollar bills that totaled $10,000 to a stack and then counted out another $6,500 in hundred dollar bills. At that precise moment, Lori Cochran, real estate extraordinaire, knew she was headed for a cruise. She worked like a demon and closed on the cottage in a remarkable nine days from the first day Max had walked in wearing those Bruno Magli shoes. It was in time with enough money to put her $1,500 over Taylor in yearly sales.

This was the first time in the last seven years Taylor hadn't won a trip. If she hadn't always been so uppity, Lori might have felt sorry for her. After all, Taylor had even congratulated her, but Taylor Reese was a bitch and Lori couldn't bring herself to feel sorry for her.

Being pampered like royalty on a cruise was very different from what she would have expected five years ago. No one in Moulton other than Helen Mitchell knew about her former problems with drugs. Helen was also the only person in Moulton who knew she had been to prison.

For five years, Lori languished in Julia Tutwiler Penitentiary for Women sentenced for accessory to murder and accessory to armed robbery. She was still afraid at times she would wake up to see those Pepto-Bismol pink walls of the area where she spent most of her time. The facility was named in honor of the "Angel of the Stockades," Julia S. Tutwiler, a noted Alabama educator and crusader for inmate education.

Now it seemed like only a bad dream. She had been high and needed money for more drugs. She and Tony, a loser she had met at a fraternity party, robbed a convenience store in Tuscaloosa. Tony tied up the clerk and gagged her neither knowing nor caring she had a medical problem preventing her from breathing through her nose. The clerk died before the next customer came in.

The drugs and booze had seemed so harmless when she first started. She had been a high school dropout who was always looking for a party and her next high. She never really cared where it came from or whom it was with, but Lori hadn't killed anyone. Tony tied the clerk up and shoved that gag in her mouth. Lori didn't have a violent bone in her body. However, she was charged as an accessory on two counts, and was soon on her way to Tutwiler and five years of torture.

Lori's long blonde hair and full breasts and hips immediately caught the attention of the wrong guards. As a result, she was violently raped eleven times during her first week of incarceration. She stood only 5'2" in her stocking feet, barely weighed in at one hundred pounds, and could do little to defend herself. The first time it happened, she told one of the female guards but quickly learned guards didn't care what happened to inmates.

After a blurred six months of almost unbearable rape and torture, she met a guard sergeant who put the word out she was his personal property and no one was allowed to touch her. Two to three times a month she did to him what his wife wouldn't do. He never asked for anything else, and the other guards left her alone.

In her first year of incarceration, she barely managed to survive. In her second year, she found the gym and worked out, toning her already beautiful body. The third year she passed her GED test by scoring one of the few perfect scores ever recorded in the Alabama penal system. Finally, she was a high school graduate who hungered for knowledge and took any available prison class. Through it all, she kept to herself and made no friends except for an inmate named Mattie Wilson who later introduced her to her savior, Helen Mitchell.

Mattie was convicted of manslaughter. She killed her mother in the garage of the house they had lived in for twenty years. Mattie drank too much tequila celebrating Mama's eightieth birthday. She had argued with her Mama over who would get that last sip of tequila left in the bottle. Mama wanted it because it was her birthday, but Mattie had bought the tequila and was determined to drink it herself. Mattie scooped the bottle up off the kitchen table and staggered into the garage as Mama tottered right behind. Mattie got in her car and cranked it up. She patted the accelerator as Mama came into the garage and stood in front of the car. Mattie raised the tequila bottle to her lips and drank that last sip of tequila as she shoved the old Buick into drive and took Mama on a hood ride that smashed through the back of the garage and ended with Mama pinned against the wall of their den.

That lone sip of tequila put Mattie in Tutwiler for fifteen years. Mattie had since seen the error of her ways and was a model inmate. She worked at the Tutwiler Clothing Factory, where inmates sewed uniforms for the Department of Corrections. She took real estate courses taught by Helen Mitchell and had talked Lori into doing the same.

Helen was a real estate broker and former teacher. Several times a month Helen drove from Moulton to Wetumpka to volunteer at the women's correctional facility. Sweet, serious, and compassionate, Helen privately tutored Lori and helped her acquire her real estate license.

When Lori served her time, Helen offered her a job. Helen also helped Lori move to Moulton, get an apartment, and purchase a vehicle. Lori was now a successful real estate agent, full of class and charm. Never in a million years would anyone believe Lori had lived for five years in Alabama's harsh maximum-security prison for women. Maybe one day she might even meet her *Mr. Right*, not those *Mr. Right Nows* who seemed to always be attracted to her.

Lori had no idea how soon *Mr. Right* would enter her life.

* * *

RUSSELLVILLE, ALABAMA

Back in 1812, a road was needed to connect New Orleans, Louisiana, to Nashville, Tennessee. The Federal Government built the road and named it Jackson's Military Road.

It passed through a town now known as Russellville which was named after Major William Russell--who helped in the building of the road in Alabama--and was incorporated on November 27, 1819.

* * *

Chapter Seven

"Good morning, Jennifer," Peter said pleasantly as he strode into Harold's reception area.

He and Lila had spent the weekend in Cheaha State Park, where they'd relaxed in a secluded glass cabin atop Cheaha Mountain far away from the questions of the media and pitying glances of well-meaning Russellville residents. They learned the word Cheaha was a Choctaw word for "high" and Cheaha State Park contained the highest point in Alabama. Before Andrew Jackson became President of the United States, he fought against local Indians in a battle that later became known as the Creek Indian War. One battle was fought at the Callabee Battle Ground on Cheaha Mountain's southeast slope. Close by at Talladega, Jackson wiped out an entire Indian village. The battles were romanticized through Davey Crockett in movies, on TV, and in the famous song, *Davey, Davey Crocket, King of the Wild Frontier.* Jackson's triumph over the Indians in the Southeast ultimately ended in the bloody **"Trail of Tears"** as the Indians were relocated west of the Mississippi River. Most Americans, even Alabamians, don't know the history behind the mountain, and only saw the mountain as a romantic getaway or a great place for church retreats or school field trips.

"Good morning, Mr. Stacia," said Jennifer, who was slightly, but not grossly, overweight. She was one of those women whose age was hard to determine depending on what she wore that day and how she fixed her hair. Last week at the memorial service wearing a threadbare black dress with her hair drawn back in a severe style she had looked at least sixty. Today, she had just returned from the beauty parlor with a cascade of loose auburn curls and sported a new, tailored blue suit the exact color of her eyes. She looked to be in her early forties.

You look exceptionally nice, today," complimented Peter.

"Thanks, Peter," beamed Jennifer. She liked Peter and he had always been her favorite of all of Harold's clients.

"Is Harold here yet?"

"No. He called and promised he would be here within thirty minutes."

"Since I have nowhere to go and all day to get there, I'll wait."

She laughed.

As Peter struggled to fit his large frame into a stiff waiting room chair built for someone half his size, he picked up a copy of a book, *Everything Men Know About Women.* Peter opened it and saw every page was completely blank. There was not one word written in the book. Peter smiled and replaced the book on the table. He then picked up a copy of *Newsweek.* As he browsed through the magazine, he was amazed it continued to have articles that lamented over all the unnecessary money and time spent on Y2K. When were they going to get over it? It had happened over five months ago. He pitched the magazine back on the table.

When Harold appeared, he looked frazzled and slightly perturbed. "Good morning, Peter," he said as he held his side.

"Good morning, Harold. Are you all right?"

"I need to catch my breath. You know how I hate to be late for an appointment. I ran from where I parked in front of the courthouse."

"You shouldn't have hurried on my account, although I am curious to know what happened to you."

"Jake Malone's kid tried to run me off the road in one of those jacked-up pickup trucks, but I'm happy to say, Nelly, my old suburban, held her ground. I have to get her a new passenger side mirror and a little paint where it seems she had a *wrestling match* with Sam Benefield's mailbox."

Peter laughed. "Sorry, Harold."

"It's okay. Go on into my office, and I'll be with you shortly."

Peter ducked his head as he walked through the doorway into Harold's office and eased into a large, comfortable armchair that fitted his 6'9" frame much better than the one in the waiting area. Within minutes, Harold entered and walked around behind his desk to sit down.

"Let's begin." Harold took a letter opener and slit the seal to the folder while Peter tried to relax. "According to these documents," said Harold, "Papa left you everything excluding what he relinquished in the will to the employees at Stacia Homes. Listed here, I see the home in Russellville on Wilson Boulevard and the farm in Vina. Also, there seems to be several bank accounts with balances totaling a little more than $1 million."

Papa had indeed bequeathed him something. Peter hadn't told anyone, but after the meeting with the employees, he'd had serious reservations about Papa's mental health in the last few months before he died. If Papa hadn't provided for him adequately, he had already decided to take the employees, Dillon, Geneva, and Harold to court to get what was rightfully his. Now he didn't have to worry about that.

As Harold went over each bank account, Peter signed a new signature card. When Peter added the amounts in the bank accounts to the properties, he figured it to total close to $2 million.

"Are there any liabilities?" asked Peter.

"No. Everything is paid for. There is an additional earmarked account to pay any bills that could come in later. After a year, I will turn over any remaining funds to you. Oh, by the way, I have an envelope Papa instructed me to give to you upon his death. It almost slipped my mind."

Harold spun his chair around to a safe behind him and dialed the proper combination. He opened the safe, reached in, and removed a large manila envelope. He handed it to Peter and said, "Papa left instructions you were not to open this in my office. You are to open it in private."

"What is it?"

"I don't know."

Peter left Harold's office as the bells of the downtown Methodist Church rang out twelve times before starting its medley of church tunes. *The Lord has promised good to me--His word my hope secures,* sang Peter waving to a group of curious onlookers headed for the courthouse. *He will my shield and portion be--as long as life endures.* This was Peter's favorite verse of *Amazing Grace.* He liked this verse because he had always felt God protected him and favored him above others. He, Eric, and Alan had all three grown up fatherless, but it was Peter who ended up with the better life. *Yes. God has given "good" to me and has been my shield* thought Peter as he laid the envelope on the passenger seat and hopped into the Dodge. Backing out onto North Jackson, his cell phone rang. It was Lila.

"Are you and Harold through with your discussion?" she asked.

"Yes."

"And?"

"And we're rich. Papa left us almost $2 million worth of property and cash."

"Since we're loaded, do you think you could stop by one of the Mexican restaurants and pick up some lunch on your way home?"

"Sure." Peter called and ordered shrimp and chicken fajitas, which were Lila's favorite. Peter pulled into the garage and pushed the button to let the garage door down. He grabbed the food, leaped out of the Ramcharger, and entered the kitchen.

Lila came out of the den wearing nothing but a smile. "Hey, handsome," she purred.

Peter dumped the food on the counter and turned around to face her. She placed her arms around him as her upturned breasts brushed lightly against him. She kissed Peter deeply and unbuttoned his shirt. She slowly tugged off his shirt and ran her hands across his broad chest. Peter scooped his wife up into his arms and carried her back to the bedroom. She, for the moment, had just what he needed.

Afterward, they lay very still, spent and totally satisfied. Peter whispered, "I love you more today than I did when I married you five years ago. Thanks for being my best friend, my lover, and my wife. I love you, Lila."

"I love you, too," said Lila as Peter noticed a look of concern first cloud her face and then recede like a distant storm.

"Lila, is something wrong?"

Smiling sweetly, but with a look of worry barely evident under the surface she answered, "No, but I do have a surprise for you."

"A surprise?" winced Peter as he abruptly sat up. "You know I hate surprises."

"I don't know if you will be pleased or not," said Lila as she also sat up and held one of his big hands in hers. "It could cause a big change."

"A big change?" he said removing his hand from hers and looking away from her moist eyes. He already didn't like the sound of this. He had already encountered enough surprises and changes for one week.

"Yes," said Lila as she stroked his arm with her long, strong fingers and reached up to pull his face within inches of hers. "My body is already starting to change. In about eight months, your life and my life will be changed irrevocably."

Like a freight train, it hit him. "You're not?"

"I am."

"You're having a baby? We're having a baby," Peter exclaimed. "That's wonderful. How did this happen?" he asked innocently.

"You can't take me ten or twelve times a week and not expect it to happen. I only hope this is the right time, especially with Papa passing away," Lila said as she turned away with her words fading into silence.

"This is the perfect time," Peter reassured as this time he pulled her face back to meet his. He stared deep into her eyes before a look of worry crossed his face and he asked. "Could we have hurt the baby? Or you?"

"No. If you could hurt me, or the baby, I wouldn't have done it. We wouldn't have done it," she said as her mood changed and she suddenly jumped up. "Let's go out by the pool and soak up some sun."

"What about work?"

"I took the afternoon off."

Peter got up and raced Lila to the pool, neither bothering to put on any clothing. They always swam nude. They dove in and expertly lapped the pool. Lila pulled herself up the pool ladder, glanced over at Peter, and asked if he was ready to eat.

"Sure."

As Lila walked across the patio and through the French doors into the house, Peter watched her perfect form with admiration. She soon emerged with a plate of steaming fajitas. Peter climbed from the pool and stepped over to the patio table as she set the food down. She went back inside and returned with their drinks and silverware.

They ate in silence until Lila blurted out, "You need to start looking for a job."

"What? . . . Why?"

"You're not going to be a deadbeat dad."

"I'm worth almost $2 million. I don't think that qualifies me as a deadbeat," argued Peter.

"Well then, go over with me exactly what you found out, and then I'll decide for myself," countered Lila.

Peter went over his visit with Harold while she listened intently.

When he finished, she asked, "What was in the manila envelope?"

"I'd completely forgotten about the envelope. I'll go get it." Peter walked off the patio through the grass to the side door of the garage. "Meet me in the kitchen," he called out. He opened the door of the Ramcharger and did not immediately see the envelope. He climbed up into the truck as its warm leather seats stuck slightly to his damp bare skin. *There it was.* Peter reached between the seat and console and retrieved it.

Peter returned to the kitchen and tossed the envelope on the table, as Lila came out of the hall carrying a pair of boxers and a towel for him. Peter lightly toweled off and put on the shorts. Lila took a knife out of one of the kitchen drawers and handed it to him. Peter slit the top of the envelope and found six typewritten pages.

Peter picked up the papers and looked at the first page. The letterhead bore the name of a company called *Navoiczyk Enterprises*. On it was a list of names for the board of directors. Peter was surprised to see the first two names.

Chairman of the Board	Peter Alesky Stacia III
President	Peter Alesky Stacia
Chief Executive Officer	Jacqueline Pamela Lowell
Chief Financial Officer	Daniel Lucias Bobo
Vice President	Richard Wade Barstow Jr.
Acquisitions Manager	Michael Dunston Jones
Finance Manager	Cordelia Leslie Hames
Sales Manager	David William Andrews
Property Manager	Laura Susan Everman
Security Advisor	John O'Leary

Lila looked at Peter and started to speak. Peter read her mind and said, "I don't know what *Navoiczyk* is."

"It this *Navoiczyk* Company included in what you learned about in Harold's office?"

"No."

The next five pages in Peter's hand listed account number after account number with dollar amounts following each account. A dazed Peter picked up the phone and called the phone number listed on the letterhead.

"*Navoiczyk Enterprises*," said a female voice on the other end of the phone.

* * *

TELL ME

Tell me why I had to suffer.
Tell me why I had to fall.
I thought I was back to normal.
Looks like nothing's changed at all.

Tell me, Tell me why I struggle . . .
Tell me, Tell me why I strive . . .
Failure always seems to find me.
Tell me why I even try.

Tell me because I need to hear it.
Tell me that you still believe.
Tell me, tell me I can make it.
Tell me you still stand with me.

Tell me there's still hope for tomorrow.
Tell me I still have a chance.

~~~Stone Ronson

* * *

Chapter Eight

"What did you tell him?" he yelled as he backhanded her across her pretty face.

"I didn't tell him nothin'," she blubbered through split lips.

"Yes, you did. I know you did. What did you say?" He hit her again and felt the satisfying crunch as her nose broke and sprayed the chair and floor with blood. "I saw you come out of the Sheriff's office. If you tell me, I'll let you live."

"Nothin', I didn't say nothin'," she cried out in pain. He then grabbed up a short aluminum ball bat and hit Georgia Hubbard several times in her stomach. *Something on the inside was hurt real bad.* Each breath brought a sharp pain as she coughed up blood. Her pain surprisingly gave her courage she didn't know she possessed.

"Dey gonna luv your white ass down at dat state pen," gasped Georgia lapsing back into the slang of her childhood. "Dem brothers gonna get you and get you good. One of dem gonna make you his toy boy. Get ready. Dem brothers, my brovers, is gonna make you wish you never touched me. Dat Sheriff . . . dat nice young Sheriff, he say he gonna lock you up good dis time. I don' tole' him everthin' . . . He knows everthin' . . . He knows you's Da' Man."

"What did you tell that pig?"

"I don' tole' you. I tole' him everthin'. He knows who's you gettin' yo stuff from. I showed 'em da tape of you and dat sorry Poleese Chief. An I'm gonna see yo' white ass 'n jail. 'Ima gonna tell de' judge everthin. You done whupped me de las' time. You be a little man goin' t' jail. Dat's where my brovers gonna get you. Make you like it too. Gonna be there the rest of yo' sorry ass life."

He hit her again.

"No. Don't. Please. Don't," she begged.

He hit her again, harder.

This time, she did not beg. Instead, she looked up at him and calmly peered into his cold blue eyes and all the way into the depths of his soul searching for a glimmer of goodness and compassion but finding only malevolence and cruelty. Georgia knew she wouldn't survive this time. She prayed to the God of her childhood to forgive her and save her wretched soul as she headed toward a bright light in which a distant figure stood with his hands outstretched.

He hit her again, and again, and again to keep from hearing that voice. It became the voice of his Mother telling him how worthless he was and how he would never amount to anything.

Why can't you be more like Peter and Eric? Why did I have to get the bad one? I wish I'd never gotten you. Each time he hit her, the sound was deafening, but he didn't hear it. He was in the zone. He had to make her stop. She had to stop. He didn't want to hear her voice anymore. She had to stop talking . . .

* * *

The first one's path went straight and true
For God's favor, he had won.
His touch was like the Midas King
He was their "Golden Son."

* * *

Chapter Nine

"I would like to speak to Mr. Daniel Bobo," Peter said to the distinctly feminine voice on the other end of the phone.

"May I ask who's calling?"

"Peter Stacia."

"Please hold, Mr. Stacia."

A different female voice came on the line and said. "Mr. Stacia, this is Jackie Lowell. Mr. Bobo is currently unavailable. Is there something I can help you with?"

"Yes ma'am," Peter replied. "My grandfather recently passed away. His attorney gave me an envelope containing documents listing me as Chairman of the Board of this organization."

"I am sorry about your grandfather," she said sounding truly sympathetic. "I've been expecting your call."

"Well then, Ms. Lowell. Maybe you can answer this question. What is Navoiczyk Enterprises?"

"We are a brokerage firm who owns and manages holding companies, commercial real estate, stocks, bonds, and various corporations."

"What companies do you manage?"

"Everything we manage is directly or indirectly owned by Navoiczyk."

"I see, so Navoiczyk is a publicly listed corporation?"

"No sir, Navoiczyk is privately owned."

"Who owns Navoiczyk?"

"According to the articles of incorporation, you do."

There was a pause.

"I see. Exactly how much property are we talking about?"

"I'm sorry, sir. I can't give out that kind of information."

"Excuse me," Peter said as he felt his blood pressure rise along with his feeling of importance. "This is my company, and you say you can't tell me what it's worth?"

"Pardon me. What I meant to say is we don't give out information like this over unsecured telephone lines. We must meet in private."

"Where are you?" Peter asked as calmly as possible.

"In Manhattan."

"You're the one who wired the money to Citizen's Bank?"

"Yes, sir."

"Okay. I'll see if my wife and I can catch a plane up there tomorrow."

"Catch a plane, sir?"

"Yes," said Peter struck by the idiocy of Jackie Lowell. "You do understand what *catch a plane* means, don't you?"

"It would be easier for us all if we sent your jet sir." Ms. Lowell asked in her continued calm and polite manner, seemingly unfazed by Peter's rudeness.

"We have a jet?" asked a surprised Peter.

"Yes. It can be there in about four hours," Ms. Lowell patiently explained.

"Be where?"

"Muscle Shoals," she answered.

"I see," Peter said not seeing at all. He hadn't known about the lake house, why would he know about a jet?

Peter looked at his watch. It was a couple of minutes past 5 o'clock. "You could have the jet at Muscle Shoals by 9 P.M.?"

"Yes, sir."

"Okay. Send the jet. We'll be at the airport at 9 P.M."

"Please hold while I confirm the times with the pilots."

While he was on hold, Peter turned to Lila and asked, "Do you have any personal leave days left at work?"

"Not really. Why?"

"We need to go to Manhattan to review financial records for Navoiczyk Enterprises. We could do a little site-seeing while we're there."

"New York? I've always wanted to visit New York City."

"Ms. Lowell will send the jet to pick us up at Muscle Shoals at nine."

"Who owns that company, and why are you on the board?"

"Apparently we do."

"We do? We own a company with a jet? You're lying!"

"No. I'm not."

"Jets cost a lot of money. How much is this company worth?"

"I don't know. That's why we're going to Manhattan."

"They won't tell you?"

"Not over the phone."

"This is really strange. When people inherit a company they generally know about it beforehand and have an idea of how much it is worth."

"Yeah. Tell me about it."

Ms. Lowell came back on the line. "Mr. Stacia?"

"Yes."

"It has been confirmed. The plane will depart LaGuardia at 7:30 P.M. our time and should be there no later than 8:30 to 8:45 P.M. Central Daylight Time."

"That's great," said Peter. "Can you recommend a good hotel close to your office?"

"It would be best if you'd stay at your residence at Seventy-First and Central Park West?"

"We have a residence in New York City?"

"Yes. You do."

"I guess we'll stay there, then."

"I will make your arrival known."

She gave Peter the gate information for Muscle Shoals after which Peter thanked her and hung up still dazed by all he had heard. To whom would she make his arrival known? What kind of bizarre nightmare was he and Lila in now? When was this going to end? When could they get back to their old life, their everyday boring and predictable life? He longed for that life he hadn't appreciated until now.

Lila called her parents at the clinic to inform them she and Peter were flying to New York and would be gone at least a couple of weeks. It still amazed Lila her father and mother had given up his successful and lucrative practice in Tuscaloosa to move back to Russellville to open this small clinic. He'd been so eager to leave as a teenager and had told his mother he would never set foot in Franklin County again. He had kept his word except to attend her funeral in '83 when Lila was eight and staying with her grandmother for the summer. She talked a few more minutes, said goodbye, and pushed the end button. "I'm free for at least two weeks."

"Let's get packed then," Peter said as Lila left the room.

Peter reached for the Bible on his nightstand. As he picked it up, the envelope with the gold keys once again fell to the floor. He picked up the envelope, opened it, and examined the gold keys closer. He turned them over several times in his hands wondering what they fit. They were unusual keys--each with a different colored jewel and an eagle engraved into the widest part of the key. As he looked closer, he noticed the eagle had two heads. *Why would there be a two-headed eagle on each key, and why was one head facing left and the other facing right? Was this some kind of special symbol or emblem?*

As he heard Lila coming back in the room, he slipped them back in the Bible and placed the Bible in his suitcase. He suddenly felt guilty about not having told Lila about the keys, but it lasted for only an instant. He surprisingly enjoyed being the only one who knew about the keys. As he watched Lila do her hit and miss style of packing, he wondered if she could sense this difference in him.

Lila was completely unaware of the change beginning in Peter, but it wouldn't be long before she noticed the man she thought she knew had been replaced by a stranger driven by money and power. She, of course, would rationalize and reason he was going through a phase and would soon be his old self.

Neither Peter nor Lila realized once a soul has traveled from innocence over the bridge of power and knowledge, it is impossible to find a path back. God hides the bridge and it is never found again with the traveling soul forced to live in its new world. Peter would soon taste the sweet fruit of *power* and lose his innocence just like Adam and Eve tasted the forbidden fruit of the tree of knowledge and lost theirs.

* * *

If God did not exist,
it would be necessary to invent him.

~~~Voltaire

* * *

Chapter Ten

Eric and his two top deputies were only fourteen miles away from where the confrontation was in progress. They huddled together listening intently to the transmission from Georgia's hairpin.

"Where are they?" asked Eric.

"He's going to kill her if we don't get to her in time," said Chief Deputy, Andy Landers.

"Come on, Georgia. Give us a hint to where you are! Why won't she say where they are?" screamed Eric as his level of terror expanded. "Has she forgotten she's wearing a microphone? Doris!" Eric yelled. "Go over the tapes. See if you can hear any mention of where they are. It has to be close."

"Yes, sir."

Over the speaker they heard:

"What did you tell him?"

"I didn't tell him nothin'."

"This is not good," said Eric. "At least say his name. We need it on tape. Tell us who he is," the Sheriff coaxed Georgia. He knew she couldn't hear him, but talking to her somehow helped him keep his sanity.

"What did you tell that pig?"

"I don' tole' you. I tole' him everthin'. He knows who's you gettin' yo stuff from. I showed 'em da tape of you and dat sorry Poleese Chief. An I'm gonna see yo' white ass 'n jail. 'Ima gonna tell de' judge everthin. You done whupped me de las' time. You be a little man goin' t' jail. Dat's where my brovers gonna get you. Make you like it too. Gonna be there the rest of yo' sorry ass life."

"Doris, do you have anything yet? We really need to know where they are," Eric yelled back in the direction of Doris as she frantically listened to the tapes.

"No. Don't. Please. Don't," they heard Georgia cry.

Then they heard a sequence of sounds that would torment them and trigger nightmares for years. It only lasted a matter of seconds, but it seemed like an eternity.

They first heard a demonic blood-curdling wail that must've been heard for miles. Then came the horrific sounds of fists pounding flesh. Thump . . . thump . . . thump . . . thump . . .eventually the sounds became splat . . . splat . . . splat . . . splat.

What disturbed them most were the uncontrollable sobs and distorted pleadings of, *Mommy, Mommy. I'm sorry Mommy. Forgive me, Mommy. I'm sorry. I'll be better, Mommy I'll be better . . . I'll be as good as them . . . I promise . . . Mommy, PLEASE!*

It all ended with a grinding sound and silence.

"It's over," Andy said unable to meet the eyes of Eric or Doris.

"Yeah," said Eric.

"It was Alan, wasn't it?" asked Andy.

"Yeah."

"I guess he found the listening device."

"Yeah."

"Sheriff, did you hear what I heard?" questioned Doris. "I heard him call . . ."

"Yeah," interrupted Eric.

They all knew what kind of mother Alan had. Louise had been a drug addict. Alan grew up with her going in and out of rehab. That's why he spent most of his childhood at Peter's house. She had died from an overdose when Alan was a teenager.

"Doris, call and wake up the judge," said Eric in calm voice, much too calm for what he had heard. "We may never understand what happened, but we have to put that behind us and take action. I need a warrant for the arrest of Alan Chipenski for murder one. I also want a search warrant for all his premises. We will search for evidence to connect him to a murder as well as any evidence connecting him to a prostitution ring operating in the area. We will look for any drugs, paraphernalia, or money that could result from any illegal operation. I also need a warrant to search his personal vehicles and residence for drugs, cash, paraphernalia, and any evidence connecting him with Chief Jim Davis. I need an additional warrant for the arrest of Jim Davis for solicitation of prostitution, sale of a prohibited substance, and money laundering. I want all his bank accounts frozen as I think he might be a flight risk. I also need an order seizing his home and other personal property."

Doris nodded and left as she still scribbled Eric's instructions on a legal pad.

"Why do you want a warrant for Jim Davis?" asked Andy.

"That's who Alan gets his drugs from," Eric said in a matter of fact tone. "I have a videotape where our fine Chief of Police exchanged drugs for cash and then paid for sexual favors, but enough of that. Andy, I need every Deputy not on duty called out. Make sure you notify the Alabama State Troopers. Call all chiefs of police in the surrounding area. I want Alan Chipenski in a cell tonight."

"Sheriff?" asked Doris as she re-entered the room.

"Yeah."

"Judge Pilgrim is on the phone. He needs verification on some of your requests. He's on line two."

"Good evening, Judge," said Eric.

"Are you sure about Jim?" asked the Judge.

"Absolutely," said Eric. "I have a videotape of a meeting between him and Alan Chipenski."

"I see," said Judge Pilgrim after a long pause. "The warrants will be ready in about twenty minutes."

"Thanks, Judge. Goodbye."

Eric turned to Andy. "Go by the Judge's house and get the warrants and then meet me at Chief Davis' house."

"Yes, sir."

Eric strode purposefully to his cruiser and opened the trunk. Methodically, he stripped off his shirt and carefully placed it on the floor of the trunk. He pulled his bulletproof vest out of the trunk, put it on over his undershirt, and slipped his uniform shirt back on over the vest. He picked up his gun belt and buckled it around his waist. After he had removed his Ruger, he jacked a shell in the chamber, released the clip, and added another round. He replaced the clip, holstered the pistol, picked up the pump shotgun in the trunk, and chambered a shell. He did all this as if he were a robot without the capacity to think about what he'd heard. He then walked to the front of the Ford and checked the rest of his equipment.

* * *

MUSCLE SHOALS, ALABAMA

Muscle Shoals, Alabama, is the largest city in Colbert County. It is known for its recording studio called Muscle Shoals Sound. Recording stars and groups such as Aretha Franklin, Percy Sledge, Wilson Pickett, Otis Redding, Rod Stewart, Eric Clapton, Lynyrd Skynyrd, The Rolling Stones, The Allman Brothers Band, Carrie Underwood, and George Michael have all recorded there.

* * *

Chapter Eleven

The drive to Muscle Shoals took Peter and Lila about twenty minutes. Since they still had a little time before they had to meet the jet, they stopped at a quiet restaurant located a few minutes from the airport. As Peter sipped his beer and Lila her ginger ale, they discussed everything that had happened in the last few days.

Later as they pulled into the airport, Lila spotted a rather large corporate jet taxiing up the runway. "Do you think that's it?" asked Lila, her eyes wide with wonder.

As Peter started to reply, the plane turned around and they saw Navoiczyk Enterprises stenciled on the plane's side. A huge N with a circle around it painted in gold encompassed its tail.

"I guess it is," he replied.

They parked and started to remove their luggage. Before they could complete the task, a young man in what appeared to be an expensive Italian suit came driving up in a small electric car similar to a golf cart. "Are you the Stacias?" he inquired with a clipped British accent.

"Yes."

"I'll take care of your luggage," he said as he motioned Peter and Lila to sit in the small electric vehicle. As they sat down, he loaded their things and apologized for not meeting them at the gate. He explained it had been short notice.

"Don't worry about it," said Lila. Giggling under her breath, she looked at Peter and mouthed. "This is the way to travel."

"You're telling me," Peter mouthed back grinning like a possum.

As they were driven to the plane, they observed it was not an average business jet. It was a rather large one. A sophisticated, fair-haired woman stood at the bottom of the boarding stairs. As they pulled up to the stairs, she smiled. Peter and Lila both noticed she was quite attractive. She was somehow familiar to Peter like he'd met her a long time ago. She wore a gray business suit cut to accent her shapely legs and figure. "I'm Jackie Lowell," she said as she extended her hand.

As Peter shook her hand, he felt a connection. He knew her . . . maybe? He looked into her eyes searching for some reciprocated recognition. "Ms. Lowell, have we met before?"

Jackie seemed to hesitate before she shrugged. "And you would be Mrs. Stacia?" asked Jackie turning from Peter to Lila and offering her hand.

"Yes, but everyone calls me Lila," said Lila as she took Jackie's hand.

"Okay, Lila," said Jackie. "If you and Mr. Stacia will follow me, we'll get this plane in the air."

She turned and Lila and Peter followed her up the stairs. Once inside the plane, Lila gasped in amazement. "We own this?" she blurted enthusiastically.

"That's correct," said Jackie.

"What kind of plane is this?" Lila asked. She had never seen anything quite as luxurious.

"This is a new version of Gulfstream, a G990 designed especially for Navoiczyk Enterprises. It isn't actually out on the market. The Gulfstream Company executives are in the planning stages of the marketing and cost analysis to see if it is worthwhile to sell a stripped-down version of this plane for less than $100 million."

Peter looked at Lila. Her eyes were almost as wide open as he knew his must be. What kind of fortune did Papa have that he could afford this plane? Jackie Lowell just threw out the $100 million number like it was a pocket full of pennies.

"Mr. Stacia, I apologize for not answering your question on the phone. There will always be privacy concerns when we are talking about billions of dollars. Navoiczyk Enterprises has a net worth of $400 billion give or take a few million depending on the market prices of property today.

I want you to know I will never hide anything from you or answer you dishonestly, but there are some things we never discuss over open lines or where it can be overheard."

"Four hundred what? How could a poor Scottish immigrant build a company worth almost half a trillion dollars?" Peter wondered aloud.

Jackie Lowell laughed and then said, "Your grandfather was not and never was a poor immigrant. And he most certainly wasn't from Scotland."

"Yes, he was. He came here from Scotland with hardly anything."

"That must be a far cry from the truth. Our records go back to 1919 when your grandfather was worth more than $100 million."

"More than $100 million? Where did Papa get $100 million and how does $100 million become $400 billion?"

"Your grandfather shared a lot of secrets with me through the years, but never that one. I have no idea where the money came from, I just know it was Family Money. Your grandfather must have come from a family of very smart people, because as far as I can tell, your grandfather never touched anything that didn't turn into a gold mine."

"Family Money?" Peter thought back to the last conversation he'd had with his grandfather, *"You must listen, Peter. I have not always been so good, you don't understand, there is more . . . so . . . much . . . more . . . You will have great power. Use this power for good . . . not evil . . ."*

"That is unbelievable. Are you positive?"

"Of course, Mr. Stacia."

Jackie then told what she knew of Papa's story. "During the summer of 1929, Papa didn't like the way the business community was operating. He pulled all his money out of the banks, converted much of it back to gold bullion, and shipped it to an unknown location where he stored his money and gold until after the stock market collapse. In fact, he was probably the reason the banks failed which in return caused the Great Depression. By then on paper he was worth $180 million.

During the Depression, he bought manufacturing facilities, apartment buildings, and office buildings at sometimes one-thousandth their previous value. By 1940, he was cash rich with no liabilities and owned one-fourth of the commercial property in New York City and the surrounding boroughs. Of the properties he purchased, he never sold a one. These properties are now valued at approximately $400 billion.

Through venture capitalism and other business speculations, he has a controlling interest in a large portion of European businesses. It's hard to comprehend, but his companies owned companies that owned other companies. Your grandfather lived a very frugal lifestyle in contrast to his net worth. Each year since I have been with Navoiczyk Enterprises, about 99.7 percent of the net profits have been reinvested in purchasing companies and real estate worldwide.

The $400 billion net worth attached to Navoiczyk Enterprises is barely a drop in the bucket. Navoiczyk is only the real estate owned in New York and the surrounding boroughs. The combined holdings of the Stacia Empire worldwide may approach as much as $500 trillion. It's impossible for me to tell you exactly everything you now own. That is something you will discover as you get into the day-to-day running of your empire.

For more than seventy years, your grandfather built an empire. He was ruthless, and he didn't play games. There was no compassion and no second chances. Papa Stacia was always in control. He never second-guessed, never backed up, or ever backed down.

It's funny how people idolize sports stars, movie stars, and singers. Last year Michael Jordan was the highest paid celebrity, not earning in a year what your grandfather did in an hour, and your grandfather was unknown to the masses."

Peter and Lila both wanted to ask questions, but somehow they could not get their brains to cooperate with their voices.

Jackie showed Peter and Lila a list of European companies that neither had ever heard of. As Peter and Lila flipped through lists of properties they saw Parmalat of Brazil, Glenshee Chairlift Company of Scotland, Bertelsmann of Germany, New Look of Great Britain, Pizza Express of St. Albans, UK, Caffe Uno of UK, Gum of Russia, Tyumen Oil of Russia, Kovykta Gas Field of Siberia, the lists continued on and on.

Peter looked at Lila, scowled, and then threw the pages at Jackie. "This is absurd," protested Peter. "There's no way any of this could be true. If Papa were so rich, he'd be listed on Forbes list of the richest."

"I agree with Peter," Lila said. "This is crazy, but then I'm already worth about that much, myself. I bought a trillion dollars' worth of real estate day before yesterday."

At first, Jackie didn't say anything as she quietly picked up the thrown papers. Upon rising, she looked into their faces and into their souls. They were still kids and didn't understand wealth and power. They had never really been exposed to it and were about to get a crash course. She suddenly felt sorry for them because she'd been where they were. "I know this is hard for the two of you to comprehend," she said softly.

"What about inheritance taxes? Won't the U. S. Government take a good portion of properties and available cash?" asked Lila.

"No. A government can't tax what it doesn't know about and doesn't control. Powerful people don't play by the same rules as the masses. We're a little bit different."

Peter and Lila looked at each other and then back at Jackie.

"You'll both learn more as the day-to-day running of the empire begins; there's a lot to learn in New York and more to learn at the compound and other places. Papa said you two had the makings of a power couple. Peter, you think he didn't prepare you for this, but he did. Take away the zeros and management is management; it is still about delegation. Welcome to Wonderland, a place where everything is possible, nothing is as it appears, and the unbelievable is probable. You are officially the top of the feudal class. Everything is yours. The masses work for you, and they will never know. You no longer answer to anyone."

Chapter Twelve

Alan took his head out of his hands. What had happened? Where was he? What had he done? He looked over at Georgia and gasped. That was impossible. He couldn't have done that! Had he blacked out again? As he studied what used to be her face, he noticed something out of place hanging from her hair. A strange looking hairpin dropped to the floor. Alan looked at the hairpin and, at first, dismissed it. Then he bent over and retrieved it. As he turned it over in his hand, Alan wondered where she got the money to buy this unusual hairpin. As he turned it over again, it sprang open, and a small battery bounced on the concrete floor. Alan picked up the battery, put it back in its proper place, and looked again at the hairpin. It wasn't a hairpin at all. It was a transmitter or a microphone. It was small but definitely a microphone. Did it have a tracking device? No. If it did, someone would have shown up by now.

Alan swore under his breath as he stroked his beard. He then dropped the transmitter on the floor and ground it under the heel of his boot. How long had she been wearing a wire? Who had heard what happened? What had they heard? It was Eric. He knew it was. That Sheriff was always meddling in somebody's business.

Now, what? He didn't tell anyone where he was going. No one knew about this little lake retreat near Belgreen. He had purchased it under a false name from a real estate agent in Lawrence County.

It was definitely time for Alan to leave this part of the world. He went into the den and walked over to the fireplace. He kneeled and removed several bricks from the hearth revealing a large open space. He quickly reached in, pulled a latch, and slid the hearth forward on its rollers. The hearth covered eight packages wrapped in butchers' paper. Seven of the packages contained ten bundles each of tightly bound hundred-dollar bills that totaled $800,000. The eighth package contained a Mississippi driver's license in the name of Randall G. Marlowe, several credit cards, a social security card, and the title to the new Silverado truck he had purchased several months ago, all in the Marlowe name. These were actual documents, not fake, not replicas, but actual documents that would stand up to any state or federal check.

What was he going to do with what was left of the girl? He went to the pantry and opened a non-working upright freezer. It should be large enough. He ran back to the kitchen, scooped up Georgia, carried her to the pantry, stuffed her into the freezer, and slammed the door shut. When he turned around, he saw the mess he'd made. He got out a mop and bucket and cleaned the kitchen.

He finished his cleanup and walked into the bathroom. The Mississippi driver's license displayed a beardless, computer-altered picture of him with short blond hair. He would have to change his appearance to look like the generated photo. He took a pair of clippers out of the cabinet, plugged them in, and removed his beard. When it was down as close as he could get it, he did the same to his long black hair. With his hair as short as that of a new Marine recruit, he took out a bottle of blond hair dye and applied the gel thoroughly. Since it took at least thirty minutes for the bleach to work, he would use the time to shave his face until it was as smooth as a baby's butt. As long as he continued to masquerade as a blonde, he would have to remain very clean-shaven since his beard was black as coal. He managed a wry smile as he couldn't help but wonder if he'd have more fun as a blonde instead of a brunette. Alan got into the shower and washed the color from his hair, as well as Georgia's blood from his arms. When he finished, he got out, toweled off, and wiped the steam from the mirror. He looked at himself in the mirror and was satisfied. Randall Marlowe looked nothing like Alan Chipenski.

He pulled a light blue, cheaply made suit out of the closet. He searched until he located a wrinkled but clean white shirt. He continued to look until he finally found the burgundy tie he hadn't worn since he attended Eric's victory party last year. *How appropriate*, Alan thought. He dressed and completed his insurance salesman image as he donned a pair of John Lennon glasses.

The only identifying marks he had were the scrapes on his face from his earlier confrontation with Peter. Alan realized he had made a mistake when he taunted Peter. He had grown up with Peter and fallen victim to Peter's malevolent temper before. *Take it back. Don't you talk about Nicole Sheridan that way,* he could still hear Peter screaming at him more than a decade ago. He still had no idea where Peter's rage came from.

It was time to go. He had planned everything except where he was going. If he were going to pull this off, he needed a job. *That shouldn't be too hard,* he thought, as he looked at his falsified papers. *Randall Marlowe had a college degree.*

He loaded up the Silverado with what he would carry with him. When he finished, Alan slipped on a pair of brown cotton gloves. He went into every room with a dust rag and wiped clean of fingerprints everything he had ever touched. He didn't want fingerprints to identify him later. He went back into the pantry and pushed the back wall until it moved forward on its rollers. Going into the passageway, he walked into a small room filled with electronic equipment. He also wiped all this for fingerprints as he looked at the videotapes. He was so sorry he would never get the chance to use them. Alan then took out the tapes loaded in the recorders and laid them down so he could take them with him. If anyone ever found this place, he sure didn't need them viewing the tapes of what he'd done to Georgia. It had been quite some time since he'd blacked out like that. He then wiped each of the stored tapes individually to remove any chance of anyone finding his fingerprints on them.

With this finished, he sat at the computer, selected several files, and sent them to a secure server. He wrote a quick computer program that would wipe the disk continuously until someone tried to turn it on. If they ever did get the computer to come on, they would never be able to get to any files stored on the computer.

He inched back down the narrow passage and pulled the wall back into place. Alan looked around the house once more. He didn't want anything tying Alan Chipenski to Randall Marlowe, but he had made one mistake that he would later remember all too late.

Seated in the Silverado, he removed his gloves and looked through a road atlas. He turned to a map of the entire United States and contemplated where he would go. For no reason at all, he chose Billings, Montana. It was a long way from Russellville, Alabama, and had a large enough population into which Randall Marlow could successfully blend.

He said good-bye to his old Trans Am parked safely inside the garage. There was no person he hated to leave, but he did hate to leave his old car. That was something he, Eric, and ole Petey had in common. They all still drove the same vehicle they had first gotten in high school. Peter's Papa had bought it for him on his sixteenth birthday since his Mother had died and her live-in companion couldn't afford to buy him one. It was the only thing anyone had ever freely given him.

Alan was going to miss Papa. Papa and Gramma Joanna were the only people in the world who ever treated Alan like he was somebody. He had seen Peter glaring at him at the funeral. He knew there was going to be trouble if he attended, but how could he not go? Papa was the only man in his life and only real example of what a man should be. He heard Papa's words once again encouraging him--*Don't borrow money because the borrower is slave to the lender. As long as you don't owe and have cash, you're richer than most. Just keep busy, and one day it'll all be clear where you belong.*

He looked around at the little cabin. It wasn't much, but it was his. How many 28-year-olds could say they owned a house they'd paid for completely? He was going to miss this tiny place. He hoped it would be quite some time before anyone found it, but, of course, that would depend on how quickly Sheriff Eric Sandusky got his name and picture out to all the cops. The only thing that could tie him to this place was that real estate agent. What was her name? Laura? Loraine? Lori? Yeah. That was it. Lori . . . Lori Cochran. Nothing he could do about her.

He theorized if he could get out of Alabama, he would be in reasonably good shape. He took a various maze of county roads until he came out on Alabama Highway 247. He turned right and headed north for about sixteen miles before he hit U.S. 72. Turning west, he assumed he was going to beat the news about him-- that was until he got to Cherokee where he encountered a roadblock that would test how good his disguise and credentials held up under scrutiny. He was extremely nervous as he pulled up to the officer who stood out on the highway. He was even more nervous when he realized he recognized the trooper. What was his name? Jack? Yes, that was it. Jack Massey. He hoped Massey didn't recognize him. As he pulled up to the officer, the trooper gave him a thorough look.

"Good evening, sir. Could I please see your license, insurance, and registration?"

"Sure thing, officer," said the new Randall Marlowe whose voice was a few pitches higher than the bass voice of Alan Chipenski.

He handed the documents to the trooper, who carefully inspected them. The trooper held the Mississippi license up to Alan's face and noticed the recent injuries. "How did you get those facial abrasions?"

"I'm a skydiver in my spare time, and a few days ago I made a jump, and fell during the landing." Alan couldn't believe he had come up with such a bizarre explanation.

"Is that right?" scowled the trooper. "You look a little too effeminate to be a skydiver. In fact, you look kind of familiar."

Alan froze.

"You look like that insurance salesman who harasses my mother and father every month to collect his money."

"I am that, too--an insurance salesman--not effeminate." Alan tried to make a joke, but the trooper ignored it.

"Why did you start skydiving? Are you crazy?"

"No. I was an Airborne MP in the Army."

"It's stupid to jump out of a perfectly good plane," remarked the trooper as he walked around to the back of the truck and wrote down the license plate number. When he came back to Alan, he commanded Alan to pull to the side of the road while he ran the plates and license.

"What's wrong? Did I do something? What's this all about?" asked Alan with a voice even higher than before.

"We had a murder tonight over in Franklin County. The suspect is a grungy, hippy-looking dude about your height and weight but with a beard and long, dark hair. In fact, he has cuts on his face," the trooper said with a laugh. "I guess there's more skydivers around here than I realized."

"I guess so," said Alan weakly as he looked at his now blond reflection in his rear-view mirror to purposely avoid the trooper's steady gaze. The glasses gave him a rather intelligent look he'd not noticed before. The more Alan studied his own reflection, the more handsome he noticed he was.

"Sit tight," interjected the trooper before he walked back to his car.

Alan contemplated stomping the gas and making a run for it. That was until he saw the trooper speak to two Cherokee city cops. One immediately reached into his car and removed a pump action shotgun. Suddenly, Alan knew it would be best to stay where he was and pray the license and plates held up to the trooper's scrutiny.

The trooper came back wearing an easy smile. Gone was the hard look he'd left with. "Here you go, Mr. Furlowe," the trooper said politely as he handed the papers back to Alan. "Even though I don't believe a word you've said tonight, everything checks out fine."

"My name's not Furlowe. It's Marlowe . . . Randall Marlowe," corrected Alan with a sigh of relief.

"Oh sure, Mr. Furlowe. I'm sorry about that and sorry about the delay."

"Thank you, sir," Alan would give up on the trooper getting his name right. "Who did you say this guy killed?"

"I didn't say, but he murdered an innocent girl. Since officials heard the whole thing on audio and Alabama's penal system sentences more people to death per capita than any other state, we'll reserve him a special cell. In other words, he's bound for Hell."

"I do hope you catch him and he gets what's coming to him," Alan lied as he thought, *what a "fool" this trooper is.*

"Thanks, Mr. Furlowe," said the trooper as he waved Alan through the roadblock. "Have a safe drive on your way back to Mississippi, and remember to drive within the speed limits."

We'll see who's bound for Hell, thought a smug Alan Chipenski. *The guy you're looking for drove right through your roadblock, and you even wished him a safe trip. They may have me on tape, but that's not Randall Marlowe's voice. That's Alan Chipenski's voice, and Alan Chipenski doesn't exist any longer. Mr. Alan Chipenski is now officially dead. Long live Randall Marlowe.* Randall Marlowe smiled as he put the truck in gear and calmly accelerated away toward Mississippi. He would drive at least to St. Louis before he stopped.

By the time Eric arrested Jim Davis, Randall Marlowe would be on U.S. Highway 45 in Jackson, Tennessee, where he would catch Highway 412 on his way to Interstate 55. After he reached Interstate 55, it would be smooth sailing all the way. He had done it. He'd escaped their net and fooled one of Alabama's so-called finest. Cops were buffoons and no match for him. He was a free man with nearly one million reasons to stay free.

* * *

COLD CONCRETE

Hard long days with nothing under feet,
Restless naps upon the cold concrete.
Dreams are good, But in a cell
Sometimes dreams can hurt like hell.

Unless you've seen,
Unless you've felt, you won't know what I mean.
There's more to what I'm going through
Than you could ever dream.

I'm not sure why I tell you this
For it is incomplete.
While warm beds wait for you and yours,
My dreams are dreamed on cold concrete.

~~~Stone Ronson

* * *

Chapter Thirteen

Sheriff Eric Sandusky and Chief Deputy Andy Landers pulled up in front of a large Victorian style home within minutes of each other. Andy got out of his car, walked slowly up to the right side of Eric's cruiser, opened the door, and sat in the car. He closed the door and handed Eric a piece of paper folded twice. "Here's the warrant, Sheriff," he said.

Eric took the paper, unfolded it, and quickly read over it. He looked at Andy and asked, "Did you get the seizure order?"

"Yeah. It's right here." Andy handed the Sheriff another piece of folded paper.

"Are you wearing your vest?" asked Eric.

"Of course," Andy replied.

"Then let's do it."

"How are we doing this?" asked Andy.

"We will walk right up and ring his doorbell," Eric said. "The Chief's probably in bed asleep."

Eric and Andy walked up the sidewalk. They climbed a short flight of stairs that led to a covered entry. Andy rang the doorbell. In a few moments, Judith Davis, a Martha Stewart look-alike, in a pair of red silk pajamas and oriental house slippers came to the door. She turned on the entry light, and as soon as she saw the Sheriff and his Chief Deputy, she opened the door. With a sleepy smile she said, "Come on in, Sheriff."

"Good evenin', Mrs. Davis. Is Jim here?" asked Eric.

"He sure is. I'll go get him," she said. "Both of ya'll just make yourselves at home." She turned and padded back down the hall.

"Do you think he suspects anything?" Andy quietly asked Eric.

"I don't think so, cautioned Eric, but be ready."

The Russellville Chief of Police came down the hall as he buttoned up his uniform shirt.

"Evenin', Sheriff. How can I be of service?" asked Jim.

Eric and Andy flanked Jim, and before he could move from between them, the Sheriff and his Chief Deputy each got an arm. Eric reached behind his gun belt, removed his handcuffs, and cuffed him. "What is this?" Jim asked.

Eric read the Chief his Miranda Rights. Then he read the long list of charges. When he got to solicitation of prostitution, Mrs. Davis turned ghostly white, then immediately as red as her pajamas. She walked over to her husband of twenty years and slapped him.

"I've been framed. I'm innocent," Jim pleaded. "Judith, honey. Please call our lawyer."

"Call him, yourself. You should have thought about this when you were out with prostitutes," Mrs. Davis said in a flat monotone voice, as she tried unsuccessfully to conceal her hurt and shock.

"Put him in the car and call dispatch," Eric said.

Eric turned to Judith Davis and said, "Ma'am I hate to do this to you, but you need to wake up the girls if they're here." He knew the Chief had twin sixteen-year-old daughters. "You have to leave. I have a seizure order for the house. You'll want to get clothes and personal items for you and the girls. Do you have somewhere to go?"

"What?" she said as tears started to form in the corners of her eyes. "We have to leave? Why do we have to leave? This is *my house--my house*--I've made every payment. Because of that cheating bastard, you're taking *my house* away from me? What makes you think you have the right to take *my house*? It's *my house*; I had it before I even married. I have made every payment! Not him--Me. Only two payments away from owning it free and clear, and you want to seize it? It's *my house*--Not his--Mine."

"Ma'am calm down," begged Eric. Even though he tried to be sympathetic, he knew it didn't come across that way. He could hear the harshness in his own voice.

"CALM DOWN. CALM DOWN? HOW DARE YOU TELL ME TO CALM DOWN AFTER YOU TELL ME I HAVE TO LEAVE MY HOUSE?" Judith Davis yelled. Not only did Ms. Davis resemble Martha Stewart, she also had her temper.

"Mrs. Davis. If it is your house, then we can't keep it. You will still have to leave until I can get this sorted out. Do you have somewhere to go?"

"I can go to my parents, I guess," said Judith Davis mildly as she realized yelling was getting her nowhere.

Sometimes I hate this job, Eric thought. *It doesn't seem right to tell this woman she has to leave her home. She most likely doesn't know anything about what her husband is doing.* In his experience, he found wives often never knew what their husbands did on the side. It was almost as if they didn't want to know.

"Go visit your parents for a couple of days. Are the girls here?"

"No. They're on vacation with Jim's parents in Gulf Shores."

"Good. Maybe by the time they need to come back, we will have this all straightened out. I'll go with you while you get your personal things." Eric knew he had definitely stretched the truth. It would probably take months or even years before any of this was straightened out. The ones who really suffered would be Jim's girls and his wife. The public would see to that. As soon as the word got out, and it would get out, the family would be ostracized even though they were innocent.

"You have to go with me?" she questioned.

"Yeah. I have to make sure you don't destroy any evidence."

"I see," she said, not seeing at all.

* * *

As Eric and Andy walked the Chief of Police through the gate into the central booking area of the Franklin County Jail, they heard a nearby train blow its air horns to warn motorists at the next crossing.

The jail's trustees didn't look at Jim that hard until they saw the chrome shackles around his wrists behind his back. The trustees immediately ran upstairs to spread the word the new Sheriff had arrested the Russellville Chief of Police. News spreads like wildfire in jails, and this time was no exception. One of the trustees called a friend collect from the pay phone located inside the drunk tank. Before daylight, half the county would know Jim Davis had been arrested.

After Eric booked Jim, he ordered the Chief to be locked up in a solitary cell. This was for Jim's protection. He didn't want anyone in the County Jail to hurt or kill the Chief. Incarceration of a fellow officer was always dangerous. Most inmates believed they were in jail because of the law officials. It could never be the fault of the incarcerated, only the fault of the incarcerator. There were always inmates that would attempt bodily harm to any officer in jail. After Eric safely locked Jim in a solitary cell away from the general population, he walked back down to the dispatch/jailer's office to find Andy.

"Are all officers assembled in my ready room?" asked Eric.

"Sure thing, Sheriff," Andy replied.

"Good," Eric said, "I need to get them briefed and out on the road as soon as possible. We've got to find Alan."

Eric walked out of the jailer's office and down the short sidewalk to a gate in the fence that led to the outside world. He punched in his exit code on a numbered keypad and waited as the gate opened. He walked the short path to the courthouse to his office and ready room.

* * *

FAMILY

One of the definitions of FAMILY by dictionary.com is:

All those persons considered as descendants of a common progenitor.

* * *

Chapter Fourteen

Feeling more than slightly overwhelmed, Peter sat back in the soft leather chair. This was not what he had expected after the reading of the will. Could they really own $400 billion worth of New York real estate? Properties worldwide? A compound somewhere? Had Jackie said $500 trillion net worth? He felt as if he were in a badly put together video game. How much is $500 trillion? It would take hundreds of years to build that much wealth. His head hurt as he tried to figure it out. Why hadn't Papa let him know about this? This was simply too much. Why hadn't Papa prepared him better? What other secrets had Papa hidden from him? Where had he gotten the money to start all this? Was Papa a criminal? How could this alleged wealth come to him honestly? Jackie had said it was *Family Money*. What Family?

Peter realized for the first time he had never heard Papa mention Family. He always said things like, "We take care of our own," and "Never forget Family; it's who you have when there is no one else." But Papa had never mentioned *his* family. He'd heard Scotland but never any mention of brothers or sisters. Neither had he mentioned parents, grandparents, cousins, uncles, or aunts. What Family? Who was The Family and *where* were they? According to Jackie, they sure weren't in Scotland. Why had Papa lied about what country he was from? It had never occurred to Peter until this moment that he had no idea who his family really was. He knew there were no cousins from his dad's side. He'd been an only child, but what about his mother? Who was she? Where was her family? Who was her family? Papa had been everything to him, and now all he had were questions.

After the jet completed the landing and had finished its taxi to the departure area, Jackie unbuckled her seat belt and instructed Peter and Lila to do the same. They walked off the plane and were met by the longest limousine Peter or Lila had ever seen. This was definitely going to be an interesting trip to New York.

The limo pulled up to an ancient looking five-story brownstone building at Seventy-First and Central Park West. Lila and Peter hopped out of the limo and walked up to the door. They were met by an attendant who opened the door to a large well-lit lobby not unlike that of a major luxury hotel. As the limo driver brought in Lila and Peter's luggage, Peter asked in what direction their room was.

"Room, sir?" questioned the attendant looking quite puzzled. "We don't have any *rooms* here."

"Well then--What apartment are we in?"

As Jackie walked up, she caught the last of the question and replied for the attendant. "Peter, this whole building is your private residence. The floors three through five is where you will reside. The first floor includes the kitchen and living quarters for the hired help. The second floor features an indoor Olympic-size swimming pool as well as a fully equipped workout facility."

"Floors three through five is where we'll stay?" asked Lila, who appeared to be in shock.

"Yes. That's the residence."

"Hired help? Exactly how many people work here?" asked Peter starting to understand what Jackie had meant when she said she had to make their arrival known.

"I really don't know. I don't handle the everyday details of hiring and firing here at the residence. I could find out if you really want to know. I do know the cooks, limo drivers, pilots, security guards, and a butler live here full time," said Jackie as she opened the elevator with a key. "I live in my own apartment not far from here."

"Here's your key to the elevator," said Jackie as she handed it to Peter. "There are only three. Jeffery, your butler, and I have the other two." They entered the elevator along with the attendant who had already expertly maneuvered their luggage into the back.

They rode up to the third floor without speaking. Peter and Lila walked out of the elevator into what resembled a huge ballroom. It was exquisitely furnished, with a staircase spiraling up some twenty feet to the next floor.

As Peter sat with Jackie on an extremely uncomfortable but expensive couch, Peter marveled at the detail of the moldings and the artistry displayed almost everywhere. The floor was a rose-colored marble or maybe granite that appeared to be seamless though Peter knew it was impossible to ship a solid sheet of marble that size. All the furnishings were extremely heavy and ornate.

Lila, on the other hand, was absolutely smitten by the quality of artwork and artifacts displayed. Original paintings signed by well-known artists were everywhere. As she wandered around, she almost felt as if she were in a museum. She entered a large, private library where she saw first editions of books and writings dating back hundreds of years. Some of the titles she could read as she read and spoke French, Spanish, and German fluently. There were others in which she wasn't sure of the language. There seemed to be quite a collection of Russian poets--especially Pushkin. She was amazed at the extent of Russian authors—Bryusov, Chukovsky, Nadezhda Dmitievna Khvoshchinskaia, Sergei Timofeyevich Aksakov, Mark Aleksandrovich Aldonov, Fyodor Mihailovich Dostoevsky, Nicolai Vasilyevich Gogol, Boris Leonidovich Pasternak, Aleksey Nikolayevich Tolstoy--the holdings went on and on. The only two besides Pushkin she immediately recognized were Pasternak and Tolstoy as she had read English translations of *Dr. Zhivago* and *War and Peace*.

"Now exactly what is your position with Navoiczyk Enterprises?" asked Peter after the attendant had put away their luggage and gone back down the elevator.

"I'm your personal assistant. I was Papa's personal assistant for the past thirty-nine years. I was recruited when I was a junior executive for Chase Manhattan. After working for Navoiczyk for eighteen months, I came to work for Papa and Joanna directly."

"You have been working for Papa the last thirty-nine years?" interjected Lila as she returned and sat near them in a matching side chair almost as uncomfortable as the couch. "You can't be much more than forty. When did you start, when you were six?"

Jackie laughed. "Sweetheart, bless you. I am sixty-five years old. What you see here is the product of good breeding, a personal trainer, and a great plastic surgeon. I look essentially the same now, if not better, than I did thirty years ago."

"You go, girl," said Lila relieved Jackie was over forty.

"How many people know about my net worth?" Peter asked.

"Three…You, Lila, and myself," said Jackie. "Worldwide there are perhaps a dozen who could put everything together if they really thought about it."

Peter had an even stronger feeling Jackie and his Papa's relationship had been more than merely that of employer/employee, and he could tell from Jackie's expression she knew that Peter knew. She had looked familiar when he and Lila met her on the plane. He was suddenly flooded with memories from his childhood he didn't know he still had. There was a time when he and Gramma Joanna had gone to eat at a little sandwich shop in Muscle Shoals close to the airport. As they pulled out to head back to Russellville, Peter had told Gramma Joanna he saw Papa with some woman pulling into the parking lot. His Gramma had said that wasn't Papa, but Peter had known it was. He had seen the same woman with Papa on several other occasions. He now realized that woman had been Jackie. Why hadn't that bothered Gramma Joanna? Something else dawned on him. Jackie had been at Papa's memorial service. She'd sat in the back and worn sunglasses and a fashionable scarf wrapped around her head and shoulders. Yes, he was sure she'd been there. Why had she not approached him then? Why did she not mention it now? Peter gave her a knowing smile as she blushed. She'd definitely had a romantic connection with Papa at some time in the past. Peter imagined Papa had provided very well for Jackie Lowell. He decided if Jackie never brought up anything about her and Papa's past, he wouldn't either.

"You mean Daniel Bobo, the CFO doesn't know?" asked Lila.

"To be quite honest, he doesn't exist. He's a name on a piece of paper. Navoiczyk is only one of many corporations under the umbrella of Stacia Enterprises. You and Peter will be in charge of Stacia Enterprises. You'll find you have thousands of *nonexistent corporations* with *nonexistent board members* to protect your monetary interests," Jackie explained. "It's practically all legal and highly intricate. When you visit the compound, it will probably answer a lot of your questions."

Jackie stepped gracefully toward the elevator and turned toward them before she inserted her key and waited for the elevator to make its way back up. "I hope the two of you enjoy your stay here in New York. Within the week, I'll submit as complete a list as possible of your companies along with assets and bank balances. You will also receive portfolios from the brokerages that handle stocks and bonds. Of course, you must understand it will be quite a matrix to figure out."

"How can you come up with information on thousands of companies in a matter of days?" asked Lila.

"I must confess I'm efficient, but not that efficient. Papa had already requested me to compile this information back in February only a month before his March accident. It's almost like he knew his time was up." Peter and Lila both noticed Jackie's eyes fill with tears and for the first time Peter saw through Jackie's expertly applied makeup that her eyelids were red from crying. "I have worked around the clock since then and am within days of having this task accomplished. That's how I was able to give you an approximate worth. Until recently, not even I knew the enormity of the combined Stacia wealth," concluded Jackie. By the time she finished speaking, she was once again composed and tearless which made Peter wonder if he'd imagined her tears and redlined eyes.

"I really hate to change the subject, but how do we get our hands on some money?" asked Lila. "If I'm in New York, I'd like to take in a few sights and do some shopping."

"The attendant will have charge cards for each of you at his desk by 8:00 A.M. tomorrow. Your chauffeur is available with the limo, or you may take one of the cars available in the garage. I will go for now. Jeffery should be up shortly to assist you." She waved as she entered the elevator and the doors slid silently shut.

"Do you believe this?" asked Lila as she got up and plopped down on the couch beside Peter.

"Not hardly," Peter replied more surprised at Papa's indiscretions than the $500 trillion they were supposedly worth.

"Did she say $500 trillion? Trillion with a capital T?"

"Yes. That's what I understood her to say. Trillion with a capital T."

"How much is that?"

"I don't know. Five hundred with twelve zeros behind it. It's probably enough money to buy most of Europe and all of the U.S."

"That's kind of what I was thinking," said Lila. "I think I'll retire and never go back to the clinic. This is better than winning the lottery." Lila had spoken those words with an award-winning smile on her face until she looked at Peter and realized he was thinking about Papa.

"I'm so sorry, baby," Lila apologized. "I wasn't thinking about what had to happen for us to be in this position."

They sat for several minutes as they held on to each other and sobbed. They would miss Papa.

The elevator doors parted as an elegant looking man in a black tuxedo stepped out to meet Lila and Peter, who quickly composed themselves as best they could. This man looked almost like a huge porcelain doll. His face was blank with no emotion. If he noticed how upset Peter and Lila were, he showed no evidence of the fact. With an accent Peter couldn't identify, he informed Peter and Lila his name was Jeffery, and he was their butler. There was something about him . . . Something. Peter knew he'd seen the butler before. Peter closed his eyes.

He was sitting in the middle of the floor. Everyone around him was so big. Papa was so young, and he was talking to a tall even younger man, "You can't, Alex! It's dangerous, and it's not time!"

The tall haughty man looked down at Papa and declared, "It's never going to be time, Pa-Pa. When do we take back what's ours? Are we so impotent? Do we allow them to hold our lives hostage forever?"

Papa was obviously angry. "You'd give up your family for WHAT, Alex? An Ideal?"

"It's my legacy Pa-Pa."

Papa interrupted, "It's NOT yours; it's mine! I rule. I'm the head of The Family. I'm the Patriarch! As long as I live, you will do as I say! You have a Family to consider! Who takes care of Family if you don't?" A door opened and a younger Jeffery came into the room, Papa whirled and coldly said, "If I'd wanted you in here, I would have called you. You don't walk in on family discussions!"

"Nice to meet you, Jeffery," Peter said as he held out his hand. Lila had already decided she didn't want to shake the butler's hand.

After Jeffery shook Peter's hand, Peter noticed how cold it felt. In fact, it felt almost inhuman. Jeffery asked if Peter and Lila would like a drink before they retired for the evening.

"Sure," said Peter and Lila in unison. Peter asked for a double vodka, and Lila asked for a glass of milk since she was pregnant.

"Very good. If you wish to have a seat in these matching French Louis XV Bergere chairs, I will return shortly with your drinks," Jeffery ordered as he stiffly shuffled away. Lila looked at the uniquely shaped scallop back of the chairs as she and Peter did precisely what Jeffery had ordered them to do.

"He makes me feel like I'm in the first grade again and have to be told what to do," complained Lila. As she studied the chairs further, she knew Peter wouldn't be interested to know such facts as how these chairs dated back to the 1920s or be impressed with the carved crest rail with its gilded rosettes or gorgeous carving on the apron of the chairs. Peter was simply glad his seat cushion was comfortable and the arms were fully padded. He also liked the green color and feel of the satin material.

"I could care less what kind of chairs these are," said Peter. "I wonder if he will explain what kind of food he gives us, too." Jeffery promptly appeared with their drinks, a tray of very small sandwiches, and various unrecognizable sweets. "Will you follow me please?" he questioned in a way that sounded more like another command, as he led them back to the uncomfortable couch. He placed the tray on a table and announced, "When you are finished with your drinks, I'll show you to the master suite."

"That's quite all right. We'll manage to find it," said Peter, who was tired of being ordered where he should and should not sit. "You may go back to your residence."

Jeffery said through an extremely tight smile, "Very good, sir. What time will you require breakfast?"

Peter looked at Lila, and she at him, and in unison they said, "Eleven."

"Very well. Breakfast will be served at eleven. If you need me, merely pick up any telephone and dial seven. I'll take leave of you now. Good night, sir. Good night, madam."

"Good night, Jeffery," they both said as Jeffery turned the key and entered the elevator. They got one last glimpse of Jeffery's emotionless face as the elevator doors slid shut. They heard the slight whine of an electric motor as the elevator started down to the first floor.

Peter didn't have a clue what was in the miniscule sandwiches on the tray and now wished Jeffery had explained what the food was. The sandwiches were all crustless bread with nothing substantial inside and so tiny they were barely a taste. Peter and Lila were famished, and it was well after midnight, so they ate every bite on the tray without even saying a word.

Peter finished his drink, stood up, and looked for the bar. Now where had Jeffery gotten that drink? As he walked around, he noticed a small, unobtrusive doorknob in what appeared to be a solid wall. He walked over, turned the doorknob, and was surprised when the wall opened inward into a large modern kitchen. He looked around but couldn't find the bar. He walked out and pulled the door shut. Some thirty feet further down the wall was a large marble column with a small ornate handle almost but not quite out of sight. As he pulled the handle, he heard the electric whine of motors as the wall behind the columns slid inward six inches. It parted like elevator doors and disappeared into the wall behind the columns. The opening looked as if it was part of the room and the columns remained. Where the wall had been was an opening into a well-stocked bar with seemingly every spirit available on display.

Peter walked around behind a mahogany bar trimmed with ebony and gold where he finally found an open bottle of a very expensive brand of Russian vodka. He filled his glass and when he turned around was surprised to see Lila had taken off all her clothes and was seductively reclining on one of the matching French Louis XV Bergere chairs. He scooped her up in his massive arms and said with lust in his voice, "I think it's time to find that master bedroom Jeffery told us about." He gave Lila a long passionate kiss. "I wonder where the bedroom would be."

"Upstairs," Lila guessed as Peter carried her upstairs to the next floor. Every other step or so, Peter would stop and kiss Lila. By the time they made it to the top floor, they were both aroused and anxious to find a place to complete what they both had imagined.

Peter tried the first door on the right of a short hallway. It opened into a large sitting room, behind which lay an immense master suite almost as large as their home in Alabama. It had to be at least 5,500 square feet. Peter almost dropped Lila at the sight of the extravagant setting. To his right, lay a bathroom the likes of which Peter and Lila had never seen. As Peter carried Lila into the bathroom, a round whirlpool tub made of solid gold bubbled as if it had known they were enroute. To its right sat an old-fashioned solid gold claw-foot tub up on a pedestal made of a single block of black volcanic glass. Even more to the right was a free standing shower stall carved out of the same type of volcanic glass with a gold trimmed crystal shower door. To the left of the Jacuzzi were two large bathroom sinks made of gold with gold fixtures set in a cabinet made of the same black volcanic glass. Every wall in the bathroom was a mirror that gave the bath an unreal, heavenly appearance. Peter strode out of the bathroom and gently placed Lila on an ancient, massive four-poster bed. All at once, he started to laugh.

"What are you laughing about?" asked Lila.

"Have you ever seen so much gold? All at once, I kinda feel like one of the Beverly Hillbillies."

"Yeah. I know what you mean."

Their laughter once again turned to passion as Peter joined Lila on the bed and gently cupped her left breast in his mammoth hand. As he kissed her, they quickly moved up under designer burgundy and gold bed covers that surprisingly had a slight fragrance of freshly cut roses.

At 9:30 A.M., Peter was the first to awaken. He slipped out from under the ornate bed covers, walked into the luxurious bath, and stood in front of the toilet. As he looked down, he smiled and thought how it seemed almost sacrilegious to urinate in a solid gold toilet.

He walked back through the bedroom into the sitting room where he completed thirty minutes of stretching exercises, a regimen of sit-ups, and three hundred pushups. He then bounded down the stairs to enter the elevator that took him to the second floor to swim his laps.

When he returned to the bedroom, Lila was still asleep. He leaned over to kiss her forehead before quietly entering the bathroom. He was pleasantly surprised to find his shaving supplies and toothbrush laid out. He brushed his teeth, shaved off the beginnings of a rough, heavy beard, and walked over to the shower unit. He turned on the water and waited a moment for the water to warm up. As he looked inside, he noticed shampoo and a fresh bar of soap laid out. Someone was really going through the paces to make them feel at home.

He stepped into the shower, shut the door, and turned on the water to wet his massive frame. As he lathered up his hair, he relaxed and enjoyed the warm water as it soothed the effects the morning exercises had parlayed on his muscles.

That was when the water instantly turned hot. To get away from the scalding water, he hit the shower door with his hand tearing it off the hinges. It burst into thousands of pieces as it hit the edge of the claw foot tub some six feet away, narrowly missing Lila, who had recently flushed the toilet. "I'm worth five hundred trillion dollars and I still don't have a bathroom where I can take a shower without getting boiled like a lobster when you flush the toilet," bellowed Peter.

"Sorry, babe," Lila said laughing slightly as his water returned to the normal temperature.

"It's not funny, Lila."

"Well get over it and don't think because you're worth a gazillion dollars you get to talk to me like a servant. I'm your wife and if you want to yell at someone get that goofy butler in here and yell at him. Don't think you can start that crap with me."

Peter shook his head as Lila stalked out of the bathroom. Lila did have a point, but she needn't worry. He wouldn't let this money thing get to him. He'd seen it happen to some of his pro football teammates in Dallas. They'd ruined their lives and those of their families. Some people simply couldn't handle the responsibilities of acquiring big money. However, he was different. He had a good head on his shoulders, and nothing could control him. Besides, he'd always had a comfortable life. He couldn't think of anything he'd ever wanted that he didn't get.

Since the bathroom was already a mess, he finished his shower. He toweled off, stepped gingerly around the broken crystal door, and strode back into the bedroom. As he entered the bedroom, he glanced into the sitting room to see his clothes hanging neatly on a gold clothes rack to the right of the door. All his clothes had been neatly pressed, even his boxer shorts, and folded neatly on a shelf up above his other clothes that hung on the gold rod. Lila's clothes were on a matching rack slightly to the left of the door. He couldn't help but wonder if her bras and panties were ironed, also. How could all this take place without seeing anyone? Peter quickly dressed in black jeans and a black pullover tee shirt. He picked up a pair of black Roper boots which overnight had been polished to a mirror shine. *Didn't these people know scuffed Ropers showed their character?* He walked back to the bed where he sat down and laced them up. Last of all, he picked up a new University of Alabama ball cap and placed it on his head.

As he admired himself in the mirror, Lila came in. After mutual apologies for what had happened earlier, Lila teased, "I had planned to take a shower, but I can't because your big butt broke the shower door. I guess I have to face the fact I can't take you anywhere nice. You are like a bull in a china shop."

"Go ahead and take a shower, anyway. What are they going to do, kick us out? I'm going down to search for a TV. I'd like to see what CNN says is going on in the world today. Dress casual since we'll take in some sights today."

"Sure," Lila said. "Sounds like fun."

Peter heard the water start as he closed the door. As he walked down the staircase, he looked out over the large, tasteful room. Once down in what was a living room or den, he looked around for a TV. As he looked around, Jeffery came in.

"May I be of service, sir?" the butler asked.

"Do you know where there's a TV? I wanted to see the news."

"That would be in the library. Follow me, sir." Jeffery opened the door into the large walnut paneled room with large plush chairs and dark, heavy side tables. Huge bookshelves covered every wall from the floor to the ceiling. An elegant looking elevator was mounted to a steel rail to make getting to the books on the top shelves easier. As Peter looked around, he didn't see a television anywhere.

"Where's the TV you said was in here?" Peter asked still slightly perturbed over being boiled like a lobster.

"Right here," said Jeffery as he walked over to one of the tables. He opened a drawer, removed a large remote, and handed it to Peter. "Would you like your breakfast in here?"

"Sure," said Peter.

"What would you like, sir?"

"Eggs benedict, fried potatoes, bacon, link sausages, grits, sourdough toast, strawberries, pancakes, coffee, milk, and orange juice," said Peter waiting to see what combination of this list Jeffery could actually bring. He was taken aback when Jeffery said, without even a change of expression, "Very good, sir. That should take about ten minutes." *Jeffery has to be joking*, thought Peter. *That kind of breakfast will not be made in less than ten minutes.*

"When Lila comes down, make sure she finds me," ordered Peter in the most commanding voice he could fake. He was definitely bewildered.

"Yes, sir," said Jeffery as he walked stiffly out of the library to see about Peter's breakfast.

As Peter watched the butler leave, he decided he would keep an eye on Jeffery. That butler was not to be trusted. Peter had always been a good judge of character and was rarely wrong when it came to deciding whom he could trust, but why had Papa trusted him? Peter sat down in one of the oversized armchairs and pushed the button on the remote marked TV. The bookshelves immediately in front of him recessed into the wall and slid apart to reveal a ten-foot screen. Peter flipped through a bedlam of channels until he found Headline News. It seemed to be the same old news–a flood here, someone missing there, and trouble in the Middle East.

As he flipped through the channels again, he stopped on a morning show broadcast with a local interest story about fine restaurants. Peter listened with interest about a restaurant called Miguel's, which offered authentic Mexican dishes, aged wines, and fine spirits in a relaxed atmosphere. Peter decided it sounded like a good place for dinner or maybe supper later on today.

As he contemplated more about dinner, he glanced around the room amazed at its furnishings. Out of the corner of his eye, he saw something twinkling and glittering. He got up and walked over to a shelf that contained what looked like glass painted Easter eggs all displayed on individual gold stands in locked cases.

Surrounded by the eggs was a jeweled box. It was about the same size as those old-timey cigar boxes he remembered Papa having. The amount and brilliance of the jewels astounded him. *Could they be real? Surely they weren't. If those jewels were real, they had to be worth at least . . .*

Peter sucked in a large breath and held it as he saw the *eagle emblem* on a medallion on the top of the box. As he looked down further, he saw the keyhole.

"What have you found, sweetheart?" said Lila as she walked in behind Jeffery. She was dressed sensibly in jeans and a t-shirt. She had pulled her hair back into a tight bun with a scarf that matched her fuchsia shirt.

"Nothing, really. I was just looking around," said Peter as he quickly moved away from the jeweled box. He came over to Lila and gave her a kiss, which she willingly returned.

The butler appeared at the door scowling as he saw Peter and Lila showing affection and quickly directed three servers pushing portable tables weighed down by food and beverages on silver serving trays trimmed with gold and what looked to be real diamonds. Lila and Peter's eyes met as they both noticed the diamonds at the same time.

There had to be enough to feed a dozen people on those trays. The first tray held a heaping plate of fried potatoes, a dozen poached eggs with Canadian bacon sitting on English muffins, and a silver container that held a gallon of Hollandaise sauce. On the second tray was an entire loaf of toasted sourdough bread, a huge crystal bowl of strawberries, a gigantic platter of pancakes, and what looked to be a whole side of bacon cooked to perfection flanked by two-dozen link sausages. To their amusement, there was even a small bowl of some kind of mush. Maybe it was supposed to be grits. The third tray held three carafes containing coffee, milk, and orange juice along with two plates, a coffee cup, two large drinking glasses, and every imaginable condiment they could possibly request.

"Hungry, babe?" laughed Lila as she patted Peter's stomach.

"Yeah," said Peter, "But not quite this hungry."

"Madame, what would you like for breakfast?" the butler asked.

"If you'll bring an additional place setting, I'll help Peter eat what he has. You can add an orange and some seedless grapes, if you have some."

"Sliced tomatoes would be nice, too," Peter quickly added.

When Jeffery, this time with only one server, returned, Peter said, "Jeffery, I broke the shower door in the master bath this morning. Have it replaced. Also, I want the plumbing inspected and repaired so I don't get scalded when Mrs. Stacia flushes the toilet."

"The shower door and plumbing will be taken care of today," Jeffery said with a slight trace of annoyance.

"One more thing, Jeffery, Ms. Lowell said charge cards would be with the door attendant this morning. Have someone send them up."

"I've already picked them up," said Jeffery as he handed Peter a stack of charge cards and a small pile of one hundred dollar bills. "I also took the liberty to proceed to the bank this morning and made a small withdrawal for you and Madame Lila."

Peter and Lila looked at each other and both wondered if it were standard practice for a butler to have *that* much access to an employer's bank accounts. Peter knew something didn't seem right and made a mental note to ask Jackie about it later. He then glanced down at the stack of hundreds. There were two neatly banded stacks of hundreds with $10,000 written on each band.

"That's twenty thousand dollars," said Lila in amazement.

"Yes, Madame Lila. It came to my attention you might take in some sights and perhaps do some needed shopping. Do you require more?" Jeffery said as he left pointedly looked at the casual clothes she and Peter wore.

"Yes, Jeffery," said Lila deliberately not hiding the contempt she felt toward Jeffery's obvious insinuation. "You are right. We will, and no this will be enough for now." She knew Jeffery realized she didn't like him and was contemptuously talking down to her.

After Lila and Peter finished eating, Peter said, "Are you ready to see some sights?"

"Sure. Do you want to drive or ride in the limo?" she asked.

"Let's go by ourselves. I'm not entirely comfortable with all this service and people clearly waiting around to do our bidding."

"Me either," Lila said as she picked up the cash and placed it in her purse. She removed her pocketbook and added the new credit cards with her name on them. While she did this, Peter did much the same, as he put the charge cards in his billfold.

Peter took Lila's hand, walked her to the elevator, inserted their key, and pushed the down button. Moments later the elevator doors opened as they stepped in. Peter pushed the button for the basement.

The doors closed and Peter felt the familiar drop of the elevator. His mind kept returning to the keys and the jeweled box. Did one of Papa's keys open the jeweled box? What was the significance of the *two-headed eagle* medallion?

When the doors reopened, they stared into a garage. There were hundreds of cars. All the car families seemed to be represented. The usual domestic automobiles were present, as well as what seemed to be hundreds of exotics, including a Dusenburg, several Bentleys, and several of which neither Peter nor Lila knew the manufacturer.

They walked through the lines of cars until Peter excitedly found a Harley-Davidson Ultra-Glide painted in a color that changed hues depending on where he was standing. The Harley was the most customized bike Peter had ever seen.

"What do you think?" asked Peter. "Are you up for a bike ride?"

Up for a bike ride? She thought, as she dubiously eying the big Harley.

"Sure. Why not?" she said as she opened the small trunk located on the back of the rugged bike and put her handbag inside.

Peter climbed on the bike and started the engine, as Lila climbed on behind him. The powerful engine fired up with the classic, distinctive sound all Harley-Davidsons display. Peter waited for the engine to warm up and glanced around for helmets. He wondered what the laws in New York City were where helmets were concerned.

He didn't think about this for very long before he decided he didn't care what the laws were. He had enough money to pay whatever ticket they could give him. He turned his ball cap around backward and waited until he felt Lila's arms encircle his waist. He put the bike in gear and let out on the clutch as he rotated the throttle on the right handlebar. The large bike eased out of its parking space as he made a left turn. They went up a gently sloped ramp to a garage door that he assumed opened to either 71st Street or Central Park West.

At the end of the ramp, a few feet before the garage door, was a large flat area. He pulled up onto the apron and looked around for a way to open the garage door. Nowhere in sight were any buttons, so he looked on the bike for a garage door opener and noticed a bright blue button labeled **gar** integrated into the headlamp switch.

He pushed the button and was rewarded with the sound of the door sliding up. When the door had opened enough for them to ride under, he once again put the bike in gear, rode out of the garage, and pushed the button to close the door.

Peter made a right onto Central Park West and went south a few blocks before he made a right onto 61st. At Columbus Avenue, they turned left and coasted down to Lincoln Square.

"Be on the lookout for the Empire State Building," said Peter.

As they continued south on Ninth Avenue, Peter looked around at the people that covered the sidewalks like ants in a huge ant farm. He didn't think he had ever seen this many people anywhere, except maybe coming or going from one of the many football games he had played in.

On their left, the Empire State Building came into view. He felt Lila nudge him. The time he had spent perusing the New York City map before they left had definitely paid off. Lila caught her breath in awe as she saw the Empire State Building.

Peter and Lila pulled up to a valet lot within walking distance. The valet looked with disdain at the big Harley until Peter placed two folded hundred-dollar bills in his hand.

"Not a scratch on it," Peter told the kid.

"Not a scratch, sir."

Peter and Lila stayed in the Empire State Building for over two hours. It was as if they had never been told about the depth and breadth of their newly found wealth. They were two kids on a field trip. Lila even bought a few cheap souvenirs to carry back to her parents.

Then they moved on to the World Trade Center.

As Peter and Lila stood on an observation deck at the highest occupied floor of the city's tallest building, they had no inkling or idea that in slightly more than a year all of this around them would be nothing but rubble. The twin towers would be erased from the cityscape, and more than 2,500 would be dead. Once again, the Empire State Building would be the tallest in the city.

Peter and Lila left the towers and wandered over to one of the smaller buildings in the World Trade Center Complex having earlier noted it contained several restaurants. They walked into a well-lit, opulent lobby and looked at the list of businesses on the building's site map. Peter quickly recognized the name Miguel's. This was the same restaurant the local interest story had discussed that morning on TV. "How about something to eat, sweetie? Are you hungry?"

"I'm not starved, but I could eat a bite or two," Lila replied.

"Mexican?"

"Sure. What do you have in mind?"

"I watched a story this morning on TV about a local restaurant named Miguel's. They offer fine authentic Mexican dishes. It's on the fifteenth floor."

They stepped into a large elevator with several other people. A few of these people looked at them with apparent disgust. The jeans each wore with tee shirts had seemed like comfortable choices when they left the building on Central Park West. They had also been a good choice for riding the bike on a sticky New York afternoon, but they were more than slightly underdressed for a meal at one of the premier restaurants in New York City.

Peter and Lila stepped off the elevator on the fifteenth floor as they held hands. They walked up to a raised podium as commanding as any they'd seen in the local Baptist church. A short, sickly Maître d', who had tried unsuccessfully to cover a bald spot by parting his hair slightly above the ear on each side of his head and combing both sides to the middle, approached them. With noticeable contempt for the couple, his high tenor voice squeaked out, "How may I be of service?"

"Table for two," Peter said as he noticed the establishment was a little more than one-quarter occupied.

"Do you have reservations?" the Maître d' asked in a condescending tone.

"No," said Peter as he looked up at the wall behind the Maître d'. There he saw a large walnut plaque that displayed the same double-headed eagle as he'd seen on the keys he'd found in Papa's Bible and on the jeweled box in the library.

"I'm sorry we don't have a table available."

Peter once again looked out over the restaurant. Of the two hundred or so tables available, less than 50 were occupied. "Could I speak to the manager or owner?"

"As you wish, sir. I'll have the owner, Mr. Michaels, come right over."

The Maître d' went around the corner and soon returned with a man who could have easily passed for a miniature version of the actor, Andy Garcia.

Sean Michaels was Italian even though his name didn't reflect it. His real name was Matteo Gambino and his relatives were originally from Trappeto and Carini, Sicily. They now mainly lived in New York City and Philadelphia. Matteo meant "gift of God" and since Michael meant "God-like," he'd changed his last name to Michaels. Sean seemed like a trendy American first name so he'd chosen that to go with Michaels. After getting into some trouble, he'd convinced his mob connections to change all his records to keep him from doing jail time. Nothing showed his true ancestry or real name. He'd even further distanced himself from his Italian heritage by owning a Mexican restaurant. The only thing he couldn't give up was his love for Italian clothes and shoes. He always dressed head to toe in expensive Italian, and today wore his favorite charcoal Armani Collezioni pinstripe suit. His black hand-made Camiceria di Como dress shirt further complemented his suit as well as the Versace basket weave signature woven silk tie designed especially for him, and Tanino Criscis Italian handmade shoes. Even his underwear was ordered from Cardano al Campo (a providence of Varese) close to Malpensa International Airport in Milan.

"I'm the owner, Sean Michaels. How may I be of service?" asked Michaels as he peered up at Lila and Peter. He was no taller than 5'2" or 5'3" and Peter figured he weighed no more than 120 pounds soaking wet wearing all his fancy clothes.

"We were told there was not an available table when I can plainly see more empty tables than occupied tables," explained Peter knowing the slick, Italian-looking owner would soon escort them to a table. They would probably get one of the best ones by the window since the owner would be naturally apologetic for their unfair treatment.

Instead, Mr. Michaels looked at Peter and Lila from head to toe without missing a single detail of their appearance. He had no respect for people from the South and saw them all as inferior. He quietly sneered, "Look, Mister. You can't afford this place. Why don't you take your ill-bred hillbilly ass and your little tramp back to the elevator and leave? We don't have any tables available for the likes of you."

Peter immediately flushed with rage and reached for the arrogant owner. Sean was quick enough to step back to prevent Peter's hands from reaching him.

Immediately, two big bodyguards were on each side of Peter. They escorted him to the elevator with Lila close behind. "Calm down, Jethro, I think it's time for you to leave," said one of the thugs on Peter's left.

"Calm down?" thundered Peter. "If the four of you will let me go, I'll show you calm."

Peter knew he could take the four of them. They were big but out of shape. With a little luck, they would be bawling like newly weaned calves.

Lila saw Peter's change in attitude and knew what he was thinking. She softly said, "Let's go, baby. There's other ways to handle this."

"We can't let you beat up on the owner," another of the bodyguards flanking Peter said. "When you get to the bottom floor, leave. If you come back, you get to spend some time with New York's finest, if you know what I mean."

Although Lila could see Peter was completely mad, the words that came out of his mouth were silver-coated ice, "Don't worry. I'll see Mr. Michaels again. He'll be asking for my time, and he'll come with an apology and his hat in his hand."

"I doubt that," smirked the first bodyguard.

"You can count on it. I do believe I own this building," bragged Peter.

"Listen to the funny guy. He thinks he owns the World Trade Center, now does he?" the biggest of the men laughed as he pushed Peter out of the elevator.

* * *

Definition of "God Complex" according to www.definitions.net

A god complex is an unshakable belief characterized by consistently inflated feelings of personal ability, privilege, or infallibility. A person with a god complex may refuse to admit the possibility of error or failure, even in the face of complex or intractable problems or difficult or impossible tasks, or may regard personal opinions as unquestionably correct. The individual may disregard the rules of society and require special consideration or privileges.

* * *

Chapter Fifteen

When Peter and Lila arrived back at their New York residence, they were surprised to find Jackie sitting on the uncomfortable couch with Jeffery serving her coffee from a jeweled coffee carafe. They hadn't expected to see Jackie until later on in the week.

Peter quickly told Jackie about how Sean Michaels had treated them at Miguel's Restaurant.

Since they had not eaten since that morning, Jackie ordered Jeffery to bring them something to eat. Jeffery bowed and left the room without making eye contact.

After making sure Jeffery was out of the room, Jackie explained she had compiled as much information as she had access to. "I have assembled the numbers for all your enterprises. Your net worth as of 2 P.M. this afternoon was $516 trillion. I've amassed the printouts of companies you own outright, but it reads like the Cincinnati phone directory."

"What do you mean by that?" asked Peter.

"There are over 100,000 companies in the U.S. alone you either own outright or control. I brought a list of the 'Fortune 1000' companies we control."

Peter picked up one of the printouts and was surprised to find that of the top ten companies, they owned eight of them outright and of the other two they owned 51 percent of one and 18 percent of the other.

"How is it we own these companies?" asked Peter. "I see these companies traded every day on the various stock markets worldwide."

"The Stock Market is a wonderful thing, it makes it possible for us to allow the public to give us money for things they will never own. Some years we pay a paltry percentage on the shares, but we always maintain control."

Peter and Lila looked at each other, then Peter turned back to Jackie, "What if I had a disagreement with another businessman. What could I do about someone who, shall we say, slandered me?"

"You wouldn't happen to mean a man by the name of Sean Michaels who owns a restaurant named Miguel's? Would you?"

"I can't seem to get over how we were mistreated."

"Mr. Stacia, you do have the power to get even, and I am the person who can help you."

"Do we own the World Trade Center?" asked Peter.

"Just the building," replied Jackie. "Technically the Port Authority owns the land, but we control the Port Authority."

"What about Sean Michaels' suppliers? Do we own any of them?"

"We own all the major restaurant suppliers in the city."

"Get me a file on Mr. Michaels. I want to know everything about him and his business."

"Peter," implored Lila, "You could let this go. The man didn't know."

"Why should he let it go?" asked Jackie. "The Stacia family is never mistreated in New York!"

"There's another way I've been mistreated," said Peter, "and this is serious."

"I'm sure I can take care of that, too," said Jackie. "Tell me about it."

"It's this couch," explained Peter. "It's old and uncomfortable. With all my money, I feel I can afford to get a new one that's more comfortable."

Jackie laughed aloud. Peter and Lila could hardly believe that simple request was so funny to her. "This is an antique Victorian Rococo Revival couch. It, along with its four chairs, form a priceless parlor group. It's a Henry Clay Pattern that is one of a kind."

I'm not sure who Rococo is, or why he had a revival, put it in storage and find me something by Lazy-Boy or Ashley. If I'm going to stay here, I want comfort.

Forty-five minutes later Peter had a file in his hand almost four inches thick. It contained a complete history of Sean Michaels. Not only did Peter now know, or rather have access to, Sean Michaels' business records, but the history was so complete it gave the names of Sean's parents, his grades in elementary school through college, as well as all the names of Mr. Michaels' love interests for the past twenty years. The file was thorough, it even showed what Sean Michaels' Mafia friends had planted.

Lila watched as Peter and Jackie planned how to get back at Sean Michaels, the owner of Miguel's. It was hard to believe this was her Peter. Several more times she tried to interrupt and bring Peter to his senses, but he was intent on revenge and Jackie was more than eager to help. Lila finally got up and left. She told Peter to have Jeffery bring her something to eat in the master bedroom. She ate alone, and for the first time since they had married, Lila went to bed without kissing Peter good night. Peter barely noticed when Lila left. The thrill of revenge had overtaken him, and it was exhilarating to plan how to bring Mr. Sean Michaels to his knees.

As they continued to look through paperwork, Jackie pointed out the suppliers Peter owned to which Sean Michaels owed money. As Jackie called out the name and home telephone number of each supplier's CEO, Peter called them. He introduced himself and instructed each to cut off all credit to Miguel's Restaurant and Sean Michaels. Michaels would only be allowed to buy if he paid in cash--no checks, store credit, or credit cards.

"Who do we have in local government here?" Peter asked.

"Which department?" asked Jackie not knowing in which direction Peter was headed.

"Health Department. I think it's time Mr. Michaels had a health inspection."

"Steve Kaminski is our contact person with the health department. I will be glad to call him as well as Sergeant John O'Leary with the New York Police Department. Sergeant O'Leary would need to accompany Kaminski in case Michaels causes any problems. You may remember O'Leary's name from our Navoiczyk board of directors list."

"That sounds great. Michaels will never be allowed in the restaurant business again."

"Consider it done."

"What about the banks?" asked Peter, "How do we handle the banks?"

Jackie briefly smiled, "You handle them like any other employee. You don't ask. You only give orders. They might not know you, but they know the name. Don't back up, and don't back down. You are a Stacia. Act like one, young prince."

Peter looked long and hard at Jackie. No had ever called him *young prince* except family. He picked up the phone and called Chase Manhattan's Bank Manager at home and introduced himself. "I want Sean Michaels' bank accounts overdrawn. Send all his un-cleared checks to the insufficient funds department. Since he's late on his mortgage and car note, begin foreclosure on the apartment and repossess his car. I want that 2001 midnight blue Mercedes in front of my residence at Central Park West by noon tomorrow. He doesn't deserve a 2001 vehicle when it's still June 2000."

"I'm sure our records will show Mr. Michaels has paid all his bills on time. Is there a problem of which I am unaware?" asked the Bank Manager.

"Change the records. This is personal," roared Peter.

"Mr. Stacia, do you understand tampering with bank records is a felony punishable by ten years in the federal penitentiary?"

"I know you've dealt with my grandfather in the past. I'm no less a Stacia than he was. Do you understand? Am I making this clear?"

"Yes, sir."

"Then you understand if you don't do as I instruct, you will be in the hot seat instead of Mr. Michaels. It's a short step from the top of the crystal tower to the sewer."

"Yes, sir," said the Bank Manager apologetically. "I now clearly see what you mean about Mr. Michaels being behind on his mortgage and car payments."

Peter hung up the telephone. He then sat back and marveled at what a wonderful thing power was. Tomorrow the New York City Health Department on Broadway would give Mr. Michaels the worst health rating in the history of New York City, and within three days, Miguel's would be out of business. Peter had orchestrated it all. *That wasn't bad for an Alabama hillbilly*, he thought as a satisfied smile of revenge slowly crept across his handsome face.

After Jackie left, Peter continued to look through the printouts. At first, he didn't understand what he was looking at, but before long his MBA training kicked in and he came up with his own system to decipher the intricate business pattern Papa had used. He now understood how Papa was able to practically control the world, not through politics, but through business. When he decided to take a break, he was surprised to see it was past midnight. This had been some day in New York City.

Peter then remembered the jeweled box and the keys. He tiptoed into the bedroom where Lila lay sleeping. She looked so peaceful. He kissed her on her forehead, but she did not awaken. He found Papa's Bible where he had hidden it and headed for the library.

His heartbeat quickened when he touched the jeweled box. As he looked closer, it was evident it did indeed have a keyhole. He took the keys from the Bible so he could try each one. The key with the red jewel was a definite match to the box.

As he turned the key, he heard a click and knew it was now open. He held his breath as he opened the lid. Inside the box was a folded well drawn ancient map of Western North America. A large block of land was parceled out of Eastern Montana with a little house drawn there. On the back were several long paragraphs scrawled in Cyrillic. There was an old black and white picture of a man in a military uniform of some kind. He was with what appeared to be his wife, four daughters and a young son whose arms were wrapped around the man's leg. Why would Papa keep a map of Montana with Russian written on it locked up in an expensive jeweled box?

However, the important thing in the box ended up being the papers. For the first time in his life, he saw something which had been hidden from him in plain sight. How had he missed it? The room started spinning, and for the first time in his life he was going to pass out. When Peter awoke, his eyes were still closed. *When I open my eyes,* he thought, *I will be in my bed in Russellville with Lila at my side. The phone will soon ring, and Papa will be on the line to tell me I've overslept and need to get on over to the factory.*

Peter had indeed blacked out. When he opened his eyes, he was not in his bed in his $150,000 residence in Russellville. He was reclining in an Italian leather chair, gazing at an original Monet in his multi-million dollar library. He sat very still for a few moments before he placed everything except the map back inside and locked the jeweled box. He set it back among a very expensive collection of Faberge eggs missing for more than eighty years. He put the map and the envelope containing the keys in Papa's Bible and headed for the solace of Lila. He would lie down by Lila and sleep. He would decide what to do with this newly found information tomorrow.

Chapter Sixteen

Sean Michaels was flabbergasted when New York City's Chief Health Inspector, Steve Kaminski, showed up with New York Police Sergeant, John O'Leary.

Kaminski usually gave Sean at least a 24-hour notice, and he never brought a police officer. Regular under-the-counter payments had always guaranteed that, along with an extremely high health rating. Michaels was even more surprised when Kaminski, without even maintaining eye contact, handed him a list of violations and swiftly exited the restaurant. As Sean read violation after violation where there were none, Sergeant O'Leary informed customers in the restaurant they would have to leave because of the hazard of communicable disease. When the last customer left on the elevator, several police officers taped off the entrance to the restaurant and declared it closed until all violations had been addressed. Members of the press from local television, radio, and newspaper organizations kept busy as they interviewed customers, took snapshots, and videotaped. Sean Michaels' favorite words for several hours had been, "No comment" and "Would you please stop scuffing up my floor?"

Sean fumed as Sergeant O'Leary handed him a card with a scribbled telephone number on it and ordered in his thick Irish accent, "Ye must be calling this gentleman before ye can reopen, even after the necessary repairs be completed."

"This is ridiculous," sneered Sean. "There aren't any repairs needed, and you know it. What is this all about?" He hated Irish immigrants with their thick Irish accents, and he hated cops. The combination of the two was sickening and almost unbearable.

"I'm simply doing what I was ordered to do. Just doing me job," explained O'Leary.

"What's this idiot's name?" seethed Michaels.

"Mr. Stacia," the Sergeant answered. "And I'll not be telling 'ya how to run yer business, but I'd not take that attitude with him when ye be's seeing him. He's a very powerful man. It's possible ye could get into trouble messing with someone with his station in life."

Sean didn't need any police sergeant scarcely off the turnip truck giving him lessons on power. He understood power. He had family and friends in the Italian Mafia. He knew the mayor and knew him well. *We'll see who has the most power,* he deduced, as he dialed the number on the card. "Peter Stacia," said the southern drawl on the other end of the phone line. Sean was so mad he didn't recognize the voice as that of the man he'd called a hillbilly and thrown out of the restaurant the day before. He started cursing. His antagonist on the other end of the phone simply hung up.

Sean called back immediately. He couldn't wait to tell Santo and Ambrosi about this guy. They'd take care of him. "Don't you ever hang up on me again," he threatened when he heard Peter's voice again. "I'll have you know I'm close and personal friends with the mayor. If you ever hang up on me again, I'll have your job." Peter's only response was the click of the phone as he hung up.

Sean was even more livid than he was when he had called the first time. He redialed for the third time. Before Sean could say a word, Peter drawled, "If you would like to discuss this, come to my office. My office building is located at 105 Central Park West. Simply give your name to the doorman, and there will be someone there to escort you to my office."

"I'll be right over, and you'd better be there," threatened Michaels. He could hardly believe he would have to waste his precious time to go over to the office of some hillbilly health official with no clue who Sean Michaels was or how much power he had. How did so many hillbillies get into New York City? All these hillbillies needed to go back to the south where they belonged.

"I'll be here until 5:00 P.M.," said Peter enjoying this immensely. *This was the most fun I've had in years,* he thought, as he heard Michaels hang up.

Peter ensconced his large frame in a huge leather executive chair behind a massive ebony and ivory desk inlaid with gold. He called down to the security office and instructed the security guard, "An outraged Sean Michaels will be arriving shortly. Treat him well--but firm."

Twenty-five minutes later, the owner of Miguel's got out of a cab dressed in a Coragliotti suit set off perfectly with an Enrico Venturi dress shirt. Michaels sauntered up to the front of the unassuming brownstone building.

As Peter watched Sean Michaels on a security monitor, he had to admit one thing about the guy--he sure did wear nice clothes. Peter chuckled as he continued to watch Michaels strut around like a bantam rooster--or a bantee rooster as folks in Alabama would have called him. Bantee roosters were smaller and weaker than other rooster breeds, but in their inflated minds they were masters of the yard! They were known for strutting around looking more important than they were. Peter leaned back in his chair to take a well-deserved nap. He'd already told the guards to keep Michaels waiting for at least an hour.

To Sean Michaels, the brownstone looked like any other government building from the outside. When he pranced into the building on Central Park West, however, he found quite a different story. This was not a government building unless the government really started customizing their buildings. Top quality furnishings were everywhere. The lobby could easily have been in one of Donald Trump's homes.

One of the security men at the front desk asked Michaels to have a seat in an antique chair in the well-appointed lobby that Michaels was certain cost more than his apartment. Sitting down, he noticed there were paintings pleasingly placed throughout the reception area. This place had the look of a Smithsonian Museum. The artwork displayed was obviously expensive. He got up and went over to what he theorized was a print of Van Gogh's *Irises*. As he got closer to the painting it was clear this wasn't a print-- this was the actual Van Gogh.

Sean was an avid art lover buying what paintings he could afford, but this was way out of his league. He knew *Irises* had brought over $50 million back in the late 1980s. He presumed it would be hanging in some place like the J. Paul Getty Museum in Los Angeles. So what was it doing here hanging in the lobby of a government building in New York City? He stood and stared at the painting, mentally capturing the whorls and bumps in the paint as well as the single white flower among the violet irises. He moved on to what appeared to be a fully nude *Mona Lisa* by Leonardo Da Vinci. He'd heard rumors Da Vinci had painted at least one nude *Mona Lisa*, but this one was the first one he'd seen. If it were authentic, it would certainly be as valuable as the Van Gogh immediately to its right.

On a wall to itself was a tapestry of the Russian Czar, Peter the Great, in a protective case. The gold medallion had the date 1720 and the artist was Giovanni Domenico Ferretti. Michaels was an authority on Italian art. He was very familiar with all of Ferretti's work. Ferretti was known for his tapestry workshops for the grand duke of Tuscany starting around 1728. Ferretti was not known for any tapestries back in 1720, especially not one of a Russian Czar. Could it be this was an unknown original tapestry made exclusively for the Russian Romanov dynasty? He knew a lot of original and unexhibited art had disappeared after the murder of Russian Czar, Nicholas II and his family back in 1918. Could this be part of that missing art collection? If so, how did it get here? He was still studying the minute details of the tapestry ninety minutes later when the security guard came up to him and said, "Mr. Stacia will see you now."

"You're damn right he will," said Sean Michaels as he looked at his watch. The man had kept him waiting almost two hours. Three security guards suddenly flanked Sean. They wore military style dress uniforms and automatic pistols hung freely in shoulder holsters that would have been out of sight had the guards' coats been buttoned.

"Time to see the boss," said the largest of the paramilitary men. The men directed Sean politely to a large elevator. They made it understood they would treat him with respect as long as he behaved himself. It was crystal clear he was not going to see some minor New York City government official. This was obviously a rich and powerful man. Normal people don't hang $50 million paintings in the vestibule of their buildings or have army commandos as security. They also didn't live in buildings of this quality. Sean knew quality when he saw it.

Sean was escorted into the most impressive apartment he had ever seen in New York. When he was walked into the office, he didn't recognize the man sitting at the large ebony desk with his back to Sean.

"Good afternoon, Mr. Michaels. What can I do for you?" Peter asked as he slowly turned his massive chair around and stood to face his visitor.

Sean was struck by this man's uncanny resemblance to Peter the Great in the tapestry he had spent at least an hour studying. He quickly put that out of his mind as he remembered why he was here. "I want to know why you closed my restaurant," Sean said indignantly as he looked around for a chair close to the man's desk so he could sit down. Peter had purposely removed all chairs so Sean Michaels had to stand.

As Peter sat down in his comfortable chair, he said, "Mr. Michaels, it has recently come to my attention you owe me a great deal of money. To be exact, it comes to $2,171,412.26. Since your restaurant is permanently closed, could you possibly tell me how you intend to repay the money owed to my companies and me?"

"I don't owe you any money," sputtered Sean as he now recognized Peter as the man he'd thrown out of his restaurant yesterday.

"Don't you now?" said his antagonist as he slid a thick sheaf of papers across the desk. As he looked down at a notepad, he said, "My records show you borrowed $2.5 million and $500,000 from Chase Manhattan Bank to get your restaurant off the ground. Then you borrowed an additional $268,000 to purchase an apartment and have it decorated by world renowned Italian Interior Decorator, Piero Fornasetti. Am I correct so far, Mr. Michaels?"

A shocked Sean Michaels was for once at a loss for words. He really needed to sit down.

"Next on the list is the $112,000 to buy a special edition 2001 midnight blue Mercedes off the showroom floor this past April at the 2000 New York International Auto Show. I believe that was at the Jacob K. Javits Convention Center in Midtown Manhattan, was it not?"

How could he know all these things about me? wondered Sean Michaels. *Is there such a thing as a Southern Mafia?*

"Also, you owe Furman Restaurant Supply almost $300,000. If you subtract the almost $1 million you have in the bank, that leaves you owing me almost $2.2 million. Since I own all these businesses, I want to hear your repayment plans. You do have repayment plans, don't you?"

"I have always made all payments on time," explained a pensive Sean, who now wished he'd treated the hillbilly better.

"Have you now?" said Peter. "My records indicate that is not the case. I don't believe you can afford to be in business."

"Nor do I," agreed Lila as she approached and towered over Sean Michaels. "What was it he said to you, baby? I believe it went something like, '**Look Mister. You can't afford this place. Why don't you take your ill-bred hillbilly ass and your little tramp back to the elevator and leave? We don't have any tables available for the likes of you.**'"

"That's right, my little tramp," interjected Peter. "That's exactly what he said. He said I couldn't afford the place. Well now. It seems I already own the place, Mr. Michaels. So it's you who can't afford the place."

"Oh, shit," said Sean.

"That's right. Oh, shit," said Lila as she moved to stand beside Peter's chair.

"This is how this is going to go down," instructed Peter in a voice that not only horrified Sean Michaels but Lila as well. "Tomorrow morning you and your four bodyguards will be back here at 10 A.M. You will bring your chefs and a server, along with a menu. You will prepare a meal of our choosing in our kitchen on the first floor. Is this understood?"

"Yes, sir."

"Would you like to hear what will happen if you are not here at precisely 10 A.M.?"

"No, sir."

"I'm going to tell you anyway. At 10:02 there will be a warrant issued for your arrest. It seems you will have passed almost $100,000 in bad checks. Navoiczyk Enterprises will evict you and the bank will begin foreclosure on the apartment. Your car has already been repossessed and you will never get it back. While you are languishing in one of the many city jails because no bond will be set and no judge will hear your case, you will be forced into bankruptcy. This time next week you will have no money, no business, no place to live, and no prospects for employment. You will face felony check charges of which you will be convicted to spend the maximum time prescribed by law in the harshest penitentiary in New York. I'll even have you paired up with an excellent cellmate. Mr. Michaels, you serve at my will. Is it understood that if you are ever in business again, it will be because I allow it?"

"Yes, sir."

"I'll see you tomorrow at 10 A.M. Oh--by the way--come with a hat in your hand and a sincere apology to my wife for calling her a tramp. I want your bodyguards to see and hear that apology. Goodbye, Matteo. Don't forget the hat." With those last words, Peter stood up and exited with Lila to the left into an elegant sitting area.

Sean's blood ran cold. No one should know his proper name. Properly chastised, Sean Michaels left with the escorting security that appeared when Peter said goodbye. That hadn't gone at all like he had planned. Peter had all the keys that opened and locked all the doors. Sean had no doubts if he didn't do exactly as the man had instructed, he would soon be locked out of everything. The only door open would be a direct route to prison. As he rode down the elevator, he wondered if Peter himself owned it all or if he was the front man for another. No. He owned it all. He didn't speak like he answered to anyone. He spoke with authority--the authority of a man that knows his wishes will be carried out no matter what. The man he saw today was a very different man than the man Sean had insulted and thrown out of the restaurant. Yesterday he had only seen a southern hick. Today he saw a man who, if he owned what he said he did, was clearly the most powerful man in New York, possibly even in the United States, or even the world. He was definitely a man with a God Complex.

As he passed the tapestry again, he wondered if Stacia was a descendant of Peter the Great. No. That was impossible. Stacia had probably added it to his collection because of his uncanny physical resemblance to the former Russian Czar.

"What will happen to Sean Michaels?" Lila asked as they relaxed in the sitting room.

"Tomorrow we will have a fine lunch and then Mr. Michaels will leave."

"Go back to his restaurant?"

"No. I will make an example of him. The scenario will play out exactly as I explained to him. The only checks that will clear the bank will be the payroll checks to his employees. The employees will be kept on payroll until I find someone else to manage the restaurant. Mr. Sean Michaels will no longer be part of New York's society life. He will be lucky to find a job anywhere. The only good news is he won't go to jail."

Chapter Seventeen

His head pounded, his stomach cramped, and his eyes, even after blinking several times, refused to focus on his surroundings. Something was wrong. Where was he? Nothing, however, was wrong with his sense of smell. A combination aroma of urine, rotten vegetables, and human sweat permeated the air around him, and he soon realized he was going to vomit. When he tried to sit up, the demon in his head slung him back down and he was only able to turn his head slightly to his left before his stomach convulsed and emptied its contents onto the worn cobblestones. He lay with the left side of his face covered with the contents of the evening's menu, which consisted of, an assortment of convenience store wines, a half cooked corn dog, a large order of chili fries, four Alka-Seltzers, and at least five Valium. To his amazement, he was suddenly overcome by a powerful and insane desire to laugh. He laughed and laughed until his bizarre laughter turned into uncontrollable sobs.

"Hey, man. Like are you all right?" he heard a voice stammer. "Like are you happy or sad. Which is it?"

His eyes slowly focused on the face of a dirty, stringy-haired homeless resident of what Sean Michaels now realized was a New York City alley. As his eyes continued to focus, he became acutely aware of the homeless populace, which stood over him and observed him with dull, nonjudgmental eyes. As he lay still flat of his back, he wiped his eyes, nose, and then the left side of his face with the sleeve of his Enrico Venturi dress shirt before he growled in a weak but threatening snarl, "I'm fine. Get away from me. Get away from me, now. The show is over."

The homeless audience slowly backed away and shifted off to their seemingly assigned positions scattered throughout the alley. Sean gradually sat up, and once again, he vomited. This time, it was little more than a bizarre combination of dry heaves and throaty gasps. He sat deathly still, for what seemed to him like hours, as he tried to make sense of this recent turn of events. He was obviously still alive, but an unwilling participant in this sordid version of Hell.

Slowly the events of the last week flooded his memory. That hillbilly had ruined him. The giant redneck had taken everything away from him. He'd lost his car, his business, and his apartment. When he went to his banker to straighten out the misunderstanding, he was told he had been forced into involuntary bankruptcy with only two hours to get what clothes and toiletries he could carry out of his apartment. When he returned to his apartment, Sergeant O'Leary, as well as three armed security guards, was stationed inside to make sure Michaels followed the banker's requests.

As Sean left his apartment, O'Leary forced him to turn over the keys to his apartment, Mercedes, and safe deposit boxes. Surprisingly, he'd not asked for the keys to Miguel's or his office at the restaurant.

Sean departed with only $211 in his wallet and one change of clothes in his leather, cognac-colored travel bag. He loved that bag. In fact, it had been the first thing he'd ever ordered online. Everyone who saw it was impressed with its Florentine quality and Sean now ordered all his Italian clothes and accessories online. He had also been interested to find out Luciano Palermo, who started the line, had started out as a vendor on the streets of Florence selling straw hats, and that his son, Stefano, now ran the business. It made Sean proud to hear Italian success stories.

As his head continued to pulsate, he was suddenly amused he could reminisce about such triviality. There was no revenge, even Santo and Ambrosi had abandoned him. He'd thought they would know how to handle Stacia, but they'd refused.

"Ma, che sei grullo Matteo," said Ambrosi. *"Ti venisse un accidente!"*

A motor vehicle rumbled behind him. As Michaels strained to turn around, he heard footsteps. Within seconds, strong hands slipped a rope around his neck. One quick jerk was all it took to break the little man's neck. A lone figure easily loaded the now lifeless body into a midnight blue Mercedes that sped away into the night as the homeless audience paid little attention.

Two days later in a small obscure corner of the *New York Times*, a one-paragraph news article stated:

> *Late last night, Sean Michaels, once prominent owner of Miguel's Restaurant, was found hanging from a wooden beam in the restaurant's office. According to NYPD Sergeant, John O'Leary, Mr. Michaels died as the result of an apparent suicide. The case is closed. No foul play is suspected.*

Chapter Eighteen

Randall Marlowe was in a no-name motel in Sioux Falls, South Dakota. After he finished his shower, he touched up his blonde hair and shaved himself baby smooth. He quickly discovered being a blonde was hard work, and he hadn't even had any "fun" yet. After he dressed, he checked out of the motel where he had registered under yet another alias.

Back when he had left Belgreen, Alabama, he fretted somewhat about carrying around so much cash. How could he spend it without arousing suspicion? As he had passed a casino in Council Bluffs, Iowa, he'd had a revelation. Taking a stack of hundreds, he walked into the casino and bought $5,000 in chips. He spent the next eight days inside the casino where he managed to buy $100,000 worth of chips. After he cashed out, he had a cashier's check for slightly more than $95,000. It was a $5,000 loss, but it looked legitimate.

Now pulling out onto I-90, he set his cruise on 65, even though the speed limit was 70. He didn't want to be pulled over for any reason. He figured he had slightly more than seven hundred miles left to go. Randall reasoned he should be in Billings in about twelve hours. He would stay in a motel tonight and find an apartment tomorrow. He would open up a new checking account with the cashier's check and immediately look for a job. Once he secured a job, he would start his hunt for a house.

Almost thirteen hours to the minute after leaving Sioux Falls, he passed the city limits sign for Billings. He would finally start his new life. He had decided along the way he would be an honest man in Billings. *I'll leave my past where it belongs*, he thought, *in the past. I have enough money for a good start. I don't have to take just any job. I don't have to make the same mistakes again I've made in the past. I didn't mean to kill that girl. It happened during one of my blackouts.*

After registering at the Holiday Inn, he walked back out to his pickup to open the back door to retrieve his luggage. When he removed the bag that contained the rest of his money, the catch on the driver's seat ripped the bag causing several stacks of hundred dollar bills to tumble out. Glancing around the empty parking lot, he quickly stuffed the money back into the bag. Once in the safety of his room, he pitched his bags on the floor and lay down on the bed. He hadn't realized how tired he was from the long drive. His eyes soon closed, and he dozed off.

* * *

A TRILLION DOLLARS

A trillion one dollar bills laid end to end would stretch from the earth to the moon and back at least 200 times.

* * *

Chapter Nineteen

Eric couldn't believe it. There had been no sign of Alan Chipenski for almost two weeks. Alan had vanished.

To make matters worse, it looked as if Jim Davis was going to walk. Even with the videotape, the prosecutor said there wasn't enough evidence to hold him without Alan Chipenski's testimony. They had seized the Chief of Police's home, searched it thoroughly, but found nothing. His bank accounts held no unusual deposits or withdrawals. Nothing except the videotape indicated any impropriety. The prosecutor had gone so far as to call it an amateur smut video to Eric's face. Jim said on the tape he had an excellent source for the drugs. Who was that source? Where were they? Eric had looked up to the Chief for years. Jim had once been his boss. He hadn't wanted to believe the tape, but he had seen it with his own two eyes. He knew the Chief was crooked; he had to be.

The tape had proved beyond a reasonable doubt to Eric that Jim Davis was not a man to be trusted, but where was the evidence? Alan had handed Jim a stack of hundreds that had to equal at least $100,000. That kind of money didn't walk away unnoticed in a town Russellville's size. Someone knew something. Someone knew where the money was. The time stamp on the tape was more than six months ago. During that time, they could have made fifty or a hundred similar transactions. It could have added up into the millions of dollars. Where was the money? Not at the house. Not in the bank. No evidence had been found he bought any property anywhere. There were no cars paid for with cash. Everything the Davis family owned had been financed. The only thing even close to being paid for was the house, and it had been financed for thirty years. Only two payments remained.

Unless something major broke, there was no doubt Jim would make bail today. When it was all over, he would probably still be Chief of Police, and Eric would have an enemy. If Eric couldn't prove Jim was crooked, he would walk, continue to be Chief, and in a few more years collect a pension for thirty years on the force. That would not happen on Eric's watch. The police force was simply that, a police force. It wasn't a license to steal and sell drugs. That was what they were paid to prevent.

Where was Alan Chipenski? Had he skipped the country? If so, how?

How could a person like Alan possibly escape? How? His picture was all over the news. It wasn't like he was invisible. He had a unique look. He had to be hiding out somewhere in the area, didn't he? If that were the case, someone should come forward soon to say they had seen him.

He didn't have any family to hide with and no friends to speak of. The people in the circle of friends he ran with would have turned Judas on him in an instant-- especially when told they would be prosecuted for harboring a criminal. They weren't that kind of friend. There was truly no honor among thieves. To save their own neck, any of them would have turned him in by now. So--where was he? All these questions and NO ANSWERS . . .

Chapter Twenty

Lori Cochran's vacation was almost over. When the cruise ship docked, she would take a cab to the airport and fly to Birmingham.

She'd had a fabulous time and looked forward to getting back to work. For two wonderful weeks, she hadn't worried about one solitary thing. All she had to do each day was lie on the upper deck and soak up sun.

As she packed, she glanced in the full-length mirror adorning the closet door. She definitely liked what she saw. With her bronzed skin and platinum blonde hair, the Caribbean had undoubtedly agreed with her. She looked better than she had ever looked, even when she had been sixteen, not that she remembered much of that year.

When the ship got to shore, a deck hand carried her luggage to a waiting taxi. She tipped him in spite of his protests, eased into the taxi, and said, "Miami International, please."

Lori arrived at the airport about forty minutes early for her return flight to Birmingham, so she visited the airport gift shop. She purchased two postcards and mailed one to Helen Mitchell and the other to Mattie Wilson, her friend from Tutwiler. As she dropped the cards into the mailbox, the overhead speakers announced last call boarding instructions for her flight. She briskly walked to her gate, up the ramp, and onto the plane. She found her seat and settled in for her flight.

Two hours later, the plane landed in Birmingham. Lori pulled her Ford Explorer out of the maze they call a parking deck onto Airport Highway. Lori got on I-59 south and after only a few miles exited off onto I-65 north.

Headed north, she reached over and turned on the radio. As she tuned to a country music station, she caught the last part of the news that told about a search for a man named Alan Chipenski. Lori wondered what that was all about. The wonder quickly faded as the Dixie Chicks sang one of her favorite songs. Driving up the interstate singing along with one song after another, she made it to Cullman. Exiting off onto Highway 157, she noticed she was almost out of gas, and pulled into the BP station as George Strait began a humorous, though slightly sad, song about seating arrangements in a bar.

She couldn't get the pump outside to accept her debit card, so she selected the pay inside button and pumped her Explorer full of gas. When the pump clicked off, she replaced the nozzle, screwed back on the gas cap, and walked inside to pay. As she handed the clerk her debit card, she looked up to see Max Partain's picture on the television behind the cash register. Lori asked the clerk to turn up the sound. It wasn't Max Partain after all. This man's name was Alan Chipenski. That was strange. He sure did resemble Max Partain.

Lori suddenly realized Max and Alan were the same person. Max or Alan, or whatever his name, was wanted for the murder of an eighteen-year-old black girl.

There was a number for the Franklin County Sheriff's Department on the bottom of the screen. Anyone with any information should please call that number.

What do I do now? thought Lori. *Do I want to get involved? If I do, will they find out I used to be in prison? I really don't want anyone in Moulton to know, but I don't want a murderer to get away.*

Driving up the lonely stretch of Highway 157, she contemplated what she would do. Lori turned into her driveway feeling slightly nauseous. She had to go to the police with what she knew. The possibility of testifying against Max made her sick. She didn't want anyone to know about her time in prison, and that's precisely what would happen if there was a trial. Any competent defense lawyer would drag up her background in an attempt to discredit her, and the whole world would know.

Why was life so unfair? Maybe she could do this anonymously. No. That wouldn't work, either. Once the cops found out about the little house, she would be dragged into it regardless. It was best to go to the Sheriff's department and get it over with. She made up her mind to talk to the Franklin County Sheriff in the morning.

Early the next morning after a fitful night of tossing and turning in which she got little sleep, Lori got up and took a quick shower. She called Helen at home and told her she would try to be in by 12 P.M., but she had to go see the Sheriff in Franklin County.

Helen asked her why. So, she explained about Max.

"I see," said Helen. "Be careful Lori. Not everyone believes in second chances."

She donned a severe business suit in an almost laughable attempt to downplay her sexuality and walked out to her Explorer with butterflies in her stomach. *This was not going to be a good day. I guess I'll simply make the best of a bad situation*, she thought, as she accelerated down Highway 24 toward Russellville. Pulling up in front of the Franklin County Courthouse, she checked her hair and makeup and prayed for strength to do what she had to do. She walked up the stairs and opened the door entering a large, cool room.

Not knowing where the Sheriff's Office was, she located a map of the courthouse and stood there looking at the confusing conglomeration of offices indicated on the map. As she contemplated her next move, the Sheriff walked around the corner.

Eric strolled around the corner to see the most beautiful woman he had ever laid eyes on. She was the perfect exposé of an angel--she was beyond beautiful. Seeing her almost made him forget the mess he had been working on for the past two weeks. She made him forget about dead girls and crooked police officers-- almost, but not quite.

"May I help you?" Eric asked.

Lori was startled by the sudden appearance of a Deputy in a brown uniform. "Oh--Uh--I'm looking for the Sheriff's office. I need to speak to the Sheriff."

Thank you, God, thought Eric. "Like I said--May, I help you?"

"You're not--are you--are you the Sheriff?"

"In person," said Eric.

"But you're so young. I expected--"

"I know. You expected some old geezer," Eric interrupted. "I beat him in the election last year. Now, what can I do for you?"

"I . . . I think . . ." *All right--get it together--stop stuttering,* she said to herself. "I think I'm the one who can help you. I may have some information you need regarding that young black girl's murder." *There--she'd gotten it all out.*

"Oh really . . ." Eric was slightly taken aback. Consequently, there was a long silence. This didn't seem like the kind of woman Alan would have anything to do with, or rather would have anything to do with him. Almost forgetting his manners, he bit back a reply and gently asked her to follow him to his office.

Lori saw the instant look of distrust on his face and felt the long silence as if it were a cold winter wind. She wondered again if she should have gotten involved. Oh well--if she was going to tell a sheriff anything--it might as well be to one as delicious as this one.

Eric walked to his office with the beautiful blonde in tow, shut the door behind them, and asked her to please have a seat. With her properly seated, Eric asked her to explain what she knew about Alan Chipenski.

She started her story and told it from beginning to end. When she finished, Eric realized he had not introduced himself or found out her name. "By the way," Eric offered, "I'm Eric Sandusky."

"I'm Lori Cochran," she replied.

Eric showed her pictures of Alan and asked if she was sure this was the same person as Max Partain. When she answered "yes," he politely asked her the location of the house on the lake.

"It's technically in Belgreen, but I don't remember the exact address without my file," Lori apologized. "I can fax you a copy of the map when I return to the office."

Eric sat pensively for a minute and then asked, "Do you remember how to drive there?"

Do I remember? Of course, I remember, she thought. Then she said, "I would be happy to ride out there and show you where the house is."

Thank you again, Oh Lord, Eric thought.

Eric definitely was not the Sheriff Lori had pictured when she had left Moulton that morning.

Eric looked at her fit form and noticed how she had attempted to hide her curves by donning the business suit. It was an attempt that failed miserably. He caught himself wondering if the figure underneath was as trim and fit as it looked with clothes on.

Lori noticed Eric appraising her. This was something she had seen before. The unbridled lust was evident. She wondered for a brief moment if she should ride out there with him. It might not be a good idea. After all, he was the Sheriff of Franklin County; and he could get away with anything. If he attacked her, no one would ever know. If she were stupid enough to tell, no one would believe an ex-con over an attractive, popular Sheriff. However, life is about taking chances and making choices. You never know what cards you are going to be dealt. If she was going to take a chance, she might as well take it with someone who looked as good as this Eric Sandusky, Sheriff of Franklin County, did.

She had found her *Mr. Right*.

Eric got into the Explorer with Lori, knowing that once he got to the little house on the lake as Lori described it, he would need to get a search warrant for the property. Eric didn't drive his cruiser because he wanted a little more time with the angel who had walked into his life. He didn't want her to get away. As they started away from the courthouse, he remembered he had left his radio in his office.

"Could you go back to the courthouse for a minute?" he asked Lori politely.

"Of course," she said. "Why?"

"I left my radio at your place. I mean my office." *Why did he say that?* This girl was definitely having an effect on him. He was normally calm, cool, and collected. Now he felt like a schoolboy stuttering all over a pretty lady.

"My place?" She laughed with an ease she didn't feel. "Really now, Sheriff. I'm not that kind of girl. Only minutes after we meet and you're already leaving things at my place."

"I didn't mean it . . . that . . . way. Well, I did mean it that . . . I guess I'd better just hush while I'm behind," Eric said clearly flustered.

"Oh, you didn't mean it? Or did you? Which is it?" She said with an amused tone in her voice as she finished making the block. She pulled back up in front of the courthouse and started to park. Eric directed her to the side of the courthouse and instructed her to park in one of the spaces marked **Sheriff's Department Only**. He got out of the Explorer before he could stick his foot any farther down his throat. "Be right back," he said.

"I'll be right here, Sheriff."

He jogged up the side stairs and with his key opened the door to the courthouse. He walked in the first door past his secretary's desk and found his radio sitting on his desk. When he noticed the battery indicator light was on, he reached behind his desk, put the radio on the charger, and took a fully charged one. He picked up the phone and called dispatch down at the jail. "This is Eric. Call Andy and have him go over to Judge Pilgrim's office. I need a search warrant. Tell him I'll call with the details later. Then call Investigator Adrian. I'll also need him." Eric walked back out to Lori's Explorer and got in on the right side. "I'm ready whenever you are," he said.

They had a nice conversation about absolutely nothing as they drove west on Highway 24. When she came to Highway 187, she made a right by Hester's Store, went to the stop sign, and then made another right onto old Highway 24. Several miles after turning left on 49, Lori crossed Cedar Creek to then make a left onto Lost Creek Rd. Soon after crossing Lost Creek Bridge she made a left onto Shady Grove Road. About a hundred feet after turning left, she made a right on a deserted gravel road. "This is the road the house is on," said Lori.

"Then stop right here, please," Eric directed as he picked up his radio, Eric said. "Thirty-three-one to Base."

"Go ahead thirty-three-one," came the reply.

"Have 33-2, 10-5, J-4, 1-0-0 Shady Grove Road. That's 1-0-0 sam, hotel, alpha, delta, yankee . . . golf, romeo, oscar, victor, echo . . . Road."

"Copy. That's 100 Shady Grove Road," said the dispatcher.

"Have 33-2 and 33-5 meet me here as soon as they get the J-4 base."

"10-4."

"I'm going to be 10-6 at the previous address to investigate a possible 60."

"10-4, 33-1."

When Eric finished with the radio, Lori was looking at him with a confused look on her face. "What, exactly did all that mean?" she inquired.

"I simply told the dispatcher to have my Chief Deputy and Investigator pick up a search warrant and bring it here, and that I would be busy investigating a possible murder at this address."

Looking over at the Sheriff, Lori asked. "The dispatcher got all of that out of what you said?"

"Yes, it's mostly 10 codes. I'm 33-1. The Chief Deputy is 33-2, 10-5 J-4 means relay paperwork, 33-5 is my investigator, 10-6 is I'm busy, and a possible 60 is a possible murder."

"If you say so. Do you want me to drive on down to the house?"

"No. Let's wait on the investigator and Chief Deputy."

"Now tell me," Lori said. "How is it a man as young as you gets to be Sheriff of Franklin County?"

"It's not that hard. I had grown up knowing about a man named Buford Barker. As a kid, I always wanted to be just like him. Buford was well known and admired for his contributions to law enforcement in North Alabama, having been Chief Deputy Sheriff of Franklin County and Chief of Police at Red Bay. Legend goes he never had to pull his gun in his 20+ years in the field. Some folks believed the *Walking Tall* movie was really more about him than that guy up in Tennessee because Barker walked tall and carried a big stick. I met Buford face-to-face when I had a part-time job in high school as a dispatcher for the Sheriff's Department. He encouraged me to attend the police academy because he believed the main reason he hadn't been elected as Sheriff was because of his lack of education. Buford helped me get a job with the Russellville City Police Department as a patrol officer where I worked until two years ago. The incumbent Sheriff was a man Buford had no respect for and was totally corrupt. With encouragement from Buford and monetary help from the grandfather of my best friend, I decided to make a difference and ran against him. I did and won. So here I am."

"You say the previous Sheriff was corrupt?"

"Yeah. Most of the deputies were as bad as he was, but there were a few good ones, like Barker, had been. Before I took office, I gave all Deputies notice I would take applications, and they would have to apply for a job with the new administration. I only kept two of the former Sheriff's Deputies--a former Army Chaplain and a young Deputy that had only been on the force for about four months."

"You fired all the rest?"

"Yes, every one of them. The former Sheriff had thirty-six Deputies--most of who were useless--and eight Jailers. I kept two of the Jailers and two of the Deputies. Everyone else got walking papers the day I took office. Some of the Deputies I fired would have paid me to keep their jobs. They would have actually worked for nothing."

"You had to hire thirty-four new Deputies and six new Jailers?"

"No, I hired fifteen new Deputies and two Jailers. We didn't need thirty-six Deputies. The former Sheriff was paying Deputies $22,000 a year and the jailers $16,000. That's not even starvation wage. My Deputies earn $42,000 a year and my Jailers $30,000. With the salaries I offered, I got the best officers this part of Alabama had to offer. I did make many city councils mad because I now have several of their former chiefs of police and their best officers. I have a better force, and I'm saving the county $86,000 a year in salaries alone. My last year's budget was almost $100,000 less than the previous Sheriff's last budget. Also, our crime rate has dropped by 9 percent. We're putting that $100,000 back in anticipation of building a new county jail."

"Wow, that's a unique way to run a government office. Most of the time people always seem to need more people."

"I'm a taxpayer too, and I couldn't see overspending for people we didn't need."

The walkie-talkie Eric was holding interrupted their conversation. "33-2 to 33-1."

"33-1, go ahead," Eric said.

"What's your current 20? Can you give me directions there?"

"Sure, go west on Lost Creek Road, cross Lost Creek Bridge and take a left onto Shady Grove Rd. We're at the first gravel road on the right."

"33-1, is that the road Ezzell Cemetery used to be on before they dammed up the creek and covered it up?"

"10-4."

"33-1, I'm 10-84, my 10-87 is about eight minutes."

"10-4, 33-2."

"What was said in that conversation?" asked Lori.

"Andy asked where I was. He then said he was in route with an ETA, Estimated Time of Arrival, of eight minutes."

"Okay, if you say so."

About ten minutes later Andy pulled up with Investigator Jacob Adrian in the car behind him. They got out of the car and sauntered over to the Explorer as another carload of deputies pulled up. The Sheriff and Lori got out of the car, and Eric introduced Lori to everyone.

"Time to go to work, boss," Andy said.

"Yeah. It's that time," said Eric. "You got an extra vest in the car?"

"I certainly do," said Andy.

Before Eric went to the car to get the vest, he turned to Lori and said. "I've got to go to work now. This could be dangerous, so you need to leave. I'm interested in seeing you again. Would you be free for dinner later this week?" *There, he had said it.*

"Call me, and we'll talk about it," Lori said as she handed Eric her business card. "Call me on my cell number." Lori walked to her Explorer, backed out of the drive, and drove away.

"What a looker," Andy said. "If you don't call her, give me her card so I can."

Jacob whistled softly under his breath. "She is a hot one. That she is."

"Okay men, it's time to go to work," said Eric walking over to the trunk of the car. After waiting for Andy to open the trunk, Eric removed and donned a Kevlar vest. The Kevlar vests they wore made them itch as if they wore a solid suit of fiberglass or maybe an undershirt powdered thoroughly with itching powder. None of them **ever** wanted to wear the vests. They knew it was prudent to do so now, even if it was like wearing a shirt made of stinging nettle.

Eric and his deputies then approached the house with trepidation. Eric and Andy took the direct route to the front door as Jacob and a young Deputy named David staked out the back entrance with direct orders not to enter unless directed to by either the Sheriff or the Chief Deputy.

"How are we doing this?" asked Andy.

"Hard and fast," Eric said as he kicked in the front door. The heat and smell of rotting human flesh assaulted him as the horrid, repulsive odor attacked his olfactory system. This was far worse than anything Eric had ever encountered. He gagged slightly and stumbled back out into the yard. His stomach seemed to be caught in his throat and he was choking on it.

It took Eric several minutes to recover from his initial entry into the abandoned cabin. He spoke through his throat mike to the chief investigator, "Ya'll come around front, Jacob, but be sure to bring your handkerchief."

Each officer quickly opened all available doors and windows and with whatever he could find to put over his mouth and nose searched for the source of the horrible smell. As Deputy David Smith opened the door to a large upright freezer, a disgusting mess of rotting flesh covered his boots with a thick black mucous fluid that contained thousands and thousands off writhing, squirming maggots. The young Deputy promptly made this even worse by vomiting into the mess that was once a pretty, young black woman.

"Sorry, Sheriff," he mumbled as he ran out of the house throwing up again before he made it out onto the porch, where he hung over the railing emptying his guts. Long after there was nothing left, David still had dry heaves. This had been David's first week on the job, and it would be his last day. Some folks were not cut out to witness what law enforcement threw their way.

Back inside, Eric looked at what was left of the corpse that had been in hundred plus temperatures for over two weeks before he walked back to the living room. "I think it's time to call in reinforcement," he said to Andy and Jacob. "I think Mr. Alan Chipenski has rabbited. His Pontiac Trans Am is in the garage, and he must have had another vehicle. He doesn't have any family here. His mother was his only relative and she died more than ten years ago. We'll catch him, but it won't be here in Franklin County. I want all the evidence to be perfect so let's call in the federal and state boys. Andy, go make some calls."

"Yes, sir."

After securing the crime scene, Eric walked out to join Andy in the patrol car. He turned the air conditioner's fan up as high as it would go and decided *it was going to be another long, hot day.*

Chapter Twenty-One

He awoke after a long, restful sleep. He got up, shaved, and reapplied his hair dye. Admiring his reflection in the bathroom mirror, he considered letting his hair grow out to the top of his ears. *I should look respectable enough*, he thought, *and I'll only have to dye it once a week, or maybe every two weeks or so to keep my roots from showing.* He had no way of getting around shaving at least once a day. His heavy beard continued to come in black as coal. He contemplated letting his hair grow back in his natural color so he wouldn't have to worry about sporting a five-o-clock shadow. No. He had to be blonde for at least a couple of years. He wasn't going to take any chances. After he showered, he put on the last of his clean clothes. He would either have to buy some new ones or wash the dirty ones. He bagged up his laundry and carried it out to the truck along with the rest of his things. This time, he was very careful not to snag the moneybag.

Today he would find a place to live. The fugitive had left his key on the dresser and hadn't bothered to check out at the front desk since he had paid cash and signed in under yet another assumed name.

Randall drove down to a local diner where he purchased a newspaper from the green box out front. He didn't purchase the paper because of an insatiable interest in current events, in fact, he rarely read the paper and couldn't imagine why anyone would waste valuable hours every day reading about what had already happened. When newspapers started predicting the future, he might be more interested in their news articles. As far as he knew, nothing reported in the news had ever affected him. He chose a booth in the back corner of the eatery. A slovenly, middle-aged waitress, at least a hundred and fifty pounds overweight, asked if he would like coffee.

"Coffee's fine."

"You're not from around here are you?" she asked noticing his heavy southern drawl.

"Naw, Mississippi," he said.

To her, it sounded like he had said Missuppi. "Really? Do you need a few minutes to look over the menu?"

Why would I need to look over the menu? They're all the same.

"No," he said, "I'll have two eggs over easy, two strips of crisp bacon, white toast, and a small glass of orange juice."

"Home fries or hash browns?"

"No, just the eggs and bacon."

"They come with it."

Why can't servers bring you what you order? Why did they have to try to force things on you? JUST THE DAMN EGGS AND BACON, he wanted to scream.

"No thank you. Just bring me the eggs and bacon," he said politely.

"Alrighty then. I'll be right back," she said as she shuffled to turn in his order.

He flipped through the paper until he finally found the classified section. The first thing he noticed was a half-page ad announcing the city of Billings needed police officers. According to the ad, they were having an open interview in two weeks. *Wouldn't it be ironic if I applied for a police job,* he thought. The more he considered being a police officer, the more he liked the idea. Even though he had always been a criminal entrepreneur, he had never been arrested or fingerprinted. With his new ID, he could pass any background check. Also, he had been very careful to wipe down the Trans Am and everything at the lake house.

No. Oh, no! He suddenly remembered the tapes he had removed from the recorders. He had left them beside the computer. They would clearly show him and what had happened.

No--It would show what Alan Chipenski had done, and he was now Randy Marlowe. Randy Marlow had done nothing illegal or immoral, as his perfect record would show.

This was actually a great idea. What better place to hide than in the police department? He would be privy to information regarding any attempt to find him. This would be the perfect place to continue his criminal enterprise. Look how profitable being in law enforcement had been for Russellville's Chief of Police and the former Sheriff.

No--He would not think about that. He was going straight. He had made up his mind. He was going to be Randy Marlowe, model citizen. He would become a police officer and then make detective. He looked once again at the ad. He noted the requirements and was glad to see he could fit the bill on all. He then began to plan how to make Randy Marlowe stand out from all other applicants applying for the police officer positions.

Later that afternoon, after looking at dozens of apartments, Randy Marlowe found a suitable townhouse in one of the exclusive areas of Billings. It was unfurnished, with two bedrooms, two and a half baths, and a one-car garage. He had wanted a furnished apartment, but all the furnished apartments looked trashy and were rented mainly to transients. After he paid the first and last month's rent, he arranged with the manager to handle getting his utilities and cable turned on. Since the cable company offered high-speed computer access to the Internet, he felt he wouldn't need a phone. He would get a cellular phone instead of a landline.

Now he needed furniture. Randy parked in front of a large furniture store, took out a packet of hundred dollar bills, pulled off the band, folded them, and put them in his pocket. Once entering the store, he selected a nice, expensive bedroom suite with an even more expensive mattress set. When the salesperson guaranteed him it could be delivered that evening, he added a moderately priced bedroom suite and mattress for the second bedroom. He called the manager of the apartments who assured him she would open his door for the delivery people in case he wasn't back in time. He went to another furniture store and picked out a couch, recliner, two end tables, coffee table, entertainment center, and computer workstation.

His next stop was an electronics store where he browsed for several hours before selecting a top of the line computer, big screen TV with a built-in VCR/DVD player, washer and dryer, and stereo system. As he left, he thought about what else he would need. He made a mental list and pulled into the parking lot of a huge discount store called Colstrip where he bought all of his pots and pans, dishes, bed linens, towels, bath supplies, curtains, silverware, drinking glasses, a coffee maker, blender, microwave, and a few other small kitchen appliances. This store was even bigger and better stocked than *Wal-Mart*. It had everything he needed. Looking at his overflowing buggy, he decided it was time to leave until he saw the clothing department. In the clothing department, he picked out several pairs of jeans, a few shirts, socks, underwear, and since the nights were quite cool, a light jacket, and a pair of hiking boots. He would get anything else he needed later.

Randy left Colstrip and drove across the road to a shopping mall. In an upscale men's shop, he purchased several winter and summer weight suits, twenty shirts, twenty pairs of dress slacks, and six pairs of the most expensive shoes they had. The suits and slacks would have to be altered, so he was assured he could pick them up day after tomorrow.

It had been a landmark day for retail businesses in Billings as he was nearly $50,000 poorer. He parked his Silverado in the garage and walked into his apartment carrying some of his purchases. Someone knocked on the front door. He opened it to find the apartment manager and the delivery people from the first furniture store. When the manager saw Randy was there, she said goodbye and walked back to the office. He let the delivery people in and directed them where to set up the bedroom furniture. Thirty-five minutes later, they were gone and he continued to unload the truck. Once finished, he searched for an appropriate hiding place for the remaining $600,000. After pondering his dilemma for what seemed like an eternity, he went into the kitchen and retrieved a large serrated edged butcher knife that he took into his bedroom. In the center of the mattress, he cut a large square hole. He removed the cotton batting from around the inner springs and pushed in the moneybag. When he saw it fit, he wedged it in tight and flipped over the mattress. It wasn't the most original hiding place he had ever come up with, but, for now, it was the best he could do.

Randy made both beds using the bedclothes he had purchased earlier at Colstrip. He made his apartment look like a home as he unpacked all his new purchases and put them up. This time tomorrow evening, it would look as if he had always lived there.

The next morning around eight o'clock, delivery people from the second furniture store showed up. As they finished unloading the furniture, Randy was pleased to see the truck from the electronics store park out front. By 10 A.M., everyone was gone except Randy.

Randy Marlowe needed to make a phone call, but he would wait until after he showered. After he finished his shower, he dressed in blue jeans and a tee shirt and put on the new hiking boots. *My first stop this morning*, he thought, *is to visit the DMV.*

At the DMV, he traded in his Mississippi driver's license for a new Montana license and was pleasantly surprised when they immediately issued him a new license. Alabama had this annoying way of giving out licenses where they gave you a temporary one and then mailed out the permanent license thirty days to forty days later. In only twenty minutes, Randall Gerald Marlowe had a new Montana driver's license as well as license plates for the Chevy Pickup.

Under the name of Gerald Randall, Randy rented a post office box. As he walked out of the post office with his new box key, he knew he had almost everything he needed. That one other thing would be delivered after he made one phone call. Randy stopped in a truck stop out on I-90, bought a calling card, and called a phone number he had memorized. When the person on the other end of the line picked up, there was no hello, no thank you for calling ABC or XYZ Corporation--nothing except silence. He described what he wanted. When he finished, a person on the other end of the line, maybe male, possibly female, informed him this paperwork would be more difficult to gather than his previous request and that the price would be $50,000. He was given a New York address before the line went dead.

The mailing address was the same address as the last time, 105 Central Park West, Apartment 2G, New York, NY 10023. Last time the fee had only been $5,000. This time, he needed a complete history.

Randy purchased a large padded envelope, stuffed $50,000 inside, and mailed it to the New York address. Now it was a waiting game.

Before going back home, he deposited the cashier's check and an additional $9,000 into an interest bearing checking account at the First Regional Bank of Montana.

Noticing an army surplus store on the way home, he stopped and bought an Army dress uniform complete with the medals and markings of a staff sergeant. He also bought several of the battle dress uniforms or BDU's, several pairs of combat boots, hats, socks, a field jacket with liner, black raincoat, and a Smokey the Bear hat. He was set, and as soon as his paperwork arrived from New York, he would completely assume his new life.

Chapter Twenty-Two

Lori thought about the handsome Sheriff Sandusky as she backed the Explorer out of the drive. She suddenly felt very light-hearted and not like she imagined she would last night after watching the evening news. She expected the Sheriff to be a gray-haired, gruff, old, pot-bellied Sheriff--all hands and no charm. She had instead found a charming, personable, gorgeous man with strong features and the body of a young Adonis. *And he was so sweet.*

She contemplated about his unintentional misspeak concerning his radio left at her place and wondered if it had been intentional. As she remembered the situation, a vivacious smile spread across her lovely face. For the first time in her life, she felt protected. There was something about him, and it was much more than him being 6' 6" and over two hundred pounds.

They were the antithesis of each other. She was blonde, blue-eyed, and diminutive in stature with elf-like features. The only things about her that kept her from being considered small or petite were her childbearing hips and full overflowing breasts. He, on the other hand, was tall and dark with wide shoulders. His long legs seemed to be well muscled and he was clearly no stranger to harsh workouts in the gym--his body showed it. He walked with the confident stride and pace of a man born to command. It was obvious to Lori; even in the few minutes she observed him with his deputies, he was not a figurehead Sheriff. He was not there to simply hold public office. He was well respected and well liked. He was a man who could have any woman he wanted. He hosted a quiet, self-assured demeanor much like John Wayne displayed onscreen.

Be real, Lori, that little voice in her head said. *What makes you think a man with all that would fall for an ex-con like you? Certainly, with a keystroke, he can find out all about your storied past. Women were probably falling all over themselves to become Mrs. Sandusky. He might even be married. He probably was married with the standard two point three kids at home and a wife who would never divorce him no matter what.* Lori was interrupted by the sound of her cell phone ringing. "Hello," she said.

"Lori, this is Eric. Would you like to go out to eat tonight?"

Lori's heart skipped a beat. As composed as possible, she said, "I'd love to."

"How does Logan's sound?"

"Sounds great."

"Do you mind meeting a couple of my friends there?"

"Of course not."

"Can you meet me at my office around eight?"

"Why there?"

"The FBI agents have arrived at the cabin, and it will probably be five or six hours before they're through."

"Okay, Eric. I'll meet you there."

Eric and Lori both hung up feeling they had finally met someone they could spend the rest of their lives with. Neither had previously believed in love at first sight, but both now knew it was possible.

Chapter Twenty-Three

The rest of Peter and Lila's time in New York City was like a second honeymoon. Lila put aside how disappointed she was in how Peter had handled the Miguel's situation, and Peter filed in the back of his mind, for future reference, what he had found in the jeweled box. They slept late, ate anything they wanted, went wherever they wanted, and purchased anything they desired. Peter soon discovered he didn't have to be in any set location or have any set hours to accomplish his work and was glad to schedule it around his and Lila's various adventures.

The second week started with Peter spending most of his time discussing business details with Jackie while Lila shopped. By the end of the week, they were ready to go back to Alabama. They really liked the apartment on Central Park West and their new comfortable sofa, but it wasn't home. When they returned to Alabama, they decided they would reveal they'd inherited a great deal of money, but would tell no one the true extent of their wealth--not even Lila's parents, or Eric.

Peter hadn't confided in Lila about the keys or the documents he'd found in the jeweled box. Since the language on the back of the map was Russian, he'd bought a Russian/English dictionary and translated what he soon learned were the directions to the compound in Montana located on property that was physically in Montana but not considered part of Montana or the United States. If he had translated the dimensions of the property correctly, it was roughly the size of the state of Vermont and built in 1792. Peter would take Lila out to Montana, but they would drive, not fly. Peter had always wanted to see the west. Driving out there was the surest way to get to see a great deal of the country. It was different seeing it at ground level, where you could actually stop and see a few sights along the way, than seeing it at 35,000 feet where everything looked the same. They would do this as soon as Lila got over the morning sickness she had recently started to suffer from.

Peter picked up the phone in his office. Jackie answered on the first ring. "May I help you, Mr. Stacia?" asked Jackie in her candied voice.

"Yes. Tell the pilots to spool up the plane. We're going home."

"Back to Alabama?"

"Yes. While it is nice here and we'll visit quite often, I don't think we'll ever live here permanently."

"I see. The jet is ready at any time. It will only take about thirty minutes or so to get ground clearance, and you will be on your way. I'll call the pilots now and have them there by the time you arrive."

"Very good. Would you please pack up anything we still have here and send it to us in Alabama? Ship the Harley-Davidson motorcycle, the yellow Hummer, and convertible Jaguar to my Alabama address. You might as well throw in that midnight blue Mercedes that used to belong to Sean Michaels. That will be a little memento of my New York City vacation."

"Yes sir, but you know you've got enough money to purchase similar vehicles in Alabama."

"Are you questioning my judgment?" asked Peter in a haughty voice he had never before used with Jackie.

"Of course not, sir," countered a surprised Jackie with a quick recovery. "I now see your point. It would be wasteful to purchase items you already possess. It would be much more cost effective to ship them to Alabama."

"I'm glad you do, indeed, see things my way, Jackie. Have the helicopter pick us up in twenty minutes."

"Yes, sir."

Peter hung up the phone with a smile on his face and started up the stairs to search for Lila. Before he got halfway up, his cell phone rang for the first time in almost two weeks.

"Hey buddy, what's up? What mountain top have you run off to see now?" asked Eric. Peter and Lila were known to disappear for a day or two at a time, but this was the longest they had been gone without checking in with him.

"It's good to hear your voice, Eric. It's the first southern voice other than Lila's I've heard in two weeks," said Peter. "We'll be back home today."

"Home from where?" asked Eric.

"New York."

"What are you doing up there in Yankee country?" Peter knew Eric was not referring to the baseball team when he asked this question.

"We flew up to finish some family business. Papa was worth a great deal more than I'd imagined, and we had to meet with a few business advisors. We should fly into Muscle Shoals in slightly more than four hours."

"Which airline flies into Muscle Shoals?"

"Mine."

"You don't own an airline, do you?"

"No," said Peter, who felt slightly guilty about telling this lie. He actually owned controlling interest in several. "But I do own a Gulfstream business jet."

"You're kidding."

"No, I'm not."

"Aren't they really expensive?"

"Yes."

"Exactly how much money did Papa leave you?"

"Let's put it this way--Lila and I will never have to worry about money."

"Hey, Pete?"

"Yes, Eric."

"I've got good news and bad news. Which do you want to hear first?"

"I'll take the bad first so we can end the call on a good note."

"Alan Chipenski killed my informant, and we can't find him."

"You're kidding," said an unbelieving Peter.

"I wish I were," lamented Eric.

"When did it happen?" inquired Peter softly.

"It must have been the same day you and Lila left for New York."

"It's been that long?"

"Yeah. Are you ready for the good news?" inquired Eric with an instant change in mood and tone.

"Okay. I'm ready."

"I've met a girl," said a jubilant Eric.

"You meet lots of girls in your line of work. What makes this one so special?"

"She's the one. I think she is, anyway."

"When do I get to meet this fantasy girl?"

"Can you and Lila meet us for supper at Logan's at say--eight-thirty, tonight?"

"I think we can do that."

"See you then," Eric said before he hung up.

Peter and Lila stepped off the Gulfstream into a smoldering heat wave. They had almost forgotten how hot and sticky it could get on an Alabama summer afternoon. It had only taken a couple minutes for Peter to sweat so much he looked like he'd been dipped in a creek. A young man picked them up in a little electric car and drove them to the Dodge Ramcharger. Peter gave him a hundred-dollar bill and told him to have a good afternoon.

Peter inserted the key in the ignition switch of the Dodge and fired it up. Immediately they noticed the A/C wasn't working. It was going to be one sweltering ride back home in this vehicle. Going north on Airport Road, they made a left at Second Street. Peter looked down at the gas hand and saw the truck was low on gas. This was great. No air conditioning and no gas. When Peter got to Woodward Avenue, he made a left and turned into the Texaco station on the corner of Woodward and Second Street. He got out and looked at one of the debit cards Jeffery had given him. He started to put it in the gas pump, but he changed his mind and jumped back into the Ramcharger.

"What are you doing?" asked Lila.

"I'm going to buy my first truck."

Back in the big truck, he pulled out onto Woodward Avenue and headed south. For the first time in two weeks, he felt like he was on familiar ground. He passed Long-Lewis Ford and wondered about the actual ownership of Alabama's oldest Ford dealer. Did he own it, too? He seemed to own everything else. As they passed Jim Bishop Chevrolet, Peter slowed down to see if the Silver ½ ton Tahoe was still parked on the front row. He was twenty-eight years old and had never bought a new vehicle. Of course, he had gotten the brand new *1988 Ramcharger AW 150* on his sixteenth birthday, but Papa had picked it out. Peter did love the Old Dodge, but it was twelve years old and . . .

Lila asked, "Where we going, baby?" as he made the U-turn to head back north on U.S. 43.

"Back to buy me a Tahoe."

"Cool, maybe the A/C works."

Peter pulled up in front of the office and went inside. A young salesperson immediately met him. "Can I help you, sir?" asked the nice young man.

"Sure, I came to buy that Silver Tahoe on the front row."

"Would you like to test drive it first?"

"No, I'll do that on the way home."

"Come on in, and we'll get the paperwork started. How much do you plan to put down on it? How much do you want for that old Dodge?"

"I don't recall saying anything about doing paperwork, and I don't remember saying anything about trading. I came to buy the Tahoe. I'll not do any paperwork. You can mail it to me when you get it finished."

"I don't have time for jokes." The sales representative had never experienced this kind of nonsense before, and it was too hot to stand out in the sun with a seven foot tall lunatic. "Come on in where it's cool. We have to do paperwork. All the banks require it for financing."

"Did I say I was going to finance it? I didn't say that, did I?" argued Peter as they entered the air-conditioned showroom.

"You're not going to finance it? How will you pay for it?" The salesperson looked at the old Dodge outside and Peter's shirt that was wet with sweat and assumed incorrectly he could not afford to pay any other way.

"Do you take MasterCard?" asked Peter as he handed over the new Chase Manhattan debit card.

The young man was definitely out of his element now. He had never sold a car this way. He wasn't sure a MasterCard could be used to purchase a car.

"Yes we do, but I don't know if it can be used to buy a car. I'll have to check."

"Then get it done. I don't have all day."

The sales representative went to talk to his sales manager. The sales manager looked over at Peter and then sent the young man back into the showroom.

"If you will come this way, we'll get the paperwork started."

"Maybe you didn't understand me. I'm not doing paperwork. Get the truck cleaned up, make a copy of my driver's license, run the card, and I'll leave. I expect to be on my way in fifteen minutes. The only thing I'm signing is the title application. You can mail the title to the address on my license."

"Hold on a minute," said the sales representative as his sales manager came over.

Before he could say anything, Peter said, "Mister, you'd better be coming out here to tell me that silver Tahoe will be ready in about ten minutes. I have places to go and people to see. If you won't sell me one, I'm sure they will come across the river at Nelda Stephenson Chevrolet. I'm not sure what the price of the truck is, but if you can get it cleaned up and have my lovely wife and me on our way in nine more minutes, I'll pay $1,000 over the sticker."

"Consider it done."

This was new to the sales manager too, who didn't believe the issuing card company would honor a transaction this large. When the salesperson brought in the invoice, he was sure of it. The sticker price was $36,313. He called back to the shop and had the boys start the cleanup. He told them they had eight minutes to finish, and they'd better have it done and up front in that period of time.

The sales manager ran the card even though he was positive it would be rejected. Debit cards usually had a $500 limit. He was sincerely surprised when the transaction for slightly over $37,000 went through. He made a copy of the driver's license and brought out the credit card slip for Peter to sign.

Peter signed the slip and handed the salesperson twenty, one hundred dollar bills. "Fix the A/C on the Dodge and deliver it to my home address. When you deliver it, bring the title to the Tahoe."

Twelve minutes later, the sparkling new Tahoe was sitting in front of the showroom. Peter looked at his watch. "They're a little late, but I guess three minutes won't hurt anything," he told Lila.

The sales manager handed him the extra set of keys and keyless entry modules and said. "It was a pleasure doing business with you, Mr. Stacia. The tank should be full of gas, and the other set of keys is in the ignition."

Peter shook his hand and walked out. His total elapsed time in the dealership was twenty-two minutes. When they drove off the lot, he was pleased with the way the transaction had taken place. It was a lot easier to buy things when you had money. You didn't have to accept any of the trouble normally associated with credit transactions.

He played with the new truck on the way home and noticed it was underpowered compared to the big Dodge. Well, he could do something about that. Hadn't that General Motors man said they were developing a new 572 cubic inch engine to go into racecars? He also supposed the Tahoe would look better jacked up a bit.

He was still thinking about this when he made the right turn onto Parks Drive to go to his house up in Hester Heights.

What he was not thinking about was how quiet the usually talkative Lila was.

* * *

THE GAME

Trusting in the lying voice,
I soiled myself.
I trapped a life.

The things I knew would mess me up,
I lost my fear.
I tried my luck.

The road I drove began to end.
I crashed into
a prison then.

It took the time to figure out,
The truth was there
Without a doubt.

The game ends, and I am free.
Just quit the game.
It's all on me.

~~~Stone Ronson

* * *

Chapter Twenty-Four

When the FBI, state investigators, and forensic teams left the little cabin, they had found little to use against Alan Chipenski.

After hours of forensic study, the investigators had recovered a short aluminum bat like children used to play t-ball, some black hair in the bathroom, and a small bandage with what looked like a dried bloodstain. They found no fingerprints in the entire house. The whole place had been wiped down before Alan's departure. Nothing except DNA evidence in the hair left in the bathroom, the testimony of the real estate agent, and the black Trans Am in the garage could tie him to this place. They may or may not have enough evidence to convict him if he were ever caught.

Eric thought of Lori and decided to give her another call when he got back to the office. As he headed toward Andy's cruiser, Andy came out of the house and called out, "Boss, you may want to come back inside. There's something you need to see." Eric strode back up to the house. As he entered, he saw Andy push on a back wall that slid silently back. As he got closer, he saw a narrow opening to the left open into a very constricted space. The hall-like room was about four feet wide and thirty-five feet long. Multitudes of cameras and video recorders mounted on the walls were connected to a large central computer that zoomed at the end of the hallway. Hundreds of VHS video cassettes were in cabinets organized and cataloged. He was surprised to see three tapes lying on the desk alongside the computer. Eric and Andy spent several minutes unsuccessfully to get the computer to come on before they gave up and picked up the three tapes to head back into the living room toward a VCR and television. Andy turned on the TV, inserted a tape, and pushed rewind. When the tape stopped, he pushed play. They were rewarded with a picture of the kitchen.

The scene was vivid. Alan walked in with Georgia. At first, she showed no sign of anxiety. She had obviously been there before. Alan reached into a cabinet and removed what seemed to be a can of starting fluid. Spraying this onto a handkerchief, he quickly placed this over her nose and mouth and held it there as she struggled. When Georgia no longer struggled, he dumped her on one of the stout oak dining room chairs where he sat her up and duct-taped her arms and legs to the chair. The time stamp in the bottom right-hand corner of the screen indicated the time was 6:54 P.M. For a few seconds the screen went blank. When the picture returned, the time stamp was 8:03 P.M. Georgia had started to come around. She was still securely taped to the chair as Alan came into the room holding an aluminum ball bat. He walked right up to Georgia and hit her across the shins. She was instantly awake.

An idea came to Eric. The system must be motion activated. It showed the complete and unfortunate scene the Sheriff and deputies had listened to previously.

Eric and Andy watched as Alan found the hairpin transmitter. The screen went blank again. When it came back on, Alan walked into the kitchen with a bloody Georgia in his arms. He then crammed her into the pantry. Eric fast-forwarded through the cleanup of the kitchen. The tape came to another blank spot. The next time the camera was activated it showed a very different picture. A young, clean-cut man dressed in a light blue suit strolled through the kitchen. He wore glasses and had his blonde hair cut very short.

"Who is that?" asked Andy.

"I think it may be Alan, but I'm not sure," Eric said.

"You think?"

"Yeah," said Eric, "I wouldn't know it was him if I hadn't gone to school with him for twelve years. The suit, glasses, and short hair are a definite change from the hippie look."

"That's all we can do today. Let's go."

Eric got into the squad car with Andy and remembered he would soon be going out with Lori. He hoped Peter and Lila would like her. Eric was ready for a big juicy steak with a gorgeous blonde. For tonight, he would forget about Chipenski.

Chapter Twenty-Five

Peter patiently sat by Lila's dressing table and watched her apply makeup. For the tenth time in the last five minutes, he glanced at his Seiko watch. It was now 8:05 P.M., and they had twenty-five minutes before they were to meet Eric and his new girl at Logan's. *This,* he thought, *was near to impossible, since it was a thirty-minute drive.*

Peter had learned, after five years of marriage, it was a hopeless endeavor to rush her. It would take as long as it would take, and no amount of threatening to leave her would do any good. She knew he wasn't serious, and he definitely would not leave without her.

By 8:15 P.M., her makeup was complete. She walked into the bedroom and looked through her jewelry box as Peter walked up behind her.

"Wear this," he said as he slipped a necklace around her neck.

The 18k gold chain was as thick as Peter's little finger. It had diamonds embedded in an overlapping chain-link pattern. At the center of the necklace hung a pendant made of three heart shaped red stones. Two of them were almost as large as grapes and one was smaller. All slightly overlapped and were set in a delicate 18k gold spider web.

"The two hearts symbolize our hearts intertwining forever," Peter said. "The third is our unborn child."

"Oh my," gasped Lila. "It's beautiful. Please tell me those aren't real rubies."

"You're right. They are not rubies."

"They're not?" she said showing obvious disappointment.

"They are red diamonds, and for you, my dear, I even have matching earrings," Peter said holding out an open jewelry box containing two teardrop red diamond earrings.

"They must be priceless," Lila said as she turned and kissed him deeply.

"If you keep this up, that pretty black dress you're wearing will be crumpled into a ball on the floor, and we will never get there," teased Peter.

"That would be fine with me, big boy," flirted Lila.

"They're not priceless; they came with a price," Peter said as he brought the subject back to the jewelry.

"How much?"

"How about a kiss?"

"No—Seriously, Peter. How much?"

"I'll never tell. Simply enjoy them."

If she knew the necklace cost almost $30 million and the earrings an additional $5 million, she would be afraid to wear them. The jewelry had been handcrafted especially for her. Peter, after consulting with Jackie, had visited a master jeweler. Peter picked the gems out personally. Red diamonds of gem quality were exceedingly rare. Lila now owned five of the only twenty in the world.

Peter watched Lila as she walked to the closet door to admire herself in a full-length mirror. The hearts lay nestled in her cleavage at precisely the right spot. She looked lovely--absolutely luminous. She far outshone any gem. Nothing could ever be as beautiful to Peter as Lila was at that precise moment.

The trip to Florence was uneventful. At 8:45 P.M., Lila and Peter pulled into a packed parking lot, and after a few minutes of driving around the lot, finally found a parking spot. The parking spot was in the farthest corner of the lot where they would have to walk the maximum distance to the front door. Peter parked the new Tahoe, walked around to the passenger side, and opened Lila's door gently helping her out of the truck. As he did this, he thought of his decision to lift and accessorize the vehicle. Peter decided while he was still going to do that, he might buy some kind of a family SUV he could fit into, as he didn't fit into cars. He would get something he wouldn't customize, something she could drive and get in and out of with relative ease, maybe an Explorer or an Expedition. Either one of those would be a good choice. Soon they would have a new addition to their family, and they didn't have an appropriate vehicle for all of them to go anywhere in. The Dodge was too tall, and the backseat was practically inaccessible for a child seat. Lila's BMW was too small, as was the Jaguar and Mercedes Jackie was shipping. The Hummer was certainly large enough and access was easy to the back seats, but it was a huge vehicle. Peter felt certain Lila would not be comfortable driving the Hummer. The more he reasoned, the more an Expedition, or *God forbid,* a minivan, seemed the most appropriate choice. They would also have to make some changes at the house. They could turn one of the bedrooms into a nursery.

"Baby! Baby! Pete! Are you listening to me?"

He suddenly realized Lila was talking to him.

"No, Hon. What did you say?" he asked absent-mindedly.

"I asked what you were thinking."

"I'm sorry. I was thinking about minivans and nurseries."

"What?" she asked sounding confused. "You were thinking about minivans and nurseries?"

"I plan to make some changes to accommodate this little one," he said as he patted Lila's flat stomach. If she hadn't already told him she was pregnant, he wouldn't have a clue.

"It's about time ya'll got here," Eric said. Peter noticed he was sitting beside a dazzling blonde who held one of Logan's pagers.

Lori looked up to see the biggest man she had ever seen. Eric had told her Peter was big, but she hadn't expected this. He was immense. Peter looked eerily like Eric's big brother. He was well dressed, yet you could see the muscles bulging under his shirt. He was almost twice as thick through the chest as Eric. His hands were as big as hers would be if she'd had on a softball glove. He had to weigh more than three hundred pounds, and not an inch of it was fat.

She wondered briefly if he was Eric's workout partner at the gym because it was clear that neither was a stranger to workouts. While Eric had the broad shoulders and lean hips of a cowboy, Peter had the look of Paul Bunyan in one of the children's books she remembered from her childhood.

Eric stood up, shook Peter's hand, and hugged Lila.

"Peter, Lila, this is Lori Cochran, my future wife," Eric said to introduce the blonde to the Stacias.

Yes! Yes! Lori thought suddenly.

Where in the world had that come from? Eric thought as he grimaced in embarrassment. *I've only known her for a few hours, and this is our first date. I don't even know if she likes me.*

Did Eric ask me to marry him? Lori wondered.

"I mean this is my date," said Eric. "Lori, this is Peter and Lillian Stacia, or Pete and Lila."

"It's good to meet you," Lori said as she glanced back and forth between Peter and Eric. "Are the two of you related? You look like brothers."

Peter and Eric shook their heads and smiled.

"People ask them that all the time," smiled Lila as she held out her arms to give Lori a hug. "Eric, what does Bess think about this future wife business? Have you told her and the kids?"

"Yes," Peter chimed in. "I'm not sure Bess will approve of another woman in the house."

Lori felt like the Titanic going down as she thought, h*e's married. He has kids. I knew it. He was too charming and too good-looking to be single at twenty-eight. I bet Pete and Lila think I'm just one of his . . .* Her shoulders slumped, and she was ready to leave.

"Lori. We're only kidding," interrupted Lila, who had noticed how suddenly pale Lori had become. "Bess is Eric's German Shepherd, who had puppies a couple of months ago. Eric, as good looking as he is, is not and has never been married. I have tried several times to marry him off to one of my nurse friends, though."

Lori was suddenly relieved. Her built-up tension and hostility now floated off in the warm summer breeze like a child's helium-filled balloon. The pager she was holding suddenly lit up and vibrated.

"Looks like ya'll got here right on time," said Eric as they started inside. "Let's eat."

The hostess grabbed a tin bucket and filled it with peanuts from a large wooden barrel at the front door. "This way please," she said. The four guests followed her back to the back corner of the non-smoking section as they walked across discarded peanut shells littered on the floor.

Logan's was the perfect place for a couple of guys to take their dates. They served great steaks, wonderful barbecued ribs, and fantastic appetizers, along with almost any beverage one could imagine. Even though Peter and Lila had eaten at several of the finest restaurants in New York, they enjoyed none more than Logan's.

"How's this?" asked the hostess.

"This will be fine," the dinner guests said.

Lori noticed on the way back to the table that neither Eric nor Peter moved with the clumsiness usually associated with the very large. Eric's stride was confident and his moves were sure, but as sure and confident as they were, Peter's were slightly more so.

Peter moved with almost a feline grace. He was a big cat, which crept like a river not really seeming to move but at the same time in constant motion. It was evident Peter was, or certainly could be, 300 pounds of walking, stomping hell and a master of all men. Yet, he treated Lila with gentleness--almost as if she were made of delicate crystal. Lori could clearly see he had a wildness about him--primitive man under the surface. That was it. He was a primeval man barely constrained by his polite manner and nice clothes.

She had seen this wildness in people in prison. They lived on a primal level and the strongest were often the only ones to survive. They had to be strong or protected by someone who was. Lori would sincerely hate to see the person who attempted to harm Lila, psychologically or physically. Peter's deference, gentleness, and mildness of manner would quickly disappear if his beloved Lila were in trouble.

Lori shifted her gaze and noted Lila was possibly the most beautiful woman she'd ever seen. Exactly what was her ethnic origin? Middle Eastern? Asian? She was too dark to be Asian. She certainly wasn't black; maybe she was Hawaiian. That's it; she was Hawaiian. The only thing that didn't fit with that diagnosis was her accent. She definitely had a southern accent, so she was probably raised in the South. Lila was tall for a woman. Lori felt like a Lilliputian among all these tall people, but Lila had already made Lori feel comfortable. As comfortable as an ex-jailbird dating the Sheriff could be, that is.

After the four were seated, the server came around and took their drink orders. Peter and Eric each ordered a beer, Lila requested water with a slice of lime, and Lori ordered unsweetened iced tea. Peter took the initiative and ordered the spinach dip and chips for an appetizer. Peter hated spinach but loved Logan's spinach dip.

When the server left with their drink order, Eric said, "My after dinner plans are ruined."

"What were your after dinner plans?" Peter asked.

"I would get Lori drunk and take advantage of her, but she ordered iced tea and ruined it," Eric joked.

"Take advantage of little ole' me?" Lori said in her best Scarlet O'Hara voice. "You don't have to get me drunk to do that. When the time is right, I will be willing enough." The friends laughed at her playful comeback to Eric's jest.

"Speaking of taking advantage, Peter and I have some good news," announced Lila with a huge smile. As Peter put his arm around Lila, he blurted out, I'm pregnant--I mean Lila's pregnant."

Eric laughed and slapped his friend on the back. "That is the best news I have heard in at least a month." As the three talked about baby names, due dates, and whether the child would attend The University of Alabama in Tuscaloosa or Birmingham, Lori noticed how much love and respect these three had for each other. She hoped they continued to allow her to be part of their inner circle.

After the server brought the drinks, Peter turned to Eric and asked, "How's the case against Alan coming along?"

"Since the murder, he hasn't been seen anywhere," frowned Eric as Peter and Lila shook their heads and sighed.

"That's how I met Lori," Eric continued. "She had information we didn't have. Lori sold him a house out on Cedar Creek in Belgreen last December under the name of Max Partain. If she hadn't come forward, we would still be looking for the place where he killed Georgia. We had it all on audiotape. Georgia was wearing a wire, but we didn't know where they were. Alan had moved out of the house he was renting out there by Kirk Cemetery. We didn't even know he had moved until we went out to serve the warrant and found a family of Mexicans living there. We had no idea where to even start to look for him."

"What's the verdict now?" Lila asked.

"If we can catch him, he's on his way to death row down at Donaldson."

"What's Donaldson?" Peter asked.

Lori did not say a word. She knew exactly what Donaldson was. It was a maximum-security men's prison in Bessemer.

"It is a prison down in Bessemer," explained Eric.

"Are you sure you can convict him when you catch him?"

"We have an audio tape of the murder, and thanks to Lori, we have the body and a videotape of the crime."

"A video?" Lila was clearly horror struck. "How sick is that? I can't believe even Alan would video a murder."

"He didn't purposely do that, he had a system set up that turned itself on with motion detectors. Apparently, he was using it as a potential blackmail for future events."

"It's still sick as far as I'm concerned."

"Peter, do you remember when he said one day he would be an important man in this county?"

"Yeah."

"We uncovered over two hundred video tapes with a whole lot of important people on them. They were buying drugs, selling drugs, having sex with children, and every other illegal activity you could think of. We even have a tape of our fine Chief of Police paying to have sex with a twelve-year-old. This goes no further than this table, but we also have the District Attorney and Circuit Judge on tape in similar uncompromising situations."

"You have got to be kidding," said Lila apparently horrified.

"I wish I were, but there is an upside to all of this. Since Alan disappeared, drug arrests have fallen by more than 75 percent. He was set up to supply the whole county with drugs, and they haven't found a replacement yet."

"Will they will find a replacement for him; I mean for the drugs?"

"Of course," said Eric. "Furthermore, the driving force behind the drug market is money. Cash is untraceable. If there were no cash involved, there would essentially be no drug market, no prostitution, and no gambling--except for maybe casino gambling. The driving force behind all illegal activities is cash."

"You're saying the war on drugs is virtually unwinnable?" Peter asked.

"Do you think there ever was a real war on drugs?" scowled Eric. "To supply the American public, the drug cartel has to move hundreds of thousands of tons of the stuff. It comes in on planes, in containers that load off trains, ships, or trucks. It comes in via personal automobiles. We are not talking about something we can't stop. However, you can't stop it as long as certain government officials can be bribed with cash. Cash to bribes is like oil to engines. It's the lubricant."

The server brought the appetizer and asked if they were ready to order. The foursome had not even looked at the menu.

"Give us another minute or two," said Peter.

They looked at the menus for a few moments then motioned the server over and gave her their order.

After the server left, Eric said, "You know I didn't come to talk shop. I'm supposed to be enjoying myself!"

"Lori, did you say you were a real estate agent?" asked Peter.

"Yes. Why?"

"I need you to make some purchases for me."

"Sure. What did you have in mind?"

"I want to purchase large tracts of land. I'm itching to be the largest landowner in the state of Alabama. I want every tract of land for sale more than 300 acres, any vacant factories and warehouses that exceed 50,000 square feet."

"Does it matter where the vacant land is located?"

"Let's start with Franklin County and the surrounding counties. On any tract of land larger than six hundred acres, I will need either railroad access or at the least access to a main state highway. I've recently come into a large sum of money, I think I will build factories on the large tracts of land, and maybe housing on the smaller tracts. I tell you what. I want you to buy any available land and be my buyer's broker. This will be very profitable for you. I'll pay the standard 7 percent on all purchases, but I will also pay you a premium of 20 percent on all you save me. In other words, if a property is listed for $1 million, and you talk the seller down to $750,000, I'll pay 7 percent on the $750,000 to you and your broker, and another 20 percent directly to you on the $250,000."

Lori had always been good in math. It only took her a minute to see the $17,000-$35,000 she would get in commission on a $1 million sale could quickly turn into $76,000 with the bonus.

"I will work exclusively with the real estate company you work with until you get your broker's license. I want more control and to give you the check instead of someone else who splits it with you."

"How many tracts are you talking about, one or two? How many factories would you start with?"

"Wasn't I clear about that? I want *every* property in Franklin County and counties that border Franklin County. Don't worry about zoning. When the time comes, I'll worry about that personally."

"What about residential property?"

I am not looking to buy every house or any house in the average neighborhood. I am looking to develop land for factories and subdivisions."

Lori was stunned. Peter had talked about hundreds of millions of dollars, possibly even billions of dollars. Eric said this man was rich, but she was thinking of a couple of million dollars. He was talking in the billion-dollar range.

She never presumed she would have an opportunity like this. It was a great opportunity, but there was one small problem. She couldn't hold a broker's license. Alabama law forbade her from holding a broker's license due to her prison record. She hadn't wanted her prison record to ever come out, but now it was clear it would. She was going to take a chance and come clean because she felt these people were the kind of individuals who were nonjudgmental. She prayed her revelation wouldn't ruin her chances to become Eric's girlfriend and business partner with Peter and Lila.

"Peter, Pete, I hate to turn down this opportunity, but I can't do as you wish. I can act as your agent through Mitchell Realty, but I can never hold a broker's license. Alabama law forbids me to hold a broker's license, as do laws of most other states. The best I can ever do for you are to act as your agent through Mitchell Realty."

As she was finished, the server brought out the appetizer. Thankful for the lull in conversation, Lori braced herself for the inevitable questions that would follow.

"What do you mean you can't hold a broker's license?" Eric asked.

She told them her story. She told of her life as a party girl and how she had been incarcerated. She left out nothing, not even the rapes. She didn't stop the story at any point. She also didn't look up into Eric's face. She was sure after she finished, she would never hear from him or any of these people again.

When she had spoken the last word in her story, Lila got up, walked around the table, and hugged her tightly. "Lori, sometimes bad things happen to good people, and sometimes even good people do bad things. From what I heard, you were never really a bad girl, only misguided. While I don't doubt if I had been on the jury I would have voted for conviction, you have served your time. Lori, you have changed, and I'm sure God has forgiven you for what you did. God's grace is deep enough to cover a multitude of sins. It took a lot of courage to tell what you did to two complete strangers and a man you have a romantic interest in. As far as I am concerned, it never happened. I'll never hold anything against you that occurred in the past. What's in the past will stay in the past."

"Nor will I," Eric said as he placed his hand on hers and kissed her on the cheek.

Peter didn't say a word

Lori could tell by the look on Peter's face he didn't believe she had changed. She knew he would do everything in his power to talk Eric out of this relationship, and would never allow her to be his broker. She knew she might as well get up, leave, and go back to prison.

Peter reached into his shirt pocket, pulled out his cell phone, and dialed a number.

"Jackie," they heard Peter command. "I have a young lady here I've offered a very lucrative opportunity to, but she needs an Alabama Real Estate Broker's License. The problem is she has a prison record. I want that record to disappear. I want it to look like it never happened. Do you understand? I want all court records to disappear along with anything written in the newspapers."

Peter looked over at Lori and said, "I need your driver's license number, social security number, and full legal name."

Lori did not know why, but she recited the required information.

Peter relayed Lori's information to Jackie, listened for a moment, and then said, "Okay. I'll tell her. Thank you, Jackie."

Peter looked across the table to Lori and said, "That was Jackie, my personal assistant. She assured me by this time tomorrow, you would have no criminal past. You will have a clean slate with a work history in place of your prison time. There will be no newspaper articles on file anywhere, not much I can do about the newspapers people may have kept, or memories they may have, but there won't be any records in the Alabama court system. The prison record at Tutwiler will be erased. Now like I was saying, I need you to get your broker's license."

Lori was in shock. *Who was this man? Was he God on earth? How did he have the power to get her prison record erased? What was his deal with the newspapers? Whom had he called? He'd said it was his personal assistant, but how could anyone's personal assistant take care of all that?*

"Peter? How can you promise her what you did?" asked an unbelieving Eric. "I couldn't even do what you described, and I'm in law enforcement. I have contacts, and you don't. Who did you talk to?"

The server brought their food and as they each took a bite, Peter told them a watered-down version of his and Lila's trip to New York. When he was done, everyone at the table except Lila was stunned.

"So--you're telling me we're eating with one of the richest couples in the world?" Eric asked.

"Yeah."

"Do you have the power to do what you said?"

"Yeah."

"Now that's absolute power. You know how the saying goes, don't you? Power corrupts, but absolute power corrupts absolutely," said Eric.

Lori looked solemnly at Peter and softly said, "Having that much money and power could give you a *God Complex.*"

"Maybe not," Peter said as he reflected on the secrets the first of Papa's golden keys had unlocked.

Lila knew Peter was indeed capable of being corrupted. She already acknowledged the beginnings of a *God Complex* in her husband. In New York, she had pledged to God she would protect Peter as best she could. He had slowly changed since Papa passed away. The old Peter would never have put someone like Sean Michaels out of business, wiped out someone's prison record, or even impulsively bought a new vehicle. The old Peter would never have done anything illegal.

Yet, Peter would be surprised to know he was not as good as he assumed he was about keeping secrets. Lila had been saddened and hurt on several occasions by Peter's clumsy attempts to hide things from her but had decided not to confront him. She would patiently wait for Peter to confide in her when he felt the time was right.

"By the way, how much time left do you have in your term as Sheriff?" Peter asked.

"Three years, but I plan to be re-elected."

"Would you consider not running for re-election?"

"Why? What do you have in mind?"

"I'm going to need good people around me, I need a right-hand man. He has to be a person I trust implicitly. You are that person. I will make it worth your while. I'll make sure you are one of the richest men in the state, if not the U.S."

"Right now there are only five people in the world that know about my position of power, so let's keep it that way. When I make these purchases, I have to do it in a way in which I am not recognized as the owner. I'm going to look like I'm working for someone else here. I will be known as the front man for Navoiczyk Enterprises and nothing more. I have good reason to keep myself unknown here." Peter paused as he took a sip of his beer.

"Lori, I want you to start a real estate agency," continued Peter. "All my purchases and sales of property nationwide will go through this company. Eric, you will launch a security company. I have people from a hundred government agencies on the payroll. I will give you two the seed money to start these businesses. Eric, would you be willing to resign as Sheriff, and let Andy become the new Sheriff? I don't think you grasp what I'm asking, but we can change the world."

"Let me think about it. Give me at least a couple of days."

Eric's head was spinning. It wasn't every day he was asked to help change the world and become one of the richest men in the U.S.

"Eric, you are my oldest and closest friend. Except for Lila, you are the most important person in my life. You are . . . The brother . . . The brother . . . I never had," said Peter as he lowered his head and choked back tears.

Peter was now transported back to the awkward moment he had opened the jeweled box to find two birth certificates that showed he and Eric were brothers. They were fraternal twins with Peter being born first.

Papa had included a one-page letter asking Peter's forgiveness for not telling him and Eric before now. There was a short explanation how Papa had made up the story about Eric's parents and how he had placed Eric with Ms. Sandusky because he and Anna couldn't take care of more than one infant. He had made sure Eric did not want for anything materially. Papa had also asked Peter to tell Eric when he felt Eric could handle it. Papa ended the letter begging Peter to share his wealth with Eric.

Lila could tell from Peter's expression what he was thinking. Lila had her secrets, too. She merely kept them better. After all, she had opened the jeweled box hours before Peter had.

Chapter Twenty-Six

Randy received his package. It contained exactly what he had requested. He now possessed a complete 201 file for Randall Gerald Marlowe. His 201 was a copy. The original would soon be in the Department of the Army's records in St. Louis, Missouri. The only things missing were a fingerprint card and dental records. The package contained a blank fingerprint card he promptly placed his fingerprints on and mailed back to New York. Three days from now his 201 with the Department of Defense would be complete. It would actually be more comprehensive than thousands of veterans' files. No one would ever know he had never served a day in the armed services to defend this great country. He would even receive veterans' benefits when he needed them.

He studied the file in a thorough fashion. He had gone through basic training and AIT, (Advanced Individual Training), at Ft. McClellan, Alabama, in the summer and fall of 1990. After he received his training in his MOS, (military occupational specialty), as a Military Policeman or 95 Bravo as it was known in the Army, his first posting was at Ft. Riley, Kansas. He was posted there for one year before he transferred to Ft. Hood, Texas. He posted at Ft. Hood for eighteen months where he rose to the rank of Specialist 4. His next transfer was to Ft. Campbell, Kentucky, right at the beginning of Desert Shield that would later become Desert Storm. After a year at Ft. Campbell, he moved on to Ft. Gordon, Georgia, with the new rank of sergeant. At Ft. Gordon, he attended the NCO school where he remained for a year. His next transfer was overseas to Camp Red Cloud in Uijongbu, South Korea, home of the 8th Army. He finally returned stateside to Ft. Dix where two years later he attained the rank of Sergeant First Class. As a new SFC, he only remained at Ft. Dix for six months, before he was transferred to Groom Lake, Nevada. Randy had to go online to look this up. He had never heard of Groom Lake. He went to the computer in the dining room. It was always signed on to the Internet thanks to his high-speed cable modem. He used his favored search engine and the computer came back with page one of some four thousand plus entries concerning Groom Lake. After a few minutes, he found Groom Lake was a super-secret Air Force Base commonly known as Area 51. What would an Army NCO be doing at an Air Force base? It seems he was posted there as NCOIC (non-commissioned officer in charge) of security. He was NCOIC security at Area 51? This file was even better than he had hoped for. He had remained at Area 51 until he had decided not to re-up this year. He came out of the Army as a Sergeant Major.

He read the file several times and studied it carefully. This information represented the last ten years of his life. If he were ever asked about his life in the Army, he would have to have at least a basic remembrance of these facts.

His DD-214 showed his honorable discharge two weeks ago. He had letters of recommendation from his former Commanding Officer and Army Major General David Maxwell, Post Commander at Groom Lake. His resume ultimately listed his supposed military training with schools attended ending with a bachelor's degree in Criminal Justice from Penn State in 1997.

This was quite an impressive resume for an Alabama kid that, despite good grades, had dropped out of high school in the tenth grade. His grades had never been the problem. It had been his family life, or lack thereof. His mother, so she sometimes called herself, had always been a good-time girl. She was always in and out of drug rehabilitation and had paraded an endless cast of boyfriends, lovers, and pimps through his early life. She had never told him for sure when it was his father died, but he couldn't remember him. He figured he must have died when he was a baby because he had never seen a picture of his father. Peter's grandmother consistently gave his mother money to help. When Gramma Joanna found out how his mother squandered the money, she tried to buy what he and his mother needed. Gramma Joanna probably even paid for each failed drug rehabilitation program his mother enrolled in.

Gramma Joanna died when he was thirteen, and Papa was not as philanthropic as his wife had been. For some reason his mother assumed the Stacias owed it to her and her son to provide for them, which was something he never understood. As a kid, he concluded his mother was blackmailing the Stacias, but now realized good people could sometimes be caught up in helping those who didn't appreciate the help. The last thing Papa Stacia had done for him was to buy him his prized black Trans Am on his sixteenth birthday. He still didn't know why Papa did this but was glad to get the car. That was three days after his mother died of an overdose. His mother had always been a whore and was sometimes a prostitute, depending on how bad the times were and who her current man of the hour was. A mother she had never been. Most days she merely tolerated him. Barely. She always threw it up to him how he wasn't as popular or as good at sports as Peter and Eric--especially Peter. Before she died, her ranting became so frequent he no longer felt comfortable at the Stacia house, and he hated Peter.

What really drove him crazy, though, was that no matter how much he hated his mother, he found himself always trying so hard to win her approval. As much as he hated her, his love for her was twice as strong. After she died, he tried to find work, but at sixteen, with no real references, no one would hire him.

He had been a straight A student. It didn't matter that he had a tested IQ that placed him in the gifted classes. It didn't matter he had been willing to do almost anything. The only thing people saw when they looked at him was his whore of a mother who had died of an overdose. The only avenue left open to him had been criminal. By his twenty-first birthday, he was already beginning to set up a network of people. Coming from the background he had, he knew the right, or the wrong people, depending on your perspective. His few, narrow escapes with the law have never resulted in arrest or fingerprinting. Alan recognized the best way to continue that from happening is to know important things on influential people. His advantages over the common criminal were his intelligence and his utter ruthlessness. He had no real morals. The woman who had claimed to be his mother had imparted few family values, scruples, morals, or honesty to impress into his conscious mind. Thus, his attacks of conscience were few and weak. What did it matter in the long run what distorted depredations he had wrought on persecuted young people? Those kids wouldn't live very long anyway.

Sheriff Justin Thyme had been the reason behind his decision to video all of these incidents. The Sheriff had requested a ménage trois with two identical twin girls, which had been abducted off a street in Mobile. The twin girls hadn't yet reached their thirteenth birthday but were already compliant. The Sheriff had taken the girls in every way possible and then had the nerve to refuse to pay.

"I ain't payin' you nothin' boy," the Sheriff had insisted.

When pressed for the money, the Sheriff hit him across the bridge of the nose with a revolver and broke his nose.

"If any of this is ever mentioned, I'll either kill ya or throw ya under the jail," Sheriff Thyme had said as he walked out owing $1,500.

Alan Chipenski may not have gotten many things in his troublesome life, but one thing he always got and that was *he always got even*. Anyone who had ever done anything to him had gotten something back much worse in return, and he made sure Sheriff Thyme had been no exception.

Fortunately, those things were in the past. He was Randy Marlowe, who would never be part of any of the sordid things Alan Chipenski had participated in. Randy would settle down, find him a sweet, sexy girl to marry, and become the proud father of at least two kids. He might even get a dog and cat to complete the happy family portrait.

* * *

Seldom, very seldom does complete truth belong to any human disclosure; seldom can it happen that something is not a little disguised or a little mistaken.

~~~Jane Austen, *Emma*

* * *

Chapter Twenty-Seven

Peter and Lila were both unusually quiet as they rode home from the restaurant. Several times Lila studied Peter's profile in the darkness and tried to read his thoughts. *Was he making plans to tell her about Eric being his brother? Lila wondered, would he ever tell Eric? Did Peter really think Eric would give up his position as Sheriff to help him without knowing they were brothers?*

The one time Peter caught her gaze, his expression revealed nothing. He only smiled and squeezed her hand, completely oblivious to her inner turmoil.

Peter, on the other hand, felt no turmoil and enjoyed being the keeper of secrets. He proudly reminisced about how he'd used his power and resources to put Sean Michaels out of commission. He hated superior, highfaluting losers like Sean. When Peter played professional football, he'd run across several others of Sean's type who made fun of his being from Alabama. During those few years, he heard every "how you know you're a redneck" joke there was. *Maybe I am a little bit of a redneck, thought Peter, but I'm definitely not a hillbilly. Michaels hadn't been the first to call me a hillbilly, and he probably wouldn't be the last. At least, Sean Michaels didn't get away with it, and no one else would either.*

Peter was now in a position to guarantee that. *I might even have to look up some of my old teammates and make sure they got their just rewards. Having money was definitely going to have its advantages, he thought, yes, it certainly was.*

Peter also contemplated about the three keys Papa had left him. *Will I ever find out everything the keys opened? Will they reveal information of an even more surprising nature? Why had Papa and Gramma Joanna given Eric to Ms. Sandusky instead of claiming him as their grandson? What will I find when I go to Montana? Will I find gold? If so, where did Papa get it? Had he stolen and hidden it all those years? On his deathbed, Papa had admitted to doing things he wasn't proud of. Should I tell Lila about Montana? About Eric? Yes, I'll tell her about Montana--but for now--not about Eric. Should I tell Eric? No! I'm not ready to share my power with another male--not even Eric.*

Lila and I will go to Montana the middle of next week--not drive like I had planned back in New York. We'll not fly in our own jet--I don't want Jackie to know about Montana. We'll fly commercially. No--I'll have my jet sent to stay in Muscle Shoals instead of New York. If the people in New York needed a plane, I'll buy them one of their own. That way I don't have to check in with Jackie. I can hire my own pilots here in Alabama. Why send my money to New York when it could stay in Alabama?

Lila decided all this new fortune would not go to Peter's head as it did with some. She would prove Lori wrong. Her Peter would not develop any kind of a complex. She would see to that.

* * *

Oh, what a tangled web we weave,
When first we practice to deceive!

~~~Sir Walter Scott
Excerpt from *Marmion*

* * *

Chapter Twenty-Eight

Randy did exceptionally well in his interview with Police Sergeant Barry Locke of the Billings Police Department. Sergeant Locke informed Randy the job was his as long as all references checked out and he passed all the academy classes. Cadet Randy Marlowe not only passed his classes at The Academy but also was consistently the top performer in each class. He had graduated with honors. Randy paired up with an older officer named Jerry Slater, as all new officers right out of the academy were. He rode with him for six weeks and was now Probationary Officer Marlowe.

Of the eighty cadets graduated from the academy, the Billings Police Department hired six. The rest went on to other jobs in other departments like Missoula, Butte, Bozeman, and Helena, as well as those hired in Sheriff Departments. These cadets would remain friends, or at least friendly, for the rest of their careers, helping out their former classmates in ways the public would never understand.

Randy Marlowe had become an honest man, an endeavor Alan Chipenski had never been able to accomplish. Randy found he liked police work. He really liked the job. It, for the most part, was 90 percent boring, but 10 percent of the time it was an adrenaline rush like no other. When he turned on the emergency lights to stop a car, he never knew what would happen.

Randy was assigned to traffic patrol. After his time riding with an experienced officer, he was on patrol all by his lonesome. This job was perfect for a single man. So far, almost every third or fourth call he went on had resulted in a sexual hookup. Right now, he was involved with four different women. Each assumed she was the only one he was seeing.

He managed to get what was left of the money into a bank account. He continued to disguise the money as gambling winnings and paid proper taxes on them. He bought a large four-bedroom home on forty acres a few miles outside of town and was more comfortable than he ever dreamed he would be.

A black Honda Civic blew through the stop sign he was sitting at. It didn't check up--the driver hadn't even seen the sign. He pulled out behind the car and pushed the large cruiser up to a speed that guaranteed he would quickly catch up. When he was behind the car, he flipped the switch that turned on the light bar atop the car. The Honda pulled over to the emergency lane.

Randy pulled up behind the car and called in his location along with car's license plate number. In a matter of seconds, he received the information he needed. The car was registered to one Amanda Greene, 3075 Seventh Avenue North, who had no tickets or warrants issued.

Randy approached the car cautiously on the left side and stopped behind the driver's doorpost as he had been trained. The windows of the car were not tinted, and he could see there was only one occupant in the car, a white female with incredibly dark hair.

"License and registration, please," he said with authority.

The woman turned around and Randy saw she was an extremely attractive young woman in her twenties. She looked through her purse and couldn't produce a license.

"I can't find my license officer," she cooed. She was not afraid to look him directly in the eyes as many women he pulled over were.

"Do you have registration and proof of insurance?"

She opened the glove box on the car and a huge pile of papers fell out. There probably was an insurance card and registration papers somewhere in there, but she couldn't produce them.

"Step out of the car, please." The young woman stepped out of the car wearing a white uniform, with a skirt stopping just above her shapely knees. She had a fine figure, and Randy saw the nametag said Amanda Greene RN. "You know why I stopped you, don't you?" Randy asked.

"No," she said as if she truly didn't have a clue.

"You ran that stop sign back there. You didn't even slow down."

"What stop sign, officer?" The young nurse was being extremely polite. She also seemed to be genuinely perplexed as to where she had run a stop sign.

"About six blocks back you ran a stop sign, and I have you clocked at 45 in a 35. Did you find your driver's license?"

"I think I left it on my dresser at home."

Randy knew he could write her a ticket for driving without her license in her possession, speeding, running a stop sign, and improper documentation. But would he?

"Please come back to the patrol car," he said, as he motioned with his head toward the passenger side. As they walked, he watched her shapely behind. She was about 5'6" or maybe 5'7" and probably a size seven. She was big breasted and her tight backside was without a doubt in motion as she walked. Randy knew she had strutted her stuff for him.

She sat gracefully in the front passenger seat of the patrol car. When he sat, he noticed she smelled the smell that he had come to associate with all patrol cars--a stale mixture of puke, sweat, and piss. So far, this was the only bad thing about this job. He hadn't drawn a patrol car yet that didn't have that smell.

Tonight he was on second shift. He worked from 5 P.M. to 1 A.M. three days a week, and from 1 A.M. to 9 A.M. the other two days. He had come to call the 1 A.M. to 9 A.M. shift *puke patrol.* It seemed like you got all of the drunks on third shift that more than likely would puke in the backseat before you could get them to the station.

Randy got out his warning ticket book. He wasn't going to give Ms. Green a ticket and hoped to get her telephone number. "Do you know your driver license number?" he asked. She surprisingly did and gave it to him. He called in the number, and the dispatcher came back with her name, address, and date of birth.

Randy quickly jotted these facts down on a notepad kept especially for this purpose. He transferred this information to the warning ticket.

"Are you writing me a ticket?" Amanda asked.

"Yes," Randy said as he noticed the top two buttons on her uniform top were undone to where he was able to get a good peek at the side of one large breast through a red lacey bra. He was starting to be turned on.

"Please don't," she pleaded. "I don't want my insurance to go up. I promise I won't do it again."

"Is 3075 Seventh Avenue North, Apartment 4A, your correct mailing address?" Randy asked as professionally as he could.

"Yes."

He wrote it on the ticket.

"Please don't give me a ticket," she begged. Randy now noticed she had wriggled around in such a way he now could get a better look at her perfectly formed thighs.

"Sorry," he said as he continued to write on the warning ticket.

He filled out the ticket, asked a few more questions, and made sure she was who she said she was.

"I need a home telephone number," he said tentatively.

She gave him her telephone number, which he also jotted down on his well-used pad.

"Work phone, and extension?"

She gave this to him as well--which he also jotted down.

"Here you go, Ms. Greene," he announced as he handed her the warning ticket. She had now been warned for going forty in a thirty-five.

She took the ticket with resignation. When her eyes focused on the warning ticket, she squealed with delight. "This is a warning ticket. I thought you were writing me a real ticket." Without warning, she reached across and hugged Randy, which made him feel uncomfortable and good at the same time. He hadn't expected that. She looked down at the ticket and asked, "Why did you need my home and work phone numbers since there's no place for them on this ticket?"

"I thought maybe I might call you?" he said questioningly.

"That sounds fantastic," she said. "I've got a better idea, though. When will you be off duty?"

"In a couple of hours."

"Why don't you come by my apartment? I'll fix us a drink. You are allowed to have a drink now and then, aren't you?"

"Yeah," he said.

"Where are you from?" she asked.

"I live right outside of town," he said.

"No silly. I mean where are you from originally? That accent doesn't come from Montana. It comes from somewhere in the south. You're from Alabama, aren't you?"

Damn. How did she know that? "Mississippi," Randy countered hoping she didn't press him further.

"It sounds more like Alabama than Mississippi. I've missed the accent," she said. "I'm originally from a small town in Alabama you've probably never heard of."

"You never know. Tell me which one," he said.

"I'm originally from Killen, but I've been gone from there for almost ten years now."

"I know where Killen is," Randy said. "That's over between Florence and Athens. How did you get here?"

"My dad moved us from Alabama to Michigan to work for the GM plant when I was sixteen. I graduated from high school there and got a degree in nursing at Michigan State two weeks before my parents were killed in a car wreck. I didn't have any family left in Michigan, so I looked elsewhere for a job. I sincerely considered going back to Alabama, or maybe Florida, before I heard they were desperate for RNs out west where the pay was good. I decided to move here and have never regretted it. It's beautiful in the summer, and skiing is heavenly in the winter with so many resorts only hours away."

His radio squawked and the dispatcher asked for his location, which he gave. The dispatcher told of a domestic disturbance a few blocks away. "I'll respond," he told the dispatcher in the language all police forces use--the language that sounded so much like gobbledygook to the average citizen.

"I've got to make a call on a domestic," he said. "I'll see you at about one-thirty?"

"One-thirty sounds good," she said smiling.

Randy watched her walk back to her Honda. She definitely knew how to make her body work. It was like watching poetry in motion. He left the lights on, made a U-turn, and headed over to the disturbance.

Randy didn't think the shift would ever end. The disturbance was simply that, a disturbance. Some kids had been shooting firecrackers. When he approached with the lights on, they scattered never to be found. He took a brief statement, which would soon find its way into the garbage can, and left. The rest of his shift took fourteen forevers. He had stopped Amanda at eleven-thirty and the next hour and a half had passed with the speed of a slug crawling across an interstate.

When his shift was finally over, he returned to the station, turned in his patrol car, and jumped into the Silverado pickup. He had driven by the apartment complex Amanda lived in several times during his last hour, so he knew exactly where to go.

Randy surprised himself when he decided to stop by the 24-hour package store on the way to her apartment to buy a moderately expensive bottle of wine. To deviate further from his usual behavior, he picked up a bouquet of flowers he had seen earlier at the corner convenience store when he was getting coffee. He had never done this for a girl before. He always expected to be on the receiving end--

not the giving. He was actually enjoying this novel experience. Not only did he arrive on time; he was ten minutes early.

Amanda met him at the door wearing a revealing robe. She apologized for not being dressed yet. She had showered and then fallen asleep on the couch. Randy apologized for being early. It was obvious Amanda wasn't wearing anything under her robe. Her hair was still damp from the shower and it was down brushing the top of her shoulders. Her hair was exquisite. A shiny coal black--so black it was almost blue.

As Randy entered, he kissed her lightly on the cheek and handed her the flowers and wine. He removed his gun belt and hung it over the back of a uniform tree he found in a corner where a couple of her nurse's uniforms hung.

Amanda had not been able to take her eyes off Randy. She watched his every move before she found the nerve to say, "I didn't catch your name before you had to leave so rapidly."

"Randall Marlowe," Officer Marlowe said, "but most people call me Randy."

"All right, Randy. I'm Amanda, but I hate that name so much I've been Mandy for most of my life."

"Randy and Mandy, that shouldn't be hard to remember."

"I know. I thought the same thing. Would you like a glass of this wine, or would you rather have a beer?"

"I'll take a beer if you don't mind," he said.

"Have a seat," she said before she walked into the kitchen. She returned with a cold Bud-Light and a glass of the wine. She bent over to hand him the beer giving him a glimpse of the most beautiful breasts he had ever laid eyes on, and he had seen more than a few.

"Tell me about yourself, Randy," she said.

Randy told her the story he had repeatedly rehearsed until it was now second nature to him. He told of a life in the Army he never lived, which ended with his time in the department.

"Sounds interesting," she said. "Why didn't you go back to Mississippi when you finished with your military career?"

"I didn't want to live there. I never knew my dad, and my mother was by then long dead, God rest her soul." *God rest her soul, my ass. I hope she burns in Hell, the rotten bitch.*

"I'm sorry to hear that," sympathized Mandy.

"It happened a long time ago. Mississippi is not a place I ever actually planned to return to. First, it's too hot and humid in the summer. Second, there's nothing to do."

"But you have a college education."

"I have a degree in Criminal Justice. The best I could hope for there was to land a job on a County Sheriff's payroll. If I didn't want to run for Sheriff, I would most likely be locked into whatever job I initially took. I don't want to do this job forever. There's not much opportunity in Mississippi."

"Like the opportunities here are any better," she said laughing.

"They are somewhat better here; plus, I like the atmosphere and weather."

"Let's see how much better you like the weather when it gets down to sixty-five below."

The atmosphere here was undoubtedly better than a six-foot by eight-foot concrete box on death row in an Alabama prison, he thought.

They chatted for the next hour. Mandy was very personable, and Randy learned she had been in town less than a year and didn't really know anyone outside work. They had become so engrossed in conversation Mandy never made it back to get dressed.

As they talked, Mandy moved ever closer to Randy. By the beginning of the second hour, she was sitting almost in his lap. *She wants it to happen,* Randy thought *but doesn't want to come right out and say it.* He liked that about her.

He leaned over and lightly kissed her soft lips. She responded, not immediately, but she did respond. Her breath was sweet and slightly acidic from the wine. Mandy used her tongue to expertly encircle his, and then did something he didn't expect. She lightly bit his tongue. It wasn't a hard bite, simply a love nibble. It surprised him, nonetheless; and he liked it.

After only a few kisses, Mandy was breathing in short, shallow gasps as she tried to unbutton his shirt. His shirt, while it retained the look of a button up, actually had a zipper. He had chosen this style at the uniform shop after he had the buttons torn off repeatedly by unruly suspects.

Randy stood, unzipped his uniform shirt, and removed it. She peeled off his undershirt and lightly kissed him. Mandy then took him by the hand and led him into a small bedroom. In the room was a king size bed that overflowed with pillows, two nightstands, a dresser, and chest of drawers. With so much furniture in the room, there was space for little else. There almost wasn't room enough to walk around the bed.

He watched her beautiful form as she walked toward the bed. She was slim and big breasted--the way he liked women. She looked like a full sized raven-haired Barbie Doll. She moved like no other woman he had ever seen. Her sexy walk exuded sexuality with an effect on men she probably didn't even realize she possessed.

She threw off pillows as she walked around the bed. When she lay down, she looked as beautiful as any Playboy or Penthouse model.

"Come here, handsome," she purred.

Randy was willing and eager to please this woman. The only problem was he didn't really know what to do. He'd been with many women before, but it was always about pleasing himself. He didn't know anything about pleasing a woman. He didn't even know if it could be done. She looked so good lying on the bed. Once again, she motioned him to come to her.

He lay down beside her. She snuggled up to him and began to kiss him. He responded in kind, as his hands massaged and explored each exquisite part of her.

Randy was totally aroused by her sweet smell. He kissed her lips, the sides of her face, and her delicate ears. He continued to move down, lightly brushing her neck with his lips. He kissed her stomach, paying particular attention to her navel. He liked the taste and smell of her body. He enjoyed it in a way he couldn't have made himself believe only hours before. As daylight broke through the ruby red lacy curtains of the bedroom, they made love in the crimson glow. Afterward, they cooked breakfast together. He made French toast while she added coffee and bacon to the menu. Randy enjoyed being able to finally relax. It was the first time in his twenty-eight years of life, he had felt a genuine closeness to another human being.

* * *

When one with honeyed words but evil mind
persuades the mob, great woes befall the state.

~~~Euripides, *Orestes*

* * *

Chapter Twenty-Nine

As Peter and Lila pulled into their driveway, they quickly spied the bright yellow Hummer as it sat on the deck of a detachable flatbed trailer. Peter looked at Lila and winked. "I think I can get used to this type of life. What about you?"

Lila smiled and winked back as she waited for Peter to come around and open her door. Even with some of the changes she saw in Peter, she was glad to see Peter was still a gentleman.

The nose of the trailer sat on the ground to make it easy to drive the vehicle onto the pavement. The truck driver had already unloaded the Mercedes and Jaguar. The Harley-Davidson was parked up against the garage door of the boat shed.

The driver was a wiry little man with greasy hair and a tattoo of a rose on his left forearm and the word *sweet* on his right. His light blue sleeveless shirt was soaked with sweat and permanently stained yellow under his arms from years of perspiration that had never and would never completely wash out.

"Good evenin'," said the driver. "You must be the Stacias."

"Yes, I'm Peter and this is my wife, Lila," said Peter as he and Lila shook the driver's hand. "And you are?"

"Mike. Mike Johnson."

"Mike, we didn't expect these vehicles to be here until Monday or Tuesday," Peter said as he watched Lila hurry over to the Jaguar.

Lila slid into the Jag and ran her hands over the leather seats. She noticed the keys were in the ignition. She let the top down and yelled out, "Hey, Pete. I'm going to ride down to Wal-Mart and pick up something for us to snack on after our swim. I'll be right back."

"Sure, hon," said Peter as he watched Lila leave the driveway in the Jag with her hair blowing sexily around her face. She sure did look good driving that car, but his Lila would look good driving a Yugo. He felt sure the Beamer wouldn't get much, if any, attention for quite some time.

"I picked 'em up at the Memphis airport a few hours ago," apologized Mike as Peter turned his attention back to what the truck driver was saying. "I hope ya'll don't mind me unloadin' 'em tonight."

"No problem at all. Would you like something to drink?" offered Peter as he walked over to the boathouse, took out his keys, and unlocked the walk-in door.

"I couldn't impose on you folks. I'll be on my way once I unload this Hummer and we get paperwork done." The driver opened the door of the extended hood Peterbilt tractor and retrieved a folded packet of papers inside a leather pouch.

Peter pushed the button to open one of the three garage doors. As the door started to slide upward, he flipped three switches on the wall, and the driveway exploded into bright light. After the driver unloaded the Hummer, Peter performed a quick and thorough check of it, the Mercedes, and the Harley. He was sure Lila was in Wal-Mart's parking lot doing the same thing to the Jaguar. Nothing was scratched, bent, or otherwise damaged.

"Notice any damage, Mr. Stacia?" asked the driver as he noticed Peter's actions.

"Not that I can find. I appreciate the great job you did." Peter was pleased Mike had undoubtedly been very particular and careful when he secured the vehicles to the detached trailer.

"It weren't nothin'--nothin' I wouldn't do for anyone. I've been drivin' for twenty-six years now. In the last decade, I ain't had even one freight claim. I try to care for other folk's things as if they was my own. It's gotten me a lot of work. Bein' careful, that is. People like to know their stuff is taken care of."

"That's good of you."

"Oh, by the way. Did ya notice that unusual stain on the leather upholstery of that Mercedes?" asked Mike. "It looks like . . ."

"Yeah. It was already there," interrupted Peter as he quickly changed the subject. "Are you sure you wouldn't like a drink? I know you can't have a beer, but I could get you a soda or maybe some tea or water."

"That's all right. I have drinks in the 'fridge in my truck. I'm like the Boy Scouts--always prepared."

Peter laughed as he took the paperwork from the driver, signed his name in several locations, took his copies, and handed the paperwork back. He reached into his pants pocket and removed what was left of the $20,000 Jeffery had given him in New York. As he handed all the money over to the driver, Peter believed there was probably $5,000 left.

"This is way too much," protested Mike as he wondered why this man offered him so much more than what he was supposed to. "I only need a thousand. There's gotta be at least five here."

"Ah, don't worry about it. I've more money than I can shake a stick at," bragged Peter.

"Thanks," said the humble driver as he leaned forward.

Peter was afraid the little man was going to hug him, but he didn't. "I like to see a man care about his job," continued Peter grateful the man hadn't embraced him. "Why don't you take the wife on a cruise or something? Do something to spoil yourself for a change. I know how hard ya'll truckers work."

Mike stood there looking pleased before he finally said, "You're a fine man, Mr. Stacia. Nobody's ever been that good to me." There were tears in the little man's eyes as he turned to walk over to the truck. He kept his head down as he climbed up into the driver's seat and backed the truck toward the trailer.

Peter watched him reattach the trailer with fascination. He had always been amazed by heavy equipment of any kind, and this was a specialized piece of equipment. It was actually made for hauling bulldozers and other earthmoving equipment.

The driver waved as he drove down the driveway. Just as Peter could use money to get back at people who had the audacity to mistreat Peter Stacia, he could also use it to reward those who deserved it and would never otherwise receive remuneration for their hard work. It gave Peter such an adrenalin rush. Like when he'd erased Lori's prison record and offered her the chance of a lifetime. (That would only be for as long as she and Eric stayed together). Next, he'd have to figure out a way to help Eric without his knowing where it came from.

His deliberations were interrupted as he saw a new fire engine red Ford F-250 Crew Cab pulling up with Lila in her Jag right in behind it. Now, who could that be coming up here at midnight? He was relieved, and at the same time amused, to find the truck contained Eric and Lori laughing inside.

At Logan's Peter hadn't noticed what Eric had driven. He assumed he still had the Blazer Papa had given him in March on his sixteenth birthday. He must have traded trucks this week.

Peter walked up and opened the door for Lila. "How does it ride?" he asked Lila with a grin of amusement on his face. Lila beamed at him and said, "Perfect! I love it, Pete. I absolutely love it!"

Peter and Lila went over to Eric's new truck; Peter helped Lori out of the four-door, four-wheel drive vehicle. Doing so, he got a good look at the inside of the truck. Pickup trucks had come a long way in the last few years. No longer were they simply a work vehicle. They were comfortable and attractive. This was an excellent truck with leather interior and a premium sound system.

"Nice truck."

"Yeah, I knew you would like it, but it seems you have one-upped me again. I expected to have the newest vehicle here, but instead you have enough new vehicles to open up a blasted car lot! What's going on with you, Petey? I see a new Hummer, Tahoe, Jaguar, Mercedes, and Harley. You're not letting all this money go to your head, are you?" said Eric as he joked at first but ended on a more somber note.

"I bought the Tahoe today, but the other three were sent here from New York," explained Peter almost apologetically.

"Can we take a spin in the Hummer?" asked Lori. "I've never even seen inside of one."

"Sure thing," said Peter as he motioned Eric to drive. He opened the door for Lori and Lila to get in the back seat before he piled into the front passenger seat next to Eric.

"Ya'll are the only ones with a Hummer in Russellville," bragged Eric, "and a bright yellow one at that!"

"I know," agreed Peter as they all laughed.

"Isn't it ironic both of you kept the same vehicle for twelve years before you got another one," asked Lori as Peter and Eric nodded in agreement. "It's almost like you have the same minds. You know, like twins do." Lori then went on to tell about a program she had recently watched on TV where twins raised separately had led similar lives. She ended with examples of how when one had gotten hurt, the other had felt the same pain without even knowing it had happened to the other.

If she only knew, thought Peter as he tuned out her expose' on twins. *It was going to take some doing for him to get used to Eric being his brother. Eric didn't know his birthday wasn't really March 31. It was the same as Peter's, which was January 22. Papa and Gramma Joanna had changed Eric's birth date so no one would suspect the truth about the boys being brothers. It had worked out fine, since Peter had always been larger that Eric, anyway. It was good, he guessed, they had not been identical like Lori was talking about.*

After a short midnight ride, Peter told Eric, "Let's head back. I need to get the Harley and Jag into the garage. Then I have to decide what to do with the Mercedes."

"Sure thing, boss," kidded Eric as he tried to do a U-turn. "This doesn't exactly turn on a dime, ya' know!" They headed back toward Hester Heights.

"Since you called me boss, does that mean you're going to accept my offer to work for me?"

"No, Petey. That's what I felt your chauffeur would say." Once again everyone laughed. They had all laughed quite a bit this Friday night. It was almost as if all four had needed a release for the tensions that had built up over the past couple of weeks.

"Peter?" called Lila.

"Yes."

"How about you give Lori the Mercedes? We definitely don't need it, and she will need it to be the high-profile real estate mogul you need."

Before Lori could protest, Peter agreed and handed her the keys. "You'll need to have a little upholstery work done on one of the seats, but you can pay for those repairs yourself with all the money I'm going to help you make."

As soon as Eric parked the Hummer, Peter got out and fired up the motorcycle, which he parked beside the boat. He then walked out to the Jaguar, opened the door, and sat sideways in the seat. When he went to turn around, he couldn't quite get his legs in. He unfolded his big body out and tried again, and again. Eric, Lila, and Lori watched his unsuccessful attempts closely. He didn't seem to be able to get his Goliath-sized body in the sports car.

He put the seat all the way back and tried again. When he still couldn't get in, he finally gave up. This Jag was like Lila's Beamer--too small for people like him. He took the car out of gear and pushed it into the garage. At that point, Eric, Lila, and Lori all broke out into a hearty applause. Peter took a bow and did a series of graceful cartwheels that ended in a round off before he shuffled over to where they were standing.

"That was some performance," said Lila as she pulled Peter's head down to give him a kiss.

"Are we going swimming?" interrupted an unimpressed Eric motioning toward the pool. "Or, are we going to have to watch you two lovebirds make out all night?"

"Ya'll go on and get started. I'll go get towels," Peter said as he started toward the house with the bags of snacks Lila had picked up from Wal-Mart. "I've need to put this sandwich meat in the refrigerator."

"Come on, you two. Last one in the pool is a rotten egg," said Eric as he ran dropping clothes behind him. By the time he reached the pool's edge, the only thing he had on was his black Stetson. As Lori and Lila walked toward the pool, Lori could see Eric was indeed built like Hercules. His muscular body was hard and tight, with clearly outlined abdominal muscles.

"Come on, Lori!" said Lila, who had jumped up on the diving board. Lori was surprised to see Lila shamelessly unzip her dress and fling it onto one of the chairs on the patio. Wearing only her new red diamond necklace and earrings, Lila executed a graceful swan dive into the pool.

Before Lori could make a decision on what to do, a nude Peter streaked by, reminiscent of his defensive end days, with several towels tucked securely under his arm instead of the fumbled football he had scooped up to run ninety yards back for the winning touchdown. After he deposited the towels on a nearby patio chair, he did a cannonball jump off the diving board that sprayed out an ungodly amount of water from the pool that soaked Lori from head to toe. Lori tried to be mad but couldn't. She laughed and was amazed to find she had felt comfortable enough to remove her clothes as well.

Within seconds, Eric, Lori, Peter, and Lila were in their own world laughing and splashing one another like school kids. Lori and Eric soon found themselves at the darkest edge of the pool where they could have some privacy. Eric kissed her deeply and Lori found herself responding to his kisses and touch. Before Lori could think about whether or not she wanted things to go further, Eric turned her around and pulled her back against him. He rubbed her shoulders and kissed the nape of her neck. She was more relaxed than she had ever been with a man. Lori was amazed this rather bizarre change of events now seemed surprisingly normal.

As Eric continued to rub Lori's shoulders, they watched Peter emerge from the pool only to dive in again. He propelled himself around the pool with the ease of a dolphin. His sleek, even strokes hardly made a splash. It was evident Peter was a powerful swimmer who spent a lot of time in the water. Lila made laps behind him, although her style was quite different. While Lila was a solid swimmer, she wasn't as quick or proficient as Peter.

After Lila and Peter finished at least twenty laps, they each wrapped up in a huge towel and went inside to shortly return with a tray of sandwiches. Instead of bringing the tray to the pool, they headed toward the hot tub.

"Why don't you two join us?" Lila said as she eased into the bubbling water with a sandwich in one hand and a drink in the other.

"Have you guys always been nudists?" Lori asked Lila as she and Eric took the drinks offered to them by Peter.

"Nudists?" laughed Lila as she sipped her glass of grape juice. "We're not nudists. We simply don't wear clothes when we swim."

"We're not ashamed of our bodies," added Peter. "We work too hard on them."

Eric then told Lori about how all three of them had a rigorous daily routine that included swimming, pushups, and sit-ups. He purposely left out part of some exercises he and Peter occasionally did.

"Don't forget to tell her about what you and Pete do in the studio," interjected Lila with a devilish look in her eyes.

"Studio?" asked Lori slightly puzzled.

"Yes, the dance studio. Peter's grandfather made them both study ballet until they finished high school. Even though Peter and Eric usually only do the stretching exercises, they sometimes go through a complete dance routine. I'm sure you were impressed with Peter's cartwheels. Eric is almost as good. No one knows about their ballet and gymnastic abilities but me and now you. Dance and gymnastics really helped them with their football moves. Peter may have been the only defensive end in NFL history who could have had a career in ballet."

Lori found this uproariously funny. She pictured the two men going through a dance routine together--Peter Stacia, with his massive frame, walking around on tiptoes making flying leaps while Eric attempted to catch him. She started to giggle.

"What's so funny?" asked Peter as a picture of him in a pink tutu popped into Lori's head. Lori then began to laugh and almost choked on her sandwich. The more she was questioned, the harder she laughed, and the more she choked.

"We'll see how you feel about it in the morning," Eric said to Lori as he patted her on the back to stop her coughing. "I'm sure Lila can find you a pair of tights somewhere. Of course, you might have to roll them up. You're not as tall as Lila."

"Not to change the subject, Lila; but you have a beautiful home," said Lori as she wiped crumbs from her face. "Have you lived here long?"

"I have lived here since Peter and I married five years ago. Peter has lived here his whole life. Eric moved in as a teenager when Ms. Velma, the lady who raised him since he was a baby, died."

"Really?" Lori couldn't imagine living anywhere for that long. The longest she had ever lived anywhere had been her years in the state pen.

"Yeah, when we got married, Papa moved to the house on Wilson Blvd. and gave us this house along with a check for $100,000 and a trip to Hawaii. When we got back from Hawaii, we kicked Eric out and remodeled the home slightly. Eric still has a room here he uses occasionally."

As Lila and Lori continued in deep conversation about Home and Garden Network and remodeling, Peter turned to Eric and whispered, "Lori may not be tall like Lila, but she is definitely as well built. She's got the best figure I have seen on a woman since before I met Lila."

"Hey there, Bubba! Remember, you have Lila. This one's mine," Eric smiled back feigning jealousy.

"I was complimenting you on your choice," laughed Peter. "She is the first woman you've dated who I truly like. She's honest too. Most women wouldn't have told what she did tonight--especially to a Sheriff she has a romantic interest in."

"I know."

The four enjoyed each other's company--laughing, eating, drinking, and joking around--for another thirty minutes before Peter looked at his watch. He got out of the hot tub and wrapped a towel tightly around his waist. "I hate to leave good company," he said as he picked up another large, soft bath towel and dried off, "but it's almost 2 A.M., and it's been a long day. I'm going to bed."

"If you guys want to stay tonight, Eric's bedroom is made up," Lila added. "We'll get up in the morning, do our workout, and take the boat out to the lake."

They all said their goodnights and Lori followed Eric into his bedroom. She had clearly had the best day and night of her life. She hated the evening to end. She looked at the center of the room, against the back wall and saw something that put fear in her heart. It was the *bed!*

She had never had sex willingly unless she was high--and none of the times she had been raped would have been considered willing. Now she wanted to be anywhere but here. Why couldn't she make a quick excuse and run? Run where? Where would she go? Earlier, Eric's friend, Peter, had offered her the financial opportunity of a lifetime along with a 2001 Mercedes. After her response to Eric's kisses in the pool, she also felt she had a chance to spend the rest of her life with Eric. She had fallen in love with the handsome Sheriff. She knew both opportunities would indeed evaporate if she broke and ran screaming from the room.

What would Eric expect of her? Back when she wandered through her life-- high to the sky with no real direction in life--she had been with many men. Lori knew what men liked. Lori knew what men wanted. All men wanted to *humiliate* and *destroy*. In her memory, she could see their sweaty and grimacing faces as they took advantage of her and raped her. She felt their rough hands and could clearly hear their threats that soon turned into moans of passion as they had their way with her. They had all been much the same. Eric would certainly be like all the rest of the men in bed. Even if he was different out of the bedroom--that had to be an act. Men only wanted to please themselves. Eric wouldn't be any different.

I need a Valium, she thought. Suddenly, the addict in her reared its ugly head. Like a snake sliding through tall grass, the need was upon her. *I need a Valium or a Xanax . . . No, what I really need now is a hit of crank.* The old feeling of hopelessness and helplessness revived the addict in her. *I will be okay if I only have one hit or one toke off a joint.* **Just one anything.**

Who am I kidding? I'm not a society girl. I'm what I've always been, a dope whore. Why did I think I could pull this off? What would a respectable, young, gorgeous man like Sheriff Eric Sandusky want with a useless druggie? Can't he see it? Can't he see the crazed need in my eyes?

Eric smiled at Lori before he turned to quietly close the door to his bedroom.

Chapter Thirty

Eric arrived at the office Monday morning around six. As usual, he was the first person on the day shift to arrive.

Today was a critical day, but he was having trouble concentrating on the task-at-hand. The Alabama Bureau of Investigation informed him arrests would be made today on evidence provided by the cache of tapes found in Alan's house.

His mind wandered as he relived the closeness he had shared with Lori. At first, she'd been unable to relax in his bedroom. When he told her nothing had to happen if she didn't want it to, she had cried. Lori then confided she had not been intimate with anyone since she'd gotten out of Tutwiler. She explained how being raped had created a phobia about intimacy.

He had held her and promised he would never pressure her. He wanted her to be ready. Holding her created stirrings in him, he had never experienced before even though he'd had numerous sexual partners. He then explained how a trauma, such as rape, often affected the sex lives of victims. Right in the middle of their discussion, they'd fallen asleep in each other's arms.

Saturday morning he had awakened to the sound of Lori showering. When he said, "good morning," she opened the shower door and asked him if he'd wash her back. He'd gotten in the shower with her, and all at once, her apprehensions vanished. His understanding and willingness to wait until she was ready had released fervor in Lori that had built up for years.

They made love slowly and tenderly yet with a raw obsession neither had ever felt before. They'd spent the rest of the weekend doing much the same, as they couldn't get enough of each other. Their passionate, fun-filled weekend was one he would never forget.

Eric tried once again to concentrate. The District Attorney and Judge Pilgrim would be arrested first. Later on in the afternoon, he would go to Red Bay to arrest Don Guilles. Don was the Assistant Chief of Police there.

The Chief of Police, Aaron Abagnale, was horrified to learn one of his officers was involved in something as tawdry as child prostitution. Abagnale was a good cop and a good man. Eric had tried his whole term in office unsuccessfully to get Chief Abagnale to come to work for him. Initially, Eric had offered him the Chief Deputy's job Andy now held, but he'd declined. Eric really didn't have anything extra to offer Abagnale.

Aaron Abagnale was a successful author of Christian fiction, with two novels on the New York Times bestseller list right now along with fifteen past bestsellers. Aaron had been the first author of Christian fiction to cross over into the mainstream. He was the first to appeal to more than your everyday Bible thumper.

Aaron was also a top officer. He had worked for the Red Bay Police Department for twenty years, and at forty-three had been the Chief for the last decade. He was independently wealthy and didn't work for the money. Eric knew he donated his salary to the Boys and Girls Ranch.

In Eric's opinion, Aaron worked for the betterment of the community. Besides being a best-selling author and Red Bay's Chief of Police, Aaron preached at the Church of Christ down on Golden Road. He coached midget football and could usually be counted on in any charitable fund-raiser.

Overall, he was a good honest man with an enviable life, a beautiful wife, and no reason to change any of it. He was a solid officer of the law with, as far as Eric could tell, no real enemies. He was genuinely liked and respected by all. Even the people he arrested held no animosity toward him and seemed to like him.

Eric was thankful he hadn't been running for office against Aaron Abagnale. Eric wasn't sure he could have beaten Aaron in an election. Aaron, though, seemed to have no desire to be more than he was. He had reached the highest point in his police career he wanted to reach, and Eric wasn't sure Aaron had even wanted to be Chief.

Eric's idol, Buford Barker, had been Chief. When he retired, Don Guilles was promoted to the Chief's position. Later on, Aaron became Assistant Chief. In the middle of some kind of scandal, the details weren't really known, Don had been demoted to Assistant Chief, and Aaron took his place as the new Chief.

Eric wondered if Lori was up yet. By now, it was almost seven. Maybe he should call her. No, there was no need for that. She had told him she rarely got up before eight and usually did not go into the real estate office until at least nine. He decided he would call her around lunchtime.

He already knew he was deeply and madly in love. He was aware that he was. He had to marry Lori. He'd didn't want anyone else to experience with her what he had.

Eric worked on paperwork for several hours and made a few routine patrol runs. He was waiting on the call that would deploy him to arrest Guilles.

He called Lori during lunch and was pleased she had a few minutes to talk. She had shown seven houses and had a contract on two. She had also lined up a portfolio of properties for Peter to consider. When she invited him over for dinner, she promised to cook for him. He had told her not to start before he got there because he wanted to help. After a short discussion on cooking, they had decided on a menu and who would cook what. Lori was impressed he not only knew how to cook but also enjoyed it. She had laughed and said he truly was the man of her dreams. Eric hoped she was serious because he already knew she was his dream lady. He had promised to be there by seven.

It was now almost two in the afternoon, and he knew any minute he would be called to go to Red Bay. For the most part, Red Bay had a good, honest police force. Except for Don, every officer Red Bay had would be a welcome addition to any sheriff or police department in the state. They were well trained and operated almost with a military efficiency. There was no doubt Aaron knew how to run a department.

The telephone rang, and Eric's secretary knocked on his office door to inform him the arrests of the District Attorney and Judge Pilgrim had gone well, as had seven other arrests. A state trooper was now outside to accompany Eric to the Red Bay Police Department to arrest Don Guilles.

It was a miserably hot day. By the time Eric and the state trooper showed up at the Red Bay Police Department, the overweight trooper had already sweated through his shirt in spite of the overworked A/C in the county squad car.

Aaron met Eric at the car seeming, as always, genuinely pleased to see him. They went into Aaron's office in the small police department and made small talk while the 3-11 officers changed shifts with the 7-3 officers.

When the 3-11 officers were officially on duty, Aaron asked Eric if one of his new officers, Josh Green, could accompany them.

"Sure," Eric said.

"Come on, Josh. You're going with us," the Chief yelled back in the direction of a young man about twenty-two, who was working on a mountain of paperwork.

"Where we goin'," asked Josh as he walked into the office.

Before he thought about it, Eric said, "To arrest Don Guilles."

"What?" asked Josh, apparently thunderstruck, as all heads turned toward Eric. "We're going to arrest the Assistant Chief?"

Eric hadn't meant to say that in the police station. Any one of the people might call him to let him know they were coming. If Don knew they were coming to arrest him, he could give them serious problems--problems only a police officer, or maybe some kind of paramilitary person, could give. Don knew the same police tactics they knew and at the very least would be carrying a firearm of some kind. Alabama law assured them of that.

Alabama law said a police officer had to be armed at all times. Whether he was on duty or off duty, it didn't matter. Eric and Aaron decided to ride together. They got into Aaron's cruiser and proceeded over to Don Guilles' home. The state trooper rode with Josh Green in the other Red Bay city car.

As they pulled into Don's driveway, Eric's instincts told him something was wrong. No, that wasn't right. Something was very, very wrong. Don's Jeep Grand Cherokee was in the drive with all four doors standing open as Aaron and Eric got out of the dark-blue police car. Eric walked cautiously by the forest green Cherokee and saw an envelope with Delta Airlines stamped on the top left corner lying on the front seat on the passenger side. The back seat of the Jeep was stacked with cash in what looked like all denominations--everything from five-dollar bills to one hundred dollar bills.

"Looks like he was getting ready to run," said Red Bay's esteemed Chief of Police. "We barely got here in time."

Josh and the trooper got out of Josh's cruiser, and Eric instructed them to go around back. They went around the left side of the house. After they turned the corner, Eric saw a flash of movement to his right. Before he could turn toward the movement, he was knocked off his feet. It felt like a sledgehammer had hit him on his right side. As he fell, he heard the second boom of a big handgun again and felt the hot burn as a bullet creased the back of his right arm. Eric hit the ground, unmoving. He struggled for breath and realized he had been shot. He heard the Jeep Cherokee crank up and accelerate down the driveway and Aaron giving their location and codes for an officer down. The Red Bay Chief fired up his car, backed out of the drive, lighted up the emergency bar atop the cruiser, and switched on the siren. The last thing Eric remembered before he passed into unconsciousness was the rapidly fading sounds of the siren.

Chapter Thirty-One

Lori looked at the man of her dreams lying in the hospital bed. His side was heavily bandaged, as was his right arm. She had been terrified when Lila called her to tell her Eric had been shot attempting an arrest. She couldn't bear to lose this man who completed her in a way she had only dreamed. Even a week ago, she would never have believed there could be a man as tender and caring as Eric Sandusky.

Suddenly his eyes opened, and she saw pain on his face. "Are you all right baby?" she asked.

"I . . . uh . . . I . . . think so. What happened?"

"You were shot," Lori said.

"If it weren't for your vest, you'd be dead. Or at least seriously injured," said a deep voice that Eric recognized as Colonel Volores.

"Shot?" He remembered being knocked off his feet. Eric looked around to see Andy and a state trooper sitting by the edge of the bed. "What happened?" Eric asked Andy. "He . . . didn't get away, did he?"

"No, he didn't get away, but it did turn out to be a very nasty situation," Andy said.

"Tell me about it," Eric said. He wanted to know exactly what had gone on.

"Four people died before we could get the situation under control, and Chief Abagnale was airlifted to UAB where he is in critical condition."

"What happened to Aaron?"

Andy told his boss about the car chase. It seemed Don Guilles had rammed an Aerostar van and pushed it under the rear wheels of a semi-truck with a load of logs headed to the mill. Three innocent people were killed in the accident--a young woman and her two young girls. For some reason, Aaron crashed his cruiser into a pine tree a few feet past the wreck. Josh Green and the state trooper continued the chase radioing in the two accidents. Josh pulled up on the slower Jeep Cherokee as the trooper shot out the left front tire on the Jeep. It flipped and rolled several times, killing the Assistant Chief.

"Is Aaron going to be okay?" asked Eric.

"At this point, we don't know. He is severely injured. A shotgun in a roof rack above his head came loose in the accident and nearly took off his head. He also has severe internal injuries. He was airlifted to ECM, then airlifted again to UAB. They're operating on him in Birmingham as we speak."

"I hope he's okay," said Eric as he said a silent prayer for the Red Bay Chief.

"I'm sure he will be," said the trooper. "It's the best hospital in the state."

"His wife?"

"We had a trooper drive his wife and girls down there. They left about twenty minutes ago. The Colonel cleared the trooper driving them down to use his lights to expedite them on their trip. They should be there in an hour or so."

Eric shifted in the bed, and the tight bandages wrapped around his chest did little to stop the sharp stabbing pain in his right side. He involuntarily let out a small cry of pain.

"It's going to hurt for a while," said Colonel Volores. "When you were shot, the vest protected you from the entrance of the bullet but did nothing for the impact. You have a broken right rib that will take several months to properly heal."

"I'm going to hurt like this for months?"

"No. It will hurt for several weeks while it mends. What you feel now is primarily pain from the bruising. Being shot, even while wearing a Kevlar vest, does a lot of damage to the body. Being shot at close range like you were with a heavy handgun is the equivalent of being hit extremely hard over and over in the same spot with a sledgehammer."

"Tell me about it," Eric said.

"It could have been worse," said Colonel Volores. "I saw much worse while I was in Vietnam. Even though our soldiers had body armor there, it didn't do much good. Body armor back then wouldn't stop a rifle bullet. Even today a light Kevlar vest like you were wearing will not stop a rifle bullet most of the time, even if they do stop handgun rounds effectively."

"When can I go home?" asked Eric.

"Anytime you get ready. A broken rib isn't exactly a reason to keep you overnight."

"I can go?"

"Anytime you're ready, Sheriff."

Eric, with extreme effort, managed to raise himself off the bed and unsteadily got to his feet. The injury to his side had become a sharp stabbing pain that made breathing difficult. The wound to his triceps on his right arm burned and made moving the arm sluggish and painful.

Seeing the obvious pain on his face, Colonel Volores offered him a prescription.

"Thanks, but no thanks. I think Tylenol will be plenty strong enough. If I decide otherwise, I'll call you."

"You do that," said Colonel Adam Volores. "Oh, by the way, Peter and Lila are coming over for dinner tomorrow night. Why don't you and your lady friend here join us? If you're able to get around, that is."

"Lori?" Eric looked expectantly at the beautiful young lady.

"It sounds wonderful. I would be honored," Lori said.

Lori found out this colossal doctor was Lila's father while she waited on Eric to wake up. He was genuinely concerned about Eric from the beginning. Even though his clinic had closed, he taped Eric's ribs and stitched up his arm. He then remained close by. She couldn't figure out why until he told her his son-in-law was Eric's best friend. With that revelation, she figured his daughter could be no other than Lila Stacia.

When she asked him if he were Lila's father, the Colonel answered in the affirmative. She told him about meeting Lila and Peter. He then said she must be special because he didn't think Eric had ever brought anyone over to Lila and Pete's house.

* * *

TO PROTECT AND TO SERVE

"To Protect and to Serve" is a common phrase used by many law enforcement organizations today.

Officer Joseph S. Dorobek submitted the phrase to a Los Angeles Police Academy contest in 1955. It won, and in 1963 became the official motto of the entire Los Angeles Police Department.

* * *

Chapter Thirty-Two

The next morning Eric awoke and turned his head slightly to the right. He saw Lori's face framed beautifully by her long blond hair. She was the vision of an angel and a picture of perfection.

When Eric attempted to sit up, he gasped in pain and knew immediately he had made a grave mistake. He felt the sharp pain stab into his side. *No sit-ups today*, he thought wryly. His arm itched where the bullet had entered. It itched and it burned. He knew from experience with other wounds--not gunshot wounds--that when it started to heal it would itch even worse, and there would be no way to scratch it.

He hadn't wanted to wake Lori up yet, but evidently, his gasp of pain had. Peter and Lila had joined forces to inform Eric he and Lori would stay in his bedroom at the Stacias until he fully recovered. Lori awoke smiling, as she had every morning since she had met Eric. "Good morning, sweetheart," she said sleepily. "Are you hurting?"

"A little."

"Maybe I could do something to make you forget about the pain," she said with a smile. She moved over atop him and instantly he was ready for her. She had to be careful of his injuries, but then, so far, she had been an attentive lover.

When they finished making love, Eric slowly got out of the bed and carefully walked into the bathroom. After he relieved himself, he turned to the sink, put toothpaste on his brush, and attempted to brush his teeth with his left hand. The injury prevented him from skillfully using his right hand. With this finished, he ran hot water into the sink while he reached into the cabinet for a fresh washcloth. Shaving was going to be difficult with his left hand. He had always been somewhat ambidextrous but had never shaved with his left hand. Somehow, it didn't seem natural. He finished shaving, looked into the mirror, and decided there was a slight possibility he could bleed to death from injuries inflicted from his disposable safety razor. It was a good thing he hadn't used a straight razor.

He turned on the water in the shower before he remembered he couldn't take a shower without wrapping his arm in a plastic bag. Instead, he ran a tub full of water and sat down gingerly in the steaming water. He washed his hair and body as best he could as he noted the massive purple and blue-black bruising on his right side. He was careful not to get any water on the bandage on his right arm. Colonel Volores had been adamant he keep it dry because he didn't want Eric back in the clinic because of an infection. He finished his awkward bath, toweled off as best he could, and walked back to the bedroom.

Lori was still lying in the bed with the covers pulled up to the bottom of her breasts. She looked delicious, and he would have liked to go back to bed and snuggle with her all day. That, however, wasn't possible. He had too much to do. Wounded or not, the cases against the DA, the Judge, and the Russellville Police Chief, among others, were going forward with or without him. He had meetings today with the State Attorney General, as well as one of the assistant attorney generals for the U.S. Since this had involved child prostitution and included crossing state lines, the U.S. Attorney General's office and FBI were now involved.

Lori helped Eric dress and kissed him as he went out the door.

"Are you sure you'll be able to drive?" questioned Lori as she watched Eric cautiously get into his truck.

"I'm sure," assured Eric. "Now don't forget we're eating dinner with Lila's parents tonight."

"I won't forget," promised Lori. "I'll be at the real estate office until three. Call me if you need me. If I don't hear from you, I'll see you back here at five."

Eric nodded as he pulled out of the driveway.

By the time he reached his office, several of the children had already been identified as children missing from as far away as South Carolina.

During the day under duress, Judge Pilgrim gave Eric an address in the Dime community where several children were held. A joint task force raided the home and found children as young as four years old chained in the basement. Most were barely alive and had been there as long as ten days without food. They drank from a barrel that caught water from the gutters on the roof. They were in poor shape, and neither Eric nor the federal authorities had any idea who some of the children were. Eric contacted the parents of those he could identify, most of whom were now enroute to Russellville.

Lori waited by the door as Eric returned to the Stacias. She could tell it had been a bad day for Eric. He had called her and told her how disgusted he'd been. It was horrible that so called civilized people could treat children that way. These kids would never grow up to be normal. Their psychological condition was too far-gone. Most would either end up in therapy for the rest of their lives or in some type of mental hospital. Some would even end up in prison. These children would forever more be a drain on society, and it wasn't their fault.

As Eric got out of his truck, she could see on his face he felt he was to blame for their condition. He had also told her how he should have arrested Alan long ago. He felt he had wasted precious time trying to build the perfect case, but he found it hard to believe his former friend had been that sick.

Eric was glad to see Lori, but he couldn't get out of his mind how he should have seen the depraved mind in the Judge, DA, and former Russellville Chief of Police. He should have known. He had worked with these people for twelve years. Why had he not seen it?

"Are you all right baby?" asked Lori.

"What? . . . I was thinking . . ."

"About the kids?"

"Yeah."

"Baby, it wasn't your fault. You couldn't have done anything else. You didn't know."

"I know you see it that way, but it shouldn't have happened on my watch. The people of Franklin County elected me to protect their children from those things. I've failed them."

"You didn't fail them. When you found out about it, you did what you could."

"It wasn't enough. You don't understand. I failed them. Not you-- didn't fail them. You weren't there. You weren't elected to serve the public. You'll never understand, and you didn't see the deplorable condition those children were in. I not only failed them, I failed Georgia, too. I should have been able to protect her. It says it on my patrol car, *To Protect and Serve*. That is not just a saying. I was elected to protect the people of this fine county, and I didn't do it. I didn't do my job."

"Do you think anyone could have done any better than you? How were you to know? Baby, you have got to quit blaming yourself."

"I know. It isn't easy. No one should have seen what I did."

"Listen, Eric. Do you think you are the only one that has seen awful things? Do you think these are the only *bad men* in the world? The world is full of them. I saw things in prison no woman should ever have to see. I had to do things in prison no one should have to do. I did my time and tried to make the best of it. Some of the prison guards that were watching me should be in jail. Some will one day make it to the other side. I have no doubts, but they weren't in prison. They were there to torture us and make sure we didn't escape. Tutwiler is where all the prison guards want to work, at least the male ones. I saw girls the guards prostituted. I saw men who came to the prison for a good time. What about *those* girls? Do you think they had a good time? Certainly some of them may have, but what about the ones that ended up with AIDS or Syphilis? Do you think they had a good time? Sometimes bad things happen, and we're left to pick up the pieces of our lives and try to put them back together as best we can. After the first six months, I was lucky. I only had one man to service, and then only a couple of times a month. Some of these girls were servicing three and four men a night. The guards let them in. It was a state-sanctioned whorehouse."

"Baby," Eric started with a sympathetic look on his face.

"No, don't start that. Don't patronize me. I don't want anyone feeling sorry for me. I did what I had to do to survive. That's what most of these kids have done. They did what they had to do to survive. Will some of them have problems later in life? Certainly. What you need to concentrate on is putting the creeps away that did these horrible acts. You're paid to look at the big picture. Right now, the big picture is to get the people on those tapes into a jail cell. That's what you're paid to do. Sometimes that is what *Protect and Serve* means. You protect and serve by putting these people in jail. You build a rock solid case so no judge in his or her right mind would ever release them. I have deliberated about it a lot in the last six years. I committed a crime, but I also served my time--every single solitary day of it. Was it easy time? No. Was I mad about it? Absolutely! I was mad about it in the beginning. Then I realized the world wasn't to blame for where I was. I was to blame. I lost my parents when I was seventeen and hated my father for trying to beat the train. I let that hatred of my dad turn me into an addict. The addict in me did a lot of bad things, things I'm ashamed of. While I was in prison, I came to realize that no one was to blame. I was the only person I could blame for my situation, so I did something about it. I educated myself. Granted, I had help. Mattie and Helen were sent from God, but even they couldn't have helped if I hadn't wanted to help myself."

Lori's voice grew softer as she continued, "When it's all over, and when everything is said and done, if these children end up in prison or in a mental hospital, it might not be their fault--but it certainly isn't yours. These kids have had a bad time of it, and they will never be the same. Can they grow up to live a normal life? Certainly! Look at you. Look how well you ended up even though you never knew your parents and always hoped they'd come back for you. God has looked after you--just as he has looked after me--and just as he will now look after these children. They may have panic attacks. They may end up in psychotherapy for the rest of their lives. That's not your fault. Understand? Not your fault. So, stop feeling sorry for yourself, and keep doing your job. I saw the first day I met you how the officers under you respect you. They believe in you and trust you completely. You are their leader. I know that is why you won the election. Sometimes people know when they see an honest man. You have the job of Sheriff, not because of who you are, but because of what you represent."

Lori sat down on the bed and Eric held her as they wept for the children. They also wept for Lori, and they wept for Eric. As their tears continued to fall, they prayed for the children. They also prayed for Lori, and they prayed for Eric.

Eric couldn't believe someone could understand him so completely. He *had* felt sorry for himself. Lori was right about another thing. The people of this county had elected him *to Protect and Serve*. When you identified a problem person, you built an indestructible case against that person. You made sure the person was no longer a problem. That's what Lori had tried to tell him.

His profession was an honorable one. Although honorable people didn't always staff it, he knew he was honorable, as was Buford Barker, Aaron Abagnale, and Andy Landers. They were all honorable. They were good people doing dangerous chores. Your average person didn't want to see what actually went on in the world. They didn't want to see the things Eric, Buford, Andy, and Aaron had to see. They wanted to believe the world and everyone in it was good. That wasn't the case. Most were good honest people, but there were the few who weren't going to adhere to what the majority of society decided was acceptable behavior. Eric had been hired by the voters to protect the population against people like Judge Pilgrim, Chief Jim Davis, and former Sheriff Justin Thyme.

Where Lori had needlessly worried about Peter acquiring a *God Complex*, Eric now realized these officials were the ones with a *God Complex*. These people had taken the public's trust and used it against the public. They'd made a mockery of their office. They would sentence a kid to life in prison for a couple of DUIs when they did things far worse. They rationalized they were above the law.

Eric and Lori wiped their eyes as Eric took off his badge and looked at it. The star said Eric was one of the good guys. While everyone that ever pinned on the star wasn't, he had to believe most were. He would be Franklin County's *Frank Serpico*. As Lori and Eric got dressed for dinner, he couldn't stop thinking about everything he had seen; but he no longer felt sorry for himself.

Suddenly he made a decision. It was a decision Pete may not like, but it was in the end his decision. He had been offered a position with one of Peter's companies. It was a position that would undoubtedly pay considerably more than his current position. In the end, though, would he still feel as good about what he did? Would he know at the end of his life he had made the world a better place for the children yet to come? He didn't think so. He made the decision on the spot. He would serve the people of Franklin County as long as they wanted him to. If he ever lost an election, he would take the position with Peter. If that position was still open, that is. If it wasn't, he was sure he could get a job with almost any police department. This job may never make him rich, but the satisfaction of a job well done would comfort him when he got old.

He was now physically and mentally ready for dinner at the Colonel's house.

* * *

Some are born great, some achieve greatness, and some have greatness thrust upon them.

~~~William Shakespeare

* * *

PART TWO –
THREE MONTHS LATER

Chapter Thirty-Three

Peter and Lila were packed for and excited about their trip to Montana. Because of Eric's recuperation, Lila's morning sickness, and Peter's increased business ventures, three months slipped by before they were able to go. Lila was almost five months pregnant, and summer had ended.

The Gulfstream waited on the runway as they drove up in the Tahoe. When they returned from this trip, the wimpy four-wheel drive would be a rompin' stompin' *REAL* four-wheel drive. It would be delivered to Memphis where the work would entail at least a new engine, interior modification, custom lift job, and exterior paint job. While Peter liked the initial silver color, he now liked black better. "The Engine" was sitting in a race shop in Nashville. Overall, the revisions to the truck would cost more than five times its original price. The new wheels and tires alone cost more than one half the SUV's original value.

The same young man met them at the gate with the same little car to load their luggage. Lila and Peter had not packed very much because they planned to go down to Billings and buy what they needed. The only thing they really bothered to pack were jeans for Peter and his one suit. His long legs prohibited him from buying a pair of jeans almost anywhere, and his immense size required any suit to be tailor made.

It wasn't as if they could ever spend all their money. They were overwhelmed when they finally figured out the true extent of how much money they had. They could walk down the road, pick up handfuls of hundred-dollar bills, and fail to pick up as much in a day as their investments earned in a minute. Lila and Peter spent money with reckless abandonment once they returned from New York. In the past three months, they bought everything they had ever wanted. Now they were sick of spending and needed something else to occupy their time.

They told no one the extent of their wealth although Eric, Lori, and Lila's parents had limited knowledge. They had told Lila's parents more than they had planned, but the Colonel and Ming Toi had gotten concerned after Peter and Lila got back from New York. The Colonel couldn't understand why Lila had quit work. Ming Toi had even encouraged the human resource manager from the local chicken plant to call and offer Peter a manager's position. Tired of being badgered, Peter and Lila elected to tell her parents that she and Peter's net worth was at least one trillion dollars. Colonel Adam Volores looked at Peter with a sneer on his face and laughed, "You're a trillionaire? You're a fool if you think I believe that. Why not a gazillionaire? Maybe they can make a video game about you called--Peter the Gazillionaire. You could play a character like Donald Trump. Really, Peter. You could have at least tried to make it believable."

Peter had felt his anger rise against a man he totally liked and respected. As much as he esteemed his father-in-law, he would not be made fun of in front of Lila. The night was one he would never forget. Not only had he had a shouting match with his father-in-law, he later on shared the secret with Lila that he and Eric were twins.

Before Peter realized what he was saying he had bragged, "Believable? Your daughter is wearing $35 million worth of jewelry. You're only jealous you can't buy something that expensive for your own wife."

"What?" Lila looked stunned as she interrupted the ensuing fight between her husband and father. "The necklace and earrings couldn't be worth that."

"I paid $30 million for the necklace and $5 million for the earrings," explained Peter as he continued to brag while the Colonel and Ming Toi shook their heads in disbelief. "I had them made especially for Lila. Natural red diamonds are rarer than any of the other diamonds. Few jewelers have even seen one. There are only twenty gem quality red diamonds in the world. Five of them are in that necklace and earrings set."

"You wouldn't know $30 million if it bit you on the ass," the Colonel countered back.

Next ensued one of the loudest and most embarrassing shouting matches in which Peter or the Colonel had ever been involved. After at least an hour with no clear-cut winner, Peter and Lila stomped out as Peter threatened to never speak to the Colonel again. Lila's parents didn't believe Peter and Lila could even have a trillion dollars, so they would never be told about the more than $500 trillion of net worth. It had been two months since the incident, and the Colonel and Peter had still not spoken to each other. Lila pleaded with each on several occasions to patch up their differences but as of yet had been unsuccessful.

When they got home that night, Peter told Lila about the keys and how he'd unlocked information from the jeweled box that proved Eric was his twin brother. He also revealed they owned a mansion and ranch in Montana. After the excitement of the evening, however, Peter's disclosures were anti-climactic, and Lila did not tell Peter the facts he had divulged was information to which she was already privy.

Now here they were climbing onto the personal jet. In five hours, they would land on the ranch in Montana. Neither Peter nor Lila had ever been to Montana. They didn't know what to expect. Peter had heard it called the big sky country but couldn't really imagine a sky bigger than the one in Russellville. Peter settled back into the big, comfortable white leather seat of the plane. Lila did much the same. They would land in Montana in slightly over four hours.

Jack Trail, who managed the compound, would meet them at the airstrip located fifteen miles from what he called *the big house*. Peter wondered about the *big house*. Could there really be a palace in Montana that covered more than fourteen acres? Over the phone, Jack said *the big house* was built in 1792 and resembled the old Byzantine-influenced palaces in Russia. The six million acre ranch was the largest in the United States and covered 9,400 square miles. The second largest, King's Ranch in Texas, covered 1,280 square miles. When Peter had first told Lila this, she had trouble comprehending it until he explained it was larger than the state of Vermont.

"Larger than Vermont?" she had exclaimed.

"The ranch covers almost 200 square miles more than the state of Vermont," Peter explained.

"How can that be when history says the first white men, Lewis and Clark, didn't explore here until 1803?"

"Mr. Trail insists there's a brass plaque set in granite with the date 1792 stamped into it. He alleges it's not technically part of the United States and it wasn't included in the Louisiana Purchase of 1803 and a bevy of treaties with the U.S. Government assures the sovereignty. I guess the French couldn't sell something that wasn't theirs."

"Whom did it belong to?" asked Lila.

"A lady named Sophie Friederike Auguste von Anhalt-Zerbst-Dornburg. I've done a little research and found out that she was a German princess who later became Catherine the Great."

Peter went on to explain to Lila everything he had found out. "A considerable portion of the palace is allocated for offices needed by the ranch and the operations center for companies such as Bozeman Meats and Colstrip. Overall, there were suites with eight thousand square feet of living space per unit. The complex covered approximately fourteen acres with about 4.5 million square feet under the roof. On the ranch alone were more than a hundred companies ranging from grocery stores to oil refineries to leather works."

What Peter did not know but would soon find out was that all 30,000 ranch and complex employees lived on site and were not allowed to leave without security clearance and protection. Security was tighter than that of the FBI, CIA, or even the Vatican. The only two people authorized to come and go freely were Jack and his assistant, Janet Cumberland. Workers grew and processed all necessary food, clothing, and other essentials. Anything else needed was flown in by company aircraft. Accredited education was provided for all. Everyone graduated college. Children were given vocational and personality testing on their thirteenth birthday and classified as one of six job categories. Some occupations such as lawyers, financial planners, mortgage brokers, real estate agents, insurance agents, travel agents, politicians, etc., were not needed as employees were well taken care of if something happened to them. All education, medicine, medical care, was provided. There was only one way into the complex and one way out. The thirty-foot surveillance fence kept all employees in and any curious tourist out. Since the facility and its acreage were not considered part of the United States, it was a protected airspace and staff paid no taxes to the United States

Government. This was another way the Stacia family had protected its income since it could not be considered as part of the United States. Only New York City-based Navoiczyk Enterprises was regarded as a United States company and paid taxes. Most workers had been born there as well as their children, parents, grandparents, and great-grandparents. Therefore, there was little need for a visitation of relatives. Every so often groups of employees, as well as their children, were flown to various vacation sites accompanied by security that prevented any transfer of confidential information. If a cruise was taken, the whole cruise boat was rented. If employees went to the beach, they were flown to a private island owned by Stacia Enterprises. Most visitors flown in were doctors, researchers, inventors, musicians, artists, and specialists that had no idea where they were. Occasionally some were allowed to stay. A few of those fortunate few brought their families, but most decided not to and were listed as missing. Papa had made it as close to Utopia as earthly possible.

Peter felt the change in the plane's engines and heard the squawk of the radio in the cockpit, "Unidentified aircraft, you have entered a Special Use Airspace, please turn your IFF transponder to Mode 6 for positive identification, if your transponder does not have a mode six, please alter your course by 180 degrees. Further incursion into this Special Use Airspace without positive identification will be considered a hostile act and shall result in anti-aircraft measures being deployed . . . I copy positive identification Navoiczyk One. Welcome, home."

Peter and Lila stepped out of the Gulfstream into an afternoon that in Peter's mind was downright cold for the last day of September. When they left Alabama, it had been a balmy eighty-five degrees. Here at the airstrip the clouds hung low and ominous, and there was a feel of snow in the air. Lila--who finally was beginning to show signs of her pregnancy--immediately started to shiver. As they stepped off the last step, a north wind began to pick up; filling the windsock at the end of the airfield, and the first snowflakes of winter fell wetly against Peter's face.

"I never considered it being cold here this early in the season," Peter said to Lila.

"Neither did I," agreed Lila, who wore a light blue skirt and a yellow sleeveless blouse.

Neither Lila nor Peter had dressed for this kind of weather. They were immediately thankful Jack Trail's four-door Ford dually pickup was close by. They sprinted over to the pickup. Peter opened the rear passenger's door for Lila, who almost ran over him as she made her way into its warm, plush interior. Peter shut the door behind her, opened the front door on the passenger side, and slid onto the captain's chair.

Peter looked over at Jack and said with a slight grin on his face, "This is a *little* cool? I thought when you said that, it would probably be in the middle to lower sixties. I wasn't expecting this."

Jack looked at Peter with a concern on his face that Peter immediately noticed and said, "When you left Alabama, it was seventy-one degrees here. The high today was to be around seventy-five. This storm blowing in put itself together in the last two hours. Ten minutes ago, the weather service issued a severe winter storm warning. Blizzard conditions are expected by dark. At the rate this storm is moving, that should occur in about two hours."

Peter looked at his watch. It said it was 2:30 P.M., which would be 1:30 P.M. Montana time. "You're saying it will be dark by 3:30 P.M.? It gets dark that soon here?"

"Normally the answer is no. Today, however, we have this storm blowing in. In an hour, visibility will be down to ten feet or less. In two hours you won't be able to see your hand in front of your face."

Peter looked down at his big hands and knew it had to be mighty dark for him not to see one of those whoppers. He glanced out the window and noticed how snow had started to fall steadily in big wet flakes. Some of the flakes were as large as silver dollars. They felt a thump as a member of the flight crew dropped the last of their luggage gently into the bed of the heavy-duty pickup.

Even as Jack put the pickup into gear, Peter saw the stairway fold up into the plane and it began to move toward a large hangar situated to the right of the runway. The snow was getting heavier by the second. By the time Jack pulled out onto the small paved road at the end of the runway, Peter could no longer see the hangar even though it was only a few hundred yards away. The snow now melted on impact with the ground but would soon accumulate.

"How far is the compound?" Lila asked from the backseat.

"Not far--only about fifteen miles."

"Oh . . . Okay," said Lila. Fifteen miles to her seemed an awfully long way with the weather conditions worsening as quickly as they were.

The first five miles were uneventful. Then out of nowhere came the biggest animal Peter had ever seen. It stood at least seven feet at the shoulder and probably weighed more than three thousand pounds.

Jack barely caught sight of the bull bison before the pickup slammed into it. The truck almost came to an immediate stop and threw its three occupants hard into their restraining seatbelts and the two front seat occupants into the airbags which had deployed on impact with the massive creature all the writers of western fiction write about in their adventure novels.

As the airbag deflated, hot gasses burned the side of Peter's face and neck. To Peter's amazement, the buffalo wasn't dead. It wasn't even seriously injured. It clambered off the hood of the once beautiful pickup and sauntered off into the snowfall that was rapidly becoming a blizzard.

Peter looked over at Jack, who seemed fine. When he looked at Lila in the back seat, he saw she was definitely not fine. She had struck her head on something that had sliced the right side of her face open to the bone. This large crevice from her temple to the cleft of her chin bled profusely.

She didn't move, and at least a gallon of blood penetrated the back of Peter's captain's chair and pooled in the bench seat in which her head lay.

Peter, almost in shock, saw--knew--she was dead. Oh, God--then no--she moved. He quickly turned around, put his knees in his seat, and leaned over the back. He felt for a pulse and quickly found one. It was strong and beat quickly, which he hoped was a good sign.

"Where'd that thing come from," snarled Jack as he turned around and saw Lila for the first time. Her head lay on the bench seat, and Jack knew she would soon bleed to death if they didn't do something about that slash on her cheek.

He picked up his radio and intended to call the house and have one of the boys hurry out, but found it smashed. Think. Think. What should they do?

Peter said in a calm voice that belied the worry he felt, "We need to stop the bleeding first. What can we use to stop the bleeding?"

Jack leaped out of the truck and opened the toolbox. He rummaged around until he found a large gray roll of duct tape good for almost anything. He grabbed it along with one of the small suitcases.

Peter could not get his seatbelt to unhook. The accident had jammed the locking mechanism. He finally removed his pocketknife from his right pocket and cut through the seatbelt. By the time Jack opened the door and got back into the pickup with the roll of tape and suitcase, Peter cradled Lila's head and held the chasm on her face together as best he could.

Jack slid into the driver's seat and thanked God the pickup was still running. He opened the suitcase and poured the contents out onto the passenger seat. It was obviously one of Lila's cases, as it held a large assortment of lacy undergarments. Jack searched through the assortment until he found something he knew would suffice.

"Here. Cut this into strips," Jack said as he handed Peter an industrial strength sports bra. Peter grasped the idea immediately and cut the cups of the bra into strips of cloth about an inch wide–thankful he'd always kept his *Case* knife razor sharp. When finished, he took a pair of Lila's favorite silk panties and wiped as much blood from her face as he could. He applied one of the strips cut from the bra to her face. It was immediately soaked with blood, but Jack taped it in place anyway. They kept this up until the entire gash was taped up and the bleeding only seeped lightly through the makeshift bandage.

By the time this task was completed, Peter, Jack, and Lila were covered in blood. Jack clambered over into the driver's seat and put the truck in gear. The truck had severe damage to the front end and was probably totaled, but it moved forward in spite of its buckled hood and dangling fenders.

Several inches of snow had accumulated while they attended to Lila's wound. Visibility had lessened to twenty feet.

The next five miles seemed to take hours, but according to Jack's watch, it only took ten minutes. Lila required immediate medical attention. She had lost a lot of blood and could possibly have internal injuries.

"I was afraid of that!" exclaimed Jack.

"What?" asked Peter suddenly worried something was wrong with the truck.

"It's overheated."

"Is the radiator cracked?"

"If it were, we wouldn't have made it this far."

"What is it, then?"

"The radiator is clogging up with snow and ice. No airflow through the radiator means no cooling capacity. Which means the truck will . . ." The engine suddenly quit almost like Jack had turned off the key. They coasted to a stop and Jack hopped out once again and rummaged through the toolbox. This time, he hurried back with a heavy snow suit, a thick pair of gloves, and a pair of rubber boots that he hurriedly donned.

Peter opened the door to surprisingly experience the coldest air of his life. It whipped through his clothes as if he were nude.

"Get back in the truck before you freeze to death," Peter barely heard Jack yell over the howling wind.

Peter did as he was told and watched as Jack secured two more items from the toolbox. One was a hat with a ski mask sewn into it. The other item was a propane heating torch.

Jack pulled the mask over his deeply lined face. He lit the torch with a striker he picked up and turned it to its highest setting. Peter watched as the foot-wide flame made little black paratroopers that swiftly drifted away. Jack staggered to the front of the truck to untangle the hoses. He could not get the mangled hood's release to work. After several attempts, he finally gave up and stood there holding the torch, with its harsh yellow flame barely visible in the blowing snow.

Peter bounded from the truck despite Jack's objections. "Whaddya need?" he asked in his southern drawl.

"I need the hood opened to get to the radiator. I need to melt the ice out of the fins."

Peter grasped the hood with superhuman strength. A sharp edge cut the palm of his hand to the bone, but that didn't deter the former defensive lineman. He'd dealt with pain before and probably would again. His muscles knotted with the effort, but slowly the buckled hood peeled away from the hinges. Suddenly with a loud crash that could be heard even over the howling winds of the storm, the hood slapped the fender on the driver's side of the truck.

"Good. Get back in the truck," yelled Jack. "Start the engine and hold the accelerator to the floor. We need to pull the hot, warm air through the radiator while I heat the other side."

Peter did as he was instructed and in a few minutes watched as the temperature gauge inched its way back to normal. He lightly tapped the horn button to let Jack know and wasn't too surprised when nothing happened. The horn was crammed into one of the cross members. Peter got out and motioned Jack to jump in. Jack slid into the back passenger seat and cradled Lila's head while Peter put the truck in gear and gently depressed the accelerator. The vehicle spun slightly sideways unable to achieve the required traction to move four tons of Detroit steel. He reached down into the floorboard and pulled the stick back one notch to engage the four-wheel drive. The pickup moved forward without any more protest. Peter's hand was bleeding profusely and throbbed with pain.

Peter saw it would be dark soon. The storm had darkened the skies considerably since they departed from the plane. He turned on the headlights even though they were useless. The right light shone directly onto the ground, and the left light shined almost directly straight up and slightly to the right.

"How much farther is it?" Peter asked Jack.

"About four miles."

The snow stopped completely after dumping at least nine inches since their arrival. This was not the fun trip he and Lila had imagined. Where was the big sky everyone talked about? All he could see was snow. As Peter turned into the drive covered with freshly fallen snow, the massive gates opened, as if by magic. There must be a transmitter in the pickup somewhere that activated the electric gates. Then he saw the palace for the first time. It was not what any sane mind would believe was a home completed here at a time of the untamed west. It did seem like one of the palaces built for some type of royalty. This place was huge, and in the fresh snow, it glittered like Cinderella's Castle in Disney World. They were still at a distance of more than a mile from the palace, and it already dwarfed everything else on the landscape.

"We're almost there," said Jack. "Drive straight ahead and we'll go down to the garage. Once in the garage, follow the blue Hospital signs. They will lead us to the emergency hospital there."

"There's a hospital here?" Peter asked almost stunned.

"It's my understanding it was built around 1914 or 1915 because of your Papa's unusual medical problem."

"Papa had a medical problem?"

"It's rumored he almost died several times before some team of experts healed him of some kind of blood disorder. My father told me your grandfather suffered with the problem from birth until he was twenty-five or so."

"That may be why Papa hated hospitals," said Peter. "He was hardly ever sick. He always made the doctors come see him and Gramma Joanna at home."

"That makes sense. Anyway, this hospital comes in handy for the 30,000 workers who live on site, and the isolation of the grounds alone necessitates constant updates of staff and equipment. It's the only capable hospital for more than a hundred miles. Some of the world's top specialists work here, and others are flown in when needed."

Lila moaned slightly. She was deathly pale, but her wound had stopped bleeding.

Peter following the Hospital signs and pulled up in the front of a rock facade with the words *Emergency Entrance* lettered onto the building set in the stone of the underground garage. Immediately the emergency room personnel rushed out to the severely damaged pickup. They seemed to be immensely capable, and an emergency room physician immediately barked out orders.

Lila was quickly placed on one of the rolling hospital beds and rushed inside. Peter followed the onslaught of nurses and doctors into a functioning area of the hospital, not a reception area. There didn't seem to even be a reception area. There were no functionaries to take insurance information or non-vital information. Instead, a capable nurse asked Peter questions, most of which Peter didn't know the answer to.

This was a hospital as it should be. A place for the healing of sick people, not a bureaucracy unduly burdened by the movement of paperwork no one would ever read. Here it seemed doctors made decisions based on the needs of the patient, not the ability of the patient to pay for the procedure. Here none of the patients had to pay for the procedure because all the patients were employees. Since it was maintained for employees of the Stacia family, hospital directorate didn't have to deal with the myriad of paperwork and budget decisions faced by the Directorate of even the smallest hospitals. Here they were concerned with only one thing and that was to make sick and/or injured people well again.

In less than twenty minutes, Lila was stabilized with an IV unit of blood. Her wound was disinfected, sewn up, and bandaged. Peter's hand also sported stitches and a bandage.

The emergency room physician made sure Lila was stable with no major injuries beyond the bad cut to her face. She informed Peter a plastic surgeon would be flown in from Los Angeles as soon as the storm was over and that Lila would incur no major scarring because of her immediate treatment.

"When will she be awake?" asked Peter. "May I see her now?"

"Certainly," said the MD. "She should be awake in a matter of hours. While she lost a lot of blood and went into shock, the units of blood we will transfuse into her system should bring her out of shock within a few hours."

"Very good."

Peter was shown to a lavishly decorated hospital room that held Lila lying quietly in bed. She still received blood while she simultaneously received a glucose solution through another IV. Peter sat in a comfortable recliner placed close enough to the bed to hold Lila's hand as he waited for her to wake up. During this wait, he pondered about what Jack had told him about Papa's illness. Papa had never mentioned it to Peter. What other secrets would his visit to Montana reveal?

* * *

WEDDINGS AND
LAS VEGAS, NEVADA

On the average
115,000 weddings are performed in
Las Vegas each year.

* * *

Chapter Thirty-Four

He pulled a small black box out of the inside pocket of his uniform jacket. As he opened the box to display a one-carat diamond solitaire engagement ring, his voice noticeably shook. He nervously asked the question she had waited to hear since she was a young girl. It was a question every little girl dreams she will hear one day. This question sent thousands each year to a wedding planner and more often than not would leave many of them with thousands of dollars of debt.

He barely got the words, "Will you marry me?" to come out of his mouth. He kneeled and prayed she would accept the ring. He hadn't known her long, but in countless ways he felt he'd known her a lifetime. Then again, there were the times he felt they'd only met minutes before.

As she stood silently and timidly over his kneeling form, he suddenly affirmed he'd made a blatant mistake. He'd asked too soon. She would turn him down. He felt embarrassed and slightly angry as he looked up into the deep green pools of her eyes--eyes filled with tears.

She remained speechless, as she tasted her salty tears. She couldn't speak. Her voice was frozen by suppressed emotion. She couldn't believe what she had heard. Had he asked her to marry him? Surely, she wouldn't imagine something like that although she had imagined hearing those words at least a thousand times since they met.

His heart fell into his socks. She would say no. His face colored with shame as he looked up once again into her lovely face filled with anguish and indecision. Tears flowed down her cheeks in rivulets that slowed only microseconds to dip in and out of her slight dimples before they continued on their journey to finally drip off her chin and disappear into the dust of the driveway.

As he fixed his eyes on hers, he suddenly became almost hyperaware. He heard every breath she made--every beat her heart made. He even heard the sound her silent tears made as they fell at their feet.

She looked down at the man who had stolen her heart. He looked not quite scared to death--but almost. She realized if she refused his proposal, it would destroy his fragile ego. She could tell her open-mouthed look of amazement at his request was doing little to quell his fears. What was the right thing to do? She had only known him a few months.

Yet here he was, on bended knee--as he held an engagement ring upward in his outstretched palm. He had asked her to marry him. He had asked her to spend the rest of her life with him. He wanted her to enter into a holy union *ordained by God*. Could she and would she pledge her life to a man she barely knew?

As she closed her eyes, she felt the hot burn of her tears on her cheeks. When she opened her eyes again, she looked down at the man she loved. That concept had not occurred to her before this moment. She loved this man. If she loved him, then the only answer would be . . .

"Yes . . . Yes. YES I'LL MARRY YOU!" she screamed in elation. She did this with the utter conviction of a southern debutante totally in love with the man of her dreams.

"Yes. I'll marry you," she almost whispered it this time. "I love you Randy, and I'll marry you."

Randy felt his heart lighten. He suddenly felt as if every burden ever placed upon him had disappeared. He no longer had any problems. All problems were washed away with her tears of love and acceptance. It didn't matter his mother never loved or accepted him. He found someone who truly loved him and would never leave him no matter what he did or didn't do.

Acceptance. For the first time in his twenty-eight years, he was loved and accepted for who he was. He was respected for what he accomplished. The officers on the force accepted him as a brother officer. *The future will only get better from here on*, he thought.

When they both ceased crying, they discussed their wedding. Since Randy had been at his job for only a few months and Mandy only about a year, they would fly to Vegas and get married the upcoming weekend. "I think I can get off for a few days," Randy told his fiancé. "I haven't taken a day off since I've been on the force. Surely, I have a few vacation days built up. How about we fly down Thursday night and stay until Sunday night?"

"Yes. I can take those days off," said a triumphant Mandy.

"Find out for sure, and I'll call my captain and ask off," said Randy. "This isn't going too quick for you? Is it?"

"What? Oh, no. It's not too quick," she said as she pressed a manicured finger lightly to his lips. "I only thought about what a lucky girl I am, and what a lucky man you are." She wore a wicked smile as she spoke the last few words.

Chapter Thirty-Five

Peter felt Lila's first stirrings. She lightly squeezed his hand as she slowly came to consciousness.

"Hey baby," she murmured barely understandable. "Where am I?" she asked as she tried to smile.

"You're in the hospital."

"What happened?"

"Do you remember the snowstorm?"

"Yeah," she whispered.

"We hit a buffalo. Anyway, I think it was a buffalo."

"Am I all right? My head hurts pretty bad. It's not a dull ache but a sharp searing pain in my face, especially when I try to smile."

"That's understandable baby. Your head was injured, and you have severe lacerations on your face."

"How bad did I cut my face . . . is it bad?"

"No. The plastic surgeon has already been here, and assured me after the surgery tomorrow morning, you won't even be able to see the scars."

"Get me a mirror."

"No, baby. You don't need to see yourself now. It will only cause you to worry. You are real banged up. The left side of your face is cut and bruised. You wouldn't recognize what you saw in the mirror anyway as the right side of your face is thoroughly bandaged."

"Okay," Lila said dreamily as she drifted back off to sleep.

The next time Lila awakened was after her surgery. "Where am I?" she asked Peter.

"You're still in the hospital."

"My baby? Our baby?" she exclaimed. "Is the baby all right? Please say it is."

"The babies are fine. Doc Alvaz assured me of this only this morning."

"Babies?"

"Yes. We're having twins--a boy and a girl," Peter said proudly.

"I guess it runs in the family--First you and Eric, and now our babies. By the way, who is Doc Alvaz?"

"He's the obstetrician."

"Twins--how wonderful," she said as she once again drifted off to sleep.

Peter walked out into the hall and had started down toward the nurses' station when he saw his father-in-law and mother-in-law walk into the hallway. He walked down to Colonel Volores and Ming Toi seeing the obvious concern on their faces. At that time, their argument was forgiven and forgotten.

"She's okay," Peter said. "She's under excellent care here."

As soon as he was able, Peter had sent the jet back to Alabama to pick up them up. They had come without a second thought, as Peter had known they would. Peter could pick up the vague look of astonishment on the face of the

Colonel. It was evident he had looked at the way the hospital was being run and approved.

"This is all yours?" the Colonel asked in amazement.

"It sure is, Dad," Peter said with genuine affection.

"I'm sorry, son, that I didn't believe you were a trillionaire. How could I?"

"Believe you me--I do understand. I could hardly believe it myself until I saw this place. It's something isn't it?"

"That it is."

"Who are her doctors?"

Peter gave his father-in-law the names of the doctors who'd treated Lila and was stunned when Adam Volores actually knew them all.

"These are the finest doctors in their respective fields, Pete. Not just one of them, all of them."

"Can we see her now?" asked Ming Toi.

"Sure," Peter said. "She fell back asleep a few minutes ago. She's only been out of surgery for a couple of hours. A lot has happened to her in the last seventy-two hours." It was then Peter realized he hadn't been away from her--or had any sleep---in the last three days. He suddenly felt exhausted. The bedlam of events the last three days had worn him down. He was suddenly very sleepy.

"Are you all right, Pete?" asked the Colonel. "Yeah. I just realized I haven't slept in three days."

"You need to get some rest."

"I know. Now that you're here, maybe I will. Come on. I'll see if I can find out where exactly in this monolith we are sleeping."

He walked up to the nurses' station and asked the nurse on duty if she could call up to Jack Trail's office for him.

Peter listened as the phone rang only once. "Jack Trail's office."

"Put Jack on the phone."

"Who's calling?"

"This is Peter Stacia."

"Certainly, sir."

Jack picked up the phone. "Can I help you, Mr. Stacia?"

"My in-laws and I need to know where in this castle we will sleep."

Jack laughed slightly before he asked, "Are you down at the hospital now?"

"Yes."

"I'll send Janet Cumberland, for you. She will show your in-laws and you to your separate suite of rooms."

"Will they be close together?"

"As close as you would like them to be. We have two suites together, and we have two other suites that are on opposite sides of the big house. We also have the main Stacia living quarters."

"Put us in the two suites that are together."

"Very well, sir. Janet will be down for you shortly."

"Tell Ms . . . Ms . . . uh . . ."

"Ms. Cumberland. Ms. Janet Cumberland."

"Tell Ms. Cumberland we will be in Lila's hospital room. She may come get us there."

"Yes, sir," said Jack as Peter hung up the phone.

Peter and his in-laws walked back down the hall and into Lila's room. She wasn't awake, as they had expected. The Colonel picked up the chart on the end of the bed and occupied his time until an extremely attractive brunette with violet eyes breezed into the room.

"Mr. Stacia, Dr., and Mrs. Volores. I am Janet Cumberland. If you will follow me, I will take you to your suites." Peter looked up into a beautiful set of violet eyes. He immediately recognized her as the woman who had handed him a tissue at Papa's memorial service. She saw the recognition and winked as her luscious lips turned up in a half-smile. Peter kissed Lila lightly on the cheek and squeezed her hand as he got out of the recliner to follow the exquisite Ms. Cumberland.

Janet Cumberland led the group out to a large Lincoln Navigator limousine. Peter watched with obvious admiration as she held open the door for the Colonel and Mrs. Volores and then motioned to him to follow his in-laws. Once Peter was seated, she slid in and sat by him. Her closeness made him simultaneously uncomfortable and comfortable. As soon as she shut the door, the driver of the limo shifted into drive and pulled out of the entrance of the hospital. The driver made several turns and soon they were coming up out of the parking garage and out into the brilliant sunshine of a gorgeous Montana afternoon. Peter looked around and saw the storm had dumped two feet of snow on the grounds. Even so, the paved parking lots and roads were scraped and salted. His workers here sure knew how to deal with snowstorms. They simply waited them out and then cleaned up after them.

As Ms. Cumberland showed Peter and his in-laws to their rooms, Peter found it hard to take his eyes off her. Janet Cumberland was the first woman he'd even been mildly attracted to since he'd first met Lila. Even though Janet appeared not to show it, he knew she was attracted to him, also. After a lingering but firm handshake that sent a surprising tingle up Peter's arm, he escorted Janet Cumberland back to the door. Their eyes met and she blushed as she turned and walked down the hall. Peter stood outside his suite compelled to watch her until she was out of sight.

Peter closed the door to his suite suddenly much too tired to marvel at his luxurious surroundings. If anything, he was too tired to even see his surroundings. He found the bathroom, quickly undressed, and washed away several days' worth of acquired grime. The hot–almost too hot–water massaged his bone-weary body. Peter stood in the almost boiling water for at least ten minutes before got out of the shower. He dried off with a towel made from the finest Egyptian cotton, combed his hair, walked into the bedroom, and collapsed on the bed, not bothering to cover his naked body. As soon as his head hit the pillow, he was sound asleep.

* * *

LAS VEGAS, NEVADA

In 1931, Nevada legalized casino gambling and reduced residency requirements for divorce to six weeks. This ended up being a pivotal year for the city of Las Vegas.

* * *

Chapter Thirty-Six

They stepped off the plane at the Vegas Airport. It had been a quick decision to get married. It did, however, seem like the right choice. They hadn't had time to plan this wedding and had decided they would not marry in Franklin County. If they married in Franklin County, it would have to be an extravagant affair in which anyone not invited would be mad for the rest of their life. It would have almost certainly made headlines in all the local papers. While Lori understood her past was in the past, Eric wasn't so sure her past could actually be erased by one simple phone call. They had decided they would fly out here and get the deed done, free from the media circus that would surely follow an official getting married in a small county. Franklin County didn't have a lot to talk about most of the time. After the child prostitution ring arrests, Eric's face was in the paper almost daily. The people couldn't believe Eric had the DA, Chief of Police, one of the judges, and the former Sheriff all in the county jail. This maelstrom caused by these arrests would undoubtedly follow him into his private life if he would allow it. So they had decided they wouldn't tell anyone about their decision to get married until it was over.

As they waited for the luggage carousel to come around with their luggage, Eric kissed his wife-to-be. Her lips were soft, pliant, and responded to his gentle caress. While they kissed, Eric and Lori each watched out of the corner of one eye for their luggage to come around.

When it did come around, they each picked up their bag, rather Eric picked up Lori's bags, and Lori picked up Eric's only bag. Eric had brought nine changes of clothes since they were going to stay nine days. Those changes fit neatly in only one bag. Lori on the other hand, in typical womanly fashion, had enough clothes for a month's stay. She had covered every possible scenario when she packed. She had clothes for every occasion--from their wedding to the coronation of any head of state that might happen to appear and invite them. When he picked her up, Eric was justifiably shocked by the amount of luggage piled on her front porch. He thought it a great joke until she turned to commence to carry them out to his truck. He'd heard Peter talk of this from time to time, but he thought his friend was joshing. He hadn't understood it was really so. Lori had insisted they take the bags--*every last one*. It seemed she had packed something of importance in every bag--along with about ten thousand items of lesser importance. She didn't have one bag she could leave; therefore, all her bags found their way to Las Vegas. As Eric walked behind Lori across the airport, he knew he looked like a prospector's donkey. He definitely felt like one.

"Do you need me to carry one of those bags, baby?" purred Lori.

Eric grinned. "No, I've got them," he said as he puffed along under the enormous load.

"Why didn't you put them on one of the luggage carriers?" she asked.

"One of the what?" Eric asked as he looked totally puzzled. Even though Eric was twenty-eight years old, he had never been on an airplane until the trip from Memphis to Vegas. He believed the luggage carriers belonged to someone. He didn't know they were there for the use of any passenger, so he stayed silent. *Better to be thought a fool and remain silent than open your mouth and remove all doubt*, he thought.

Lori looked at her husband-to-be in anticipation of his answer. She saw him shrug his shoulders under the load of her bags. At this, she inwardly smiled. He hadn't known about the luggage carriers, but he had wanted to please her. Oh, how she loved this man.

They checked into their hotel room and were assigned a room that overlooked the strip. Eric had indeed sprung big time for this room. She didn't even dare ask how much this suite cost her fiancé. They had one of the finest views of the "City of Lights." She knew he couldn't afford it, but she could. With the real estate transactions she had completed for Peter the last few months, she had managed to put away a very nice sum into the bank. Since Peter had given her a Mercedes, she had sold the Explorer. In Citizen's Bank, she had accumulated an amount most people in Alabama couldn't earn in their lifetime. After they were married, she would get Eric's credit card bill and pay it before Eric ever saw it.

When Eric finished hanging up all Lori's clothes bags, he turned to Lori. "Do you want to get married today or tomorrow?"

Lori turned from the window where she admired the magnificent view of the city. She bounced across the room to one of the garment bags Eric had hung on a rod. She unzipped it to reveal a stunning silk designer gown. While it was not the traditional wedding dress, it was stunning. She hung it next to the door and unzipped another pocket in the garment bag. It contained a pair of white hose and a matching pair of shoes.

He hadn't known she'd packed a dress. With her back to him, she shimmied out of her jeans and blouse and stood only in her bra, panties, and pink socks. She removed these items still standing with her back to him. Now she was fully nude. Her saintly form mesmerized Eric as she started to dress. She put on the white hose first. She still had not said a word since Eric's question. She then unzipped the back of the dress, gently removed it from the hanger, and stepped into it. After she had arranged herself in the dress, she walked back across the room. Eric looked at her. The dress did amazing things for her body. Her body was already perfect in his eyes, but the dress lifted her breasts provocatively and caused them to appear even larger than they already were. In the center of her cleavage was a large open heart shape. The dress squeezed her breasts together making her cleavage look as deep as the Grand Canyon, only much more enticing.

"Zip me up?" she asked as she turned around to reveal the dress zipper dropped to the cleavage of her beautiful backside. Eric grasped her slim waist, pulled her body close to his, and gently kissed her on the right side of her neck slightly below her ear.

Lori stiffened. She wanted him to continue, but . . . "No–not now. We have something to get out of the way first. Zip me up. Get dressed while I do my hair and makeup."

Dressed? "I didn't bring a suit," he said somewhat embarrassed for this brain cramp.

"Eric! You didn't bring a suit? You didn't bring a suit? You knew you were here to get married, and you didn't bring anything to get married in?" she pouted with a disappointed look that clouded her eyes. "Please tell me you're kidding."

"No. It never even crossed my mind. I don't know what I thought," he said in his most apologetic voice. "I'm sorry, baby. I was so excited when you agreed to marry me. I . . . Well, I . . . Guess I never thought," he trailed off sheepishly.

She pretended to be angry, but she couldn't quite pull it off. She walked back across the suite to another bag. She unzipped it to reveal a tuxedo Eric had never before seen. It was made of silk that perfectly matched her dress. She removed the obviously expensive suit along with a snow-white silk shirt, black bow tie, and matching cummerbund. From the bottom of the bag, she unzipped a pocket to reveal a pair of men's socks and a gleaming pair of black shoes.

"How do you know it will fit?"

"Because it is tailored to fit."

"Tailored to fit me?" he asked, "I didn't go to a tailor to be measured."

"No. You didn't. I didn't want to ask you, so I carried your good suit--you know the one you wear to court--to a tailor. He took all measurements from it."

"The jacket of that suit is a little tight in the chest."

"I know," Lori said understandingly. "I noticed that, so I had the tailor add an inch to the shoulders and chest of the jacket. The pants were simple to take care of. He measured them and made these just like the pants from your good suit. Everything should fit perfectly."

He looked at her in awe. When had she the time to get all this done?

"Put it on while I do my face. Everything should be fine."

Eric looked down at himself. "I need to take a shower before I put on that," he said. He knew if he tried to put on the solid white tuxedo before he took a shower, it would be black before he got to the front desk of the hotel. He picked up his bag and darted into the bathroom of the suite before she could give him any argument. He shaved and got a quick shower.

Lori sat at the dressing table with her makeup bag. She expertly applied her makeup quickly and efficiently. She hadn't worn makeup for the flight out. This made making up her face go a little slower, so Eric had plenty of time to get his shower.

When he walked out of the shower, Lori had applied the finished touches to her makeup. He slipped on a pair of underwear and dressed in the tuxedo. By the time he sat on the edge of the bed to pull on his socks, Lori's makeup was complete. She started to comb out her long blonde hair. When she had it combed out, she pulled it over her right shoulder, tied it with a simple ribbon about three-fourths of the way down, and flipped it back over her shoulder.

Eric pulled on his jacket as she turned from the mirror. Her whole persona radiated sexuality while being tastefully demure at the same time. The effect was stunning--she was stunning.

"Ready, baby?" asked Lori.

Eric was speechless. He couldn't believe this woman, this angel, was prepared to marry him. This woman, this vision of perfection, was willing to marry him--a simple law enforcement official. She could have anyone she wanted.

She saw the love in his eyes. He looked at her in a way no one ever had. She wasn't an object to him but a person--a person he truly loved. His open-faced admiration and love poured out of his every pore. He almost glowed with it. Finally, she had her *Mr. Right*.

Eric called down to the front desk. The concierge assured him upon check-in there would be a limo available to transport them to a wedding chapel of their choosing. He even said he could recommend a chapel. The concierge again on the phone assured him the limo was available.

They walked out of the suite. Arm in arm they looked very elegant. They looked as if they were going exactly where they were--to get married. Eric liked the way Lori left her hair down. He thought the way most brides put their hair up in some type of severe bun looked too businesslike. The way she wore her hair, while simple, really showed off one of her most attractive features. As they stood in front of the mirrored elevator doors, Eric pushed the down button and they waited for the express elevator to begin its descent of more than seventy floors. "Do you have any idea where or in which wedding chapel we're getting married?" Eric asked.

"The limo driver or the concierge can tell of a place that is suitable. I want a place that is appropriately elegant."

"In other words, you don't want to be married by a midget Elvis?"

She laughed as she replied, "No, I didn't want a church wedding in Russellville, but I do want it to look like a wedding. I want pictures, too."

After a short limo ride, they walked arm in arm into a small wedding chapel highly recommended by the concierge. As they were shown into an office, Lori noticed a wedding already in progress. She stood and looked at the backs of a couple turned slightly, facing one another.

"*Do you, Amanda Green, take this man to be your lawfully . . .*" she heard as she walked into the office behind her husband-to-be.

She wondered about the couple getting married. Who were they? Where were they from? How long had they known one another? As she wondered these things, she wished them well in her mind. She hoped they would be as deliriously happy in their marriage as she knew she and Eric would be.

"Come on in, Mister?"

"Sandusky," Eric said, "Eric Sandusky."

Not thirty feet away Randy Marlowe's blood ran cold as he heard a voice from his past. He had to get out of here, NOW.

"*And do you Randall Marlowe take this woman . . .*"

What was Eric Sandusky doing here? Had he somehow found out about his alias? Had he tracked them here through credit card transactions? He, of course, had to use the card for the plane tickets and the hotel room. He hadn't paid for the wedding with the credit card. He had the cash on him to pay for it. Did they have his alias? Were they doing real-time tracking on his credit cards? I have to get out of here. If I bolt now, Mandy will think it very strange.

"Baby, you okay?" whispered Mandy.

"What? Oh . . ."

"Answer him."

"Who?"

He suddenly remembered where he was, "Yeah, I do," he said.

"Then by the laws vested in me by the State of Nevada, I now pronounce you man and wife. You may kiss the bride."

Randy bent down and kissed his beautiful brunette wife. When they were done with their kiss, the man who married them handed them a signed copy of their marriage certificate. Immediately, Randy began to look for an exit. The only exit was beyond the office door and was the one Eric had come in through.

They walked back up the aisle as they held hands. Randy pulled his new wife along slightly past the door where he knew Eric was seated. When Eric found he was there, he knew Eric would take him down.

They walked out into the brilliant warm sunshine of a Nevada afternoon. The limo was gone.

"Where's the limousine?" Mandy asked.

"I–uh–well--I don't know."

"I'm going back in to call the hotel. They'll send it back. I'm sure they will," promised Mandy.

"Let's take a taxi," said Randy as he stepped out to flag down a passing cab that had its available light on.

Randy helped his new wife into the cab and sat down as he closed the door. As he turned to look at the small wedding chapel, he--through the glass door of the chapel--saw Lori Cochran looking out the door at him. He turned his head away from the woman and hoped she didn't recognize him. That's why the Sheriff was here. *He was marrying the dope whore.* Eric was marrying an ex-con. How fitting the great Sheriff of Franklin County had hooked up with her. When he was Alan, he had looked all her information up before he bought the house down on Cedar Creek in Belgreen. He knew she went to prison and served five years on accessory charges. He'd even read the case file. He couldn't believe Sheriff Eric Sandusky, Mr. Perfect, was mixed up with a little tramp like that. *He's not any better than I am,* thought Randy. *Look what he's going to marry.*

Randy's thoughts were interrupted as he saw Lori look once again out the glass at him.

Who was the man who stared back at her? She felt a flash of recognition. She knew him--but from where? She had watched him as he got into the cab. He moved in a familiar way, and he looked familiar. The familiarism faded rapidly when a nice young man tapped her on the shoulder.

The photographer introduced himself as Charlie.

"Miss Cochran, you wait here. Start down the aisle when the music starts."

When the wedding was over and they were Mr. and Mrs. Eric Sandusky, they sat through almost two hours of photographs. When the photography session was over, the photographer informed Lori if she gave him an address, he would send out a set of proofs for her to pick her favorites for her wedding album. By ordering the pictures of the wedding from the on-site photographer, the chapel would also provide a DVD of the wedding.

They walked past a row of slot machines as they entered their hotel lobby. Eric had never been a gambler, but today he felt lucky. Above the machines was a screen with a number flashing--*Almost eleven million dollars*. Eric saw they were quarter machines. He reached into his pocket as he stood at the last machine in the row. He pulled out his pocket change. There were three quarters and an assortment of dimes, nickels, and pennies. He dropped the three quarters into the slot machine. He pushed the button to play all three quarters and pulled the handle. The first dial from the left stopped on a red seven, the second stopped on a white seven. The final wheel slowed and stopped on a blue seven. *Three sevens*, he thought, that has to be good. I only wish they had been all the same color. Suddenly a siren went off. The noise seemed to come from everywhere. Lights flashed atop the machines.

Eric looked around for the screaming siren. Was someone trying to rob the place? Suddenly an army of casino employees surrounded him. He looked up at the screen above the bank of machines. The number above the bank of slot machines had stopped. It no longer was a steadily growing number. Now, the number was flashing. He couldn't have. Eric looked at the number-- $10,984,731.24. That was almost $11 million. Eric looked at Lori. She looked as stunned as he felt. *Eleven million dollars?*

"Sir? I am Xeno Canniphilous. Please press the cash out button, get the receipt, and come this way. We will get you paid."

Eric stood there and looked at the machine. He couldn't believe it. *Eleven million dollars? ELEVEN MILLION DOLLARS!* He looked down at the machine and found the button marked cash out. He pushed it and waited as the machine made clicking sounds. It then whirred as a printer printed somewhere inside the machine. The slot spit out a slip of paper that looked like a cash register tape. On the tape was the number that had flashed on the screen. Eric looked up at the screen. It was no longer flashing the amount of money he had won. Instead, it must have started over. It now had $100,000. The cents amount was rolling up.

$100,001 . . . $100,001.01 . . . $100,001.23.

"Come this way Mister?"

"Sandusky."

"This way, Mr. Sandusky." Xeno led Eric and Lori down a corridor and to an elevator. He inserted a card into a slot where the buttons should be, the doors to the elevator slid open, and they walked in. When they stepped out of the elevator, Eric saw they were in a large office with one wall of solid glass that looked out over the main casino floor. There were several important looking people in the room. One of them held a large cardboard check with the amount Eric had won. It was filled out in its entirety except for Eric's name.

"I need your driver's license and social security card," a casino employee commanded.

Eric got out his billfold and quickly removed his driver's license. He had to go through several things before he could come up with his social security card. He handed the folded, barely recognizable card to the employee. Eric was lead to a table where a man with horn-rimmed glasses filled out some official looking documents with an official government look. The man looked at the license and asked, "Is this your correct address?"

"Yes."

The man wrote on the form and filled in every blank. While he did this, a calligrapher filled in Eric's name on the huge cardboard check. A fascinated Eric watched the artist. While his handwriting was readable, he had always thought this way of writing was beautiful. He heard the man's pen scratching as he filled out forms behind him.

"Mr. Sandusky? If you would sign here, we'll get the checks cut, take your photograph, and let you be on your way. We have a safe available for the checks, if you wish, or we can hold them in the casino bank until you are ready for them. We also can wire the money to any bank in the world. If you wish, we can hold the money for you indefinitely. Our bank pays one of the top rates of return of any bank in the country. It's your choice."

Eric signed the papers. They seemed to be some kind of Federal withholding forms. Then he looked at another paper. The amount on that paper was only slightly over $7 million. He thought he had won $11 million. "I thought I won almost $11 million," Eric said as he held the paper.

"You did," Xeno said. "The federal government requires we hold out 36 percent to pay your federal income taxes. Be careful with your money, Mr. Sandusky. You will handle the taxes in your home state, and you could be responsible for more federal taxes than the amount we hold out."

"I see. I think I would like it if you held the money in your bank until I figure out what to do with it. I need to contact my financial advisor for a few suggestions."

"Certainly," Xeno said. "We will hold the money for you until you ask for it. You have a line of credit in our casino equal to the amount you have on deposit."

"Is there any way I can access this money outside the casino?"

Xeno had an answer for this. "We will give you a checkbook and debit card. The checkbook and debit card will be available in the morning. If you need money, present your driver's license at any money cage in the casino. They are authorized to give out any amount of money less than $10,000. Do you need any money now?"

"Baby?" Eric looked over at Lori, who had been ignored for the last few minutes. "Do we need any cash?"

"I don't think so. Besides, I don't want to carry around a large amount of cash, do you?"

"Not really. Mr. Canniphilous, we have enough pocket money for now. If you give me contact information on the bank, I will instruct them later."

"My assistant will go over all pertinent information with you."

Eric stood for the photo with the huge check and left with a new briefcase full of papers. As he walked back toward the elevator, he looked out over the casino floor.

Suddenly Eric saw him. He saw Alan Chipenski walking across the casino floor with a striking brunette. It had to be him. He moved like Alan and looked like Alan. He was dressed casually with short blonde hair.

"Lori? Is that who I think it is?" he asked pointing to Alan down on the casino floor.

Lori looked down and didn't see anyone she recognized. She followed her husband's finger, but couldn't quite figure out whom he pointed to. She didn't see anyone she recognized.

"That's Alan Chipenski."

"Who?"

"Alan Chipenski?"

Eric was suddenly on the run. He ran to the elevator. When he got there, he cursed. There was no button for him to push--only the slot for the card. "Mr. Canniphilous get this elevator door open."

"Is there a problem?"

"You have a murderer on your casino floor. Get the Las Vegas Police Department on the phone. There is an outstanding warrant for his arrest in Alabama for murder as well as several federal warrants. I don't want to let him get away."

Suddenly Eric knew his vacation was over. His honeymoon was over. The officer of the law had taken over, His wedding was forgotten about. Eric ran out of the elevator doors and out to the casino floor. He scanned the floor. He looked everywhere. Alan had vanished.

Forty-five minutes later, Mr. and Mrs. Randall Marlowe boarded a plane and settled comfortably into the large seats in first class. Twenty minutes after that, the jet lifted off for Billings.

Chapter Thirty-Seven

He had felt the ministrations of his wife before he was fully awake. He felt his maleness lubricated by a sure and succulent mouth. He didn't bother opening his eyes as he recognized the mouth of his lover. When he was sufficiently lubricated, she gracefully slid up and lowered herself on him. He felt her gasp as he thrust upward. She moved side-to-side grinding her pelvis against him. He kept his eyes closed as he dreamily enjoyed every second. The pressure was almost unbearable as it continued to build.

Lila moaned. *That's funny*, thought Peter, her *moans sound like little girl gasps, not the full throaty moans Lila usually makes.* As Peter continued to approach his climax, he put that thought from his mind. "Oh baby, that's right. Oh yes. Oh yes," Lila said as Peter felt the first hot gush spray into her and run down to further lubricate his stiffness. The feeling was so magnificent he found it difficult to catch his breath. He continued to thrust as Lila screamed. He screamed. Lila screamed again. Then they both screamed together.

Peter's eyes flew open. As they came into focus, he saw a stranger with violet eyes writhing in either pain or ecstasy. This small-breasted brunette was definitely not Lila. He had to be dreaming. He decided to close his eyes and finish this dream. Even though sex with Lila was always great, this was by far the most intense experience he'd ever had. Peter lay panting with his eyes still closed. If he opened them, he knew the dream would be over.

Petite hands caressed his face and ran tenderly through his hair. He ran his fingers up and down the slim body of this mystery woman. Flashes of Janet Cumberland crisscrossed through his mind like lightning on a warm summer night. He brushed her lips with his as she whimpered. He was overwhelmed with passion and astonished to be aroused so quickly after what he knew to be the best climax he'd ever had.

This time, he would be the aggressor. He pushed her hands back over her head and entered her. She arched her back and rose up to press her tender lips against his. He stroked her hot breasts as she began to whimper. He was out of control like a downhill train with no brakes. Almost unbearable sensations pulsated through him. How could this dream woman bring him to this point of passion again? As her succulent lips once again pressed against his, he erupted with a fervor he didn't know was within him. He felt almost possessed. He did not want this to end. He thrust as she screamed again. He screamed and thrust until he was hoarse and could no longer move. The demons finally left him as he rolled away from the equally satisfied, Janet Cumberland. Without opening his eyes, he fell back asleep.

Three nights in a row, he had the same, almost identical dream. He continued to keep his eyes tightly shut, but not so tight as to occasionally sneak a glimpse of violet eyes brimming with passion. Peter refused to wake up in the middle of such passion.

Chapter Thirty-Eight

As Randy filled out an accident report, the fax machine rang and buzzed as another fax machine next to it tried to connect. When the connection was established, it rolled out a series of papers. He glanced up and saw the insignia of the FBI on the cover sheet.

He stood and walked around to the fax machine. He was a little surprised to see his name--Alan Chipenski--rather his old name--on the top cover sheet. He looked around. The department was busy, and no one looked his way. He stood at the machine as if he were waiting to send a fax while the machine spewed out several pieces of paper. The second one it sent was a perfect photo of him and his new wife, Mandy.

How had they gotten that picture? It looked as if it were taken from some overhead camera. Maybe it was a surveillance camera in one of the casinos. How would they know to send it here? How did they know to send it to Billings? He got his answer quickly. They had sent the photos and charges to every police department on the west coast and the western states. He glanced around when the fax on the other end hung up. There was no one watching him so he picked up the photos and accompanying paperwork and put them with the other papers he was holding. If anyone from the Billings Police Department got these, they wouldn't get them from these machines.

As he sat in his patrol car that afternoon, he looked at the papers that had been faxed from the Las Vegas Police Department machine. They gave a detailed description of him, along with a detailed description of Mandy. They didn't have any fingerprints on any of the sheets, but they did have the alias Gerald Randall. They had nothing, nothing except a picture no one here could connect with him if they didn't see them. There was a possibility they couldn't connect them, or rather wouldn't connect them if they did see them. While, there was no doubt it was him in the picture, who would ever think a felon on the run would think to hide out in a police department? Still, he didn't need anyone raising any doubt at this time.

* * *

Good night, good night!
Parting is such sweet sorrow.
That I shall say good night till it be morrow.

~~~William Shakespeare, Romeo and Juliet

* * *

Chapter Thirty-Nine

To say Janet Cumberland was confused was an understatement. For the second time in less than a year, Peter had made an enemy. First Sean Michaels-- and now Janet Cumberland.

Peter had let her stay after their third night of passion. The other two nights he had gently picked her up, carried her to the door, and opened it for her to leave. Last night, however, she had slept in his strong arms and awakened several times to see him smiling at her. Even though she had instigated their first sexual encounter, Peter had been an enthusiastic and affectionate lover. He had been the first man with enough stamina to satisfy her, and she sensed he felt the same.

At dawn, they made love yet again. The only difference was this time it wasn't in the dark. After over an hour of satisfying each other's every want and need, they both lay still and looked up at the mural of hand-painted angels on the ceiling. Then suddenly, Peter turned and looked at her as if it were the first time he'd seen her. With one quick swipe, he threw her to the floor and asked who she was. She jumped up thinking it was a new game and responded she was whoever he wanted her to be. To her astonishment, he had actually snarled and asked what she was doing in his private quarters. He even accused her of raping him.

She opened her arms and walked toward him ready to play whatever character he wanted her to play. Instead, he glared down at her naked body with disdain and delivered an emotional speech about how she couldn't take him any time she wanted and how he was a happily married man. He coldly advised her to leave immediately or he'd have security remove her.

Peter left Janet standing dumbfounded in the middle of the bedroom as he entered the bathroom to take a shower. She beat on the door and pleaded for him to explain why he had changed so drastically. He opened the door barely enough for her to see his glaring eyes. He'd threatened to get rid of her if she mentioned to anyone what had just happened.

Just happened? Just happened? What's his problem, she thought as she stormed out of the suite of rooms slamming the door as hard as she could. *He acted like he was some kind of saint. He acted like I'd made a mistake--acted like he didn't enjoy every second of the last three nights.* As an enraged, naked Janet Cumberland sauntered down the hallway past the other suite, she was too preoccupied to see a startled Ming Toi standing in the doorway.

As Peter showered, he deliberated about the Janet Cumberland situation. Even though he had enjoyed every moment with that woman, he had been raped and he wouldn't let it happen again. This time, he had literally thrown her from his suite. He would not give up his comfortable life with Lila for a relationship he hadn't even started. None of this was his fault. He hadn't asked that woman to force herself into his bed. She took it upon herself. He hadn't really even known who she was. In the last vestiges of a good night's sleep, he assumed it was the ministrations of his wife. *That little tramp.* She had come to his room three nights in a row when he was sound asleep, and he had been obliged to participate. He knew he had to do something before she did. Peter finished his shower and walked back into the bedroom of the suite. He picked up the phone to call Jack Trail. He would make sure he never had to see Janet again. He looked down at the phone and realized he didn't know how to reach Jack. He pushed the zero button and waited. "You've reached Colstrip's corporate offices. How may I direct your call?"

"Jack Trail."

"Whom may I say is calling?"

"Peter Stacia."

"If you will please hold, I'm certain he will momentarily accept your call."

"You're not the only one that's certain of that," Peter barked. "If he's not on the phone in about twenty seconds, I assure you that both you and Mr. Trail will find yourselves demoted to a new position not nearly as prestigious as the one you're in now."

After only a few seconds of listening to a Mozart Opera, he heard the gravelly voice of the CEO. "What can I do for you today, Peter?"

"We need to talk. I have business that needs to be taken care of immediately."

"Certainly."

"Where is your office?"

"North wing--seventh floor."

"How do I get there?"

"I'll send the driver."

"Excellent. Don't send that assistant of yours."

"Why? Is something wrong with her?"

"She will need to be in your office when I get there. No. Have her wait outside your office. I need to first talk to you privately."

"Yes, sir. The driver is on his way."

"Thanks, Jack," said Peter as he hung the phone up.

As Jack hung the phone up in his office, he wondered what in God's name Janet had done to incur the wrath of this man. He wasn't a man you wanted angry at you.

Peter put on his one suit. It was a dark gray wool suit cut to fit his form, and it did so nicely. With a cream shirt and Crimson Tide red tie, he looked very proper while he retained the proper mix of masculinity. As he finished tying the knot in his tie, there came a knock at the door. Peter opened the door to see the driver.

"Come this way to the car, sir."

"Do we have to take the car? Can't we walk over to Jack's office? We don't have to go outside, do we?"

"No sir, we don't have to go outside, but it is quite a walk."

"Good, then let's walk."

As Peter followed the driver, he was surprised the driver went a different direction than Peter had ever been. They went through a succession of narrow hallways that Peter had not been through before. They passed through a reception area Peter didn't recognize. "Driver, I didn't get your name."

"It's James."

"James, have I ever been in this area before?"

"No sir, we came in through the south entrance."

Peter gasped as they walked past a door with a jeweled inlay laid out much the same as the box he had seen in New York. Peter opened his briefcase that contained his Papa's Holy Bible. He took out the keys and found the one with the purple stone opened the door. As the door creaked open, Peter told James to come back in a few minutes. James left after he embellished he had never seen anyone go through that door in all his thirty years of living in the complex.

Peter walked into a room at least as big as a football field with a domed crystalline glass roof set at least one hundred feet above the main floor giving it natural light. Peter stared up in wonder at the ceiling as he started down another long wide passageway lined with paintings and photographs. On the right were the Presidents of the United States, beginning with the President that adorned the dollar bill and ending with the current president. On the left, was a group of portraits of people Peter didn't recognize. All were in some type of military uniform. The first portrait was of a man listed as Michael Romanov--funny that last name rang a bell. Where had Peter heard it before? There were two sets of dates below the portraits. Below Michael's portrait, there were the dates 1596-1645 and then 1613-1645.

Peter wondered about the significance of the dates. Then he looked over at the right side of the hallway and saw that the president's pictures had two dates under them. Looking at President Lincoln Peter saw that the former president's portrait had the dates 1809-1865 and 1861-1865.

Realization suddenly dawned on him. These were world leaders. On the right were the leaders of the United States. On the left were? With the name Romanov, they had to be the Czars of Russia, didn't they? That's if he remembered his world history correctly. Why were there pictures of the Czars of Russia on the left?

As Peter continued to look at the pictures of Russian Royalty, he saw a picture he greatly resembled. It was of Peter the Great. He even had the same birthmark on his right cheek. No wonder his grandmother had told him it was like the one Peter the Great had.

As Peter passed a daguerreotype of a man identified as Nicholas I, Peter paused and looked at the oldest photograph he had ever had the privilege to see. Then he walked on down to look at a photograph of the last Czar of Russia–Nicholas II. Here was a picture depicting the Czar, his wife Alexandra, and their five children–the four Duchesses and the young Prince. The photo was familiar, it was a larger version of the one he'd found inside the box in New York.

Then Peter saw lighter areas on the walls that used to be covered by portraits. Where were those portraits and who were they portraits of?

Peter pondered. All his life he had believed his grandfather had been a poor Scottish peasant that immigrated to America to have the possibility of a better life. After his grandfather's death, he had found out that was not the case. His grandfather had come to America with over $100 million in gold. Could it have been plundered from the Russian coffers? On the other hand, could it have been that some of the Romanov children had survived and had lived their lives in the United States and had shared their wealth with Papa? Could Papa or Gramma Joanna have been one of those Romanov children? Their ages matched the ages of the youngest two, Anastasia and Alexei.

Anastasia? *Joanna Stacia?*

Papa had always called her Anna, never Joanna. *Anna Stacia?* Anastasia?

Was it possible Papa had married Anastasia Romanov and they had taken on a name that resembled her name? That would explain the ability for Papa to have accumulated trillions of dollars. The Romanov Dynasty had been in power in Russia for hundreds of years accumulating wealth. It was definitely possible to accumulate trillions if you had started out with hundreds of millions of dollars and invested wisely.

Look at how much Bill Gates and Sam Walton had collected in only twenty years when they had started out with nothing. What if they had started out with hundreds of millions? Was it possible Anastasia had somehow escaped to the United States with hundreds of millions of dollars in gold and other treasures? This palace, after all, had been in the Romanov family since the 1700s.

For the first time, Peter noticed all the artifacts and jewels that lined each side of the hallway. Many of the artifacts had the two-headed eagle on them. He went further down and saw several rooms filled with more jewels and then he saw the room with the gold. He did not know how much was there, but he did notice much of it had a marking that was probably the Romanov emblem. This was too mind boggling for Peter to handle. He had to get out of there before he suffocated.

Peter ran back up the hall and let himself out breathing heavily. As he locked the door back, he saw James walk back up.

"Are you all right, sir?" asked a concerned James, who noticed Peter seemed a bit disoriented.

"Yes, I'm fine," lied Peter. "I'm still a little worried about my wife. That's all."

"Anything in there?"

"There's nothing in there but a bunch of old clothes and other worthless junk," lied Peter for the second time in less than one minute.

"At least the door looks nice," said the driver, "All those jewels and all. I've always wondered if they're real."

As Peter walked behind James, he wondered why Papa had lied to him about being from Scotland. Why would a man he had never known to lie about anything, cover up something that important?

Suddenly he remembered one of his conversations with Jackie. She had said--
People worldwide deal with the Stacia family with respect, simply because of who you are. The most powerful people trust your family because of what your family represents. Things haven't really changed that much in the last three hundred years.

Had that meant people in power knew something that Peter hadn't known? Did they trust the Stacias because they were royalty? Had they been royalty? If his Gramma had been royalty and was the only heir to survive the massacre, would *that* make him royalty? Was he actually a prince, like his grandparents, had called him all these years? *It had only been a pet name. Hadn't it?* He was going to look for some answers as soon as he handled this Janet Cumberland situation.

"Adam, I'm telling you, I know what I saw," argued Ming Toi. "Are you going to take his side when Lila finds out? What are you going to say? '*It's simply in his nature. It's okay. All men do it.*'"

"I know Peter too well, and he's not the type."

"What is the type exactly? Let's see. It couldn't possibly be a highly motivated, business executive that craves power more than anything else, or a goal-oriented trillionaire who inherited an enormous sum of money and a castle? How could that not be the profile?"

"I don't care what his profile is. He's simply too loving. He heaps affection on Lila. They have an almost perfect marriage. He wouldn't mess that up."

"You didn't even speak to him for two months, and now you're defending him."

"This is entirely different. Adulterers hide things from their partners. They have unexplained periods. They generally won't meet your eyes when asked a direct question. Peter does none of this stuff."

"Maybe he thinks that now would be the time to get rid of a half-breed wife and a mixed set of twins."

"Ming Toi! You don't believe that any more than I do."

"Don't I? I know what I saw. I saw that Cumberland woman come out of his quarters early this morning--nude--with sex still running down her legs. What would make you believe it, Adam? Seeing what I saw? Would you have to actually see him in the act?"

"Ming Toi, you know things aren't always that simple," said Adam Volores, exasperated. "Everything isn't black and white. There are many shades of gray. I believe you saw what you say you did. I also believe you don't have all of the facts."

"If he had intercourse with that woman, he's an adulterer. What other facts do I need?"

"I guess what we need to do is wait, watch, and see what happens," he said as he let the irritation he felt finally show in his voice.

"Do we tell Lila?"

"At this juncture, I would say the answer is no. We don't actually know if anything happened. If something did happen, we don't know the details."

Peter finally walked into the reception area and headed for Jack's office. It was a vast and well-appointed room that commanded a beautiful view of the estate via two solid glass walls facing the south and east respectively. As Peter walked by the receptionist, he noticed Janet Cumberland sitting in a plush armchair directly across from Jack's door. She smiled at him with mixed emotions on her face. Peter tried not to look at her but was unsuccessful. He felt an unusual stirring as he peeled his gaze from her and tried to stay focused. He would not let this beautiful creature with those violet eyes ruin him and what God's purpose for him would be. Peter opened Jack's door without speaking and walked into the most commanding office he had ever been in. Jack sat behind an immense desk made from mahogany and polished to an almost mirror finish on the parts of the desk that Peter could see. It was almost entirely covered with paperwork, which testified Jack was indeed earning his money.

Jack's office was the mirror image of the reception area where the outline of the Rocky Mountains was visible as well as gently rolling hills. Peter knew the Rocky Mountains were several hundred miles to the west. The view to the north was of the grounds of the estate. Right beyond the fenced estate, lay a large lake impossibly blue against the snow-covered rolling hills. It stretched almost as far as Peter could see. Peter would have enjoyed the gorgeous setting more if he hadn't been on a mission.

"What's up?" asked Jack.

Peter told the story of how he was awakened last night leaving out the two previous encounters.

Jack listened patiently. He, unlike Peter, didn't find the facts as maddening.

When Peter finished the story, Jack looked across his desk at his new boss. "You're upset about this?" he asked with a look of incredulity on his tired time-lined face.

Peter stared across the desk, a loss for words, as Jack continued. "You'd better get all you can while everything still works. There will come a time when you won't be able to get a woman like Janet into bed with you for any amount of money, and if she did--it wouldn't matter anyway."

Peter understood exactly what Jack said, but he was married. He was happily married. He did not need anything extra. Lila provided him with all the sexual satisfaction he needed. She satisfied him like no other could. He'd had his chances since they married. Although he'd had some stunning women offer to grace his bed, he had never taken any of them up on their offer--nor had he wanted to. Peter sat in silence for a moment as he looked out at the distant mountains. His red-hot anger at Janet Cumberland had cooled slightly. She probably was trying to please a new boss. He was an unknown. He was a boss she didn't know. She probably assumed it was in Peter's nature--but she should have asked him first. It was in so many influential people's nature to cheat on their spouses, but it wasn't in his. She probably hadn't meant any harm.

As long as Lila or her parents didn't find out about his and Janet's relationship, he really didn't want any harm to come to Janet. He would be able to tell if Lila's parents suspected anything when he saw them later on today. He simply didn't want her around where she could cause him any problems.

"I want her out of here," said Peter. "Move her to some out of the way place where I will never see her or hear from her ever again. Do we have a place like that?"

"We are opening another luxury hotel in Vera Cruz."

"Mexico?"

"Yeah."

"I said I want her in a place I will never see her again. I want her someplace I don't have any desire or reason to visit. Is there a place like maybe . . . I don't know . . . Maybe Siberia?"

"We have a large lumber mill in Sault Ste. Marie, Michigan that would welcome her talents."

"Where exactly is that?"

"The upper peninsula of Michigan."

"Is it security controlled?

"Yes."

"That sounds perfect. Send her to Sault Ste. Marie. Handle it Jack. That's what I pay you for. If I ever come in contact with her again, I will not hesitate to dispose of her."

Peter pivoted and exited Jack's office. As he walked from the office, Peter felt Janet staring holes in his back. She would soon be in a place he would never go. No one would ever know about their steamy encounters. He would never visit Sault Ste. Marie.

When Peter had left the floor, Jack called Janet Cumberland into his office. He calmly told her of Peter's plans to have her banished to Sault Ste. Marie.

"I am not going there," exclaimed Janet. "I am not going to be shuttled off to some forgotten part of the world."

"Janet, you have no idea how much power this man has. Peter is probably worth almost a trillion dollars--several hundred billion in the least. I work for him, and I'm worth nearly a billion."

"I don't care how much money and power this man has. I am not going to be sent off to some backwater logging camp like a rebellious child. I like it here and here's where I'll continue to live."

"Janet," he said, "I don't think it's negotiable. That's where you are going. It will only be for a couple of years. Then this will be forgotten, and I'll bring you back here."

"This is the only place I have ever lived or worked. I don't want to go to Michigan."

This wasn't going as well as Jack had hoped it would. He knew it wasn't going to be easy. She was making it hard, but he did have a job to do. "The boss said Michigan, Sault Ste. Marie. That's where you're going. No more objections, young lady."

"Daddy. I'll not be a prisoner, and I'll not go to Sault Ste. Marie. Do whatever you must, but I am not going there."

Damn, thought Jack. *She's as hard headed as her mother.*

"Janet, you are going to Michigan. If not, he said he would *dispose* of you."

"What does that mean?"

"You know what that means. You have seen people disappear from here that never were heard of again."

Janet made a sour look with her face and began to cry. She knew this would sway her father. He, like most men, couldn't stand to see a woman he loved break into tears. She had manipulated him for years. She had studied psychology in college and used all of her electives to explore a subject most of her business major friends concluded was useless. She, however, understood if she knew how people thought, she could get them to do whatever she wanted them to do. It was even better if you could make them believe it was their idea.

"Pop, isn't there any other place I could go that's a little more exciting than Michigan? What about the new hotel in Vera Cruz?"

"That has already been discussed. He strictly forbids me to send you there or anywhere else he might ever consider going."

"What about the *Duchess Tatiana?* She should be ready to sail out of St. Petersburg sometime this month. I rather think I would enjoy the cruise from Russia to Tokyo. I may not enjoy it forever, but it would get me out of your hair for a few years until all of this cools down. Russia is about as far away as I can possibly get."

Jack eyed his daughter dubiously. He knew she manipulated him. She always did, just like her mother did before her death two years ago. Like all daughters did, she held a special place in her father's heart. He really couldn't deny her anything, no matter what the boss said. *The Duchess Tatiana* was as out of the way as he was ever likely to find, and as long as he kept her away from Peter, he would never know she wasn't in Michigan.

Peter walked into Lila's room. Peter's in-laws sat at her side. He looked at his mother-in-law. She had an uncharacteristic sour expression as her eyes met his. He knew then she had seen Janet leave his room this morning. He had to act fast. He asked if she and the Colonel could come out to speak with him in the hallway. He would confide how Janet had raped him last night.

Lila's parents were as close to being his parents as any could be. He would explain the situation, and they would understand. Even though he wasn't the cause of the problem and had dealt with it as best he knew how, he would ask for their advice on whether he should tell Lila about the little problem or keep it to himself.

When Ming Toi and the Colonel walked into the hallway, he told them how Janet Cumberland had raped him. He left out what had happened on the two previous nights. He confessed like they were his priests. When he concluded, he was relieved to see the look of compassion on his mother-in-law's face. He had won her over to his side.

His father-in-law's face was harder to read. It was almost expressionless. He knew Ming Toi believed him, but wasn't sure about the Colonel.

"You didn't invite this woman into your bed?" questioned an incredulous Adam Volores.

"No. When I woke up this morning, she was on top of me, and I thought I was dreaming. Since I'd had very little sleep for almost a week, I had taken a sedative one of the doctors here had prescribed and was completely out of it. I made no advances toward her. I tried to stop, but I couldn't. Then it was too late," said Peter as he managed to conjure up one tear to slide down his face.

"See. I told you. I told you there was an explanation," the Colonel said as he looked at his wife.

"I know. I jumped to the conclusion that seemed to best fit the situation."

Peter did his best to put a puzzled look on his face. "Ming Toi saw that woman come out of your room this morning," confessed the Colonel. "She jumped to the conclusion you had cheated on Lila. I didn't believe it. I couldn't believe you would cheat on my baby girl."

"You saw her?" Peter asked Ming Toi as he feigned surprise.

"Yes," acknowledged a relieved Ming Toi. "But what happened?"

"I banished her to a small town in Michigan where she can never bother me again," stated Peter flatly as he glanced at the Colonel.

"I think you did the right thing by telling me and Ming Toi," said the Colonel. "I, however, do not believe you need to tell our daughter. She does not need to know any of this."

"I agree," Ming Toi said.

"You already answered my next question," confided Peter. "I was going to ask if you thought I should tell her. So you think I should forget about it then? Make it a part of the past?"

"That would be my suggestion. Are you traumatized by the incident?" inquired Adam Volores, who seemed a little more distant than usual.

Peter could tell by the Colonel's body language he didn't completely believe what Peter had told them, but Peter felt sure the Colonel didn't want to stir up trouble. Until the Colonel fully believed him, he would play the pretend game. He would play for as long as it took.

"I guess I am more angry than traumatized. It's hard for me to believe someone would do that kind of thing to me. I felt like I've been used," Peter decided it was time to lay it on thick to get sympathy. "I feel dirty, but I think it will pass in a few days. I never understood how a woman feels when she is raped.

Now I think I do. Even though that woman wasn't strong enough to physically force me into anything, she forced me by deception."

"You may need to see a counselor. This is something that happened you couldn't control. You need to document in case anything ever comes up. You also need to think about going down to the hospital here and being checked out for any venereal diseases."

"I don't think I need to see a counselor. I know I can handle this on my own. I have spoken to a doctor about the situation and think that I will ignore his advice that I seek additional counseling." He lied as he looked squarely into Adam Volores' questioning eyes. "I will do as you say, though, about being checked out for venereal diseases. Thank you, Colonel."

When they walked back into the room, Lila was awake. In spite of her bandages, she looked bright-eyed and bushy-tailed. Her sunny disposition had returned, and she was smiling as best she could underneath the bandages.

"How long did the doctor say it would take it to heal?" she asked her father.

"He said it would be a couple of weeks for the wound to completely heal. You did not have any significant internal or external injuries. You lost a lot of blood and were in shock when you were brought here. You are able to leave whenever you want. If you check out tomorrow, we can go on a helicopter ride to celebrate. There's a chopper outside sitting on a helipad. It looked like it would seat more than four people including the pilot."

"That sounds like a good idea," said Lila. "I would like to see the ranch and what better way than from the air?"

"Are you sure you're up to it?" asked Peter concerned she wanted to go straight from the hospital bed to a helicopter ride.

Lila and her father looked at each other.

"I'm one tough cookie," declared Lila. "If Dad thinks I can make it, I'm ready."

Lila was indeed one tough *cookie*. Peter and her parents didn't realize she already knew her way quite well around the complex, thanks to a young male nurse and an electric wheelchair. A helicopter ride would be a piece of *cake*. With all these references to food in her mind, she was getting hungry. She buzzed the nurse for a snack.

Peter, Lila, and her parents enjoyed the helicopter ride immensely. Peter hadn't known until now there could be a helicopter as nice as this one. It was even more ornate than the one he had in New York. He guessed it must be an executive helicopter--if there was such a thing. He really shouldn't have been surprised. Everything else was extravagant. Why not the chopper too?

As they walked away from the chopper, he held tight to his briefcase that held the keys from Papa's Holy Bible. He was afraid to let the briefcase leave his sight. As soon as possible, he wanted to take Lila to the room the second key had opened and share with her what he had found out about the Romanov gold.

When Lila asked him what he was thinking about, he said he was thinking about how much he loved her.

They walked back to one of the entrances to the mansion. The balmy forty-degree temperature was quite a contrast to the zero degree day of the blizzard a week ago. As they walked into the garage, Lila saw several Snow Cat snowmobiles.

"Could we?" she asked as she pointed to the machines.

"Do you think you're up to it?" asked Peter as he shook his head in amazement.

"Yes, I do. I think it would be fun," said Lila who was back to her energetic self. "Those things are fast. Even though it is only forty degrees, the wind would freeze us in only a few minutes without snowsuits. Why don't we ride or fly down to Billings tomorrow and pick up a few snowsuits? Then maybe we could fly down to Vegas for a couple of days. Maybe we could call Eric and Lori and send the plane for them. They would enjoy a short trip to Vegas. I don't think Eric has ever been anywhere--anywhere that required a plane flight, that is."

"Mom, Dad?" Peter turned to his in-laws whose mouths were wide open unable to fathom the speech they'd heard come from their daughter who'd had major surgery to her face only three days earlier. "Do you think you would enjoy a trip to Billings, a snowmobile ride, and a Las Vegas adventure?"

"What do you think, sweetheart?" said the huge doctor as he turned to Ming Toi. "Do you believe that we could get Sam Hammock to cover for us for a couple more weeks?" Sam was young doctor from Red Bay, who had been trying to buy out the Colonel and Ming Toi's interest in the Russellville Clinic for the past several months.

"I would love to stay longer and visit Billings and Las Vegas," replied Ming Toi. "I may skip the snowmobile ride, though. I prefer to be indoors."

"It's settled," said Lila. "Let's call Eric and Lori."

Eric answered his cell phone on the first ring. "Hey Pete, What's going on?"

"We were thinking of flying out to Vegas, and were . . ."

"How did you find out we were here?" came the astonished voice of Eric Sandusky.

"Find out you were where? In Vegas?"

"Yeah, Lori and I got married yesterday."

"Thanks for the invitation asshole. I seem to remember inviting you to my wedding," Peter said as he pretended to be hurt. "I seem to remember your being the best man."

"Well . . ."

"We'll fly down there. Don't you go anywhere."

"I'm not going anywhere right now, but I am not sure this would be the best time for you to come."

"Why not?" Then the realization of what Eric had said hit Peter. Eric didn't want him down there because he was on his honeymoon. "I'm sorry. I didn't mean to intrude on your and Lori's honeymoon."

"It's not that. I'm not sure if I will have time to do anything with you and Lila. This has turned into a working vacation. It would, however, probably be a good thing if you came down. At least, you could be company to Lori. I have kind of left her to fend for herself the last twenty-four hours."

"What do you mean you've left her to fend for herself? Where are you?"

"I'm at the Las Vegas Police Department. We're going over tapes right now."

"Tapes? What kind of tapes?"

"We're looking for Alan Chipenski on surveillance tapes from one of the casinos."

"Why? Do you think he's in Vegas?"

"I know he is. I saw him last night. I was within fifty feet of the SOB and couldn't get to him because of a security door."

"I bet Lori is mad. You just left her there?"

"No, I didn't just leave her there!" said Eric, who by now was getting a little irritated that Peter was treating him like a child. "I didn't leave her there. I had someone escort her to our room. I have talked to her several times today, but . . ."

"You left her there? I can't believe even you could be so insensitive as to leave your new wife on the night of your marriage," interrupted Peter. "This police work will wait. You get back to your new wife. There is nothing as important as she is right now. You get back to that hotel room and spend the next couple of days with her. If you are going to find him, you can do it after your honeymoon is over, or you can delegate the authority and send for your investigator. That's what you have him for--isn't it?"

"I guess," Eric replied as he realized Peter was right.

"You shouldn't guess, you should know. If you can't trust the people who work for you, get some you can trust. Get Jacob or Andy out there and let one of them do the job. You need to enjoy your vacation. It is the first one I have ever known of you to take."

Eric sighed. It wasn't often his friend chastised him. This time, he guessed it was well deserved. He could have a vacation. He needed a vacation. He didn't want the trail getting cold. Not after what Alan had done. He had to catch him, and this had seemed like his only chance. This was his first lead in over three months, but his friend was right. Jacob or Andy could handle it.

"All right," Eric said, "I'm on my way now. I'll have Jacob and maybe Andy take a flight out tonight if they can get one."

"Don't worry about that," Peter said, "I have a plane that's coming out here from New York I can have it swing by Muscle Shoals and pick up Jacob and Andy."

"That's too much trouble."

"All I have to do is make the call."

"At least let me pay you for the flight out."

"Certainly not. I'll take care of it. Consider it a tax-deduction for me. Alan needs to be caught before he does something like that again."

"I know."

"Get back to your wife. How long had you planned to be there?"

"Nine days total."

"Okay, Lila and I will be down there in two days. When we get there, I don't want to hear a word from Lori that you've ruined her honeymoon. If I do, I might have to whip your scrawny little ass."

Eric looked down at his muscular body and laughed. Peter was one of the few men on the planet that could call him scrawny and make it seem so.

"Okay, okay, I'm on my way out of here now. I'll call Jacob and Andy and make sure they can come."

"I'll have the plane in Muscle Shoals in about five or six hours. The pilot will call the Sheriff's office with the details."

"10-4."

"See ya in a few days, partner," Peter said as he pushed the end button on his cell phone.

* * *

Sad that our finest aspiration
Our freshest dreams and meditations,
In swift succession should decay,
Like Autumn leaves that rot away.

~~~Alexander Pushkin
Russian Poet, (1799–1837)

* * *

Chapter Forty

Lila and Peter enjoyed their visit to Las Vegas with Eric and Lori. The next month went by fast as Lila felt great and looked great. She and Peter were able to thoroughly enjoy Montana. They made several trips to Billings as well as back to New York and Las Vegas. They had decided to keep Montana as their main home until after the twins were born and Lila had sufficient time to recover.

Lila's parents enjoyed Montana so much they retired from the Clinic and sold their interest to Sam Hammock, the young doctor from Red Bay that had taken over for them when they first came out because of Lila's accident. The Colonel and Ming Toi accompanied Peter and Lila on many of their trips, and Peter and Lila encouraged them to stay as long as they wanted. It was a special time for Lila having her parents around with the time and money to enjoy them.

Peter and Lila took pleasure visiting their secret room. They called it the "treasure room." Every time they entered, they found something new and amazing. On one such adventure, they found an underground stone vault that contained hundreds of showcases of jewelry. Each showcase contained a complete matching set of earrings, bracelet, and necklace make of expensive and exquisite gems.

Another time they had found a room of swords and sabers dating back hundreds of years. Then, of course, there was the "gold" room filled with gold bullion and gold coins. Peter soon found out many of the gold coins were priceless. Undoubtedly during the early 1930s, all countries stopped the circulation of gold coins and demanded they be turned back in. Peter and Lila found sovereigns from the first production for Henry VII back in 1489 and half sovereigns made for Henry VIII in 1544. That room would be heaven for numismatics.

They had both decided to learn Russian as they had so many original Russian books and artifacts. They wanted to read Pushkin's poetry as it was written in Russian instead of translations as well as the works of hundreds of other Russian authors and poets. Every day was an exciting and hopeful day. Peter was understanding and enjoying his role of running the Stacia Empire more every day.

Peter never discussed with Lila his belief he was Russian Royalty, and Lila seemed to be happy to enjoy the wealth without questioning where it all came from. She probably theorized Papa had come by the wealth dishonestly and had decided not to embarrass him by pressing the issue. She would never imagine Gramma Joanna was probably Anastasia. He was so busy in running the Empire; it would probably be years before he would have the chance to further research what had really happened to bring his Gramma to this country.

Then came the day Peter got a telephone call from Janet Cumberland. He had not seen her nor talked to her since his meeting with Jack Trail over a month before. Each day since, he had struggled to put her and her violet eyes out of his mind. Her conversation with Peter was short and to the point. She told Peter she had urgent business to discuss with him, and she had to talk to him in person. It could not be done over the telephone. Before she hung up, she urged him to meet her at her hotel room in Billings the next day. As Peter sat in his Montana office and looked at her room number written on the folded piece of paper, he felt the same animal stirrings he'd had for her when he first met her. He also remembered the passionate nights with her he'd never been able to forget. What could be so important that she had to see him? He was torn on whether or not to go to Billings. After hours of analyzing the situation, he tore up the piece of paper and threw it in the garbage can in his office.

That night he slept little as he continued to contemplate what to do. When he got up that morning, he had made up his mind. What could it possibly hurt to visit for only a few minutes and let her say what was on her mind? He at least owed her that much after their hours of passion.

When Janet opened the door of her hotel suite, her violet eyes once again enraptured Peter. Before he had a chance to control himself, he picked her up and carried her to her bed as he passionately kissed her lips and eyes. As he undressed her, he continued until he'd kissed and enjoyed every inch of her luscious body. She did not discourage him and he was once again impassioned by the sound she made as she enjoyed his every touch. He could not have felt any hotter if he'd actually been on fire. The more he strove to please this violet-eyed woman, the greater the height of his own pleasure. After they'd both satisfied themselves and each other, she had softly and tearfully told him what she could not tell him over the telephone. She was pregnant with his child. Even though it should have been bad news, he was secretly pleased.

"What do you want me to do?" he gently asked.

"If you could give me enough money to raise the child until he or she is twenty-one, I'll not ask for anything else from you. I know you have a wife and twins on the way already. I won't do anything to jeopardize your business or your personal life," whispered Janet, "I have told no one but you about this."

"How much do you believe is acceptable," Peter tentatively asked.

"I'll leave it up to you. You can base it on whatever lifestyle you would want your child to have. There's an envelope on the table you can take with you as you leave. The envelope contains my Swiss bank account number and instructions on how to wire the money to it."

"That seems fair," Peter said as he traced the outline of her eyes and lips with his forefinger. "I'll do that."

"Will you promise me one thing?" she whimpered.

"What?"

"If anything ever happens to Lila, will you find me and give me a chance to be your wife?"

"I promise, Janet."

"Thank you, Peter."

Peter picked up his clothes and went into the bathroom. As he showered, his tears mixed with the water that hit his face from the showerhead. When he returned to the bed, Janet was asleep. As he gazed down at her beautiful face, he could see tracks her tears had left on her checks. He ached for the life he could have with her but knew would never be. He ached for the child he knew he would never hold or be able to acknowledge as his. Peter sighed as he gently removed the envelope from the nightstand and quietly left the room.

* * *

Children are the hands
By which we take hold of heaven.

~~~Henry Ward Beecher

* * *

Chapter Forty-One

She couldn't believe it. She simply could not believe what the doctor had told her. She was sterile? Not sterile. Sterilized. How could that be? She had never had an operation of any kind. Her mascara and eyeliner mixed with tears that streaked down her face and made her look like a morose clown. Tears also dropped onto her blue silk blouse ruining the expensive designer garment. How could this be possible?

"You will never have any children, Mrs. Sandusky. You've been sterilized," Dr. Dempsey had said. "You should have known this. You would have had to authorize such a procedure."

There had been no procedure. When could it have occurred? Could I have been? No. It couldn't have. Surely it wasn't . . . Yes . . . It had to be the abortion. It had to be the abortion she had been forced to undergo in prison. The wonderful prison system with all its infinite wisdom had decided it couldn't possibly let an inmate in her first year of prison become pregnant. There couldn't be any children born to prisoners who were allowed no outside contact with men. It was as simple as that. Mattie had warned her about the doctors, but she hadn't supposed they could be as sorry as to sterilize her. Why would they do that? Did they expect her to stay there forever and be their personal love toy? That's what she had been during her first six months. That's how she had become pregnant to begin with.

How was she going to tell Eric? She couldn't tell him this. Once again, the need was upon her. She needed something to help her get through this. She looked down at the piece of paper the receptionist had handed her as she walked out through the door crying. It was a prescription, Valium, 10 mg. She looked at the writing not believing what she held. It was exactly what she needed right now.

Twenty minutes later, Lori Cochran Sandusky walked out of the drugstore. *Now I have what I need,* she thought. She took the first one before she even got to her car. It didn't matter that she didn't have anything to wash it down with. She waited until she pulled into the driveway of the farm she and Eric had purchased before she swallowed the second one, this time with a soft drink that had been in her car since early that morning. Fifteen minutes later, she swallowed the third and fourth Valium with a swallow from a light beer she had gotten out of the fridge down in the basement.

An hour and a half from the time she'd taken the first Valium, Lori Sandusky was feeling good. She took another of the blue pills out of the bottle, and as she swallowed it with a sip from her fourth beer, she saw there were only five of the ten pills Doc Dempsey had prescribed still in the little brown bottle.

Lori decided she would like a swim. Thank goodness, the pool was heated year round. Even though it was the first week of December, today was one of those unusually warm winter days. It was actually seventy-two degrees. She stripped out of her clothes. She admired her body in front of her full-length mirror in the master bedroom of the house. Her breasts were full, but the rest of her figure was slim, but as she remembered what she'd found out in the doctor's office, she slumped. What good is this body if it can't bear Eric a child? What good is living? She might as well as be dead. She picked up a small statue on a table close by and slung it into the mirror scattering shrouds of glass throughout the room. One piece of the glass clipped the side of her face narrowly missing her right eye. She reached up and felt something sticky she knew must be blood. The pain felt good. It felt right to hurt on the outside. She shouldn't only hurt on the inside. This new inside pain was unbearable. Worse than the pain and embarrassment of the rapes.

She walked out to the second-floor balcony of the master suite and looked down at the pool. It was only a short jump away--Six feet out and ten feet down. *Only a short distance . . . And everything would be over. No more pain.* Lori climbed unsteadily onto the railing, swaying back and forth, clawing at the cut on her face. *Only a short distance . . . No more pain . . .* The clear, calm water beckoned to her. *ONLY A SHORT DISTANCE . . .* She screamed as she hurled herself off the balcony into the pool.

Chapter Forty-Two

Adam and Ming Toi Volores boarded the plane for Alabama. They would be back in Russellville in five hours. They had thoroughly enjoyed their time at the Montana ranch and would be back next month to be with Peter and Lila when the twins were born.

The Colonel had gotten in touch with Dr. Bill Porter, a doctor friend of his in Billings. He and Ming Toi had spent a few days with Bill and his wife, Lorraine. Dr. Bill, as everyone called him, had his pilot's license and insisted on flying Adam and Ming Toi back to Alabama.

Lorraine had never been to Alabama. The Porters would spend the weekend with Adam and Ming Toi in Russellville before going on down to Tallahassee, Florida, to spend a week with their daughter, Annabelle, who was expecting a baby within days of Lila's due date.

In five hours, they would be all be dead. They had no idea they would never get to see the grandchildren they had so anticipated. They would never be able again to hold their daughters or argue with their sons-in-law.

Adam and Ming Toi sat in their seats, buckled up. Neither was afraid to fly. They had flown hundreds of times and this time would be no different. They had faith in Doctor Bill's ability to get them safely to Alabama.

* * *

The second one's path went up and down
He stumbled, but no one mocked.
He did not fall and so they bragged
"He's solid as a rock."

* * *

Chapter Forty-Three

Eric turned off the highway and onto his driveway. It had been a terrible morning, and he had decided to take the afternoon off. He had gone to visit Officer Aaron Abagnale, who had been moved from UAB to a nursing home facility in Red Bay. It had been over four months since the accident, and Abagnale showed no hope of coming out of his coma. It was such a waste for a fine man like Aaron Abagnale to be incapacitated. As Eric made the turn to the farmhouse, he was pleased to see Lori's car. Since it was so warm, they could take a swim and relax beside the pool. He would cook tonight. He would cook Lori's favorite dinner that consisted of cubed steak with gravy, mashed potatoes, slaw, Italian green beans, deviled eggs, homemade biscuits, and sweet tea. He had finally convinced Lori her girlish figure wouldn't be harmed if she drank sweetened tea instead of unsweetened.

He smiled as he thought about Lori and how much he loved her. He couldn't wait until they had children. She was going to be a great mother.

He might even crank up some of Bon Jovi from the 80s and he and Lori would dance while he cooked. He couldn't wait to feel her body pressed against him. The thought of spending time with Lori had cheered him up.

As he drove closer to the house, something did not seem right. The driver's side door of Lori's Mercedes was wide open. Why would she leave the door open?

At that precise moment, he heard a scream followed by a loud splash. He got out of his patrol car and ran to the pool. Lori was floating face down in the middle of the pool. "Lori? Lori?" Eric screamed. She couldn't be dead. He pulled off his gun belt, hat, and shoes and dove into the pool. He pulled her out and administered mouth-to-mouth resuscitation until water sputtered from her lips.

"I don't want to live. I want to die. No more pain," she moaned almost incoherently. Eric was beside himself with panic. "What are you talking about, Lori? Lori, I need you! I need you. You can't die."

"Hold me. Hold me, Eric," sobbed Lori.

"What's wrong, Lori?" pleaded Eric as he held her tight. "Tell me, baby." By now he could tell by her eyes she was on some kind of drug. What had happened to bring her to try to kill herself? She had not even had so much as a sip of wine since she had been out of prison. What could have happened to make her slip back into the life she so hated?

"I'm so sorry, Eric," sobbed Lori. "I'm so sorry."

"It's okay, honey. Everything's going to be all right. I promise."

"Eric? Eric? I've failed you. I've failed you."

"No, you haven't. Tell me what's wrong. I promise everything will be all right if you'll tell me what happened."

"I'm worthless now, Eric. I'm worthless. You might as well put me back in the pool and hold my head under."

"No, you're not. Now come on and tell me what you need to tell me."

"I'm sterile, Eric. Dr. Dempsey said I couldn't have children. I can't give you any children, I'm worthless."

"How can you be sterile?"

"In prison they got me pregnant and then performed an abortion against my will. They must have sterilized me also. I'm so ashamed."

For at least twenty minutes, they sat on the edge of the pool and Eric held her as she wept for the children and grandchildren they would never have. Finally, Eric gently picked Lori up and cradled her in his arms as he carried her inside to take care of her. "Lori, you have nothing to be ashamed of. We'll work this out. We'll go in and call Lila and Pete. They'll help us figure out something."

Lori realized she would spend the rest of her life thanking God for sending her this sweet, compassionate man who loved her despite all her imperfections. He loved Lori Cochran Sandusky, for who she was *now* and for who she *had been*. She loved him so much it hurt. "I love you, Eric. I love you so much."

"Lori, I love you, too," said Eric as he gazed down into the eyes of the most perfect woman he would ever meet. She was the only woman who loved him for who he *had been*, for who he was *now*, and for who he *would be*. He thanked God for sending him this angel and prayed for the strength he would need to continue to protect her.

Chapter Forty-Four

The plane was lined up for the approach to Runway One at Muscle Shoals Airport. As the small plane started powering down for approach to the landing strip, something unexpected happened.

Coming down Wilson Lake in his new boat, the angler saw what appeared to be a promising cove to fish in. As he maneuvered the light powerboat into the cove, he startled ten mallard ducks that sat peacefully on the water. The ducks immediately took flight right into the path of a small plane on approach to the Muscle Shoals Airport.

"May Day. May Day. This is Doctor Bill Porter on approach. We have lost number one and number two engines. We are a dead stick tower and coming in with no power. Repeat--we are a dead stick tower."

The air traffic controller alerted the fire crews. He had a plane coming in with no engines. The air traffic controller watched in horror as the aircraft hit the runway too fast, cartwheeled, and burst into flames as it continued to roll repeatedly over and over. He would have to find out who was on that plane and tell the family. Sometimes he hated his job.

Peter listened to the man on the other end of the phone. "What happened?" he asked.

"It looks like the plane's engines each ate a duck. There was a bunch of ducks in the air."

"Okay, good, thanks for letting me know." *Now—how was he going to tell Lila this?* He called their suite where she was resting.

"Baby, we have something we need to talk about," he said. "I'll be there in a few minutes."

As Peter entered the master bedroom where Lila was lying propped up with pillows, Lila could see the look of sadness on his face and tears that slowly seeped from his eyes.

He sat down beside her, put his arm around his wife, and pulled her close.

"What is it?" she asked. "What is it?"

"It's your parents. They've . . ."

"What about my parents? What's happened?" she asked as her eyes filled with tears.

"Baby," he said as he pulled her even closer. "Thirty minutes ago, Dr. Bob's plane crashed at Muscle Shoals. There were no survivors. All of the bodies have been identified, and two of them were your parents."

"What? . . . No . . . No . . . No . . ."

"How could this have happened? What happened? No . . ." She barely got this last part out before the tears became a torrent. "NO . . . NO . . . THIS CAN'T BE HAPPENING," she wailed. "NOOOOOOOO . . . NOOOOO. This can't be," Lila broke down in sobs as her husband held her.

* * *

In this, our age of infamy
Man's choice is but to be
A tyrant, traitor, prisoner:
No other choice has he.

~~~Alexander Pushkin

* * *

PART THREE -
ALMOST TWO YEARS LATER

Chapter Forty-Five

Mandy stood and looked at the bank statement in awe. That figure couldn't be right, could it? There was almost $5 million in a Chase Manhattan account. She didn't even know this account existed. Where had Randy gotten $5 million? Why had he kept it from her?

She was still on maternity leave since the birth of their son, Alan. As she stayed home each day, she found out several things she may have been too blind to see before. In her hands, she now held records for a bank account with almost $5 million and a cell phone for which Randy had never given her the number.

As she looked back over the deposit records, she saw where there were regular deposits made to the account. Until about a year ago, the account had been almost inactive. It had carried a balance of slightly over $600,000 with the only change to the account being the interest added every three months. Then nine months ago regular deposits started to be made to the account. That almost coincided with his ascension to detective. Sometimes it was a few hundred dollars, but most of the time, it was several thousands of dollars. She looked at the figures. It didn't make sense.

Where did a detective who only made $40,000 get that kind of money? Several of the deposits on the statement were for $10,000 with many coming very close to that amount. As Mandy continued to peruse the account, she saw the name on the statement was Randy's middle name as the first and his first name as his last. Why was the social security number on the account different than Randy's? Why would Randy use Gerald Randall instead of Randall Gerald Marlowe? Why were the statements addressed to a P. O. Box in town? She didn't have any knowledge that Randy had a Post Office Box for an address. Why would he even need a P.O. Box? Why did he have a cell phone for which she didn't have the number? Something wasn't right.

Since he had been promoted to vice-squad, he'd worked an enormous amount of overtime. Mandy didn't worry about the late nights because Randy wouldn't cheat on her. Except for a few things, like forgetting to put the toilet seat down and not picking up his underwear, he was a perfect husband and father. He absolutely doted on little Alan. It was as if he never expected to have a child. Other than the birth of their son six weeks ago, nothing had really changed in the two years they had been married. They had taken several extended weekend vacations, mostly to small towns and resort areas. They had even taken a wonderful cruise on the Princess Sophie, from Seattle to Anchorage and back that lasted two weeks.

They had not returned to Vegas since their marriage. She had mentioned once she would like to go back for a few days, and he had told her rather harshly he would never be back in that town. Why? She had wondered aloud. Why would he not go back to Vegas? He had replied he wanted to keep the memory of the city on the day they got married, not some later time. Since Vegas changed daily, she had accepted that explanation. Now, however, she wondered if that was the right reason.

Was he taking trips there and gambling? If so, why didn't he tell her how lucky he'd been? Could he have won over $4 million in nine months? It was possible. No--there had to be some kind of mistake. Maybe he had some rich uncle named Gerald. Randy had never mentioned a relative of any kind, except for his Mother. At least once a week he would have some sort of nightmare where he cried and called out for his Mother. When Mandy gently touched his face, he would smile and go right back to sleep. They had never discussed the nightmares. She knew he would confide in her when the time was right for him.

She had found the bank statement by accident looking for a cleared check in the filing cabinet when the drawer fell out onto the floor and spilled its contents. When she put the contents back into the drawer, she noticed a small hole drilled in its bottom. When she held up the drawer, she immediately saw the hole didn't go all the way through. She stuck her finger in the hole and pulled up. She found documents hidden there. As she went through them, she got the feeling she shouldn't look at them. He was her husband, however, and his business was her business.

She put the documents back in the false bottom of the drawer and put the files back over the top of them. She would ask about all this when he came home. Randy would have a logical explanation for everything. Mandy knew he would.

Chapter Forty-Six

"The final vote count is in," Peter announced to the cheering group of supporters for his best friend, Sheriff Eric Sandusky.

Eric's convictions of everyone in the child prostitution and illegal drug ring had certainly boosted his reputation. He had won every case and the shortest sentence given out had been fifty years. The former district attorney would be the first up for parole, but that would not happen for at least fifteen years. The only sore spot had been their inability to capture the ringleader, Alan Chipenski. No one had heard from nor seen Alan Chipenski since Eric saw him in Las Vegas. The case had been dead for two years. The only thing they really had was the alias, Gerald Randall, and neither Alan's description nor Alan's social security number matched anyone by that name in the United States. Alan Chipenski appeared to have dropped off the face of the earth.

"Sheriff Eric Sandusky has received 9,434 votes," Peter yelled over the PA system. "His closest opponent has only 700 votes. It's another landslide victory." The crowd of well-wishers cheered and clapped as Eric took a bow. Peter gave Eric a hug as well as Lila, Lori, and others close by.

Over the last two years, things had gone extremely well financially for the Sheriff. Following advice from Peter's advisors, his $7 million casino winnings had been turned into over $70 million and Lori's $49 million earned through her real estate brokerage company turned into almost $300 million. Eric was the richest politician in Alabama, which wasn't bad for a thirty-year-old public servant and his ex-con wife.

He and Lori had been devastated when they learned Lori could not have children, but through some of Lila's connections, they had adopted an adorable son when he was only one week old and named him Michael. Michael was the light of his and Lori's life. When Michael was six months old, they also adopted a pair of twins who had been part of Alan's child prostitution ring. Their parents had never been found, and Lori and Eric couldn't bear the thought of them going in and out of institutions and foster homes as unwanted and loved children their age usually did. Their names were Jenny and Patrick, and they were now eleven.

The first few months with all of them together had been rocky, but now things were finally on track. Lori's friend, Mattie, had been released from Tutwiler and lived with them. Mattie had become a mother to them and a grandmother to Michael, Jenny, and Patrick, and they were the children and grandchildren she'd never had. Jenny and Patrick called Lori--*Mom*, Eric--*Papa*; and Mattie--*Granny*. Michael accepted them as his own brother and sister. He called them Sissy and Brubbie, and they adored him. They both thought he was the smartest little brother in the world. Eric, who as a little boy had spent so many Christmases and birthdays crying for a family, finally had a big, wonderful family of his own. Lori had gone into semi-retirement to be a full-time mom, and Eric's heart was so full of love he sometimes was afraid it would burst.

Eric thought about all of this as he prepared his acceptance speech. Through a series of trusts and corporations, no one knew of his true net worth. Not that he would hide it from anyone. He didn't believe his financial successes should be broadcast. He still drove the Ford pickup he had bought right before he met Lori. It was almost three years old now, and he hadn't seen any need to change. Lori drove the same midnight blue Mercedes Peter had given her. The only thing they had really changed financially was that they had bought up the land around his farmhouse that now amounted to over two hundred acres. It was a non-working farm with a few head of horses and a few cows, but they didn't really want any more than that.

After he gave his acceptance speech, he excused himself from the gathering of well-wishers and escaped to the Hummer with Peter. "You seem to be pretty popular. Maybe you should run for another office," Peter said.

"Like what?" asked Eric.

"The governor's race will begin in about a year."

"Governor?" Eric laughed. "Who would elect me governor? I don't have that kind of experience or a college degree. I only have a police academy diploma."

"Who said you need a college education to be governor? It's not one of the requirements."

"You are kidding. Right?"

"I am not kidding. We can get you elected. You have an excellent history here in Franklin County. You cut spending back to the bare minimum while providing even better and more streamlined services. People like you are needed in government service on the state level and maybe even the federal level later on."

"Federal level? What in the world are you talking about?"

"I spoke to one of our senators only two days ago who informed me he would not seek reelection his next time. He pledged to support whomever I thought was the best candidate. If I get you elected governor in two years, then three years later you will announce your intention to run for the Senate."

"I can't be a senator. I don't know anything about being a senator."

"Lila was on the phone with Jackie today. She assured her by the time you are elected governor, you will know how to be a senator. Lila has someone who can train you how to talk, think, and act. It is not as hard as you would believe to get someone elected senator. We have big plans for you if you are willing."

"You, Lila, and Jackie are some kind of trio! If I didn't know better, I'd think the three of you ruled the world."

You don't know how close you are to the truth, Peter thought to himself. "How about it, Eric? Are you up to the task?"

"Which do you want me to become? The next governor? Next senator?"

"Both."

"Peter, what if I don't have the ability to be a governor or senator?"

"What if you do and aren't willing to take the chance? I would trust you with my life, the life of my wife and twins. I trust your decisions. I trust your analytical ability to work out problems and come up with the best solutions. Besides, we have advisors to help you."

"You're not kidding. You're actually serious."

"Absolutely."

"You're setting me up to run for president, aren't you?"

"Who knows? It's possible."

"I know I could never get elected to that post. You have to graduate from Harvard or Yale to get there."

"What makes you think that?"

"What kind of time frame are you talking here?"

"Fifteen years. Maybe less."

"What makes you think you could get me elected to the highest office in the country?"

"How do you think our president now got there? Luck? He's there because Papa and my companies wanted him there."

"How could Papa possibly get a man elected President of the United States?"

"Where do you think all of those campaign contributions come from? Do you think that presidential candidates go to the voters for the money to run these massive campaigns? No. Someone finances them. If I want someone to be president, all I have to do is have my radio, television, and newspaper outlets give him or her good press, and, of course, lots of money. Remember, I own most of the media outlets in this country and all of the important ones. I also own a good portion of the manufacturing facilities. Money has greased many a squeaky wheel. Besides, it's not as if the money doesn't come back to me anyway."

"What is your part in all this? What exactly do you want from me?"

"I stay in the shadows. I will never tell you what to do. That is your decision, but I want you to listen to my suggestions and the suggestions of my advisors from time to time. I will want certain bills passed, and certain legislative actions enacted. In the end, though, it will be your decision," encouraged Peter.

"It's something to think about. There's no doubt about that. So far, you have never steered me wrong on anything. I also appreciate how you financed and ran my campaign. Thanks--even if I could have done it on my own."

"You're welcome. So--You'll think about it?"

"Of course. How could I not think about it? It's a very lucrative offer. I would have the chance to change things in this country for the better."

"Not only for this country but for the whole world. Hopefully, for the better for all of us," Peter said smiling inwardly. "We will need to know your decision in the next few days. If it is positive, we will get major media outlets up here to begin statewide coverage for you. Once you are governor, we will have the national media help you out. It really doesn't matter what you do as long as it looks good in the papers. Good press coverage helps that. Remember, we have the ability to have you interviewed by Barbara Walters and Larry King. I can make you look like the smartest person in the world. Just think about it. Okay?"

* * *

Author John Steinbeck had admiration and respect for other states, but he had true love for Montana. He was quick to also point out how difficult it was to analyze love when you're in it.

* * *

Chapter Forty-Seven

"Hey, baby," Mandy said as her husband came through the door. It still seemed out of place to see him without the uniform. Even after a year, she expected her husband to come home wearing the blue. Now he usually wore a gray suit. He didn't wear the badge out on his chest anymore. It stayed clipped to his belt instead.

"How's the most beautiful woman in Montana?" Randy asked as he kissed her on the cheek. "Where's little Alan?"

Mandy had never understood why he had insisted on calling their son Alan. He had been adamant about it. She had picked out the name Peter Erickson Marlowe. Peter was her grandfather's name and Erickson was her mother's maiden name. When her husband had heard that, he had actually blanched. He eyed her suspiciously and told her there would never be one of his kids with the name Peter or Eric. Therefore, in the name of peace, they had named him Alan Shane Marlowe. Randy had been inflexible about his son's name. Now that they had him, it seemed to her like her husband was right. Alan was a good name. It appeared to fit the boy perfectly.

Randy went to little Alan. He looked down at his son who smiled up at his father with bright blue eyes. He was a beautiful baby. He wasn't like all of the others Randy had seen all of his life. This baby--his baby--was the most precious kid in the world. Before his child had been born, he had never understood what all the uproar was about. He couldn't understand how someone could love something that only ate, cried, pooped, and threw up. Now he knew. This was/would be the most loved baby in the world.

"Come on Randy. Supper is on the table." Randy looked over at the dinner table almost surprised to find steaming bowls of food. How did she know when he would be home? He didn't realize that supper had been ready for nearly two hours. Mandy had placed the dishes in the oven to stay warm. She had only removed them when she saw her husband's lights turn off the highway and down their long drive.

Randy sat at the table and filled his plate. They ate fried potatoes, turnip greens, pinto beans, ham steaks, cornbread, and banana pudding. "Mandy, you're going to kill me with all of this food," Randy said between gulps of sweet tea. He looked down at his midsection. For the first time, he was beginning to get a little pouch in the middle. He had always been trim. With his comfortable job and good food provided by his wife, his indulgences showed.

She laughed and said, "I'm trying to fatten you up some. You were too thin when I met you."

While he ate, she got the baby out of the crib and held him to her breast. As little Alan nursed, she sang softly. Randy stared in wonder. His life had changed so much in the last few years. Randy thought about all of the decisions he had made in his life. The best decision he'd made was to marry this woman. She was beautiful, sweet, and just dumb enough for him to carry on his extracurricular businesses and affairs right under her nose. She thought she was the only woman he was having sex with. She had been stupid enough to believe he had been celibate for her when she was too sick during the pregnancy to have sex and for these six weeks after little Alan was born. He had just come from an afternoon delight at Kim's house.

After more than two years, Mandy still didn't know a thing about the affairs or the money. He had finally worked himself around to the vice squad. After taking the Sergeant's exam, he'd had his choice of assignments. He chose the one in which he could make the most money. Not legal money, mind you, the other kind. After not even a year on the vice-squad, he already had more than forty high-class call girls working for him. He got half of the money they brought in. He also protected a man running a child pornography ring. That business was lucrative beyond their wildest dreams. Not only could they sell the pornography, they could prostitute the children and blackmail the participants on the prostitution side. Nine kids aged seven to twelve were bringing in almost $250,000 a month. His take on that was 75 percent. He was also back into the drug business in a big way. This time, he didn't buy most of the drugs. Because of his contacts, he pressured the movers and shakers to pay to protect themselves from a raid. Overall, he should do almost $4 million every year. Not bad for a high-school dropout. His Mom would be proud.

Randy finished his supper, sat down on the couch, and quickly spotted the remote control to the television. He looked at his watch. It was almost nine o'clock. He picked up the remote and turned on the TV.

Mandy put little Alan back in the crib and sat beside her husband. She kissed him. "I went to the doctor for my six weeks check up today, and he gave me the go ahead."

"I don't feel like it tonight," said Randy. He knew he had experienced only hours ago what she offered him now.

"I feel like it," she said slightly hurt. "I think I can make you feel like it. It's been over two months since we've . . ."

"I said I don't feel like it tonight," interrupted Randy. When he saw tears in her eyes, his tone softened as he said, "Baby, I—well--I guess I can."

Randy led Mandy back to the bedroom and started to remove their clothes. When they were finished and lying in each other's arms, Mandy softly said, "Randy?"

"What?" he murmured sleepily.

"I have a question for you."

"What?" he asked annoyed. He was almost asleep and was not in a mood for mindless chitchat.

"Today I was cleaning in the study. I found a bank statement that showed a balance of over $4 million. What's that about?"

Randy was immediately awake. He sprung up and glared at Mandy. "Why did you go through my stuff? That's my stuff. You stay out of it."

"I . . . Uh . . . I didn't mean . . ."

"I said you stay out of my stuff! Do you understand?"

Mandy couldn't figure out why he was yelling.

"Do you think you will get some of that money? What other things of mine have you gone through?"

"I haven't been . . ."

Randy slapped her with everything he had. Her lip split against one of her teeth.

"Randy . . . I didn't . . ."

"You little whore. You think you can go meddling in business that isn't yours? Huh. Answer me. I said, answer me."

"No. Randy, I didn't mean to . . ."

Randy grabbed her by the hair, pulled her off the floor, and hit her again. This time, it was with his closed fist. "Don't you ever go through my stuff," he yelled. "Do you understand me?"

"Yeah. Baby. I . . ."

Randy hit her again. It felt so good. He enjoyed it. It had been years since he had been able to do something like this. He had forgotten what a rush it was. He hit her repeatedly.

Mandy couldn't understand what was happening. *Why was Randy so mad?*

"I guess you think you know everything about me. Don't you? Do you think you know me? Answer me, bitch."

"Nooo," she wailed, "I . . ."

Randy hit her repeatedly. The sight of her swollen face increased his pleasure. He'd show this little whore what it meant to mess with him. She was exactly like his mother, always criticizing him and meddling in his business. Once again, he heard her voice ridiculing him and comparing him to the other boys who were better behaved. Comparing him to Eric and Peter. The louder her voice was in his head, the harder he hit Mandy.

"Please don't hit me again," Mandy begged through split lips. Her left eye had swollen together. She could barely see through it now, and she saw no possibility he would stop.

Randy suddenly realized that he was more aroused than he had been in three years. He was more aroused than he had been since he'd killed that black whore in Alabama. He couldn't kill this one, but he could break her. Randy forced her to her feet and threw her onto the bed. She begged him not to hurt her as he raped her. She was a bleeding, crying little whore like his mother.

When he had finished, she said coldly, "You better hope you enjoyed that, you son-of-a-bitch. It'll be the last time you ever touch me."

"Oh really," Randy said sarcastically, "Is that what you think? I'll take you whenever I wish. You're another whore like the rest of them."

"If you ever touch me again, I'll kill you."

"Think so?" Randy asked. This wasn't the first time he had heard this threat.

Randy walked back out into the living room. He returned with his service automatic. He handed her the pistol. "Go ahead. Shoot me. Pull the trigger."

She pointed the pistol at him as her hand shook. She prayed for the nerve to pull the trigger.

Randy grabbed the gun from her shaking hand. "That's what I thought. I didn't believe you had the balls to pull the trigger on me. Don't think you'll get any help from anyone, either. I'll kill you and your bastard child if you do. Do you understand? I'll kill you both and bury you in the backyard. It will be years before anyone misses you. If anyone asks, I'll tell them you moved off somewhere else and took the child with you because he wasn't mine."

"I will leave you. I will take little Alan and leave you," she blubbered. "First thing in the morning I will file for divorce and leave you."

Randy beat her until she was unconscious. *Leave him?* She would never leave him. He would make sure of that. He got up and walked out into the garage. Her Honda Civic was parked in the garage. He opened the hood and jerked off all the wires to the distributor. Then he went to the telephone box and jerked all of the wires out of it. First thing tomorrow morning he would cancel the phone service at the house. She wouldn't be able to go anywhere or call anyone. If necessary, he would fix up a room she couldn't get out of while he was at work. He really needed her to take care of his son. The threat against the child was only a threat. He would never hurt the little boy. He loved him too much.

He walked down to the basement. The basement in this house was almost another house. The wonderful thing about it was it had no windows a person could crawl through. There were two bedrooms, a bathroom, and a kitchen down here. This would be the perfect place for him to keep Mandy. There was no reason for Mandy to ever leave. *His Mom had left him, but Mandy never would.*

There were only two exits from the basement. The one to the outside had a deadbolt on a heavy steel door. The deadbolt was keyed on both sides, and Randy would keep the only key. The other door exited up into the kitchen.

While Mandy was unconscious, Randy handcuffed her to the bed and drove the fifteen miles back into town. He went down to Colstrip and bought three more deadbolts keyed on both sides. He also purchased a week's worth of groceries. The refrigerator downstairs did work, but the only things they'd ever kept in it were a few bottles of beer and a box of wine. If he kept her down there, she and the baby would need groceries. This was perfect. He had allowed her too much freedom, anyway. Because she had snooped around and learned about the money, she didn't warrant any freedom. She would learn to be happy down there. She could clean it up and fix it up like she wanted.

Chapter Forty-Eight

"What did he say?" Lila asked Peter. "Will he run in a few years?"

"He said he would think about it."

"Do you believe that we can control him? He has always been rather independent."

"I think we can. Eric trusts us, and he trusts our decisions. He still believes this country is a democracy. In one sense, I guess it is. We do hold elections, but our people, one way or the other, control both sides. By the time they are in offices at the federal level, most realize this and quit fighting it."

"Will we ever tell him about the gold in Montana?"

"Probably not. Why does Eric need to know? It's enough that we know."

"You're going to continue to keep all the money from your brother and use him to achieve your own agenda?"

"Papa didn't leave him the money, he left it to me. I don't see any reason to cloud things now. I am the oldest, after all, and Primo Genitor laws would apply. He doesn't know, and I don't see how it could possibly help things. Especially if he ever finds out we knew and didn't tell him. He's well enough off since our casino allowed him to win that big payout in Vegas. Our advisors turned that money and the brokerage fees we paid Lori into almost a half billion dollars."

"I understand now why Papa picked this area as a control center. No one could imagine it could be possible to run the entire world from a place in rural Alabama. It's so far removed from the hub of things, and recent advances in telecommunications make it possible to run things from anywhere."

"Does Eric have what it takes to be president?"

"I don't know right now. He is smart enough. Where Eric is as solid as a rock, our current president is as dumb as a rock. Obviously, one of his ancestors jumped into the gene pool when the lifeguard wasn't looking. If it weren't for our advisors telling him every move to make, he couldn't tie his own shoes. In fact, he doesn't tie his own shoes. He even has someone do that for him. He does, however, look statesmanlike."

"Is there anything else Congress is working on now?"

"There is one other thing. They are in the process of drafting an amendment to the constitution that will repeal the second amendment. It is going to be one of the least popular amendments ever."

"There's one thing that really bothers me."

"What's that?"

"After all this time Eric hasn't caught Alan. There seems like there would be a way to catch him."

"We'll put him on America's Most Wanted."

* * *

Freedom is not worth having if it does not include the freedom to make mistakes.

~~~Mahatma Gandhi

* * *

Chapter Forty-Nine

She thought about her mistakes. She hadn't thought she'd made any until she'd found that bank statement. Now she couldn't believe the mistake she had made. Here she was locked in the basement of what used to be a happy home with a nine-week-old baby. She also believed she was pregnant again.

She couldn't believe things could go so wrong so fast. She couldn't believe she had misjudged Randy so badly. Hadn't he been in the Army? Hadn't his job always been to protect and defend? First as a soldier and now as an officer? She still didn't know after three weeks exactly what she had done wrong. She had to do something to get out of here.

The baby was asleep. She walked around the basement again. She was looking for any sign of weakness. So far, she hadn't found one. The door to the outside was a heavy steel door. Randy had installed two deadbolts on it. Since it opened to the outside, he had also installed a crossbar on the outside of the door. Trying to get out that door was useless. She looked at the door that connected the basement to the kitchen. It wouldn't do any good to try it either. She had tried that all day long one day about two weeks ago.

Had she been here that long? Yes. She had. It had taken her a week to get over the injuries of the beating. When she awoke the morning after, she was in a strange place. It really wasn't a strange place. It was one of the basement bedrooms. No matter how hard she had tried the two doors, neither would even budge. There had to be another way. She didn't want her child to grow up in this dungeon. There was no telling how long he would keep her here. So far, he hadn't shown any sign he would let her out.

The only time he even came down here was to get the baby--or when he wanted sex. Sex now wasn't what it had been only three weeks earlier. Now they didn't make love, he raped her. She could almost deal with that. She did still love him, and she had hoped things would get better--but they hadn't. She knew women had been used this way for hundreds, even thousands of years, but it wasn't supposed to happen to her, not in America. Why had he changed toward her? What had she done to him? She didn't want the money. She wanted it to go back to the way it was. However, she didn't think it would ever be possible.

She continued to search the basement again for an escape route. She looked at the windows set high in the basement walls. She could get to them, but they weren't large enough for her to crawl through. There had to be a way out of the basement.

After searching the basement again, and again, she gave up and sat on the edge of the bed to watch television. She surfed through the channels until she found a program called America's Most Wanted. The lead story was set in Russellville, Alabama. She watched with interest as they described a man that had run a successful drug and child prostitution ring. He escaped without detection after killing a black prostitute in 2000. He'd only been seen one time since then and it had been in Las Vegas in October of 2000.

When they showed the last picture of this man, she stared in horror. It was Randy. The last picture of him they showed was a picture of Randy and--it's me, she thought as she stared at the TV. The last picture they had of him was obviously from a security camera. It showed Randy and her walking past a bank of slot machines. "This man may be using the alias, Gerald Randall." She listened as they gave the man's name--Alan Shane Chipenski. Alan Shane? Was that why he had been so adamant about little Alan's name?

"If you have any information about this man, the Franklin County Sheriff's Department would like to hear from you," the announcer said before giving out the number. She wrote down the number, as well as the name of the Sheriff, Eric Sandusky.

Now all she had to do was get out of here. She walked around the basement again. Then she saw something she hadn't really noticed before. On the right side of the furnace was a new brick wall. Why was there a new brick wall right there close to the furnace? She stepped into the opening beside the furnace. It was about two feet deep. She walked around to the left side of the furnace and saw it was more than six feet to the back wall of the basement. There was a difference of almost four feet. Was there any significance to that? She looked at the wall. It seemed to have been a recent addition to the area. The bricks here were newer than any of the others in the area. Why did that seem to matter? She measured again. Yes. There was four feet of difference.

She went back to the kitchen area of the basement where she had hidden a claw hammer behind the refrigerator. She looked at her watch. It was almost 7 P.M. He would be home in less than two hours. She decided she would wait until tomorrow morning to see about this wall. She didn't want him to walk in on her as she escaped. There had to be something behind that wall that could help.

It was 7 A.M., and she had heard Randy start his pickup and drive off. Now she would see about that wall. She went behind the fridge and got her claw hammer. She also had a screwdriver hidden in the bottom of the cabinet beside the fridge. She took her tools over to the wall and began to remove the mortar from around one of the bricks. It was a tough job, but after several minutes, she had the first brick removed. When she pulled the brick out of its hole, she felt a slight breeze blow from the hole. She put her eye to the hole, but all she could see was blackness. It couldn't be any worse than here, she concluded, as she removed the second brick.

By 9 A.M., she had a hole big enough for her to crawl through. She went back to the kitchen. On the top of the refrigerator was a flashlight. She picked it up and hurried back to the wall beside the furnace. She shone the light into the area behind the wall. She could see a small room.

She crawled through the hole into an area black with coal dust. This must be where they stored coal years ago before the furnace had been changed over to a natural gas furnace. If there was coal here at one time, then there had to be a way to get it down here. There had to be a coal chute. She shone the light up around the ceiling. About six feet up was an opening large enough for her to climb through.

Could it be? Should she get her hopes up? She wasn't tall enough to get through the hole from the ground. While she could reach the lip of the hole, she didn't have the upper body strength to pull herself up. She continued to shine the light around the floor. In one corner of the small room was an old Coca-Cola crate. She pulled it over and stood it on its end. When she stood on the Coke crate, she was barely tall enough to bend over at the waist and pull herself into the chute. She hoped there weren't any creatures in there. She wiggled up through the chute while shining the light out in front of her as she crawled until she came to a small door. She pushed against the door, but it seemed jammed against something. It wouldn't open. *So much for that idea.*

As she started to slide back down the chute, she saw the latch for the door. She quickly shinnied back up the chute and forced up the catch while she pushed the door outward. There still seemed to be something against the door. She pushed with all of her might and the door opened a crack. When she saw daylight for the first time in more than three weeks, she pushed even harder. There was something on the door--dirt. The door had been covered over with dirt. She pushed and pushed, with the door giving away an inch at a time until it finally flung open. She climbed out into the chill of the morning air. She was thankful there was no snow on the ground. This was October, and it could snow any day. She pushed the door closed and with best of her ability, covered the door back up with the dirt and sod. She didn't want Randy to know she was out yet.

She had a few things to take care of before she let him know she had escaped. It might take several hours, possibly even a full day.

She went to the front door and removed a key from behind the light fixture. She opened the door and then placed the key back above the light fixture. She walked into the living room and was surprised to find all the keys hung by the door where they always were. She took what looked to be a new set of keys and went into the kitchen. She tried the keys in the door and was pleased when the deadbolt turned effortlessly. She went down into the basement, stripped off her filthy clothes, and threw them in the washer.

When she was once again dressed, she went to her baby and got him dressed for a trip. She went into the office and removed the paperwork for all accounts in the name of Gerald Randall from the filing cabinet. She sat and studied the papers. She found the account numbers and a signature card. She had been signing Randy's papers for two years. After only an hour or so of trying, she could mimic the signature on the signature card. She looked through everything and found the account balances could be moved to another bank via a code phrase and a release number. She picked up the papers and went to the phone.

When she picked up the phone, she was again pleasantly surprised. There was a dial tone. Randy had lied when he told her the phone service had been removed from the house. She called the number listed on the paperwork. When she had a person on the phone, she gave the account number. The person on the other end of the phone asked for the code phrase. When she had given it to him, he asked, "And how may I be of assistance today?"

She gave him the account number of her checking account. After he assured her the entire balance had been transferred, she asked for a confirmation number and was given one. She then called her bank and asked if they had received a wire from Chase Manhattan in the last few minutes. The bank manager assured her that they had indeed received a wire from Chase Manhattan. She asked when the funds would be available.

"They are available now."

"Very good. I would like to transfer all of the funds, except for five thousand dollars to a savings account at Killen National Bank."

"Could you give me the city and state please, along with the routing number?" She had been expecting this so she pulled out her savings passbook that was from the first bank account she had ever had. Until now, it had kept a balance required to maintain the account. Twenty-five dollars. Finally, she called the Killen National Bank. After a few minutes, the Vice-President told her that the wire had indeed come through. She was out of here! Let the bastard come looking for her!

Chapter Fifty

Eric was ecstatic when he called Peter. "I need a plane," he said breathlessly. "Is your jet at Muscle Shoals?"

"Yeah. What do you need it for?"

"I'm going to arrest Alan."

"Where? Did you get a call from the TV show?"

"It's better than that. I got a call directly from an officer in Montana. He said he went to the academy with this guy. Claims his name is Randall Marlowe, who is a detective sergeant with the Billings Montana Police Department."

"He's a cop?"

"Yeah. He's a detective with vice. Can you believe that? Someone like him in the vice squad?"

"Meet me in my office in twenty minutes. I'll have the pilots warm up the plane. It will be ready to fly when we get to Muscle Shoals."

"No! You're not going," Eric said.

"What makes you think that?" Peter said.

"I can't let a civilian go on a trip like this. Chipenski is an extremely dangerous felon, and he's on the run. More importantly, Lila would have my head. Besides, you can't go. You know it's official government business."

"If I don't go, neither does my plane. If you try to get a commercial flight out there, I'll call the airlines and make sure no plane flies within three hundred miles of Billings for the next seventy-two hours."

"You wouldn't?"

"I would."

"I'll deputize you on the way to Montana."

"I am going to be a Deputy now? Do I get a badge?"

"I'll bring one on my way."

"What about a gun. Do I get one of those?"

"Yes, you can have a gun too," Eric said with a nervous laugh. "We will meet the FBI in Billings."

"I'll call ahead and have them waiting," said Peter.

Five hours later, Sheriff Eric Sandusky and newly sworn in Deputy Peter Stacia stood in the Billings office of the FBI. As they gave the information to the Special Agent in charge of the Billings office, the man stood shocked.

"I know this guy. He's a damn fine officer."

"He may be a damn fine officer," interrupted Eric. "He's also a damn fine murderer, kidnapper, child molester, drug pusher, blackmailer, liar, and a hundred other things. He's damn fine at everything he attempts."

"This is too hard for me to believe," said the SAC as he pulled up the file on Alan Chipenski. He compared photos to the driver's license photo of Randall Marlowe. "We do a thorough background check for the Billings Police Department any time they hire new officers."

He held Randall Marlowe's file. He had personally reviewed the candidate. "I checked out all his references." He showed Eric a file almost half of an inch thick. "He was an Army NCO with top commendations along with a letter of recommendation from Army Chief of Staff, David Maxwell."

"Recommendations or not, this is our man. I think DNA evidence will make that clear."

"Very well. Let's go down to the Billings Police Department."

The FBI agent walked into the Billings Police Department followed by Eric and Peter. They talked a minute with Randy's captain, showed him the evidence, and asked if he would call Randy in. Peter sat down in the back of the room out of sight from anyone who walked into the captain's office. Eric sat with his back to the door where Alan wouldn't see his face until after the captain called him by name.

Twenty minutes later, they heard a knock at the door. Sheriff Sandusky watched as the captain held up his hand motioning Randy to come in. As Randy came in, the Captain said, "Have a seat, Alan." Alan walked around the chair and sat down. "Alan, this man here has some fascinating allegations about you. He seems to think you are Alan Chipenski, not Randall Marlowe." Until the last words came out of the mouth of the captain, Alan had been unaware the captain had called him Alan, not Randall or Randy. He turned to look at his accuser, confident, whoever he or she was; he could convince everyone he was Randy Marlowe--not Alan Chipenski. Who he saw was not merely any accuser. It was Eric Sandusky.

Alan jumped up, pulled his pistol out of the holster, and pointed it at Eric Sandusky. The captain wasn't armed. He never was. Right now, the danger in this room was the Sheriff. As he backed the hammer and prepared to shoot Sheriff Eric Sandusky, he never heard the soft, catlike footsteps behind him. He backed the hammer and started to pull the trigger on a man that so far had never moved--who only smiled up at him. Then his head exploded. He felt the blow as he went down. The last thing he felt was a size fourteen shoe step on his wrist and kick his pistol away.

"Have you ever seen anyone hit that hard?" said Eric as he looked at the captain.

"I didn't believe you when you said your Deputy could take him down with one blow. I know he's big, but that was some kind of punch," the captain said, thankful he wasn't on the receiving end of the blow.

"I've been waiting to do that for years," said Peter. "Ever since he called my wife a *nigger whore*. When I found out about the kids, it made it even worse. All my life I knew he had mental problems. I didn't know how messed up he was until he murdered that poor girl. I'm a father, Captain. Do you understand how it feels to get to hit someone that has seriously injured a child? Let me tell you--it feels good--damn good."

"The honor is yours," said Eric as he handed Peter a pair of handcuffs. Peter reached down, pulled Alan's hands behind his back, and clamped the bracelets on, not quite tight enough to cut off circulation. The captain called two patrol officers off the squad room floor. "Carry this man down to a holding cell, strip him out of those clothes, and find him a jumpsuit. Book him under the name Alan Chipenski. He is a felon on the run. The State of Alabama has already filed extradition papers. I expect Montana to approve them in the morning. He is going home to stand trial for capital murder among other things. Get this monster out of here."

* * *

The third one's path went straight downhill
He stumbled and then he fell.
He could not pick himself back up
And he was bound for Hell.

* * *

Chapter Fifty-One

"What do you mean you can't use the audio tape?" Sheriff Eric Sandusky asked.

"It's a copy. I need the original. This version has been edited for content. I need the entire taped conversation before the murder," said prosecutor, Keith Collier.

"I can't get you that." Eric didn't understand what difference it made.

"Then I need to interview his wife. What's her name?" Collier asked as he checked through his notes. "Amanda Marlowe? Was Marlowe the name he was using?"

"Yes. Randall Marlowe. Concerning his wife--neither you nor I can interview her."

"Why not? Is she going to take the spouse's privilege?" asked Collier. "She will testify, won't she?"

"No."

"Is it because she can't fly here? If it is, you can fly up to Billings, interview, and fly back."

"You know that's a lovely idea. I wish I had thought of that. It would even be a great idea if she were in Billings. She's missing. Amanda Marlowe and her young son are MIA. She hasn't been at her job in almost three months, since before the birth of her child, Alan Shane Marlowe."

"What do you mean, she's missing?"

"Exactly what I said. Is the word missing that hard to understand? You do understand English, don't you? Neither the wife, Amanda, nor the child has been seen since Alan's arrest."

"Think he murdered them?"

"Possibly."

"Think they fled?"

"Possibly."

"Where would they have gone?"

"She wasn't originally a resident of Montana; she was born in Flint, Michigan. Her name was Amanda Greene and she graduated from High School in East Lansing. She went on to receive a BS degree in Nursing from the University of Michigan. After college, she moved to Montana. She's an orphan with no family we know of. She could be anywhere," said the Sheriff of Franklin County.

"I don't like this," the prosecutor snapped at Eric. "Find her. I need her to finish the state's case against him."

Eric looked at the young prosecutor. Keith Collier couldn't be more than twenty-seven, and this was his first year on the job. He was already known for being brash and hard to work with. In Franklin County, the Assistant Attorney General didn't carry half the political weight as the Sheriff. Eric bristled at the tone of the prosecutor's voice and bellowed, "Who do think you are talking to?

Do I suddenly work for you? You'd better not ever speak to me in that tone of voice again. Do you understand?"

Keith Collier suddenly realized the Sheriff was standing--actually towering--over him. When Keith entered the Sheriff's Office, Sheriff Eric Sandusky had been sitting. Keith hadn't realized until now that this was one of the largest men he would ever meet. The Sheriff, in his estimation, stood somewhere in the neighborhood of 6'6" and weighed at least 250. This was indeed a formidable man.

"I am an elected official. I answer to the people of Franklin County, not a little wimp like you," Eric continued. "Now get out of my office, and go do your job!"

The state prosecutor appeared to want to say something but then thought better of it. He turned and like a snake, slithered out of the Sheriff's office.

Eric stood up and walked around his desk. He took a deep breath and left his office. Outside he looked up at the magnificent oak trees that shaded Limestone Street and realized some of them had to be more than 100 years old. Their job for all these years had been to shade the pedestrians that walked to and from the Franklin County Courthouse, main parking lot, and County Jail. When he reached the gate for the County Jail, he punched in his code. The electromagnet buzzed, and he pushed open the chain-link gate. In only a matter of seconds, he had crossed the sixty or so feet from the fence to the building of the County Jail. He opened the door into the dispatch/jailers' office and was assaulted by the jail smell of bad body odor, urine, and other things most of the civilian population never thought about. "Bring Mr. Chipenski down to the interrogation room," Eric told the jailer. "I want to speak to him."

Eric went into the interrogation room and waited. He didn't bother turning on any of the observation equipment. He knew Alan wouldn't say anything to incriminate himself; he wouldn't even admit to being Alan Chipenski. Once again, as he had so many times in the last three years, Eric contemplated on what could have happened to turn his once close friend into a killer.

The door opened and the jailer led Alan into the room. He wore the typical orange jumpsuit, and his wrists were handcuffed to a chain around his waist. He wore leg bracelets that had only ten inches of chain between each bracelet. The short chain made it impossible for him to run. Alan came in with the shuffling gait all prisoners soon learn after they've had the honor to sport leg irons.

"Sit down," ordered Eric.

"What do you want this time, Sheriff," stated Alan in a voice a bit higher than his regular voice.

"I was only curious," smiled Eric.

"Curious about what," asked Alan, who had also added a nasal tone to the already higher tone to his voice.

"Why did you do all those things, Alan? Could you tell me why? What possessed you to do all this stuff? I can understand running the drugs, even the prostitution ring. But the children? Why the kids, Alan? I would have never believed even you could do the things we found on those videotapes."

"I have a question for *you*, Sheriff," sneered Alan. "Why do you insist on calling me Alan? I've told you a hundred times my name is Randall Marlow, Randy to my friends, of which you never have been and never will be."

"Oh, come on, Alan. I know who you are. We grew up together, remember?"

"I don't know why you insist I am some loser named Alan Chipenski. I am not. My name is Randall Marlowe and until your Deputy knocked the hell out of me, I was a detective for the Billings Police Department."

"Please, Alan. You're not going to bore me with the 'I spent twelve years in the Army' crap, are you?"

"Sheriff, I assure you if you'd check, you will find a complete 201 file on me in Army Records in St. Louis. I spent twelve years in the Army as MP as I completed my Army career at Groom Lake as the NCOIC security. From there, I went to Billings, Montana, where six weeks after I left the Army I entered their police academy. Until I stepped out of your squad car, I had never been in Russellville, Alabama."

"Alan. We have pictures to prove who you are. There are at least a hundred people here that will say you're Alan Chipenski."

"Then there are one hundred people that would be wrong. I am and I have always been Randall Gerald Marlowe. I was a Command Master Sergeant in the Army and a detective on the Billings Police Department staff. I had never heard of this little backwoods part of Hell until I stepped off the plane." Alan rubbed his face. The entire right side of his face was black and blue. The color had started to change slightly to a yellow. "Who was that Goliath-sized Deputy that hit me so hard?"

Eric ignored Alan's last question and continued with his questions. "It seems strange you named your son, Alan Shane Marlowe. Is it only a coincidence he's named after a killer here in Franklin County?"

"Sheriff. I don't care what you believe. The only thing I can say is that I'm going to beat these charges. When I do, I will sue you, that Goliath that hit me, and all of Franklin County for everything all of you together own or will ever own."

"Yeah. Yeah. Like I haven't heard that threat before. We'll see how well you sue from Donaldson."

"What's Donaldson?" asked Alan, who knew Donaldson was a maximum-security men's prison in the state.

"That's where you'll be sitting on death row."

"I would like to see my attorney now. I don't think you can harass me in this way."

"This isn't harassment. This is a friendly conversation off the record. I simply wanted to know why anyone would do those things. This isn't an interrogation. Nothing said here can be used in court. We have enough evidence to convict you.

Do you really think our case is so weak that we need a confession? You can be like all the other guys on death row and proclaim your innocence right up until they inject you with . . ."

"Like I said before," interrupted Alan. "I've finished talking. I want my attorney."

"You don't have to talk. I thought you might need to bare your soul. You know if you confessed to this, we probably let you off with life. You would probably only do seven years before you were paroled."

"Or I could fight and prove my innocence. I would get time served. It's obvious I will spend all my time here in this County Jail until my trial. That became evident when the judge denied bail."

"The judge denied bail because you have proved you are a flight risk."

"A flight risk? I guess I am a flight risk. I need to fly back to my home, wife, and son, I have a job to do, which includes raising a young son."

"Murderers and child abusers like you don't deserve to have children of their own. Your son's better off to never see your face again. Oh, and about your job-- what was it? Oh yes, I know. A detective in vice. What better place could a former drug dealer ask for than the location with the most money to be made? How much did you make working ten months in vice? One million? Two? Five? How much?"

"Honest cops don't do things like that."

"I know honest cops don't. Who said you were honest, Alan? I never did."

"I wish you would call me by my real name--Randall--Randall Marlowe."

"Yeah. Yeah. Whatever. I wish that were the truth. For your sake, anyway." Eric stood and walked around behind Alan. He knew this was Alan, but somehow, he didn't act like him. It really didn't even look like him much. In the time he had been in the County Jail, he hadn't altered his story one iota. Not one syllable of his story was different from the first day he'd been here. He had an army record. Eric had even looked through the file. It was true, if he had been presented with a file on a former military man that looked as thorough as "Randall Marlowe's" file did, he would have hired the man in a heartbeat. His 201 was without a doubt one of the finest forgeries Eric had ever seen. He wondered how Alan had gotten the file into the hands of the FBI. Had he paid a courier to deliver it? How?

"I guess you can go back to your room, or should I say cell. It's obvious I 'm not going to hear an explanation from you today."

"I've already told you I haven't done anything."

"If you haven't done anything, then where is your wife and kid? They haven't been seen or heard from since we found you in Montana. Did you murder them, too?"

So Mandy hadn't turned him in, thought Alan. It must have been Peter's half-breed wife. He'd seen Lila snooping around several times in Billings. When he got out of this place, he'd take care of her. She'd get what was coming to her.

When Eric saw the anger that flared up in Alan's eyes and expression, he knew he'd gotten to him, and he also felt Chipenski hadn't killed his wife and kid. Little by little, he'd break Alan. Maybe next time he would run the cameras. Technically, he couldn't do this. He couldn't question a prisoner after he had asked for a lawyer, but who would ever know? It wasn't on tape, and he wouldn't have used it if it had been. He didn't really expect Alan to break down and tell all. He really did want to know what made a thing like prostituting those kids out in the Dime community seem like a good idea. Why would a man do such a thing to defenseless children? How could you tie kids up in the basement of a falling down home, only to clean them up and prostitute them out? Alan was one sick, son-of-a-bitch.

"Jailor. Get him back upstairs," Eric said as he left the interrogation room. "Let him enjoy some of the amenities of jail life since it won't be long before he's on death row and on his way to Hell."

* * *

Life always offers you a second chance.
It's called tomorrow.

~~~Anonymous

* * *

Chapter Fifty-Two

Mandy's plane touched down in Memphis. She didn't have any luggage. The only things she had with her was her young son and her bank book and credit cards. She rented a car and put her young son into a baby seat she had also rented.

She made the two and a half hour drive to Killen. This was where she had grown up. This would be where she would live out the rest of her life.

She went down to the bank and transferred a sizable amount out of her passbook savings into a checking account she opened. With her bank business done for a few days, she drove back over to Long-Lewis Ford in Muscle Shoals, which was twenty minutes from where Randy sat in jail.

There she purchased a new Ford Explorer from a nice young man named David Smith. As she talked to the nice young man, she learned that once upon a time he had been a Deputy for the Franklin County Sheriff's Department. Yes. He knew Eric Sandusky. "He's a fine man," the salesman said. "Solid as a rock."

"Why aren't you still a deputy?" Mandy asked.

"Did you ever hear about that guy that ran the child prostitution ring?" David asked.

"I might have heard something about that."

"You know he killed a young black girl?"

"Yeah."

"I found the body. It was during my first week on the job. I quit the next day after that happened. I'm not cut out for that kind of work."

"I'm sorry," she said. "That's horrible."

As she started to leave, she asked David if he knew of a good realtor. "Sheriff Sandusky's wife is a realtor," said David. "Maybe she could help you out."

"Do you know her telephone number?"

David looked through his desk for a moment, before he finally came up with a card. "Here's her real estate agency's number. Give her a call. Tell her David sent you."

"I'll do that. Could you possibly return my rental car?"

"I don't believe that would be a problem. They have an agency out at the airport. If I can't run it by, I'll have someone else do it."

"Could you recommend a hotel? It has been a long time since I've been here."

"Try the Comfort Inn right down the street. I don't know how good it is, but it looks clean from the outside."

"I'm sure it will be good enough."

"Would you like to eat with me tonight," David blurted out as he felt his face burn.

"I think I would like that. I'll check in at the hotel and leave information for you at the desk. What about eight?"

"Sounds great," said the grinning David Smith.

"I'll see you at eight."

"See you at eight."

He watched her walk out to the new truck. She was without a doubt a beautiful woman on the inside as well as the outside. Even her kid seemed well behaved. He liked kids, anyway.

Chapter Fifty-Three

Peter walked in through the doorway to his home. Lila greeted him with a kiss, and his twins toddled toward him as they screamed. "Pa-Pa. Pa-Pa."

"Yes," said Peter. "Papa's home. Papa's home." Alesky was the more rambunctious of the two, while his sister, Anna, was a bit, but not much more, subdued. In a couple of months, they would be two years old.

"I have a surprise for you," Lila said that night after the kids had been put to bed. Peter saw a look of concern first cloud her face and then recede like a distant storm.

"A surprise? You know I don't like surprises."

"I don't know if you will be pleased or not. It will be a significant change."

"Change?" Peter seemed to recall they'd had a similar conversation once before.

"Yes, my body is already starting to change, in about eight months, your life and my life will be forever changed."

"You're not? Are you?"

"I am."

"We're having another baby? You're having another baby?"

"I am."

"That's wonderful. I can't wait."

"Peter, would you do something for me?"

"Anything. Lila, I will do anything for you."

"Promise me you will never cheat on me. Promise me."

"I promise you I never will."

"Thank you. I love you, Pete." Peter looked over at the woman he had married almost eight years ago. Every passing year he felt a deeper affection for her than the year before. He truly loved her more now than he had yesterday or the day before. "I love you too," he said with meaning that could never be expressed with mere words.

* * *

A lie told often enough becomes the truth.

~~~Vladimir Lenin

* * *

PART FOUR –
A FEW WEEKS LATER

Chapter Fifty-Four

Lila slipped into the study to relax. If she could simply take a short nap, she knew she would feel better. The events of the last couple of years had taken their toll.

As she melted into her favorite chaise lounge, she intertwined her fingers and placed them behind her head. With closed eyes, she tried to focus on pleasant, peaceful thoughts.

Lately, it had been more of a challenge to manipulate Peter. Yet, it still amazed her how through her tone of voice, a light touch to his hand, or a wistful smile she could guide Peter to do what she wanted him to do. She was the grand puppet master. He was the pliable puppet. Lila moved the strings, and Peter performed.

When they first discovered the extent of their power and wealth, Peter had gone overboard; but Lila immediately knew what to do to save him. She steered him expertly away from the unrealistic business ideas and power schemes he had concocted. She encouraged him to be more diplomatic and discreet. Their lack of discretion had almost gotten him killed September 11. She developed and cultivated his philanthropic image and provided much-needed assistance in decisions to which public officials would be re-elected and which would be defeated.

On days like today, she found her secrets and manipulations a heavy burden almost impossible to bear. This morning after she arose to sunshine and the sound of sweetly singing birds she decided today would be the day she would tell Peter everything. I will end my pledge to God to protect him at any cost. He is strong enough to bear his own cross. However, she had sighed as she pictured her kind, trusting husband who loved her unconditionally. She pictured the innocent eyes of the man she loved more than life itself that were the color of the sky on the clearest of days. To keep those eyes innocent, she would continue to be the keeper of the secrets.

Did Peter know the extent of her power? Lila knew in her heart of hearts he had no idea. Lila was only the current in a long list of other strong, influential women given the charge to preserve the wealth and bloodline of the world's richest dynasty--the Romanovs. Yes, the blood flowing through Peter's veins, and those of her two, and soon to be three, children, was indeed that of Russian Royalty.

Peter's beloved Papa was Alexei, son of Nicholas II, the Czar of Russia; and Joanna, Peter's grandmother, was not his grandmother but rather his Grandaunt, the Grand Duchess Anastasia.

Their parents, Czar Nicholas II and Czarina Alexandra had not been the weak and hopeless figureheads history had portrayed them to be. They successfully pulled together a small network of loyalists that included one of the children's tutors, a Navoiczyk family from what is now Belarus, three influential leaders of the Russian Orthodox Church, two Polish/Russian inventors, an American physician and researcher, and the wife of an American President to safely transport their two youngest children to the United States of America.

Nicholas II and Alexandra gathered immense strength from their belief that as long as there were children to carry on their bloodline--especially a son--anything was possible. The Czar and Czarina had successfully orchestrated a plan to create the means to an end that would never be revealed to the masses.

After Germany had declared war on Russia and Nicholas II left St. Petersburg relinquishing much of his power to his beloved wife, Alexandra, their plans had already been laid. Under the smoke screen of Rasputin and the war with Germany, Alexandra transported gold under the Stacia name to banks in London, Paris, San Francisco, and New York City.

More gold and other Romanov treasures were sent to the Romanov palace in Montana. A hospital with state-of-the-art facilities was built at the Montana Palace and doctors were hired to accommodate her cherished son and heir to the Romanov fortune. It was there that Alexei, after five grueling years, was finally cured of his afflictions. He didn't have hemophilia, as documented in history, but only a similar yet curable disease.

Rasputin, prophet and advisor to the imperial family, had seen the vision of the Romanov family controlling the world from a new location. That location would be the United States of America. This vision had given Czarina Alexandra the courage to activate what she had to do to cure and protect her precious son, Alexei, and preserve the Romanov bloodline.

Nicholas, Alexandra, and the three Duchesses—Olga, Tatiana, and Maria--had given their lives for Alexei and Anastasia's freedom. Because of this knowledge, this proud family faced the Bolshevik firing squad with a fearless, unflinching gaze the executioners did not understand.

Vladimir Lenin, head of the Bolshevik party and later head of the Soviet Government, was perplexed when told Anastasia had disappeared only hours before the execution but infuriated to discover the young boy executed with the Romanovs was not Alexei but rather a sickly peasant boy who only resembled Alexei. This young boy had also gallantly given his life to protect Alexei. Lenin spent what little was left of his wretched life searching for the two children believing he would someday find them along with the Romanov gold. He lived less than six years after having members of the Romanov family massacred.

Lenin, Stalin, Trotsky, and other leaders of the Bolshevik party had plotted and killed for years, but it wasn't for the party or the people. They had done it all for the gold and riches of the Romanov family. Each blamed the other for letting it all escape their elusive and greedy hands. After Lenin's death, Stalin had Trotsky exiled and later killed. Stalin never found the missing Anastasia or Alexei. His unsuccessful search for the missing Romanov gold and riches cost millions of lives and secured his place in infamy as one of the cruelest dictators in history.

Lila knew this because she had read several passages from Papa and Gramma Joanna's diaries. The key with the green jewel had unlocked Papa's volumes of secret diaries. Lila had found them in an enormous jeweled trunk on her and Peter's first night in New York City. She transported the trunk to a secure, fireproof location in Russellville of which Peter was unaware.

Lila decided that first night in New York City not to let Peter know the complete truth about his being a Romanov. Peter actually thought Papa had somehow stolen the wealth from the Romanovs. He had no clue Papa and Gramma Joanna were brother and sister instead of husband and wife.

At Papa's memorial service, Harold handed her an envelope yellowed by the passage of time with the words, "Deliver to Peter's Wife after Papa's Passage," written across its front. Inside she found a safe deposit key and a short letter. The safe deposit box was in New York City and contained Anastasia's secret diaries. The letter was short and to the point.

Lila had memorized every word.

My Dear One:

> **I know you are indeed chosen of God to continue the pledge of which I have committed my entire life. That pledge is to protect the Romanov Dynasty and wealth. The Romanov men have always known how to pick a strong, Godly partner, and I know that is why my Peter chose you. Read and learn of my life. Please know I am in heaven and, with God's help, will guide you in whatever you must undertake. ~~~Anastasia**

These diaries were also in a secure place in Russellville.

Anastasia's diaries were full of heart-wrenching testimony of what she had seen and accomplished.

When she and Alexei moved to Alabama, everyone assumed Alex was their child and they were married to each other. Since Anastasia's one true love had been murdered years before, she had already resigned herself to the fact she would never marry. She willingly devoted her life to protecting her brother, so she let the rural Alabamians believe what they wanted. Papa, on the other hand, began a love affair with Jackie that endured until the end.

Anastasia had also successfully planned the boating accident in France that killed Peter and Eric's parents. Anastasia had known these people were unworthy of the Romanov name and could not be entrusted with the secrets.

This knowledge of what Anastasia had done to protect Romanov power and wealth had given Lila the strength she needed to protect Peter.

As soon as Lila had found the keys in Papa's Holy Bible, she had made her own copies. Her first charge in protecting Peter was to remove one birth certificate and one full page from the first small, jeweled box. Papa had carefully placed three birth certificates there. Fraternal triplets, not twins, were born to Peter and Eric's parents before their accident in France.

Horror of horrors--Alan Chipenski was also Peter's brother. Papa had also written Peter a one-page letter about Alan. Papa had given Alan up for adoption to Stuart Chipenski, one of Papa's closest friends, who had recently married a sweet girl named Louise Chandler. Twenty years younger than Stuart, Louise had not been mature enough to handle a new marriage along with the adoption of an infant. When Stuart died only three months after they'd married, she snapped and never recovered. Papa and Gramma Joanna kept planning to take Alan away from her, but Louise would cry and promise to change. They would always give her another chance. After Gramma Joanna and Louise had died, Papa realized Alan was already too far gone to be helped. After he bought him a vehicle, he practically gave up on the boy.

Toward the end of his life, Papa had undoubtedly grieved over breaking up the three boys and wanted to make amends. He had left Peter the responsibility of whether or not to reveal the truth to Alan. Papa also encouraged Peter to help Alan financially. Lila hated Alan, and there was no way Alan Chipenski would ever have a place in their lives. Once she heard about his sad background, she was still not moved to feel any differently toward Alan. She would see to it Peter never found out Alan was his brother.

Lila had known all about Alan's whereabouts and activities ever since she had run into him in Billings on her first trip there after her accident. When she and Peter looked for snowsuits in Billings, she spotted Alan and wrote down the description of his truck and tag number. With very little effort, she found out the original Mississippi tag number and gave it to Jeremy O'Neal Jenkins to report to the authorities in Franklin County. It was in evidence Jeremy had seen a man fitting Alan's description with short, dyed-blonde hair leave the Belgreen cottage. This was within an hour after Georgia's death. Jeremy O'Neal Jenkins described the vehicle as a Silverado truck with a Mississippi tag number that matched Alan's original Mississippi tag. Whenever Alan's trial started, Jeremy O'Neal Jenkins' testimony would be the nail in the coffin to incarcerate Alan Chipenski for good.

Jeremy was Mattie Wilson's nephew and only surviving relative. He had not seen Alan there, but when the time came, he would gladly give false testimony in return for the $100,000 he had received from Lila and what she had accomplished to release his great-aunt from Tutwiler.

Lila had even found out who had provided Alan with the documentation for his new life. This had been one of the most shocking discoveries of the past two years. Their butler, Jeffery, in New York had been running quite a scam. She had known when she first met Jeffery that he was not one to be trusted, but she hadn't expected he was intelligent enough to weave the web of deception he had. She had taken her almost a year to methodically trace Alan's information back to Jeffery. That butler even had the nerve to conduct his illegal activities through Peter's office in New York City. It had been easy for her to set Jeffery up for stealing one of their Faberge eggs. Jackie had helped instigate that endeavor, and Jeffery had been in the penitentiary for the past year. He would remain there for the rest of his miserable life. The evidence she had against Jeffery could be used to put yet another nail in Alan's coffin, if necessary. Alan continued to proclaim he was Randy Marlowe; a person whom Lila could prove didn't even exist.

As long as Alan hadn't made trouble for Eric and Peter, Lila had been satisfied to let him live as Randy Marlowe in Billings. If he had stayed straight, he could have been free indefinitely. For a year, he had actually been a changed man. He had married Mandy, who Lila liked and respected immensely. About a year ago, however, he had slowly returned to his old and familiar routine of corrupt behavior. The last straw was when he beat Mandy and locked her in the basement. Lila knew then it was time to take action. Very gently, she led Peter to feature Alan's picture on America's Most Wanted. Lila had also subtly monitored the success of Mandy's escape and departure from Billings. Lila knew where Mandy was now and would gently lead her to testify if necessary. As long as she wasn't needed, Lila would allow Mandy and her son to enjoy her new life. Lila would keep Mandy and little Alan safe from Alan Chipenski.

At this point in time, Lila could not let Peter ever know the third key had opened the trunk containing Papa's diaries. Even though she knew Peter for two long years had steadfastly looked for what the last key opened, the diaries detailed too much information about Alan. Similar information was also contained in Joanna's diaries.

When Peter discovered the concealed ballroom in Montana, Lila had already removed and hidden several portraits from the walls that would reveal to Peter he was indeed Russian Royalty. Peter never had a clue she had already found the jeweled door and gone inside before he had. For a split second, Lila thought Peter looked at her suspiciously, but Lila realized it was probably the shock of seeing pictures of Russian Royalty along the walls. Peter would probably never know Papa, Peter's father and mother, and her and Peter's portraits had hung on the wall to signify the succession of the Romanov men and their spouses.

Janet Cumberland had not gone meekly away when Peter paid her the blackmail money. Lila knew all about that situation, too. Janet shouldn't have taken advantage of her precious Peter that night like she did with him being asleep and on a sedative. Ming Toi had told Lila all about what that little tramp had done to Peter. When Lila traced a wire of $100 million to Janet's Swiss bank account, she immediately knew Janet had blackmailed Peter. Lila knew Janet had to be taken care of quickly or she would be a permanent albatross around Peter's neck.

Poor Janet incurred a nervous breakdown that resulted in her permanent commitment to an expensive and discreet mental institution. Since no one knew about her pregnancy or baby's birth, Lila put the baby up for private adoption. Lila tested the baby's DNA and found with 99.99% certainty he was indeed Peter's biological son. This same child was now Eric and Lori's adopted joy, Michael Sandusky. It had been relatively easy for Lila to direct the entire scenario. She smiled as she thought about all her accomplishments and how much better she'd made the lives of the people she cared about.

Once again, so many lives had been made better. Lila loved Michael and so did Peter, Alesky, Anna, Lori, Jenny, Patrick, Mattie, and Eric. Her and Peter's newest addition would be named after Papa's sister, Maria, and would learn to love Michael, too. Michael had been and would continue to be raised in a healthy, loving environment.

The only thing she'd done to protect Peter that still gave her nightmares was how she had handled the Sean Michaels situation. Sean had contacted her several times and threatened to have the Italian Mafia destroy Peter if she wouldn't pay him $5 million. Lila followed him in his own midnight blue Mercedes to the New York City alley that night. She hadn't meant to actually break his neck when she yanked the rope, but her adrenaline level had increased when she had seen her chance to scare him. As a man, he was so petite she hadn't even breathed hard when she lifted him and put him in the Mercedes. The suicide setup was easy to accomplish and no one even questioned its authenticity. She hadn't known for sure if the stain on the Mercedes leather seat was Michaels blood or not, but when Peter had given the car to Lori and encouraged them to redo the seats, she knew she was home free. She still felt badly that she had accidentally killed the poor man, but after all, it was an accident. She hadn't done it on purpose, and he had been so distraught that he probably would have committed suicide at some point later on, anyway.

Anastasia's diaries revealed how weak or troublesome family members were handled in the history of Russian Royalty. They were sent off to do life service in convents, died in secluded castles of undetermined diseases, permanently visited Siberia, or were horribly tortured. In the United States, these types of people were killed in boating accidents, spent life sentences in prison, set up to look like they committed suicide, or ended up in mental hospitals never to be heard of again.

Yes, Lila had completed a very busy but productive two years. Even though many times her soul did feel tortured, she wouldn't have changed a thing. As far as she was concerned, everything had turned out as God meant it to. She knew God was on her side. The only thing other than what had happened to Sean Michaels Lila regretted was that her parents weren't here. She missed her mother and father so much. She hated they had never seen nor would ever see any of her children, but every day the ache she felt for them got a little bit duller. Perhaps they were in heaven and could see their grandchildren, after all.

Lila was relieved to finally feel the tension leave her body. She felt a peace she hadn't felt in almost three years. All of the pieces of the puzzle had finally fallen into place.

She recounted a comment Lori had made during their first meeting about how so much power and money could give Peter a *God Complex*.

Lila smiled with pride as she dozed off because she knew she had prevented that from happening. Peter was the same man as before his unsolicited acquisition of money and power.

What Lila didn't realize, though, was that one didn't have to be a man to develop a *God Complex*.

* * *

... To marry then? Of course it's hard.
But why don't marry, in a whole?
I'm of the young and healthy sight,
Ready to work for day and night;
I'll someway find the good repose,
The simple and shy place, at last,
Parasha will be there composed.
The year or, maybe, two will pass –
I'm in position, to my dear
I'll give all family to bear
And bring our children up, at once ...
Such we'll start life, at last repose,
With hand-in-hand, such we'll come both,
And our grandsons will bury us ...

~~~Alexander Pushkin
Excerpt from *The Bronze Horseman*

* * *

Chapter Fifty-Five

Peter Alexei Romanov entered the study. He saw his beloved Lila asleep on the chaise lounge with an angelic smile on her lovely face. He loved her and all his children, born and unborn, and knew the satisfaction of having that love returned. He gently bent down and kissed the top of her head.

What Lila did not know and would probably never know was that Peter was much smarter than Lila gave him credit for being. He knew about *all* of Lila's secrets.

He even knew about the diaries--even though he'd only read a few pages from each. When he tried to read the words of the two people who had lovingly raised him, he became emotional and couldn't help but resent how they had lied about who they were and who he was. There were far too many Family Secrets. He felt sure the day would come when he completely forgave them for their deceit. At that time, he would read about how they'd been able to escape what had befallen the rest of their royal family in Russia and what their early life in the United States was like.

He had not at all been pleased at how Lila had handled Janet Cumberland and his child, but then it occurred to him that children weren't at all hard to come by. As long as Lila believed Michael was his biological child, she wasn't likely to go looking for Janet and his son Nicholas. He thought of Janet's violet eyes and how he had promised to give her a chance if anything ever happened to Lila. She didn't really need a chance. She was his, forever and always, and whenever he wanted. He would be spending time with her and Nick next week in New York City. Lila hated it there and rarely went. Why did he need to divorce one for the other? Peter could take care of both and ten dozen more if he needed them. Divorce was for common people, and he was no longer a common person.

What he had marveled at was how she had disposed of Sean Michaels. With only a little help from Sergeant John O'Leary, he'd been able to sufficiently cover all Lila's tracks.

As long as Lila continued to be on his side and looked out for his best benefits, he would let her do and act as she pleased. She was his secret weapon. If this ever changed, though, he could and would step in to rectify the situation. Not only could Romanov men pick strong, loyal women, they also had the psychological edge of knowing they allowed these women to think they had the upper hand. That was how the dynasty had survived for more than three hundred years and would surely last at least three hundred more.

Lila believed she had hidden Alan from him, but Peter knew everything Lila knew and more. After all he was a Romanov, and she was only married to one. In every organization, there was a little good, a little bad and a whole lot of mediocrity. An organization as large as his needed some evil--he needed Alan, and soon he would no longer be sitting in Holman Correctional Facility. He had to do it the right way or Eric and Lila would know. Jeffery was more than a butler, much more. Lila was right not to trust Jeffery. He was a snake in the grass and a superbly trained master of deception, but he was loyal. Why not be? He was working for the organization which controlled everything, and he had almost unlimited power. Today he was quietly running numbers and putting people in place. Peter couldn't let a direct attack against him go unanswered. He had stood in the conference room and watched as Flight 11 flew at 466 miles per hour and hit 1 World Trade Center less than a hundred feet below where he stood. He had been knocked to his knees, but before flight 175 hit 2 World Trade Center, Jackie, and the other eight people in the conference room were inside his helicopter and on the way to LaGuardia where the Gulfstream waited. He'd been stupid. That Middle-Eastern group had almost gotten him. Now he knew why Papa was here in the small town of Russellville, Alabama. This was an ideal place to hide when the dogs came out, and they were going to come out. They believed that since Papa was gone they'd strike, however, they didn't realize the grandson was as ruthless as the grandfather.

His grandmother had said it best the first day he really met her: *He was ruthless, he didn't play games, there was no compassion, and no second chances. Papa Stacia was always in control. He never second-guessed, never backed up, or backed down.* Lila believed a woman named Sandra was his grandmother, but Peter knew his grandmother was Jackie Lowell. A simple DNA test had confirmed it.

He quietly strode over to sit in his favorite leather chair. As he faced a multitude of books, he thought about how many times in the past two and one-half years he prayed he could roll back time to before Papa died. Back then his life had been good. No. It had been great, but it would never again be the same. Peter could handle it, and would take care of it because he understood and appreciated the responsibility of carrying forth the Romanov Dynasty. Even with all the mistakes Romanovs had made in their collective attempts to control the world, there was one mistake they never made. They never made the mistake of giving up. They were not quitters, and neither was Peter.

Chapter Fifty-Six

The souls of hundreds of Romanovs, gathered over hundreds of years, felt a renewed and intense burst of pride as they looked down upon Peter. At that precise moment, *a dramatic, brighter-than-ever-before-seen flash* exploded through the October sky in Russellville, Alabama.

That *act of God* would be talked about, not only in Alabama but also throughout the entire world until the end of time. Meteorologists worldwide who studied the satellite pictures of the phenomenon would debate the cause without ever being able to explain it.

The Romanov Dynasty had finally been rewarded for all their sacrifice and heartache. The culmination of all their good qualities was now synergized in Peter Alexei Romanov. Whether portrayed in history as *strong or weak, hunter or hunted, torturer or tortured, conqueror or conquered, man or woman, young or old, tall or short*--they were all in agreement that this was the right Romanov to indeed rule the world. Ironically, it would be through games of business rather than games of war.

Even though Peter thought he was in charge, the Romanov spirits collectively knew they were the ones in control, because they managed Peter. They, and only they, had allowed him to know all about Lila's adventures.

They knew God's power had always been with the Romanov Dynasty and had guided them in their endeavors. They were able to now enjoy the certainty that they had finally prevailed. It had been a long and arduous journey. These once restless, but now triumphant souls were finally *put to rest* because of a *humble* Alabama boy.

Chapter Fifty-Seven

Jehovah God, with a divine sense of amusement, watched the whole scenario of Lila, Peter, and the Romanov spirits' wretched attempts to plot and command like gods.

Earth humans always supposed they were in control of their own destinies.

Even though **HE,** *Hashem,* has explained how everything is predestined and is according to HIS will and HIS will only.

Those humans seemed to never learn.

Jehovah-- . . .   יהוה   . . .   --is in control of the earth.

Not merely the earth--but also the entire creation of all universes--as it always has been and as it always will be.

Moreover, **HE,** *Adonai,* doesn't have a *complex.*

Because **HE** is **GOD** . . .